THE PATH

BARRY RICHARDS

This is a work of fiction. All of the characters, organizations, and events portrayed in this novel are either products of the author's imagination or are used fictitiously.

THE PATH. © Copyright 2023 by Barry Richards. All rights reserved. Printed in the United States of America. For information, address B Rich Media.

www.brichbooks.com

Cover design by Barry Richards

The Library of Congress has cataloged the paperback edition as follows:

Names: Richards, Barry, 1972 - author.
Title: The Path : a novel / Barry Richards.
Description: First Edition. | Atlanta : B Rich Media. 2023.
ISBN 978-0-9978307-6-7 (paperback)
ISBN 978-0-9978307-7-4 (ebook)
Subjects: LCSH: Science fiction. | BISAC: FICTION / Action & Adventure / General. FICTION / Thrillers / Technological. | GSAFD: Suspense fiction.

First B Rich Media Paperback Edition: April 2023

*For Aunt Joyce.
Thanks for all your help. I couldn't have
done this without you.*

THE GOOD LIFE

1

"Well, class of 2057, our time together is almost over," remarks the gentle, middle-aged professor as he slowly rounds the open center of the large, circular classroom floor. Fitted in a sheer, white bodysuit and smiling benevolently, he glides effortlessly on mobile shoes like a roller skater. Collaborative work sectionals filled with pupils, holographic replicas of remote classmates, and life-like robotic aids encircle him. All wearing digital mixed-reality visors called AllVu, his students hang on to his parting words with mechanical smiles as their waning moments of education come to an end. With only minutes left on this final day of instruction, this delighted high school instructor proudly prepares to send his scholars off into the cradling arms of The Path.

While he continues to survey the room in silence, digital, bold black words of happiness fade in and out across his chest. This basic virtual experience is common today, as augmented (AR) and virtual (VR) reality has seamlessly integrated into everyday life. With the use of AllVu technology, simulated objects and haptic sensations, such as touch, smell, and taste, have become natural and sometimes indistinguishable parts of the real world.

The professor takes an extended break as the all-caps letters "P-R-O-U-D" display on his shirt in progression. Then, with a genial grin, he cups his hands. "I'd like to leave you with a few words," he begins, which is the hallmark of his brief signature speeches to which his students have become accustomed.

"Your worlds are expanding every day, far beyond what your ancestors could have even imagined. No longer are we bound by gridlock, waste, indecisiveness, and misdirection. The Human-NonHuman Partnership we have embraced has allowed us to experience the fullness of our being. Now, more than ever before, our life experiences are richer in pleasure and meaning. We are a connected chain of unity and prosperity. It's a good life! So, before you exit this building for the last time, either in person or virtually, I would like to be the first to say: on behalf of the Federal Department of Efficiency and Compliance and this great nation – Welcome to The Path!"

He pauses again for a reflective moment while the reserved students calmly applaud. "And thanks to Mr. Richmond, for sharing so MUCH of his World during his stunning final presentation," the Professor ribs while cutting his eyes to the ceiling, "Life Simplified 103 will never be the same again."

With humorous flashbacks, fellow classmates chuckle as the resident joker, Rony Richmond, reclines in his curved rocker. He pushes his green spiked hair back, then shrugs devilishly. "Told you I'd leave my mark, Professor," he jokes as a winking cartoon emoji drifts high above his head and then poofs into smoke.

In response to Rony's wise-cracking spectacle, the room fills with snickers as a series of "thumbs-ups" pop around the room like live thought bubbles. The professor calmly spins around, slips his hands in his pockets, and eases until he's standing right beside Rony. With the quick command "Hide AllVu," his digital AllVu visor evaporates from in front of his eyes as he peers down at Rony. "Mr. Richmond," he begins while sighing with exasperation. "Let's just hope your Track is not Life Enhancement," he jabs and then playfully pats Rony's shoulder, "or we're ALL in trouble." Finally, the restrained students loosen up and erupt in full laughter. High ratings of 9s and 10s fly in the air as the professor victoriously struts around the room with "CHAMP" boastfully illuminating from his shirt.

Meanwhile, sitting in the back row and almost unconscious of the comical events is Rony's good friend, Jolem McKay, gazing dreamily at the long glass exterior wall at a passing bird. The colorful creature perches on a thin tree limb, looks around, then takes flight back into the air. Its effortless glide through the still wind captivates Jolem's imagination. He would love nothing more than to be soaring alongside. With a thought command of his AllVu, virtual reality makes his daydream come to life.

Just then, subtle vibrations pulsate from the small, flat, black AllVu orbs attached to everyone's temples, signaling the end of the day. "In-class education is now complete," echoes throughout the building by the warm voice of the school's artificially-intelligent administrator. The black entryway doors become translucent, then swiftly slide open. "To all of our graduates," the administrator continued, "we'd like to congratulate and wish you great success in The Path. Your guided future of peace and prosperity awaits you. It's a good life."

"Much happiness to you all," remarks the professor to the lively, departing crowd. As they pass, they launch heartfelt visuals into the air. These augmented words and/or images, known as "cheer," offer a quick expression without the utterance of a sound.

"I hope you are awarded the Life Tracks you desire," he continues heartily. On the day they were born, their individual birth size/weight, respective families' history/financial situation, and many other variables all contributed to their Societal Impact Valuation (SIV), which ultimately landed them in his care. The SIV is a fluctuating estimate of an individual's value to humanity. It helps to appropriately group children with like minds and circumstances. It is also a primary factor used to determine Life Tracks in the Path.

Jolem attempts to slide inconspicuously through the dispersing group, hoping to leave unnoticed. To Jolem's dismay, the professor abruptly interrupts his conversation with one of his other students.

"Ahh, Jolem – may I grab your ear for a moment?" he calls out, lifting his pointer finger.

Jolem stops, rolls his eyes, and drops his head. Over the years, the professor has been a leading advocate, hoping to spark a fire under Jolem's sluggish ambitions. The professor has recognized signs of huge potential in his quirky student. However, to the professor's disappointment and confusion, his mentoring has routinely fallen upon Jolem's deaf ears.

The professor smiles brightly, shakes the hand of the student with whom he was conversing and quickly wishes her well. His elation at launching another class into The Path is written all over his face. After a nostalgic grin, his attention shifts back to Jolem. Jolem lumbers over, head down and hands stuffed into the pockets of his shiny, body-hugging pants. "Hello, Professor…" he mumbles through twisting lips.

"Ahh, yes, yes. Jolem, have you put any thought into our discussion from the other day?"

"Well…yeah, but I don't know," Jolem says, looking off to the ground. "Life Simulations might not be for me."

With an abrupt shift of emotion, the professor's face falls, exhausted by all his fruitless efforts. "Jolem, I don't understand," he says, gesticulating with bewilderment. "Why are you sabotaging your future? You could be well-positioned in the resource pool, but I'm afraid your eligibility for gigs will fall far short of your capabilities. Your competency and adaptability are fine, but you will have to work on cooperation and likability to improve your SIV."

"Professor, I do appreciate your words and all your support, but…," Jolem begins while reaching uncomfortably for his words. "I don't care about my SIV... or The Path for that matter. I just feel trapped."

Instinctively, the professor's eyes shift back and forth, spying to see if anyone overheard Jolem's unadvised declaration. "Jolem! Please! Those are very dangerous words," he whispers with immediacy.

"I know…I know, but…,"

"Well – be very careful. The Path has brought us through very troubling times. Don't be selfish, Son. The Path is good – for everyone."

Shaking his head, the professor gazes at Jolem searchingly. "I don't understand. There is peace and harmony, all because of The Path. Why do you fight it so?"

"Uhh…"

"Because of The Path, the world is a better place, and you should be excited, not resistant to the prospect of joining its ranks. Soon, you'll learn your track in life, and I'm sure you'll see it first-hand, but you MUST protect your SIV. It is your ticket to happiness. You also don't want to risk deviation."

Jolem nods. "Maybe you're right," he murmurs dismissively.

"Your Path Advisement iisss – next Tuesday, correct?"

"Actually, I pushed it back a couple weeks."

"Jolem, Jolem," the professor remarks with suppressed exasperation. There's a puzzling condescension in his tone. His eyes spin towards the ceiling as he rubs the stubbles of his shadowed beard. "Celey, why wasn't I notified of this change??" he questions out loud. Accustomed to regular alerts from his digital AllVu Assistant, he's not sure how he has overlooked this important update.

"Professor, perhaps the excitement of another graduation has gotten the best of you," she chides politely like an elementary school teacher. "I've reminded you of this recently... twice already, in fact," she continues, laughing softly.

Like a faithful friend, his AllVu Assistant offers insight, suggestions, and consistent companionship. Powered by the Halcyon life-navigation operating system, she functions as a second set of refined eyes, constantly scanning and analyzing the Professor's surroundings. She responds to his voice, touch, smell, and even emotions, intuitively delivering relevant information on the fly. Without the need for headphones or earplugs, she speaks in his ears, and unless broadcasted, only he can hear her sound. At birth, all citizens receive a Personal AllVu Assistant, whose name, voice, language, and other settings can be customized. They are ingrained necessities in today's mixed reality, and society relies heavily on them.

"Why, Jolem??" the professor asks.

"Professor, you know we have up to three weeks after graduation to have the Advisement. I'm just not in a hurry."

The professor's head drops back as he releases a heavy sigh. Then, while scratching his scalp, his eyes drift back to Jolem. "Wellll... Jolem, most people are so excited to choose their Track, their Advisements are scheduled as soon as possible."

"I received a summer gig that I start next week. I'm in no rush to enter The Path."

"Jolem, these little gigs were fine to provide you with credits during education, but…The Path is here now. At this time, society could use a greater contribution from your talents." The professor rubs the skin of his cheeks as his lips tighten in befuddlement. He is stumped. "Hmm… of all my students, you've been the most challenging. It's hard for me to understand individuals like you, Jolem. Your life could be full of joy and adventure in The Path, but for some reason, you fight it. I know you still question the Human-NonHuman Partnership, but those arguments are over."

The professor places his hand on Jolem's shoulder and smiles. "Remember, you are an important piece of a greater whole… a link that helps hold the chain of humanity together. Humans, NonHumans --- how we collaborate is fundamental to all our survival. Trust in The Path, and follow its wisdom. It will set you free."

Jolem looks the professor in the eyes kindly and gives him a firm handshake. His respect for his instructor is much deeper than he lets on.

"Thanks, Professor."

"Please, Jolem, you seem to enjoy flirting with the edge, but youth is over and it's time for you to accept your place in The Path. Smile, laugh, play, and stay on Track. Follow the advice of your assistant. It will serve you well. It's a good life," the professor reiterates. "Welcome to The Path."

Sliding his hands back into his pockets, Jolem turns toward the exit, where his prankster buddy Rony is waiting. Leaning against the wall with his arms crossed, he taps his foot impatiently. A 3D yellow "unhappy" face floating above his head, pouts like a child, and then razzes its tongue.

"C'mooon Sola!" yells Rony, opening his arms. "Good times are outside these walls. Let's get outta here!" Corresponding to Rony's actions, the "unhappy" face morphs into elation, expands like a balloon, then ignites into fireworks.

"Right behind you, Sola," Jolem replies, echoing the modern-day slang.

2

"We're finally FREE!! Life is great!" shouts Rony as he launches out of the building into the bright, sunny day. For the young men, education is complete, and the graduation ceremony is just on the horizon. While arching back his head, he inhales the summer air, then leisurely releases his breath into the atmosphere, "Ahhhhhh…"

"'Free,' huh? That's an interesting way to put it," Jolem replies cynically, approaching slowly from behind. His lackluster response to graduation is a far cry from his friend's excitement. "'From one cage to the next' is the way I see it," he says as he runs his fingers backwards through his thick, dark, curly hair. As he gazes into the distance, details such as temperature, date and time digitally overlay the sky.

While Jolem and Rony thread through the throng of disbanding students, the softly vibrating hum of rolling IGliders resonates louder than any conversation. Moving at velocities of no more than six miles an hour, these mobile shoes glide people smoothly from one place to another. They're safe, efficient, and the most common form of short-distance transportation. Rony spins around Jolem in a small circle. Over the years, he's accepted Jolem's strange nature and unusual aversion to The Path but doesn't support nor understand it.

"C'mon, Sola – you gonna start that again?" replies Rony, throwing his hands up in the air. "I don't get it with you and The Path."

Tilting his head downward, Jolem peers at Rony, who's a few inches shorter. "Sola, if you don't get it by now – I'm just wasting my breath."

"You're like an old man in a young man's body. You ever listen to yourself?? You sound crazy, like one of the Freedom Fighters, always complaining about The Path," Rony huffs, shaking his head derisively. He moves close and pats Jolem on the chest. "I'm telling you, give that up. My gramps tells me about times before The Path; it was CHAOS. Listen, my SIV is goin' through the roof JUST from likability – alone! You better get with it for real. Deviation is not something to play with."

Jolem lifts his right hand, preparing to respond, but before he can eke out a word, an abrupt series of soft, seductive sounds ring in Rony's ears, grabbing his attention.

"She's hot for me man, ahhhh," Rony suddenly blurts out as he views a "for his eyes-only" message. He grins mischievously while floating augmented hearts and pulsating smoochy lips form his name in the sky. "She's trying to invite me into her World," he chuckles.

Socializing has moved well beyond short messages on mobile apps and social media websites. In today's mixed reality, AllVu Worlds are virtual reality social spaces where people congregate. Just a verbal or thought command away, these simulated environments provide an alternate universe for interpersonal interactions. The sky's the limit in these creative Worlds, which allow individuals and groups to do almost anything and be almost anyone.

Rony flashes a large ear-to-ear smile while he keeps his flirty friend on hold. "She's crazy," he laughs, "sitting on a sofa with her arms crossed in the middle of the ocean. 'Accept invite,'" he finally says, which sends his digital self, or SimMe, into his admirer's World. Although still standing right next to Jolem, Rony's thoughts drift far from the conversation in which they were just engaged. While in VR, his body goes into semi-autopilot and is navigated by his AllVu Assistant in order to prevent unsafe body movements. It's common to see people move around like zombies as their consciousness plays in their virtual Worlds.

Jolem glances pathetically at Rony, shakes his head and sighs. He reaches into his bag strapped around his shoulder and pulls out an angular metallic board similar to a short skateboard without wheels. He drops it, but before hitting the asphalt, it suspends in the air, hovering about six inches off the ground.

"We're meeting up later at Wyth Island, right?" Jolem asks, dismissing Rony's last comments as if they weren't even spoken.

"Huh…??"

"Wyth Island?"

"Oh – oh yeah – that's right, Sola! Everybody's gonna be there. Zones from all over town. Tonight's goin' to be STRATOSPHERIC!"

"Stellar…" Jolem replies calmly, bobbing his head. "Okay – I'll meet you later. Gotta make a stop."

"A stop?? Jo, what's up?"

Jolem's eyes drift toward the ground. "I'm going…to see my father," he replies somberly.

As Rony slowly nods his head, there's a moment of silent reverence. "Ahhh, okay."

Rony moves in closely, slips out his hand, then Jolem returns with his own. The backs of their arms slide against each other and then the fronts, ending in tightly locked fists.

"I'll catch up with ya later," says Jolem, as he leaps onto his AirBoard and propels away without a helmet or any other protective gear.

3

"Watch out for the protruding stone, ten feet ahead," warns the helpful voice from Jolem's AllVu. "Jolem, I seriously recommend that you slow down. Gliding at this speed is extremely dangerous, especially without proper head protection. I really wish you'd cease this childish activity. You know you're paying a small fortune in Detrimental to Your Health Taxes for these little stunts."

"Thanks, Li'l J. They can take those DTH taxes and kiss my ass. I'll do what I want," he replies, as his body shifts back and forth to avoid the road disruption. "Li'l J" is the affectionate name he's given to his AllVu Assistant, that has been his lifelong faithful companion. Attempting to guide Jolem from harm's way, Li'l J's "voice of reason" is always present but often ignored. AllVu enabled components, such as visors, communicators, digital fibers, etc., are all interconnected to their host and a national cloud of shared information. Whenever at least one of them is in his possession, their symbiotic connection allows him to communicate with them all at the same time.

On a whim, Jolem dips low, grabs the edges of his board with his fingertips, then flips, feet into the air. In an instant, he's upside down, performing a handstand on his dynamically shifting foundation. Most would not even attempt such a maneuver for fear of how it might negatively affect their record. They're comfortably aware that the country's wireless surveillance system monitors and records just about every move.

After clasping tightly for a few seconds, he pushes his momentum forward, attempting to return back on his feet. Then, after an awkward landing, he realizes he has miscalculated. His right foot completely misses the board and is now dangling loosely in the air. As he desperately tries to regain his footing, it is clear he can't prevent the imminent collision course ahead. Before he can even react, he's hurled headfirst into a barrier of hedges.

A moment later, Jolem is propped in the bushes with his legs stretched into the sidewalk. Fortunately for him, he escapes with just a few scratches, a bruised thigh, and a small tear on his shirt. He releases a puff of air that blows a large leaf from his face. While continuing to toss twigs and other foliage from his hair, he looks around to see the fate of his board. To his relief, when analyzing the prospects of damage, it pulled itself back from the crash. Off to his left, the board is floating in wait and completely unharmed.

"Jolem, do you require assistance?" questions Li'l J.

Jolem smirks, then shakes and scratches his head. "No…I'm fine," he says, as he replays the embarrassing experience captured by his constantly recording World Cam. Immediately, the event becomes a conversation piece in his World as ratings and comments pour in. Most would enjoy the temporary celebrity, but he quickly regrets his spontaneous action. The less attention, the better for the reclusive young man.

Jolem sighs, then attempts to lift himself out of the hedges, but suddenly, he winces from a sharp pain in his lower back. In a quick response, his shirt sends an electric nerve stimulation to relieve the pain. Within moments, he feels none. The smart nanofibers of his clothing monitor his heart rate, body temperature, and a host of physical states. They detect viruses or illnesses before any symptoms are evident. If he's cold, they will warm; if he's hot, they will cool; if he is embattled, they alert the proper authorities of his condition and location. In the event of an emergency incident, his mom would be immediately informed. Smart fibers were initially designed for athletes, the elderly, and those with underlying health conditions, but now all mainstream clothing is made with them.

'Uhgh…" he grunts when he notices the rip in his shirt. He hates the thought of another lecture about irresponsibility from his mom, should his fibers report the incident. Annoyed with himself over the results of the risky maneuver, his next move is even less predictable than the stunt. As he slips his board back into his bag, he takes a small step forward and then just…walks.

For the next twenty minutes, one labored stride after another, Jolem moves through the streets immersed in thought. As his eyes survey the happy community, he takes note of all the carefree faces engaged in discussions with their AllVu Assistants or immersed in their Worlds. They are so consumed that they appear unaware of anyone or anything around them. It seems an airplane could fall into the middle of the street, and no one would even notice.

Jolem tilts back his head and then sucks in a deep inhale of the fresh air breeze. With his sights in the sky, he notices the typical scene of various-shaped drones casually sailing back and forth. Some high above and others close enough to touch. As common as birds, they zip from one direction to another. Many of them scout for security, some for transport, and others expeditiously deliver parcels like modern-day carrier pigeons. In the evening, they light up the skies like shooting stars. As the captured air blows out of his mouth like a motorboat, he grows bothered. Although privacy has become an abstract concept in today's world, the thought of one of the drones looking down on him at this very moment irks him.

His head drops, and he stalls with his hands resting on his waist. Slowly, he takes a curious panoramic view of his surroundings. On the sidewalks, people move in unison as they would on an escalator, without rush or worry. On the roads, emission-free, self-driving cars glide efficiently from place to place. Feeling oddly like a man imported from another place and time, he reflects on his young life. As far as he can remember, he's felt different or out of place in typical social settings. For reasons unbeknownst to him, the enduring bliss most enjoy eludes him. Why is he so stubbornly resistant to the norms that friends and family accept so freely? The origin of his discontent is a mystery he is unable to solve nor dismiss.

Jolem takes a shortcut, climbing a hilly terrain after passing through the backside of a large empty lot. When he was younger, he and his friends would take this course because of its drone blind spots beneath its many trees. As he comes to the top, he slips under an old barred fence, then continues through a quiet rolling landscape. Finally, his steps slow as he approaches the landmark of his destination. Standing still in a sea of headstones in a graveyard, he looks down with emotion at the one dedicated to his departed father, Michale.

Michale died when Jolem was only ten, but his strong influence remains. He was just a regular man with an abundance of wisdom and determination. His life's teachings of liberty and independence ring loudly in Jolem's everyday thoughts and actions. "Jolem, don't get so lost in your World that you lose sight of the world around you," he'd always say. Although years have passed since Michale's premature death, Jolem still struggles to understand it. What he knows is fuzzy, and he longs for a sensible explanation for his departure.

"Li'l J, shut down my World," he calmly instructs. "I want to go dark for a while."

"Okay, but I just want to remind you that you are approaching your weekly dark limit. Your credits are low to cover more fines."

Jolem sighs. "Hmmm…okay. Continue anyway."

"Well, okay then. Would you like some music?"

"No. But play the last experience with my dad. I know I've seen it a million times, but it seems appropriate right now. Start from when I got home from school."

"Sure, Jolem."

Going dark shuts down his World Cam and social tracking mechanisms, but digital monitoring systems remain active. His family or friends will not be able to find him or see what he's doing, but should an emergency arise, support systems could pinpoint his location immediately. As he crouches down, he swipes away the dirt and dust that has collected across his father's name on the memorial plaque. "There we go," he proudly remarks as he plops to the ground beside it. He leans back on his forearms, tilts his head up to the sky, and his eyes slip shut.

"Well, Pop – Path, here I come," he murmurs with resignation as he releases a depressed exhale. In the high swinging grass, Jolem sits overlooking the rolling mounds and single winding road of the cemetery. Alone among the silent souls of the deceased, he replays his recorded memories of his father. Here he finds a peaceful refuge from the unrelenting noise of the living.

4

Hours later, as the light of the sun transitions into a dark night, the popular hangout, Wyth Island, is hopping with excitement. From the outside of the building, a sound can hardly be heard, but inside, the DJ's AllVu, music is blaring in the ears of the celebrating crowd. They jump up and down behind the flashing lights while the highly anticipated Regional Drone Race Finals begin. Throughout the energetic hall of youth, color-changing mood outfits light up the dim hall. In this large, converted warehouse, graduates from all over the city converge to commemorate the days between the end of education and the entrance into The Path. It's a rite of passage that is, for the most part, overlooked by authority as minor indiscretions are ignored.

This is Gen Phoenix, the first generation born and raised in the age of The Path. Allegiance to its ways is the only life they know. Long gone are the reckless days of indiscriminately sharing videos of bathroom fights and underaged, drunken nudity captured at rowdy parties. These adolescents are much more conscious of the effects of irresponsibility and are extremely cautious when taking risks. After 18 years of restraint and careful attention to their SIVs, they're ready to find out their rewards in The Path.

The night's festivities are just getting started, but the growing Wyth Island crowd is in a frenzy. Local favorite, Zoe Phenon, uses her mind to remotely control her drone from her command center. Twisting and turning, she experiences the haptic bumps and vibrations as if being in the actual cockpit. Her drone hurtles around a tight corner at over 100 miles per hour. The finish line is in sight, and all she must do is maneuver beyond her rival's aircraft to claim the opening-round lead.

"Zoe Phenon's angling for position, but it looks too close," screams the animated announcer as Zoe's glider edges a cement wall. Fans brace in anticipation with an up close and personal AllVu vantage.

"OHHHHH, that's it!!" the announcer shrieks. Within a split second, the left wing clips the wall, sending the racer spinning. Zoe Phenon tries hard to gain control, but her aircraft collides and then shatters into a blaze of digitally-simulated smoke and fire. Fortunately for Zoe, the only harm to her is her ego. She shoots from her command center seat and throws up her fist in frustration at the destruction of her beloved drone.

"Shit, man --- did you see that?" yells Lateria, while swinging her short silver hair and dangling, strobe-light earrings to the banging music. The AllVu augmented sounds are so loud she can hardly hear her own words. Flashing room lights reflect off her fluorescent, glistening lip gloss and AllVu "bling." Petite and full of sassy energy, Lateria rounds out the tight threesome, along with Rony and Jolem. She turns sharply to Rony. "Jolem's been dark all afternoon," she continues. "I've sent, like, four invites to my World. What the hell, man?"

"Jo's okay," Rony yells back. "He's paying his respects."

"Ahhh, okay – he's at the cemetery again. I get it. But he's been dark for a looong time. He's definitely over his limit…again. Doesn't he even care about his SIV?"

"Yeah. I know," Rony says curiously, crinkling his lips. "Give 'im a little time. He'll get it together before he enters The Path."

In the midst of the celebration, Lateria's arms fall to her side, while her demeanor grows somber. "Yo, stop showing your World --- I need to ask you something."

"Teri, you know my people might want to weigh in; what's up?"

"Rony, hide LiveView please?!"

"Okay, okay... what's up?"

"Silence music," she says, and while people continue dancing, to her, the room grows quiet. "Sooo, what's the deal...and be honest, Sola --- is he still messing with Incubus??"

Fidgeting uncomfortably and ruffling his high hair, Rony stalls before responding. "Teri – I don't know."

For those seeking a quick escape while bypassing the limitations imposed on virtual reality, Incubus is the sedative of choice. Any decent hacker can develop a basic Incubus program, and its mind-altering effects are typically short-lived. They appear like tiny clear pills, leave no physical trace and their after-effects usually subside after a few minutes. Most stay far away, fearful of the illegal recreation. Those daring enough to engage typically experience intense psychological pleasure with few drawbacks. For those not so lucky, a bad program can send the mind into a horrible delirium between reality and fantasy, from which some never break free.

"He needs to stay away from that stuff," Lateria offers.

"C'mon Teri, it's not that bad."

"ARE YOU CRAZY???" she wails. "Don't make me replay the experiences. You remember what that shit did to him."

"I know, I know...I'm just saying lots of people do it with no problems."

"Rony, my cousin got lost in one of those programs for weeks. It's no joke."

As if on cue, suddenly Jolem's LiveView becomes active again. "What's up, cronies?" he asks as his World Cam footage appears in front of them.

"Whooo, Jolem! What up, Sola?" shouts Rony.

"Heeeyy, Joleyyy!" follows Lateria, sticking her tongue out like a lizard.

"I'm almost in the building."

"Well, hurry. This party is fierce!" says Rony, hopping up and down. "Lots o' love in here too, Sola, so try to loosen up and have some fun. WHOOOOOW!!" he shouts, raising his arms.

"Okay, Sola. I'll see you in a min," Jolem chuckles with a twisted smile and goodbye salute.

Jolem's LiveView disappears and Rony and Lateria return to the energetic party. "HOW DO YOU FEEEEL!??" shouts the MC, and the room instantly illuminates from the glow of mood, wearing fabrics shining bright as the sun. "I FEEL GOOOOD!" they yell, as the background bass bangs thunderously. The crowd goes wild.

The psychedelic experience continues, and out from the smoky darkness, Jolem floats slowly on his AirBoard. He hops off as Lateria throws her arms around him, hugging like she hadn't seen him in years. Although extremely close friends, most of their interactions are virtual. She lives in a zone on the south end of town, and they are rarely in the same room together. Jolem spins her around, embracing her tightly, and then reaches out to slap hands with Rony.

As the night wears on, the large congregation of segregated zones converges into one giant liberating celebration. It's a colorful assembly, with a mixture of ethnic and cultural backgrounds which represent the mulatto face of modern-day America. Mind-altering stimulants flow through the electric room, elevating the sexual intensity as they purge years of bottled-up restraint. Throughout the city, festivities outlast the night and keep going well into the morning hours.

5

Early afternoon the next day, Jolem awakes in his bed, almost unaware of how and when he made it home. The night's party was intense, and as he wrestles his eyelids open, he feels the aftermath effects.

"Good AFTERNOON, Jolem," quips Li'l J. "It was a long night --- how are you feeling?"

"Li'l J --- now THAT was a party," Jolem mumbles, rubbing his eyes. "What time is it?"

"It's 12:44 PM, and a warm 76 degrees. Your mom and Liz are downstairs eating lunch. Shall I prepare your meal and let them know you're on the way down?"

Jolem props himself up on his elbows and stretches his neck backward until he's looking up to the ceiling. "Hmmm, I really don't feel like hearing my mom's mouth right now," he cracks. "All she wants to talk about is The Path. Does she know about my shirt?"

"Well, it was just a minor incident, and I sent it out for repair. Your account was low but had just enough credits to cover the costs. You need to do a few good deeds to get your credits back up. Your mom wasn't alerted, so no need to involve her. However, I'm not aware if she's seen the experience. It was very popular."

"Okay, good. I guess we'll just have to wait and see…"

"But Jolem – the nightmare you had last night…"

"I know, I know," Jolem interrupts. "Believe me, Li'l J – that was the last time."

"I hope so, but the chances you will use Incubus again are great. Let's get help."

"NO – no, I can kick this. Trust me."

"As you wish."

Jolem drops his legs off of the side of his bed and blows out a gust of air. "Okay, show AllVu," he mutters and instantly, invisible items around the room come to life. As he lethargically slips onto the floor, his smarthouse responds to his movements. Around him, his grungy, synthesized music begins low, then progressively bumps like a live orchestra. Out of his bare walls, his creative digital doodles of superhero characters, ghouls, and strange shapes display vividly. He extends his pointer finger into the air and draws a screaming face with Xs for eyes. He smirks contentedly, nods, then tosses the image in place with the others.

Like a snail, he inches from his bedroom into the hall on the way to the bathroom. As he walks, he's greeted with dynamically changing positive thoughts and affirmations that leap out of the clear walls. "It's a good life, Jolem," "Today's going to be a great day!" a few say, while soft sounds and sweet smells follow his steps. Even the temperature surrounding him adjusts to his personal liking.

His earthy, modern house is powered entirely by renewable clean energy, as are all structures built after the Natural Energy Act of 2029. Most of its interior and exterior walls are made of dense glass. They react to the sun, allowing natural light to flow from room to room and also obscure appropriately for privacy. Innovative designs usher fresh air throughout the house from the outside. With these systems, homes are adaptively cool in the summer and warm in the winter without the use of high-energy intensive devices.

After a quick wash up, Jolem finally makes his way downstairs. "Well, look who decided to come out of his room," his mother, Kirame, remarks sarcastically as he turns the corner into the kitchen. His sister Elizabeth, "Liz" for short, beams when she sees him step into the room. Without saying a word, a large, sparkling smiley face appears on her shirt, while a small pink heart pulsates and explodes above her head. Seven years younger than her brother, she idolizes him, and she is the light of his life.

Jolem cuts his eyes at his mom but flashes a quick wink to his sister. "Hey, squirt," he says, cracking a smile as he strolls to reach for his chilled drink, which suddenly appears out of his refrigerator's camouflaged front panel. Unseen until requested, the hidden wall appliance individually preserves, monitors, and recycles items separately.

"Jolem, please have a seat. You know I'll get that for you," softly scolds the family robot assistant, commercially known as a HumanAid. With life-like features and motions, late model HumanAids are almost indistinguishable from real people. "You continue to do these things on your own," the humanoid politely admonishes as he attempts to intercept the beverage.

"Don't worry, I've got it," Jolem scoffs, refusing his help. Swiftly moving past him, he reaches out and grabs his own drink.

"Congratulations, Solar," his mom says beaming, then ruffling her fingers through his curly hair. "Isn't it a good life?"

"'Sola' not 'Solar.' You're so square," he laughs, shaking his head condescendingly before taking a large gulp.

"Okay, sorry I'm not stellar enough for you," she cracks. "I am so proud of you."

"C'mon, Mom, it's not that big a deal," he replies, pulling his head away.

"Jolem. It is a VERY big deal. The Path awaits you, son."

Jolem smirks awkwardly, turning away from his mom, then casually moves over to the table. He plops down into the seat next to Liz and grabs a whole-wheat pastry off a center plate. "So, Squirt, what's up with you?" he asks nonchalantly while taking a bite.

Smiling affectionately, she doesn't have a care in the world. "Ah - nothing," she replies without looking his way. She abruptly giggles and then slaps her hand on the table. "You were supposed to ride the bubble up to Sector 5, not EXPLODE it!!" she blurts out, then bursts into laughter.

"Liz – you know there's no VR at the table. Leave your World immediately," Kirame calmly, but firmly instructs.

"Oh, c'mon Mom. We're up to SECTOR 5. You know how long I've been trying to get there??"

"I don't care. Pause it, and tell your friend you'll be back after you eat."

"But mom – I can't just leave her in my alternate. She doesn't even know what she's doing!!"

"LIZ – now."

Twisting her lips, Liz sulks in her seat. "Ooookkkay. Mom," she sighs. "You better get out before the Cynocephalus bites your head off," she says to her across-town classmate. "Give me about 10 minutes, and I'll be right back."

After quickly hiding her AllVu, she begins to cram her food into her mouth until her cheeks are stuffed like those of a chipmunk.

Chuckling, Kirame shakes her head. It seems every day, she needs to reinforce her house VR rules. She can still recall the days as a young child when people were glued to their cell phones and tablet computers. Today, clunky devices are like dinosaurs. With her arms crossed, her attention shifts casually to Jolem as he sits, twisting a loose piece of bread between his fingers. Kirame is more than puzzled. She leans against the kitchen wall like a mannequin, with one hand on her chin and the other resting on her waist.

"Jolem...aren't you excited about your Path Advisement??" she questions, baffled by his apathy. He appears carefree.

"Oh," he replies without a moment's pause, "no."

"What do you mean – 'no'?? This is one of the most important meetings of your life, and all you say is 'no.'"

Growing increasingly irritated, Jolem drops his hands to his side, and he throws his head back. "C'mon Mom, not now…"

With her arms still folded, Kirame moves in close. "Jolem, after all we've been through, it's here; you've made it," she states, swinging open her arms. "I know you have never been extremely enthusiastic about The Path, but you're in a good position now. Your SIV is fine. You just have to lighten up a little, build some relationships, get some high ratings..."

"'Never extremely enthusiastic,' huh? I think that's a li'l understated. I don't care what people think about me," he mumbles under his breath as he stuffs his face into his hands.

Kirame stands, hands on hips, and gazes at Jolem. He is the spitting image of his father, and his stubborn aversion to The Path is painfully familiar.

"So, what do you want to do, Jolem? Live off the grid in a Unicorn... or worse, become one of these idiotic Freedom Fighters?? It's a good life. Stop fighting it."

"Idiotic Freedom Fighters? How can you say that??" Jolem lashes out. "Freedom Fighters are activists. Maybe they have a point."

"Jolem, please," Kirame smirks derisively. "What's their point? They're fighting against their own interests. There is no point."

"I just think it's unfair to have such a rigid viewpoint, Ma...this IS still 'The Land of Liberty', right??" he argues. He drops back down into his seat and turns toward the end-to-end window wall overlooking the backyard.

Kirame releases a belabored sigh. She moves forward, reaches out her hand and places it lovingly on his shoulder. "To hear you talk like this scares me, Son. You sound just like your father."

"And is that so bad??" he murmurs with his head down.

Instead of returning a sharp reply, Kirame bites her bottom lip and contemplates. She's had this debate many times over, but they remain at an impasse.

"Jolem, I'm just afraid sometimes. Like your father, you're strong, and you're a fighter...but there's no need to fight anymore. It's a good life! No wars. No hunger. No poverty. The Path has set us free. Why can't you see this?"

"'Free,' Mom?? Really??"

As if clearing the room from overhearing eavesdroppers, Kirame cautiously glances back and forth. "Jolem, just last week, two Compliance Control Officers – not one, but two visited the Perrys' house."

Jolem's eyes and mouth pop open wide. Swinging around in Kirame's direction, he props himself up in his seat. "REALLY? They were looking for Mr. Perry, right? What did he do??"

"I don't know, and I don't care. This is the second time officers have visited him this year. You know the FDEC doesn't send them unless someone is in deviation."

As his mom passionately appeals, a sense of sudden sadness and conflict overcomes Jolem. His thoughts take him to a troubled period in his past. At the young age of thirteen, Jolem abandoned his life of convenience and escaped to an Unconnected Community (Unicom) far from home. Unicoms are self-sustaining villages iSolated in rural dead zones located outside of The Path's nationwide wireless signals. With typical numbers of no more than a couple hundred people per village, Unicoms are largely left alone by the government. Most of these communities are peaceful havens for the recluse, while others serve as a refuge for deviants or vagabonds looking to disappear.

When Jolem prepared to run away, he knew he had to rid himself of all AllVu technology to avoid being tracked. Even shedding most of his clothes was necessary because of the signals from their digital fibers. With some help from friends, he managed to stow away in an old supply truck headed west to a Pennsylvania village aptly named "Refugio del Mundo", or "World's Hideaway."

Powered by home-grown, patchwork natural energy contraptions, Unicoms are rare places, still using old local connected networks. Their buildings are enclosed in conductive metal to provide extra protection from wireless signals and unwanted visitors. While Jolem's thoughts continue to wander, he recalls sitting completely immersed in conversation with the senior resident, Jeremiah, as LAN technicians worked through the night to restore the community's network that was lost after a storm.

"Jolem," Jeremiah began in a low, raspy whisper. "Technology and The Path have created mindless zombies, incapable of tying their own shoes without instruction," he lamented passionately. His strained words were eked out through pre-prohibition chain-smoking vocal cords. "They are nothing more than living, breathing, and shitting puppets. Don't trust it, Jolem – don't trust it! At the end of the strings, there's always a master."

For three days, Jolem basked in the congeniality of the tight-knit community. Attentively, he listened to narrated historical stories resembling tall tales. They were spoken with the exaggerated detail that today's microwave attention-span minds are almost incapable of following. However, refusing to debunk his own intelligence, he challenged their wisdom. "But what's the alternative?" he questioned, "Why collect all this information – innovate, if not to use it to help lives? Isn't society better?"

Jeremiah sat on a rug with his legs crossed. His thick, hanging, gray dreadlocks raked the ground. He peered impressively over to his life partner, Salam, and then back to Jolem while sucking through the empty spacing created by his missing front teeth. He was indeed intrigued by the astute young man, with insightfulness well beyond his years. "You're a smart guy, aren't you??" he chuckled as he sized up his young challenger. "I wish I had all the answers," he continued before clearing his throat. "In many ways, you have to make up your own damn mind. But the turmoil you feel bubbling inside is real; it is human. Humans and NonHumans are not the same. I don't give a damn what the agreement says. I don't care what "logic" says. We must fight for our humanity. We must fight for our sapience and all the mighty bestowed abilities. If we do not have the burning passion to fight for these things, we are truly no more than machines."

Jolem's thoughts return from his daydream back to the present, and his posture deflates like a balloon pierced by a tiny pin. His fallen eyes lift from the ground and shift in the direction of his mother. From the intensity of her stare, she appears as if she's attempting to solve a game show puzzle.

"I hear you, Mom," he concedes after the long break, "but don't you ever want more? We live in a bubble. When is the last time you've been out of this town?"

"Wha'?? In the midst of all that's going on in Europe and other parts of the world? We had an amazing trip in Paris; didn't you enjoy it?"

"Well yeah – but, we didn't actually go," he comments.

"Hmm – what do you mean?"

"Mom. Those were simulated environments, Alternates. We weren't actually there."

"Jolem – what difference does it make?? We have wonderful memories from the trip. In our Worlds, we can go anywhere..see anything. My Track helps preserve the air we breathe. It gives me purpose and fulfillment.

I remember when I was your age. I had just finished school, but I had no idea what to do with my life. The livelihoods of everyone I knew, including Nana and Grandpa, were all being replaced by NonHumans. There weren't any jobs, no direction. I was frustrated, angry, and confused. Everyone was. Crime was high, and many were afraid just to leave their homes. That year, President Mendoza was elected, and we figured out how to coexist with NonHumans. Soon, she introduced The Path and life…became beautiful."

"But…"

"Listen, it might not seem like much to you Jolem, but I'm happy, healthy, and safe. I have everything I need right here… and so do you. It's a good life."

While nodding slowly, his head is scattered with competing emotions. Maybe conformity would not be so bad, he considers. For all his gripes, he can't deny that things are good, and after hundreds of years of violence and wars, the country has been quieted by peace. Following his father's passing, his innate guardian qualities kicked into high gear regarding his mother and young sister. He would do anything to protect and keep them out of harm's way.

"Maybe you're right," he whispers. With both hands, he grips the side of his chair, pushes himself up from the table, then heads out of the room.

"Jolem??" Kirame calls, concerned about her embattled son.

"I'm just going to my room for a while," he says, attempting to mask the anxiety from his voice. "I'm sure I'll get it together before my Advisement. It'll be okay, Mom."

Standing still and watching him walk out of sight, Kirame's thoughts are riddled. Jolem has always been a unique soul, even as a child. Most graduates are enthusiastic about knowing their Track in The Path. They have been preparing for it throughout their adolescence. It's extremely frustrating to see her son squander his potential without explanation. Deviants of The Path become social outcasts or worse, and Jolem's stubborn opposition gives her chills. She's clueless about how to help him.

When he returns to his room, Jolem plops onto his dual-purpose sofa that morphs into a full-size bed upon request. "Privacy," he says. Responding to his command, his clear sliding glass door seals tightly and darkens to shroud any view inside. As he touches the corner of the bottom drawer of his desk, it slides open. Reaching inside, he carefully pulls out an item as if embracing a precious, delicate gem, then places it on his lap. As he traces his fingers across its brittle surface, his eyelids become heavy while his mind wanders to faraway lands. His hand scrolls from the leftmost edge across to the right, then his fingers tenderly lift open the cover of a – book.

Out of popular circulation for a generation, books typically only exist in museums or are stored on the shelves of wealthy fanciers. Nowadays, periodicals and other communications are all digital. Paper is a luxury and in very short supply. The need for print-outs is nonexistent; even handwriting is seldom seen or performed, as it has been replaced by dictation.

Jolem reclines in his seat and flips through pages, caressing the felted sheets as he becomes engulfed in the simple story of a young man's backpacked hike down the Nile. He's read it so many times that the words are already ingrained in his mind, yet each time, it feels new. He recalls how the historic document landed in his possession years ago during his childhood hideaway in the Unicom. Jeremiah presented it as a memento in response to his profound thirst for knowledge of the past. To this day, Jolem cherishes it as one of his most prized possessions.

After laying the brittle hardcover gently down, he walks over to the long-mirrored door of his closet and stands firmly in front of it, as if challenging himself to a duel. His fingers ball into tight fists hanging down from his lanky frame as his brow crinkles into a knot. "You can do this, man," he proclaims. "You have to do this."

He prods himself into submission, scowling and pounding his fist against his chest like a gorilla. Abruptly, his internal battle is disturbed.

"Jolem, there's a visitor at your door," alerts Li'l J.

"Who is it?"

"It's Liz. Shall I allow her in?"

"Hold on," he replies as he swiftly but discreetly slips his book back into its secret compartment. All paper publications are to be declared to the state so that they can be admitted into the national registry. He doesn't want anyone to know, including his family and friends, of its existence.

"Okay, Li'l J, let her in."

Instantly the black glass door becomes translucent and slides open. "Hi, Jolem. Whatchu doin'?" she says, with a full smile wrapping her round, butterscotch nose. She releases her long, dark hair she had been twisting between her fingers and pops into the room.

"Just thinking," he replies, waving her in. Floating next to him, she bounces onto his sofa bed and kicks her feet up.

"About what?" she asks, looking around. Through her AllVu, she can see a vivid scene covering his empty walls. "Ha – that's stellar! Did you just design that?"

"What?? Oh, the space station? A couple days ago. You like it, huh?"

"Yahh, it's way-out. Imma share it," she says, as she swings a series of thumbs up at the wall. When it hits her World, others also pay tribute, and his SIV gradually ticks up.

"Thanks, Squirt."

"So, whatcha' thinking about?"

"Wellll…," he begins, pondering, trying to weed through all his random thoughts; he's at a sudden loss of words. "Very soon, things will change. I'll enter The Path."

"Yeah, I know... but what's goin' to change?"

"You know... I'll pick my Track, get my own place; before long, maybe even start my own family." Looking up at the ceiling, Jolem wipes his forehead as he contemplates what to say. The thought of the mundane is as welcome as a bullet to the head.

"But those are GOOD things, right?" she asks, confused.

During the following moments of silence, Jolem gets lost in her inquisitive eyes, as they seem to grow the size of saucers. Quickly, he snaps back when he notices the beginnings of her distress.

"You're right! Everything's goin' to be just fine," he declares. "Everything is going to be great!"

At the time of their father's passing, Jolem was ten, and Liz was only three. She has a few years of stored memories of their dad, but mostly having him around is a blur. Jolem has been the dominant male figure in her life. She was so happy to see him return after being missing during his brief escape to the Unicorn. After his three-day stay, Jolem found his way back home, mainly with the vision of his distraught young sister in his mind. Most of his cherished memories from this period have only been shared with a select few, and he has never returned. However, he does long for the distance from the public's grasp that he experienced during that short visit. For just a few days, he felt he was indeed soaring amongst the birds without the "Big Eye" following his every movement. When he left, the community extended an open invitation, and he vowed one day he'd be back.

Jolem tickles Liz as she squirms around on the sofa like a fish out of water. She's a felicitous spirit with a genuine passion for just being, like most children her age. With the world at their fingertips, they have no concept of hard work or struggle. Used to being in command, their thoughts are shallow, and instant gratification is their expectation. The ability to critically analyze is covered by technology, so for people, the skill is hardly cultivated. As the loving siblings share the tender play, Jolem finally embraces the carefree moment. Liz, his greatest source of strength, is also his most powerful weakness.

6

"Jolem, you missed my World show this morning. What gives?" Rony asks two days later, as they glide through the entryway of a local lounge store. Featuring warm, colorful walls with personalized digital messages of greetings and joy, the atmosphere ushers them in. In cushioned seats, people hang out casually, enjoying the beginning of another relaxed day. Some interact with in-person companions, while others are off in the ethos of their social Worlds.

As soon as Jolem and Rony enter the building, they're immediately halted by the open hand of a friendly holographic store representative. She slowly nods and waves her finger disapprovingly, like a mother chastising her child caught jumping on the bed.

"Welcome back, Mr. McKay! I'm sorry, but as you know, Airboarding is prohibited in the building," she remarks, planting her hands on her waist. The vivid, three-dimensional presence of today's holograms is remarkably realistic.

Jolem grunts, hops down, quickly scoops his board under his arm, then glances back at Rony.

"Thank you, Jolem," the greeter replies graciously, then swipes her hand inward. "Please let us know if there is ANYTHING we can do to make your experience with us more pleasurable today," she continues and then disappears as they pass.

"Uhh…I forgot what I was saying," Jolem replies, frowning after dismissing the greeter's interruption. "Oh ye---your show. Liz and I were on a Kenyan Safari. I've been promising her all week we'd go."

"I hear ya."

"You have enough fans anyway, Sola," Jolem cracks.

"Jo, we had a CRAZY convo in my World! Lots of people there. My likability is climbing through the ROOF! I can't wait to enter The Path," Rony utters, overjoyed and shaking his clenched fists. While cackling like a banshee, a round, ogling face leaps out of his head and bounces around the room.

"Man, you're a clown. Not that again, pleassse," Jolem says, cutting his eyes to the ceiling.

"Whatever, man. I can't believe I let you talk me into pushing my Advisement off. I could've found out my Track last week. Now, I have to wait till Friday."

"Sola, that was your decision," Jolem says, shrugging. "You didn't have to follow me."

"C'mon, man! We're a team!"

"Yeah, whatever."

"But this morn, there was this one little glitch," says Rony, wincing. "It only happened for like a few minutes, but my World just locked. My assistant went 'loco.' He just kept saying 'you've reached your destination' over and over. I couldn't interact with my World or nothing."

"Yeah, that's happened to me a few times. They say it's nothing big; just a li'l' malfunction in Halcyon. I'm better than that."

"What do you mean?"

"It's clearly a hack."

"Whattt? I doubt hackin' is a thing anymore, Jo. Like you said, probably just a malfunction," shrugs Rony."

"Rony, Rony, Rony…" Jolem sighs. "Nothing bothers you, huh?"

"Jolem, life is great. It was a short interruption – just like that, Juko popped back. He apologized for the system malfunction, and we were back on."

"So, hackin's not a 'thing' anymore? You think it all just went away."

"Hell no. But I believe The Path takes care of it all."

"Oh really?" Jolem says cynically, glancing at Rony. "I'm just remembering some of the wild things we used to do, just for the hell of it. You know... when I was hangin' with Gank and them boys."

"I know, man. My favorite was that experience in middle education. Ya know that stunt next to the FDEC building. You boys were INSANE..., especially Gank. You still in touch?"

"Haven't seen him in a while, but we catch up every now and then."

Rony stops in his tracks, turns and looks at him sternly. "Jo, man – I've been meaning to talk to you about something," he says abruptly, shifting his demeanor. "Juko, hide LiveView."

"What's up?"

"You're still getting that stuff from Gank, aren't you?"

Jolem's head drifts off and he releases a heavy sigh. Nervously scratching his face and running his fingers through his hair, he'd clearly like to avoid this conversation. He turns back to Rony and confidently replies, "It's nothing, man – don't worry."

"Jo, you gotta leave it alone – for real. Incubus is no good. Teri's worried about you."

"I know, I know. I'm done. Believe me."

"I don't understand. Is it really that much better than VR Alternates?"

"Rony, man...even your alternates are monitored. They tell you how long you can be in a program...they even restrict what you can do. With Incubus, I can truly do ANYTHING; go ANYWHERE. I can't even describe how good it feels. It's like the intensity of all your fears and passions colliding. Sometimes, it seems you're gone for years, but in reality, only hours, or sometimes minutes, pass. It takes you places you can hardly imagine. It's an unbelievable experience. And the best part is, Big Eye is outta my head."

"That stuff can be really dangerous, though??"

"I know man, but Gank writes these programs. He comes up with some wild experiences. I just needed to get through this year. Believe me – I'm good."

"You sure?"

"Yeah"

"Okay. Stella."

For the time being, they slap hands and put the contentious issue to rest as they continue through the store. While they browse around creatively-arranged product displays, personalized advertisements reach out to them.

"Hey Jolem, don't you want to take me home," seductively suggests an animated 3-D Juice Blast. "It's been such a long time, and you enjoyed me soooo much."

When he passes, the quick presentation evaporates as the next appears with its own pitch. "Jolem, you don't have to worry about my price today. I'm on sale this week," comforts Lemon Jolt X. "Mmmmm... remember how great I taste."

Jolem lifts the cool, lemony beverage and holds it securely while he considers his purchase. His eyelids close, and for a few seconds, he experiences the virtual sensation of the sweet drink teasing his taste buds. "Man Rony! I had forgotten how much I liked these – have you tried one?"

Rony's head jerks toward Jolem after being sidetracked by his AllVu conversation with Lateria. "Huh??" he asks.

"Lemon Jolt X – have you had one before??"

"Ahhh – nope. It's gotten great reviews from my World, though. Teri, you??"

"Here," remarks Jolem, and then tosses the can over to his buddy.

Rony's fingers wrap around the chilled drink, and his face lights up. "Shit, you're right! Is there sugar in this?? Teri, try this," he says, then shares the virtual sensation with his remote friend.

"Wow! That's great!" she says, throwing a thumbs up.

"Yep, it's got a Li'l sugar," says Jolem. "The Detrimental to Health tax is pretty high, so I haven't had one in a while, but they're on sale. You know I'm getting one today."

"I hear that!"

Jolem grabs the juice can and walks around the display rack. "And this too!" he exclaims as he snatches a Chocolate Bomb.

"You high-rollin' today, huh? The DTH on that is ridiculous!"

"You only live once, my friend, and my mom gifted me some extra credits for graduation. For the next two weeks, imma do whatever the hell I want."

As Jolem pumps his fist, Rony bumps it with his own. "I hear that, Sola!" Rony replies, then focuses back on his live audience. "Get you one of these Lemon Jolt X, my peeps. The next two weeks is gonna' be stratospheric! You hear me? STRATOSPHERIC!!"

The boys carefreely pass through the exit of the store, joking around. Without a thought, their purchases are automatically finalized, and payment is rendered from their accounts. Jolem rips open his small, square snack and ogles the sweet chocolate morsel held high in his fingertips. He slowly lifts it up to his nose, then takes a whiff as if he was holding pure heaven. It's been months since he's tasted sugar, and substitutes are still just not like the real thing. The Detrimental to Health taxes on risky foods and behaviors are extremely high. As a result, cookies, candies, cakes, and the like, are luxuries reserved only for special occasions.

"Oh man, let me just have a tiny piece," Rony begs, reaching out his hand. As if entranced by a nugget of pure gold, his jaw drops.

"Are you crazy?" Jolem exclaims as he recoils. "You know how much this cost??" He turns away from Rony, then drops it in his wide-open mouth in stride. Melodramatically, he stops as if stunned with satisfaction, closes his eyes, and chews completely to savor every second of the pleasurable experience.

"Ahhhh, I get it, man. Don't rub it in," bemoans Rony.

"What, you didn't think that was funny," ribs Jolem, cracking up. "I thought everything was funny to you. Look at his face, Teri!"

"Jolem, you're a FOOL!" screams Lateria, interacting remotely. "He got you, Rony! I'll catch up with you guys later --- gotta quick gig and need them credits," she says, and then her LiveView disappears.

Jolem nudges Rony mockingly, but then his playful expression changes. As he gazes into the sky, he suddenly inhales deeply, then slowly exhales through his flared nostrils. The vision of a routine low-hanging observation drone captures him once again.

"Jolem – you okay??"

Without a quick reply, Jolem sucks in another gulp of air. Through all the years he's known Rony, the two have never seen eye-to-eye on surveillance. Contemplating whether he should even bring up the subject, he pauses for a moment and then peers back.

"Rony, let me ask you something, man."

"Okay, what's up?"

"Wait, hide LiveView for a min."

"For what?? It might be something my World wants to weigh in on."

Jolem's AllVu visor evaporates, then he elevates one eyebrow above the other. "Man, you and your damn World. Hide for a minute."

"Okay – 'Juko, hide LiveView.' What's up, Sola??"

Rubbing his hands together with hesitation, Jolem looks down at the ground. "Soo – NONE of this bothers you, huh? None of it?" he asks.

"None of what??"

"The drones, the cameras, the digital trackers... any of it."

"Nah, man --- not again. You made me hide my LiveView for this??" Rony asks, brushing Jolem away. "They keep us safe...and you know this. Would you rather be afraid of bombs in alleys or at live experiences?? What about Liz? What if she was lost? What then?"

"You're right. I don't know. I don't have all the answers, and I know things weren't great before The Path. But people were alive back then; they lived."

"'They lived??' – what's wrong with you, Man?? The country was on the edge of collapse, don't you remember? Viruses, youth revolts, violence, and crime. We're now living the BEST LIFE, Sola. I don't get you."

Rony steps toward his conflicted friend and pats him on the shoulder. "Listen, Jo – we have two weeks of uninhibited fun until we enter The Path. Let's make them legendary. I pushed my date back for you, bro, but I'm looking forward to it. This is all easy... just follow your guides."

Nodding his head, Jolem chuckles. "Maybe you're right, Man. Or maybe I'll just move to a Unicom," he jokes.

"Jo – you're crazy. You know that, right?"

"I'm crazy?? Sometimes I feel I'm the only sane person on the planet."

"What you really NEED is some love. I mean, Jolem, what's the deal? When's the last time you connected?"

"Whatever, Man. I don't know. When I connect with someone, our probability metrics always start high, and then we quickly fizzle out. Maybe I'm destined to be alone."

"You just take everything too seriously. Lighten up. Your likability is terrible!"

Jolem nods out into the distance, rubbing the fuzz on his chin. "I don't know – maybe you're right," he snickers. "I guess we'll have to see."

"I guess so…"

The two friends pal around en route to Rony's house until something brings the light-natured fun to a halt.

"Wait!" warns Rony, holding out his arm. "What's goin' on over there??" he questions as they quickly dip out of sight. Peering around a row of hedges, they notice the activity of Compliance Control Officers once again at their neighbor's house. The chilling vision of Compliance Control canvassing the Perry family property sends fear into the hearts of all onlookers. Peeping out of their windows, people inconspicuously maintain their distance in hopes of remaining unseen. No one wants attention from Compliance Control. These ominous figures don't say very much as they creep in their matte grey bodysuits and mirrored facial shields.

"What in the world is goin' on over there?" wonders Rony, gawking. "People say – they're Non Human."

Witnessing a Compliance Control visit is as attention-grabbing as a blaring fire truck rushing down the street. Discretion is not their goal, as fear is one of their leading weapons.

"My mom said they've been to his house a couple of times already," whispers Jolem. "Mr. Perry is definitely in Deviation."

"I've got to make sure my World sees this," says Rony as he zooms in on the encounter.

While the boys watch from afar, the Perry door slides open, and the three officers enter the building. Neither Jolem nor Rony say a word as they stand stunned, awaiting the outcome. Tense moments pass. A short while later, the door slides open again. The compliance officers emerge from inside, dragging Mr. Perry's limp body to their black-matted utility vehicle. They toss him in, then zip out of sight.

With his mouth and eyes open wide, Rony slowly turns to Jolem. "Did you see that? Mr. Perry wasn't even moving," he says.

"Yeah, that was insane."

The experiences of Compliance Control visits are legendary, but this is the first time they've actually seen one in person. The display is a startling reminder for Rony to stay in line or face The Path's consequences.

"See, Jolem, that's what I'm talking about. Don't mess with The Path," Rony stresses.

As he folds his arms, Jolem turns towards Rony confidently. "Man, they don't scare me," he proclaims defiantly.

PLAYTIME IS OVER

7

About a week after Jolem and Rony's Compliance Control encounter, Jolem stands on the sidewalk, facing the Federal Department of Efficiency and Compliance's Northern New Jersey District 7 Building. Surrounded by various municipalities, the unassuming white structure sits in the center of the quaint downtown metropolis. It's 9:15 AM, Tuesday morning, and 15 minutes until Jolem's scheduled Path Advisement. With his AirBoard stashed under his arm, he's been planted in the same spot for so long he resembles a statue.

"Jolem, you know the door's not going to come to you. You'll actually have to go to it," quips Li'l J, but Jolem doesn't say a word. He looks forward to this meeting as much as another one of his mom's long lectures. His lips curl, and fingers tap rapidly against his thigh until he's unable to stall any longer. The time has come for him to face his future.

Jolem lags up the white cement ramp leading to the building entrance. As he slowly advances, he spies the sliding front glass door with contempt, as if it is an old enemy. When he's within feet, he drifts to a stop. "Okay, Li'l J, here we go," he sighs. He runs his fingers through his hair, and his slouching posture straightens. After a strong exhale from his puckered lips, he then continues inside.

The door shuts behind him tightly as he pauses with his arms hanging to his side. His sights slowly pan the massive white lobby. Its interior is much more impressive than its exterior would suggest. At first glance, it appears vacant, with no one in sight. Just then, about 15 feet ahead of him, an attractive holographic figure wearing a light gray, shiny bodysuit appears out of nowhere, standing with a bright smile and arms open in an embrace.

"Good morning, Mr. McKay!" she says in a cordial welcome. Entering the structure, his presence was detected, identified, and confirmed.

"Ahhhh…good morning…" Jolem replies, startled by her abrupt appearance.

"Welcome to the Federal Department of Efficiency and Compliance. We've been awaiting your arrival," she says pleasantly, then gestures in the direction of a small waiting area off to the side of the lobby. "Please have a seat, and your advisor will be with you in just a moment."

Jolem acknowledges with a nod, then slips his hands into his pockets and shrugs. Dragging his feet, he lumbers over to the closest seat, plops down, then his thoughts drift. As he fidgets impatiently, he twists in his chair with hopes the appointment will be over quickly. Fortunately, his wait in the lobby is not long. Less than a minute after he settles into his seat, a woman in a similar gray bodysuit and hair wrapped in a tight bun strolls in front of him.

"Good morning, Mr. McKay," she says calmly as she smiles and extends her hand to greet him. "I'm Mrs. Bolder, your FDEC Advisor. It is a pleasure to make your acquaintance. It's a good life, isn't it?"

"Oh – hello…ahh…yes, it is," replies Jolem, promptly lifting himself out of his seat to shake her hand. She entered so suddenly he didn't see her coming.

Her eyes scan from his feet to his head. "Hmmm…we are sooo happy to have you here," she says, displaying a smug smirk. "Please… follow me."

As they proceed down a narrow bright hallway, there is noticeable silence. Mrs. Bolder glides mechanically at a slow pace while Jolem tails closely behind. The endless white floors and walls of the hall are spotless. A quarter of the way down the corridor, she stops at a dark glass door, which slides open at her touch. "Please enter and have a seat," she says, motioning inward.

Moving into the room is like entering a different dimension, as bare, dark office walls surround him. They're a deep contrast to the lucent hall from which he entered. In the middle of the room, a white, curved seat resembling a cracked egg faces a long glass desk. He takes a few tentative steps forward, and as he approaches, the chair swings around in his direction. Hesitantly, he slips down and drops his hands into his lap.

In her continued, unhurried manner, Mrs. Bolder strolls around the desk, slides into the seat facing Jolem, then lays her hands flat on the table. Her lips turn upward, forming a large smile before she clears her throat with a couple of quick coughs. Finally, after a deep inhale, she speaks.

"Mr. McKay, before we begin, please silence your AllVu Assistant if you have not already done so. I'm quite sure you know how this works, but here is a quick outline of what to expect during your visit today. First, we will view a short presentation. Secondly, we will recap your background. Thirdly, we will discuss your future in The Path. There will be ample opportunities throughout to ask questions."

Her demeanor is stoic, almost robotic. Her smile looks crafted and painted in place like that on a child's doll. Although her words are supportive in nature, her undertone has the undeniable quality of an intolerant parent. After previewing his history, she already knows he's going to be a challenge and that he is classified as a "pre-deviant."

"So, before we proceed, are there any questions?" she asks.

Shrugging, he quickly replies, "No."

"Good…now let's take a look, shall we?"

Leaning back in her seat, Mrs. Bolder clamps her palms and shifts her attention to an adjacent wall. As the room dims, the beginning of an extravagant presentation bursts out of the darkness into the open space in front of them. "Decades ago, in a not-so-distant past," a grim announcer commences, as somber images of life before The Path begins to appear.

"The United States of America's ingenuity, innovation, and economy all stalled. Technology had outpaced its outdated educational system. Information and misinformation were flowing at an incredible and unmanageable rate. Healthcare was expensive and woefully insufficient, as diseases, obesity, viruses, and other invisible enemies menaced. Racial and civic unrest from the cities to the suburbs prevailed. And years after the nation recovered from the historic 2008 Great Recession and 2020 Pandemic, the unemployment rate again skyrocketed."

The announcer pauses for reflection while the prelude fades into black. After a few moments of silent nothingness, montages of happy families and loving friends working and playing emerge, accompanied by a charged soundtrack.

"Fast forward to today!" the announcer continues in an upbeat pitch. "All US business sectors are booming. Its educational system is envied across the globe. Healthcare is effective and available --- free to everyone. Social networks are organized. Violent crime has been eradicated. The United States of America's might has been restored while EVERY U.S. citizen has renewed purpose and fulfillment. Peace and happiness abound from sea to shining sea!"

The introduction concludes with a large community holding hands, beaming, while the American flag waves vigorously in the background. The announcer, proudly and victoriously, declares, "The turnaround was nothing more than miraculous, and we attribute this United States of America resurgence to – The Path!"

Jolem's left eyebrow lifts as he peers with confusion at Mrs. Bolder; she appears oddly amused as if it's her first viewing. With a faint sigh, he slowly turns back to the display, puzzled. He's heard stories of The Path presentation and knew what to expect, but having a front-row seat is even more awkward than he had envisioned.

Following the intro, the room brightens, then, out of thin air, emerges the holographic greeter from the lobby. "Hello again. I am SEE, the FDEC's Systematic Efficiency Engine," she says. "I hope you enjoyed our introduction to 'The Path.'

Mr. Jolem Ellius McKay," she continues, while visuals from Jolem's life appear like a movie behind her, "we congratulate you on the completion of your education. Although there have been some ups and downs over the last 18 years, you have become a fine young man with extreme potential. We are positive The Path will give you the tools you'll need to become a standup citizen and model contributor to society. I'm sure you're excited, but before you can begin your blissful journey, let me give you a little background on why The Path was created and how it has revitalized the United States of America."

She pauses briefly, grinning as her face bobs softly from side to side, then continues her presentation. As she moves in front of a stunning display, she points to life-like optics which correspond to her words.

"At the turn of the century, the world experienced a technological evolution with the commercial introduction of the Internet, also known as the World Wide Web. The masses marveled at the ability to connect with people and businesses across the globe with a simple click. Far-off lands instantly arrived at household front doorsteps, offering intimate access to the world and beyond like never before. Information was collected and stored, available for use whenever and wherever desired...and automation of laborious manual processes made it easier to complete complex tasks quicker and with fewer resources. Companies and forward-thinking individuals thrived.

These momentous achievements created opportunities that earlier only existed as fantasy in science fiction stories. The world instantly sped up, and a bubble of prosperity followed, which, unfortunately for many, was soon to burst. Despite all the positives the new reality created, there were unintended consequences of such swift progress. Due to various factors, disproportionate segments of the population were ill-equipped to benefit from this boom. As the world adjusted to doing more with less, many manual processes became obsolete, as did the workers who used to perform them. Those unprepared or unwilling to adapt to the rapidly changing times found themselves hopelessly unemployable and desperate for help. They were labeled 'The Displaced," and by 2030, their numbers were over 100 million and growing.

SEE pauses after the somber illustration. "How did the nation avoid complete disaster? Let's take a deeper journey to understand how we arrived at this cataclysmic moment," she says while gesturing with her hands like a game show host. Out of the shrouded darkness, a holographic earth expands in the air. While it slowly rotates, legions of white beams shoot from numerous locations and land all across its surface.

"Every day, from sources throughout the world, limitless data is gathered and stored in the endless ether of the Internet. Your family history, schedule, finances, restaurants, experiences you've enjoyed, people you've met in passing or friends you've known for years, music... fashion...food...so on and so on! This information adds to an infinitely growing universe of data which makes you... YOU. Your digital identity.

Through AllVu technology, today, all of our systems work together seamlessly to organize and manage our digital world. Decades ago, this was not the case. In the unorganized environment of the past, people were bombarded with an unrelenting flow of information...and they had to try to make sense of it all. I know it's difficult to imagine, but contemplate for a moment how challenging life's decisions would be today without the helpful guidance of your AllVu Assistant. Scary, right?

Years ago, consumers had to manually perform Internet searches and sift through endless results, at times fruitlessly, in pursuit of what they desired. Companies were forced to discover obnoxious and intrusive methods of advertising their products and services, often to people who had no need or interest in them. Colleges and universities were filled with undecided students, unsure of how best to use their talents. Workers spent countless hours accomplishing unnecessary tasks that produced little result or value for their employers. Worst of all, the proposed solutions to many of life's most complex challenges were based on politics, someone's intuition, or "gut feelings" instead of math and science. Think of all of the time, energy, and finances wasted with this global system of inefficiency.

Inefficiency. I'm sure you are sitting there with one question on your mind. 'Why?' Why, with all the technology, resources, and effective capabilities available, could this scenario exist? Why was society relying so heavily on inherently biased, often self-serving, and misinformed decisions made by humans? Why not use science and technology to help solve these formidable problems that humanity has struggled with for so long? It is the same question that baffled the minds of a growing group of progressive people. They sought to change this.

In the early 2020s, important technological advancements spawned the birth of first-generation 'NonHumans,' artificially-intelligent quantum systems with the capacity to think, learn, and adapt. For many, this was the breakthrough they were seeking. Across the country, NonHumans helped solve the unsolvable. However, while NonHumans transformed corporate infrastructures, employing humans became an illogical option in many professions. This led to the big wave of 2026. Millions of workers lost their jobs during this evolution.

Understandably, those displaced resented the NonHumans and the people embracing them. They rioted and protested in the streets, often violently. In November of 2028, as this growing chaos besieged the nation, the country elected the Progressive Party's Julia Mendoza as its president. She vowed to end the distractions and futile battles with technology. She promised to usher in a new relationship between people and NonHumans, based on a common goal: a target of cooperation that would give ALL citizens a better standard of living. This vision won the imagination of a fractured nation and resulted in the Human-NonHuman Partnership Agreement. Mankind accepted the unbreakable bond between man and machine.

In 2030, in coordination with a unified Congress, the President formed the Federal Department of Efficiency and Compliance. The FDEC's top priority was to advance the implementation of Human-Non-human partnerships throughout the nation. It was theorized that these re-imagined collaborations would revolutionize decision-making and streamline the life experience. Life's conclusions could be made without the influence of human bias or emotion while also leveraging natural passion and understanding when appropriate. The first one of these such Human-NonHuman teams included yours truly: SEE."

The congenial hologram smiles and tips her head before continuing.

"Although I appear before you in human form, I am actually the digital engine that drives the FDEC's operations. My capabilities are quite vast. My team was given an audacious goal. To use people and technology to create an efficient life experience that simplifies a complicated world.

We started this process by evaluating the data from government entities. All agencies and programs were scrutinized. Redundancies were merged, and inefficiencies were enhanced. Unnecessary or outdated departments were dismantled. Excessive spending and waste were trimmed. The federal government budget was cut by more than half, and its debt was eliminated. These measures and the mandatory "Re-Invest in America Program" have provided the government with the necessary financial resources to support bold initiatives like the universal living wage.

Next, we began assisting private corporations, schools, and other institutions in establishing efficient Human-NonHuman partnerships. Clunky corporate organizations of the past were filled with expensive full-time staff, even if there was no work for them to perform. Workers were typically bound to one company and often one boring job for years. In the 2020s, the emergence of the gig economy helped release businesses and employees from this archaic system. This flexible structure allowed employers to request and receive help for projects or "gigs" only when needed. It also freed employees to diversify their lives with unique and exciting short-term work experiences.

Then, all we had to do was streamline the process of connecting the workers to work. To do this, a National Resource Pool was created. All skills were classified as either "human" or "NonHuman." Those abilities requiring empathy were identified as uniquely human, while others requiring impartiality and physicality were determined better suited for NonHumans. All humans and NonHumans were subsequently positioned in the resource pool according to their individual skills and abilities. Employers no longer needed to scour for qualified workers, and employees no longer needed to search for gigs. The resource pool would automatically connect the appropriate talent to the need when requested. Between gigs, citizens were supported by the universal living wage. The displaced were no more.

As you can imagine, this cultural evolution reset the expectations of man at home and in the workplace. While most intensive tasks were assigned to NonHumans, the minutiae of the day were minimized for humans. People discovered leisure instead of labor and were able to focus on more important things, like family, friends, and pleasure. In a very short period, we had achieved our goal of creating an efficient and simplified life experience. However, this restructuring left many uneasy about man's true value on the planet. They wondered: if the NonHumans did all the work, what was the role of man?

Hard work and competition have been a cornerstone of the American ideal. Historically, society had placed significant value on what an individual produced and/or achieved. All the while, everyday acts of kindness or broader contributions to humanity often went unnoticed and rarely rewarded. It was time to change this perception of value to society. After centuries of war, pollution, and other abuse, the world needed champions. People needed a new purpose. The marriage of opportunities was obvious. Therefore, we developed the Societal Impact Valuation. Attached to AllVu, the SIV provided us the ability to easily identify and compensate for acts that benefit humanity. All positive ratings and observations contribute to the growth of an individual's SIV, while negative ones could slightly drop it. Finally, it was rewarding just to be good.

Now, to The Path.

Jolem, we had simplified the life experience and also provided purpose, but many still lacked direction. Therefore, the FDEC had a new question: how could we help individuals to best use their unique talents and skills to make life more fulfilling? Not just fulfilling on a personal level... fulfilling as a collective? We had a theory: By tapping into the totality of a person's thoughts, ways, and actions, we could predict future conditions and subsequently guide him/her to the best possible outcomes. This was the basis of our voluntary program called "The Total Life Path" or simply 'The Path.'

The early results of The Path were tremendous. If individuals were on the verge of ill-advised decisions, we simply offered alternatives that would serve them better. Soon, we enhanced this program by creating Life Tracks for people to follow. These Life Tracks not only aided with decision-making, but they also steered the decision-making process. With The Path's insights, life's challenging choices became thoughtless.

The Path worked wonderfully for those who participated in the program. However, life's tracks constantly intersect. The decisions you make affect your neighbors', and theirs affect you. To make this program truly effective, we needed a universal system. In 2035, all United States of America citizens were required to participate in this revolutionary program. President Mendoza's vision was fully realized, and America was reborn!"

SEE pauses while Mrs. Bolder offers short, gleeful applause. "Okay, whew... now that was a mouth full," SEE jokes. "So, Jolem, at this point, are there any questions?"

Jolem lifts up in his seat and rubs his cheeks. "Ahh – well, the Re-invest In America Program. What is that?"

"Well, Jolem, in order to support all the country's citizens, we have capped the earning potential for individuals and corporations. Once these limits are reached, excess earnings must be contributed to the Re-invest In America Program."

"Hmm..."

"Is there anything else?"

Jolem's lips curl as he fidgets in his seat. His eyes circulate the room; then he turns back to SEE. "Well – some say... The Path is – biased," he stutters, and Mrs. Bolder is stunned.

"That not all are treated the same. Is there any truth to this?" he continues.

"Jolem," SEE snickers. "I can assure you there is no reason for concern. The Path is a utilitarian program using a predictive algorithm. Its recommendations are based on one simple principle: that an action is right if it promotes happiness and benefits the greater good of all. This principle is what guides the binding Total Life Path's Laws of Conduct.

We are a connected chain of unity and prosperity."

"But…"

"In less than a second, The Path considers millions of interconnected variables to foresee outcomes. A decision may appear to be biased, but it is actually the result of this infallible process. Trust in it, and it will set you free."

Jolem leans back and sucks in his bottom lip. "Okay," he sighs reluctantly.

"Wonderful! Now that you have a background on how and why we created The Path, we'd like to summarize how we arrived at the Tracks that are best for you. Please relax as we highlight some of the more notable events from your adolescence."

Anticipating embarrassing events on the horizon, Jolem sits up in his seat and rests his chin in his palm. His heart starts to beat rapidly when the showcase begins, as if a jury's verdict is about to be read. His colorful background is marked with youthful indiscretions that he's not too excited to have on display.

"You were born September 29, 2039, in Morristown, N.J., to father Michale McKay and mother Kirame McKay. Being an inquisitive child, you asked many questions. You preferred Mind Challenge Queries instead of Alternate Games and had an extremely vivid imagination. Throughout your elementary education, you were a model student and excelled in your academics. You exhibited an advanced understanding of Virtual Attachment, an area in which many of your peers struggled. You cooperated well with others and interacted with a very positive attitude.

Then, at the age of ten, came the unfortunate and untimely passing of your father. We know this period was very difficult for you and your family…and we understand how such an event can complicate a young impressionable mind. However – some of the ensuing behaviors of the next several years altered your Track trajectory."

Jolem grimaces and begins to rub his forehead as he again shifts uncomfortably in his seat.

"At the age of twelve, you were restricted from education for three days as a result of a system breach conducted by yourself and a few others. It may have been a childish prank, but it came at the expense of your hapless headmaster. Resolving this fiasco required several programmers and suspended instruction for an entire day."

Jolem smirks as he fondly recalls the words "Headmaster Foyle bites nuts," overtaking all classroom board displays for hours while he witnessed typically well-behaved students overcome with laughter. It's a nostalgic memory he and his old band of friends continue to crack up about.

"A year later, you caused a small panic when you hid away in one of the Unconnected Communities for three days after receiving a reprimand from your mother. You knew wireless signals could not detect you there. If not for your voluntary return, you may have never been found."

For the next several minutes, SEE continues to flash back moments from Jolem's past, some positive, others not so, until it finally comes to an end. The display evaporates, and the dim lights restore their luminance. SEE takes a few steps toward Jolem until she is standing only a few feet in front of him.

"Mr. McKay, you have been assigned four Tracks from which to choose. These choices have been designed uniquely for you and are accessible from your World. You will have five business days to review your options. I highly recommend you consider wisely, as your selection will begin your Track in The Path.

Once you enter The Path, monitored navigation will begin, and you'll be on your way to happiness. You'll be repositioned in the national resource pool immediately and be requested when organizations have needs that match your skill sets. In between assignments, you'll have full access to VR training courses, so you may obtain additional skills at your leisure. Every waiting opportunity is a learning opportunity. Remember to be very positive and nurture your SIV. Also, be aware that on-the-spot life tests can pop up at anytime, anywhere. These interactive tests, will be indiscernible from real world experiences.

Throughout your days in The Path, I will remain almost unnoticeable, but in the event I am needed, I will be there to offer guidance. Should you veer off-track, I will give you a subtle Advisory Alert. Simply use the advice to adjust, and you will be right back on track.

Mr. McKay, this concludes my presentation. I know this has been a lot of information, so your FDEC Advisor, Mrs. Bolder, will now answer any questions you may have. It has been my pleasure assisting you today. Welcome to The Path!" Then, as suddenly as she arrived, SEE waves, walks towards the wall, and then disappears.

Mrs. Bolder spins her chair back toward Jolem with a smug grin stretched across her face. She cups her hands and positions her chin on top of her extended thumbs. "That was fun, wasn't it?" she quips. "So, we are almost finished here today. I just need to make sure you understand a few guidelines, and you – will – be – on – your – way.

Mr. McKay, my job is simple. I am here to ensure your success in The Path. We are one big chain of prosperity and happiness. Therefore, YOUR success is ALL of our success. Subsequently, YOUR failure is ALL of our failure."

Jolem flashes a brazen smirk. Her suggestions seem personal.

"So, Mr. McKay, before I continue --- are there any questions so far??"

Sitting back, Jolem drops his head as he rubs his eyes and then takes a deep breath. Many thoughts are running through his mind, and he feels like shouting out, yet he remains calm. As he exhales, he slowly tilts up his head and looks Mrs. Bolder in her eyes blankly. "No," he replies, shaking his head, "I don't have any questions."

"Gooood. Now Mr. McKay, keep in mind: The Path is a life-efficiency program, but you are free to live your days as you choose. We provide the basic structure for success, and the rest is in your hands. However, in order for you to experience the fullness of life's possibilities, it's highly recommended that you follow The Path's advice exactly. Its scientific formula is infallible and the easiest way to continue to improve your SIV.

For instance, your choice to consume a meal that is not good for you or your decision to skip an assignment offered by the pool, The Path will overlook. We expect that your AllVu Assistant would dissuade you from these activities and offer more prudent directions; however, your daily decisions are up to you and, for the most part, calculated into The Path. Imagine The Path as a flowing stream. If you toss in a small pebble, the water will adjust and continue forward.

BUT…should you make a habit of consuming foods that are not good for you or consistently skip assignments, those activities WILL be considered deviations, which are very dangerous to The Path. To illustrate that point, now imagine that same stream, but this time a large boulder is inserted. That could bring the entire flow to an abrupt stop. So, should you deviate, an alert will be triggered in SEE, and you will be summoned to a local FDEC office for a Track Realignment. If your deviations continue, reeducation will follow.

Now, Mr. McKay, this is important, so please listen closely: in the event you receive a summons, you have 24 hours in which to respond. Should you NOT respond within these 24 hours, a Compliance Control Officer WILL be dispersed to escort you to this office. So, should you receive a summons, it is highly recommended that you respond promptly. Believe me ---NO ONE wants a Compliance Control Officer to appear at his or her door."

At this point, Jolem can no longer contain himself. "So – what if I choose to take my OWN path? What if I want to go my own way??" he snaps.

Mrs. Bolder flinches in response to his sudden outburst of defiance. She needs a few moments to gather her composure before continuing. "Mr. McKay," she begins in a high pitch, then clears her throat. "The Path was designed to help, not hurt. But – it does require a universal acceptance that we are connected; we are a chain of prosperity. If you break the chain, your deviation will not only be harmful to yourself, but the impact could also hurt your family, friends, and neighbors. The Path is the law. If you are to live within its bounds, you are required to adhere to its regulations…or face its consequences."

"So, why not just start The Path at birth? Why even give choices?"

"Mr. McKay, the United States was founded on the principle of independence for all. From the moment we are capable of thought, we are faced with a series of decisions: what to eat, what to wear, what to say, where to go. How we respond to these choices… how we react to the circumstances of our lives is largely what determines our fates. We are not attempting to circumvent this process of CHOICE; therefore, we allow the immature impulses of a child to evolve into the mature and thoughtful actions of an adult. It is only then that your digital identity is truly formed."

Mrs. Bolder again rests her chin on the knuckles of her arched palms as she briefly pauses from the intense standoff. She knew Jolem was going to be a challenge, but even she underestimated to what extent. For the vast majority of the population, the Path Advisement is a celebratory event.

Jolem sits firmly restrained in his response. There is a brief moment of silence, clouded by a thick wall of tension separating the two. Mrs. Bolder changes tactics, hoping to minimize the confrontation and appeal to his practical sensibility. Suddenly, her gritty disposition morphs as she becomes warm and genial. She hides her AllVu, then leans up in her seat.

"Mr. McKay…will you please hide your AllVu," she requests, looks ahead, then waits for an unobstructed view directly into his eyes. "Jolem," she continues calmly, "you are a very intelligent and astute young man. And as a person with such intelligence, I'm sure you can appreciate what I'm about to say."

She pauses momentarily. "It is a scientific fact that following The Path will direct you, your family, and your community to happiness, peace, and prosperity. Deviation from your Track will only lead you and others affected by your deviation to…let's say unfavorable outcomes. I highly suggest that you keep this in mind."

Jolem again slowly nods his head.

"So, Mr. McKay, before I send you on your way, let me ask again; are there any questions??"

Sitting in silent contemplation, he reaches up to softly scratch the tip of his nose, then brushes his hand down his face towards his chin. "No – no questions," he replies.

"Goooood," she remarks slyly, with the assured confidence of a cat eyeing a cornered mouse. "Welcome to The Path."

8

Jolem glides down the city streets after leaving his Advisement. His mind is riddled with strange, ominous thoughts. The routine trip home he has taken so many times before feels somewhat surreal --- like being in the middle of a strange dream. Glancing to his left, he sets eyes on two siblings playing carelessly in their front yard while their delighted parents watch close by. It's a heartfelt scene, straight out of a 19th-century Impressionist painting. These happy-go-lucky kids play unaware that their every move is monitored and scrutinized like a science experiment. Parents are encouraged to allow regimented playtime and wholesome eating as a result of the national initiative for healthy living. The children are accustomed to bland meals and snacks which are devoid of sugar, salt, and processing chemicals.

"Is everything okay, Jolem?" asks Li'l J. "You seem agitated."

Jolem again takes a deep breath, then deflates. "Well, J.... I don't know," he sighs. "I really don't know."

After rounding the corner onto his street, Jolem drifts to the glass front door of his home. His AirBoard slows to a halt, and he hops onto the ground while it remains hovering. When he approaches the door, it automatically unlocks and slides open. Without even breaking his stride, he continues forward as his board follows closely behind him.

"Would you like your usual beverage?" asks Li'l J.

"Okay, sure."

As if a routine day in his life, Jolem drags into the family room and drops onto the long-curved sofa. Its soft cushions contour to his frame as he sinks into its surface. He kicks his feet up onto the spherical table marooned between him and a long wall. "Enter World," he instructs. Instantly, the solid walls and structures of his room slowly transform into the wide, enigmatic atrium of his virtual World. As his body remains idle on his family room sofa, his SimMe is transported to his simulated playland.

"Hello, Jolem. Congratulations on the completion of your education," salute The Path's well-wishers as they stand by clapping. "The Path is very excited to welcome you. You're almost there." The propaganda of The Path is ever-present.

Worlds are completely and easily customizable, allowing people to creatively erect walls and rooms on the fly. With gestures and commands, visitors to Worlds can be removed or blocked. However, FDEC AI representatives cannot be deleted. These helpful guides dressed in all-white sheer bodysuits are available upon request but also appear out of nowhere without warning or advance notice.

Jolem's World is a maze of activity, with shared experiences from a mix of friends, family, and acquaintances who casually browse about. Some appear as themselves in everyday gear, while others are represented by imaginary characters in outlandish garb or unrecognizable masks. He moves through his unique hallways and hidden rooms, acknowledging some and ignoring others. With a quick thumbs-up or digital "cheer" that he throws their way, their SIVs get a little boost. Many return the favors. It's a routine daily experience.

After a short period, he becomes bored, and when approached, he swipes each aside cavalierly. "This was hilarious! Check it out," says a friend who walks up to his side, but he brushes it out of sight. "Jolem, I can't wait to hear about your Advisement…" begins a message from his mom until he gestures it away also. His passions are suddenly and finally triggered.

"I'm right here in front of the nation's FDEC Headquarters Building in Washington, DC, where a massive Freedom Fighter protest just erupted," dramatically remarks an on-site witness. The view from her World cam presents like a movie. "You can hear them chanting 'NO FREEDOM. NO PATH. Government cut these strings out of my BACK!'"

The angry group, dressed in black with their signature white "Big Eye" logo in the middle of their chests, wields their collective fist in the air.

"What's wrong with them?" questions an upset responder in his network.

"We shouldn't be angry. They're all sick! They need help," comments another.

"How unpatriotic…"

"Anti-Path is Anti-American!! Get out of our country!"

Beginning to cluster like an angry mob, the confused and sometimes enraged commenters cry out until finally, Jolem yells, "Enough!" Instantly his lively World disappears, and he's back in the peace and quiet of his home. Aggravated, he drops back into his seat and begins to rub the tension building in his forehead. "Li'l J…I need to go dark."

"Is everything okay, Jolem?" asks Li'l J. "You're already over your limit."

Jolem's mouth contorts as he contemplates. "Well…ahhh – no, everything is not ok," he sluggishly replies.

He slumps over, then spins a small container about the size of an old zip drive in his hand. His thoughts run wild as he wrestles with many emotions. After a while, a concerned Li'l J calls for resistance, and the contents within his grasp whisper his name like an overheated seductress. Incubus's enticement has been on his mind since he left his Advisement, and he's trying hard to fight its temptation.

Jolem slips up and lethargically moves through the house until he makes his way to his bedroom. "Privacy," he commands in a monotone whisper, which again enshrouds his glass door and walls with a dark tint.

"Jolem, you know you have a problem," warns Li'l J. "It is not too late to reconsider," he argues, but Jolem has made up his mind. After falling back into his sofa bed, his thumb presses the curve of the container corner, and its top slips open. He holds out his other hand and extends his fingers. A clear, oval pill resembling a live cell under a microscope falls into the crevice of his palm. Absorbed in thought, he mechanically rubs the long, orange hairs of his chin back and forth, spinning them around between his pointer finger and thumb. He raises the pill to his eyes in contemplation. "This is REALLY...the last time," he mumbles, reclines deep into his seat, then slips it in his mouth.

The effects don't take long to kick in as Jolem drifts off within seconds. While his eyelids remain wide open, his pupils dilate and then rapidly shift back and forth. Suddenly, a huge smile overtakes his face. His fingers grip his seat cushion as if he's attempting to hold on. Abruptly, tears of joy trickle down his cheeks uncontrollably, as if he had just encountered the returning face of a long-lost loved one. The euphoria is mind-blowing. As his limbs fall limp, he slips into unconsciousness.

9

"Jolem??? Are you awake?" a familiar sound whispers from the dark. Struggling to open his eyes, Jolem peers out into the deep black space. He's not sure who's talking.

"Uhhh – yeah," he replies hesitantly.

"Man, that was weird," the voice continues. "You had this crazy look on your face, and then you just ran off – FAST!"

"Seriously??"

"Yeah, man. Are you okay?"

Squinting, Jolem peeks around. There's comfort in his company's speech, similar to that of his departed father. But as he surveys his surroundings, he sees no one.

"I – I think so. I feel strange, though, like…like my head is really cold, but my feet are burning up like they're on fire. And my heart is racing. You ever felt that way?"

"Sometimes I do, but after a little while, everything just goes back to normal."

"Ahh, okay," Jolem replies peacefully, then reclines, looking out into the vast lunar sky. "Maybe I just need to give it a few minutes, then."

"Yeah, I think so."

Looking above, Jolem is captivated by the magnificence of the full moon. Following the curves of its hills and valleys, he feels as though its landscape is right in front of his face. "Isn't this a stellar view, though??" he calmly remarks.

"I knooww. The moon is AMAZING tonight! It's so big and bright. I bet you I can touch it."

"That's funny," he chuckles.

"What's funny?"

"You. Touch the moon...that's crazy."

"What? You don't think I can do it?"

As the odd conversation becomes even stranger, Jolem suddenly feels troubled. "Huh? Can you?" he asks.

"Me??? Jolem – so can you," proclaims the stranger. In the midst of the previously light conversation, Jolem was at ease; however, now he's completely confused. He pops up.

"Whaat?? Wait – who ARE you?!" he cries out as he searches feverishly for his hidden companion.

"Who am I?? Are you okay?? It's me – I'm Jolem." Enraptured by an Incubus-induced vision, Jolem comes face-to-face with himself.

The strange encounter jolts Jolem back to reality. His eyelids blink erratically, open halfway, then fall. A moment passes, then they open again. As he scans the room, he attempts to identify the fuzzy objects surrounding him. When his view reaches the window wall, the sun shining through instantly repels him. "Uhhhhhh," spews from his mouth as his eyelids squeeze shut again. "What the??"

While in a daze, his long-time bedroom appears foreign. "Where am I??" he mumbles., He discerns a faint echo, "Jooooolllleeeemmm, Joooollllleeemmm..."

"Huh??" he questions, still battling confusion. Within moments, the soft voice quickens and becomes louder.

"Jolem...Jolem..."

"Uhh – Li'l J??"

"Jolem, you've been out for over an hour."

"Ohhh shit."

"I hate to say, 'I told you so,'" chastises Li'l J. "Incubus...again."

As Jolem lifts up and onto his forearms, he slowly returns to coherence. "Wow, that was intense," he comments, rubbing his eyes. This latest program was one of the most realistic he's experienced, and he's in awe of its mystical adventure. Touching his fingers together, he focuses on the subtle ridges of his skin to test his reality. He's pretty confident he's awake and not still in Incubus's spell, but he's not entirely sure. "I know Li'l J, I know," he says, exhaling in relief.

Jolem takes a few deep breaths and lightly rubs his eyes until his hazy vision becomes clear. The after-effects of Incubus usually only linger a few minutes, and before long, he's feeling like himself again. His fingers glide through his hair while he stretches his neck. He's ready to engage his World.

"Okay, Li'l J, enter World," he instructs. As suddenly as the words exit his mouth, he's transported again to the lobby of his World. "Jolem, where are you, man?" questions Rony on a recorded feed. "I'm headed to my Advisement!! YEAHHH!! Dying to know my Tracks. Imma hit you after."

"Jolem?? I can't wait to hear about your Advisement," says Kirame. "Come into my World as soon as you can, okay??"

"'Brothers and Sisters of Life' is seeking volunteers. Jolem, you could use cooperation points to help boost your SIV. This is a great opportunity," comments one of the group's outreach committee members.

Then, from a celestial galaxy, a translucent yet muscular figure appears, landing in front of Jolem. The deity-like man pumps out his chest and propels his pointed finger into Jolem's face. "Dark Adaption Version 8 is now available, Jolem. You thought "Version 7" kicked ass. Wait 'til you experience THIS!!" he roars.

"Hell yeah! I've been waiting on this," Jolem exclaims as he grabs the game's icon and throws it into his virtual storeroom. His World storeroom is full of products and services he wants to revisit. Throughout the days, they'll smartly promote to him during times he'll most likely be interested in them. He has always had a deep fascination with space, time, and actuality. With a command, access to the psychological gaming experience can be purchased and become a part of his ever-expanding World.

Jolem navigates his World as normal, but this time he notices an added feature. As he drifts about, a small flashing timer follows him from above. Moment by moment, it counts down to his Track selection deadline. He's in no hurry to initiate the Track Commencement Ceremony, so his focus remains on all the other activities surrounding him. However, while he attempts to ignore the persistent alert, sensory vibrations send mild reminders through his body. They will remain and intensify until this high priority receives his attention.

After a couple of hours of World interaction, Jolem's bedroom is quiet. He's outside of his virtual reality, but the blinking alert remains, hovering near the ceiling like a black cloud that won't dissipate. He's tried to get rid of his annoying ticker by hiding his AllVu and going dark. The augmented visual disappears, but the sensory vibrations persist. No matter what he does, he can't break free of the stubborn reminder.

Jolem inhales quickly and then exhales, allowing the pent-up air to gust out of his mouth. "Li'l J…Commence Track Decision Ceremony…" he mutters reluctantly. In an instant, his room erupts like a New Year's Eve celebration. Eye-popping red, white, and blue lights appear around him festively as a patriotic chorus sings a rousing tribute. For several minutes, the salute plays while happy visions of American citizens enjoying the spoils of a carefree and fulfilling life swirl around him. It's a glorious salute to The Path.

The awesome exhibit slows, and the room darkens. Four outlined, fluorescent green squares expand in the air; one hovering above the other on the left and the same on the right. The stacked blocks separate, and then out from an illuminating pathway between them appears SEE, with open arms and a blinding smile. "Hello, Jolem McKay. Congratulations, and welcome to the Federal Department of Efficiency and Compliance's Total Life Path," she greets. "Once again, I am SEE, and I'll be assisting you with your Track Commencement Ceremony. It's great to SEE you again," she continues, stopping to give him a quick, friendly wink.

"You are in for a treat today, so sit back and let's get started. We're very excited and have customized four AMAZING Life Tracks, which we believe will offer you the greatest opportunity for success and happiness. Your Tracks have been customized for you based on your lifetime of thoughts, ways, and actions... your digital identity.

A thorough examination of your history, along with your SIV, has provided The Path with everything it needs to create the perfect life experience for you. And remember, as your SIV grows, so do your opportunities for rewards and advancements. So, keep those positive ratings coming in!

It is now 3:15 PM, Friday, July 26, 2057. You have until Friday, August 3 at 11:59 PM to make any changes and complete your decisions. At that point, your choice will be non-reversible. At 9:00 AM on Monday, August 6, 2057, you will officially enter The Path. I encourage you to lean heavily on the wisdom of your assistant when considering your options."

Jolem sits quietly, listening to SEE's introduction of the Track Commencement Ceremony, then responds to her preliminary questions. He is initially disinterested, but as the moments pass, his curiosity peaks.

"I will begin by giving you an overview of each of the four Life Tracks. If you'd like to receive more information about a Track, simply ask, and I'll go into broader detail. We can even give you up to a ten-year projection of your potential future, adjusting to accommodate multiple scenarios, such as getting married and/or having children. Your world - no pun intended- is totally in your hands. Now, if there are no questions, please say 'continue,' and we will proceed to your Tracks."

SEE smiles politely and interlaces his fingers in front of her as she awaits his reply. Jolem's sights lift to the ceiling, and he inhales through gritted teeth. "Continue," he says while the air puffs out of his mouth. His command initiates the top left outlined square, and it quickly expands, consuming everything around him. In a flash, his bedroom is transformed into an expansive, simulated high-tech office environment. SEE's head motions forward. "Follow me," she instructs, then leads him into the wide-open space.

Walking side-by-side, they journey through meeting and lounge spaces filled with small clusters of friendly co-workers.

"Okay, Jolem," starts SEE. "The first EXCITING Life Track selected for you begins by accepting an entry-level role as an AllVu Systems Technician. This role has great potential, utilizing your creative and intellectual..."

Jolem dispassionately nods as he listens to her short summary of the life opportunity. The interactive presentation acquaints him with the basic roles and responsibilities of the profession as well as earning potential and expected lifestyle. It allows him to feel the reality of an AllVu Systems Technician as if it was his real life. The simulation concludes with a glimpse of a cozy apartment home with an affectionate redhead nestled on the sofa by his side. The entire staged experience is designed exclusively for him, considering his historical likes and desires. The Path is well aware of the features that attract him, and even SEEs appearance is custom to his World.

As they exit the building, the environment morphs back to his bedroom. The first square deactivates, while the others remain illuminated. SEE beams, as if she can hardly contain her excitement. "That was great, wasn't it?? And the fun is only beginning. Unless there are any questions, we'll jump right into the next Track."

Her eyes focus on the bottom square to her left, and like the first, it bursts into the air. "You're REALLY going to like this. Your second potential Track is an interesting opportunity as a Simulation Designer..."

They again begin forward, and the room morphs into a technical learning environment. Surrounding them, enthralled students collaborate at interactive whiteboards with holographic models. When Jolem and SEE pass through these work groups, the students stop, wave, and beckon to him. The space is full of activity, and as he glances around, he's captivated by an excited trio brainstorming. Off to his other side, an overjoyed young woman thrills as her project shows results. "Jolem, you'd love this," she declares, nudging him on.

SEE grins at Jolem. "It looks like an interesting challenge, doesn't it? You know everyone loves a simulator."

The allure of The Path is hard to resist. As they traverse the distinct life opportunities, Jolem's iron walls of resistance slowly fall. Like a game show winner being awarded a grand prize, he's mesmerized by the spectacle of his Tracks, with each becoming more appealing than the previous. After previewing his third Track as a Cold Energy Engineer, the best is saved for last. Back in his room, SEE stands still with her hands cupped while the fourth box to her top right illuminates alone. With a sassy twist of the neck, her left eyebrow lifts above the other, and she smirks. "Okay, Jolem," she whispers seductively. "Are you ready for your final Life Track?"

She crosses her arms and stares ahead confidently. Finally, the last square explodes, transforming the room into a deep, celestial abyss. In the dark, stars sparkle around iridescent planets out beyond, and Jolem becomes mystified.

"Jolem, only a select group of individuals have the opportunity to join the Outer Rim Explorers," SEE begins. And just as her comments come to an end, a slowly approaching space station halts right behind her. "Please – follow me."

Since he was a child, Jolem has been enamored with the idea of blazing new depths and exploring uncharted destinies. For decades, the Outer Rim Explorers have set the standard for space exploration.

"Welcome aboard," a staunch space station Lieutenant greets, with her hands on her waist. Wearing a special metallic AllVu helmet and glistening bodysuit, she resembles an old comic book hero. "Here... have a seat," she says, extending her arm and motioning to an empty solo cockpit.

When Jolem settles into the sloped, sleek command center, it envelops him like a blanket. "Welcome, Commander McKay," salutes his command center, as the sky-blue holographic dashboard activates. "It's a great day for an adventure."

Jolem canvasses his environment like a child secured into his first amusement park ride. "Is that – Mars?" he questions in awe of the sight of a monstrous, orange orb. With an up close and personal vantage point, the subtle crevices of its massive form are as distinct as the patterns of his fingertips. He's enamored, and this time, he spends an extended period locked in the simulated environment.

As they stride from department to department of the large space station, SEE breaks down the benefits of life as an Outer Rim Explorer. In passing, a site engineer, engulfed in a challenging task, stalls, looks Jolem's way, and gives a quick thumbs up. Jolem cracks a smile, slowly lifts his fist, then returns the sentiment.

"Jolem, hold on to your hat for this one," SEE advises while they move into the back of a training room. In a tight circle ahead of them, a young group sits in the attention of an animated instructor.

"What's going on in here? What are they doing?" Jolem whispers.

"Well, Jolem," SEE says, almost unable to contain her excitement, "They are preparing for their trip."

"Trip?? Where?"

"Okay – you're going to love this! Starting this year, all Outer Rim Explorer cadets are sent on a two-week Observation Exercise conducted on the Lunar Colony! Isn't that great?! This opportunity is literally Out-Of-This-World!"

Jolem is unexpectedly speechless. The opportunity seems too good to be true. For a few excited moments, he rubs his hands together, bouncing up and down on his heels. Suddenly, he looks over to SEE and pauses. "Soo – all this sounds really great, but – is there anything I should know? I mean, is there anything negative??"

SEE's genial expression becomes more serious. "Well, Jolem, I wouldn't say 'negative,' but there is one thing about the Outer Rim Explorer project which may be of interest to you," she starts. "So, as you know, being an Outer Rim Explorer is a major opportunity. Many people would die for this Track, but they weren't chosen, and you were. You should be extremely honored to be considered as a candidate. Just imagine the success and happiness you could have."

Suspiciously, Jolem peers at SEE. "Okay..." he utters.

"Keep in mind, Jolem, this is a high-security environment. And due to this, The Path monitors the actions of ORE professionals with higher scrutiny. Nothing too intrusive, but certain behaviors which would normally go overlooked will initiate concern if performed by an ORE."

As SEE continues, Jolem's hopeful thoughts begin to fade. This blissful promise of The Path is offered with a caveat: to enjoy its pleasures is to yield to its grip. The simulation concludes, and the aerospace-inspired alternate dissolves. Back in the reality of his bedroom, he's again surrounded by his familiar walls and furniture. He was excited for a period of time, but now his cynicism has returned.

SEE stands patiently in the middle of the four boxes that remain floating in the air, then opens her palms. "Well, Jolem, we've come to your Track Commencement Ceremony conclusion. Now there is one last item remaining on the agenda. As you know, within these boxes await four unique and exciting Life Tracks for you to choose from," she reiterates. The labeled boxes illuminate responsively as her finger points in their directions.

"#1 – Accepting an entry-level role as an AllVu systems technician...

#2 – Enrolling in secondary education for simulation design...

#3 – Initiating the cold energy engineer program...or...

#4 – Joining the Outer Rim Explorer Training Program

Now the power is in YOUR hands! Remember, this is only a preliminary choice. You have until Friday, August 3, 2057, at 11:59 PM to ask questions or change your mind. Sooo – have you made a decision??"

Jolem contemplates silently. Pacing, he mulls the options presented to him, then slows to a stop. "I guess I am ready..." he mumbles and sucks in a deep breath. Slowly, he exhales through his nose before he grumbles, "I choose...AllVu...systems...technician."

Of the four Tracks available to him, Jolem selects the least challenging with the lowest prestige. After cringing at the thought of additional monitoring by The Path, his instinctive choice is freedom over pleasure.

"Hmm, okay, very good. This is an excellent decision, and I am sure this role will provide you stability, prosperity, and purpose in society. Now, to continue your journey into The Path, I will need you to accept the following agreements by saying 'I agree' or refuse by saying 'I do not agree.' Okay??"

"Okay."

"Number 1: My decision today is being made willfully."

"I agree."

"Number 2: I intend to fulfill my Life Track responsibilities to the highest of my ability?"

"I agree."

"Number 3: If I receive a Path summons, I will respond to the FDEC within 24 hours after its receipt."

"I agree."

"And lastly, Number 4: I understand my total compliance with the rules of The Path is necessary in order to be successful, and I pledge my full allegiance."

Jolem hesitates while his chest drops. As if his throat passage is obstructed by rocks, his final words are difficult to mutter. "I…I…a…gree."

"CONGRATULATIONS, Mr. McKay. On behalf of the FDEC, President Tamerson C. Tore, and The United States of America, welcome to The Path!"

WELCOME TO

THE PATH

10

Behind the shade of her AllVu visors, Leema's giant brown eyes enlarge as she hangs on to her co-worker's words. "So, what happened next??" she asks, slowly stirring her mug of hot tea in her office break room. "Did you accept his invite into his World?"

Her newly acquainted associate contorts her lips and then quickly shuts down the suggestion. "Ha! That's a laugh. His SIV was something like 4.5. I can't even believe he invited me. How rude."

"Are you serious?"

"Yes! I thought by being nice, I might earn a few points, but my SIV didn't tick up at all. For kicks, I watched some of his experiences --- incredible. I simply deleted his invite and moved on. I'm sure The Path would've gone crazy over that one. Oh, my cosmos!"

"You're hil – arious. Well, like my dad always says, his 'SIV is low for a reason,'" laughs Leema. "So, I'm off to my first presentation. Wish me well."

"Oh, girl, you got this. Stay on Track and follow all your aids. You'll do just fine."

"Thanks! I'll visit your World later."

Cradling her mug in her left hand, recent Path entrant Leema glides out of the break room en route to her office pod. She slides by colleagues collaborating in mini-groups, waving her other cupped palm like a beauty pageant winner. As she passes, her friendly co-workers toss digital hearts and expressive emojis. It's the second week of her happiness ambassador internship at GreenView Industries, a leader in Solar and wind energy. With numerous satellite offices up and down the Eastern Seaboard, New York City-based GreenView Industries is one of the largest and most powerful business conglomerates in the country.

Leema slows as she moves into an offset, open room of wide-eyed and excited young professionals gathered at a 3-D digital whiteboard. Within a year, they'll develop the ins and outs of happiness ambassadorship through the University Ubiquitous Living Learning Program. This immersive instruction has largely replaced the historical University system. It takes advantage of social interactivity and life's situations to create learning opportunities instead of relying on boring lectures and general tests. Scholastic institutions still exist, but in today's mixed reality, education has expanded well beyond the bounds of the classroom. Constant internet connectivity creates conditions for personalized learning anytime and anywhere.

Now among her peers, Leema sets her mug down on a glass table and clears her throat before entering into the lively discussion. The diverse cast of six includes all high SIVs, 7 and above, who are products of very controlled and responsible lives. High SIVs are typically leaders, executives, owners, or other highly regarded professionals. Because of their ranks in society, The Path has systematically rewarded them with the most sought-after careers and personal opportunities.

"Is everyone excited?" Leema enthuses. "Life is not just good --- it's GREAT!"

The stoked bunch receives her words like high school cheerleaders from the past. "Life IS great!" one of them replies. "Let's share the joy."

Following spirited applause, Leema glides backward, then a holographic young Thought Leader emerges by her side. He grabs a word from the digital board, then enlarges it with his pinched fingers. "Okay. Today's lesson plan is all about PERSPECTIVE," he begins while the eager group waits for instruction. "Let's get started." Meanwhile, as this engagement continues on the 20th floor, in a dim pod 13 floors below, Jolem McKay's thoughts wander once again.

It's been a little over a month since he first entered the towering New York City headquarters of GreenView Industries to begin his first gig. The initial days of The Path were challenging, as he just tried to fight his natural resistance, but to his surprise, things have slowly become easier. One of GreenView's top priorities is employee satisfaction, and he was welcomed in grand fashion. His brief but interactive orientation was interesting, informative, and somewhat fun. Now actively engaged, he has settled into his role as a Level 1 AllView Systems Technician. Unfortunately, today he can't seem to maintain his focus.

"Hey, Jolem, we're heading to lunch... you coming?" asks Jolem's system's tech team lead, who heads their five-man work pod.

"Uh... okay, sure," he remarks, popping up in his reclined curved seat when he's jolted back to reality.

His lead moves closely and pats Jolem on the shoulder. "Everything good?" he asks.

"Yeah. Everything's functioning normally. All good."

"No – I mean here. At the office. How's it going so far?"

"So far, everything is..."

Flashing a satisfied grin, Jolem pauses, looks around, and nods his head, "– pretty good," he says, then throws up a digital thumb.

"Fantastic! Just let me know if there's anything more we can do to assist with the transition. We're very excited to have you here for this project. We provide a valuable service to the operations of this great company. Hopefully, you'll learn a lot during your time with us."

"Okay, thanks."

"EX – CELL – ENT. Then, let's get to it. I'm starving."

The life of an AllVu system's technician is neither glamorous nor exciting. For the most part, connected systems maintain themselves with intelligent programs, machines, and automated processes. If a problem is identified, alerts trigger and responsive NonHumans disperse to intervene. His main responsibility is to provide perspective to an AllVu conflict when humans are involved. NonHuman judgment continues to lack full empathy.

"I'm right behind you," he says and quickly follows his co-workers out of the room on their way to the elevator. Like him, two of the other three members of his team are also recent graduates on their first gig. Although ecstatic about the new opportunity, each would've sacrificed an arm to go into the popular simulations program if they were given the choice. Jolem smiles tightly and attempts to lampoon with the others as they swiftly descend the clear, spherical elevator. He hopes that in time, he'll feel camaraderie with his teammates, who've quickly developed a chummy bond.

The company's dining lounge extends the full circumference of the building's garden level and features recreational activities throughout. VR alternate games, digital body massages, food, and numerous other perks are free of charge and available to all. In the center of the expansive floor, a beam wrapped with a forty-foot display spouts corporate praises and repetitive homage to The Path. "Thanks to The Path, GreenView Industries powers the country's future," echoes loudly and proudly. "For the tenth year in a row, GreenView has reached the maximum earning limit and continues to contribute enormously to the Re-Invest In America Fund. Enjoy your lunch. Enjoy your work. Enjoy your life."

Lagging slightly behind the others, Jolem surveys his energetic surroundings. Throughout the open space, there is a palpable feeling of euphoria as people are truly blissful and content. His eyes continue to wander, and a hint of a smile forms. "Maybe it won't be so bad after all," he thinks.

"What about you, Jolem?" asks a coworker, interrupting his peaceful consideration.

"Me? Huh? What?"

"Ha, you spaced out again, Man. The Path – life is good...right?"

"Well...ah, yeah," he replies awkwardly, scratching the back of his head.

"I hear that," proclaims another colleague. "Sit back, and let The Path be your guide."

Without a care, the crew glides over to a table sectional identified by an augmented arrow pointing down from above. Within minutes of settling into their seats, their pre-ordered food is delivered fresh and hot by courteous, uniformed work bots. The group's attention is immediately split between reality and their fantasy lands. Shifting back and forth from AllVu to live conversation, they pick up bits and pieces as if spanning social media video bites. A little laughter and some quick comments... chatter is short and constantly interrupted. Even communications between people only feet away are sent virtually, using animated memes and expressive emojis.

In the midst of the lunchtime experience, a beaming caravan of happiness ambassadors enter the cafeteria and then disburse in an orderly fashion throughout the room. They move about, launching cheer into the air like flower girls tossing rice at a wedding. While Jolem picks at his food, an enthusiastic young ambassador with luxuriant dark hair and large eyes approaches. She smiles through clenched teeth. Elatedly, she tilts her head, connects her fingertips like a tepee, and then begins to offer kind words of greeting. "Hello, Jolem. My name is Leema, and I am a happiness ambassador intern. We're so glad to have you with us," she says, with the barely perceptible tenderness reserved for an old friend. "How are you enjoying your time here at GreenView?"

He has occasionally noticed ambassadors' rounds as they've mechanically moved from table to table, person to person, but this is the first time he's been personally acknowledged. He peers at Leema, and his eyes wander from her hands up to her shiny white teeth. "Well, thanks," he utters calmly while casually lifting his fork of food and slipping it into his mouth. "Yeah – so far, it's been good," he continues, nodding softly.

Puzzled by his laid-back reaction, Leema winces. "Hmmm – only 'good'?" she asks, with a furrowed brow moments later, her joy rebounds. "Well, I'm here to collect smiles...sooo. Let's see it!"

Jolem looks around the table and notices all eyes are on him. With giant grins and starry-eyed, they sit eagerly awaiting his response. "C'mon, Jolem! Let's see them pearly chops," urges his team lead.

"Yeah, Jolem. Don't be shy," another calls out.

Jolem sighs and slowly turns towards Leema. "Okay, okay." He pauses his eating, sits back, then shuts his eyes. "CHEEEESE," he cracks, clenching his jaw and flashing his teeth.

"Well, okay then," snaps Leema, flinching. The unexpectedly snarky display from Jolem catches her by surprise. "I see we have a strange one here."

She turns uneasily toward the others at the table. "And how about you? Can I have those smiles?"

Without hesitation, everyone poses, showing off their best profiles as if taking a graduation photo.

"WONDERFUL," lauds Leema while sending high ratings their way. "That's what I'm talking about!" She continues clapping until Jolem interrupts. "Hey – but what about me??"

Leema's laughter diminishes, and her grin falls. "Hmmm," she murmurs while contemplating an appropriate response. This is the first time she's encountered resistance to her chants. "Well," she begins before a labored pause. "I believe we have some work to do on that smile."

"Really?"

"Yes, really. But that's what I'm here for. To share happiness. We'll get that smile," she says, waving to the table. "It's a good life!"

"It's a good life," they reply in unison.

"Have a great rest of the day in The Path!" she cheers, then rolls off to the next table.

11

Throughout the flexible business day, many casually enter the Icon building to perform gig tasks and then leave afterward. Others interact virtually from their homes based on their personal schedules. It's a calm, stress-free, yet productive environment where NonHumans roam the halls as much as people. Long gone are the extended 50 to 60-hour work weeks that used to hold belabored employees hostage. In today's Digital Reality, the previously standard 8-hour workday has been reduced to around 6, and days per week down to 3 or 4. It is the result of an intelligent world that essentially runs itself.

An hour later, back in Jolem's office pod, his eyes drift up to the ceiling, and his roaming thoughts again slip away. A message from one of his teammates pops in front of him, interrupting his daydream. "Hey, what was that about?"

"What was what?"

"You know – at lunch. Leema. Your smile."

Jolem twists and swivels towards his coworker and eyes her curiously. "I don't know what you're talking about."

"Well, it was kinda – strange. You do believe it's a good life…right?"

Jolem hesitates, but only for a moment. He's trying hard to fit in and not draw unnecessary attention to himself. "Oh, of course. You know, I was just being comical. Ya know," he laughs, waving off the idea.

"Ahhh – yeah. I thought so," she chuckles and then tosses a few smiley faces his way. "Good one."

When early afternoon arrives, and office activity slows, the mass of cavalier employees glides out to their awaiting rides. Car ownership has become almost obsolete while most rely on a ride-when-needed network called Zumer. In constant circulation, these auto-piloted cars, air, and watercrafts quickly pick up passengers, drop them off at destinations, then move to the next request. It's an easy and efficient system of transportation that keeps the nation on the go.

While people move like ants toward the multi-laned Zumer corral, Jolem rests silently on the sidewalk, scanning the typical scene. Co-workers pass and augmented thought gestures spring in the air. These expressions have largely taken the place of spoken salutations, allowing people to engage without saying a word. With an ambivalent smirk, Jolem takes note of their mechanical movements that are almost indistinguishable from NonHuman bots, then he sighs. Suddenly, the familiar approaching presence of his newly acquainted happiness ambassador, Leema, captures him. He's so uncomfortable with their earlier encounter that he turns instinctively trying to hide.

"Jolem?" she calls out when she spies him dipping behind a nearby couple. She grips her waist, and her head tilts in confusion.

"Oh hey, Leema," he murmurs, then clears his throat with a few sputtered coughs. After being spotted, he moves awkwardly from his cover and then out into the open.

"Were you – hiding??"

"Oh no. Nooo. I didn't even see you."

"Ohhh, okay. Strange," she comments, tightening her lips. "Swipe," she says, quickly moving to the next subject. "Ya know, for a brief moment today, you had me stumped," she continues.

"Really?"

"Yes, really."

"Why??"

Leema's eyes close slowly, and her head tilts back as she inhales deeply. Then, as she exhales softly, her eyelids widen. "Jolem, look around," she says while proudly presenting their surroundings. "What do you see?"

Jolem scans the relaxed scene of individuals casually sailing back and forth. "I – I don't know what I'm looking for," he says, scratching the back of his head.

"You know what I see?" she says, starry-eyed.

"Uhh – nooo."

"I see joy. Complete happiness. And that's not what I see when I look at you."

Jolem's lips curl, and he begins to fidget. "I'm…happy," he replies uncomfortably, dropping his head to the ground.

"Well, that didn't seem convincing. I mean seriously."

"I suppose."

Leema leers at him with the same befuddlement as his mom. She doesn't know what to make of his odd behavior. "You are – different from most people I encounter."

"No. I'm just like everyone else," he says again, scratching his head and looking off into the distance.

"No. You're not."

For an extended moment, Leema stares strangely without saying a word. "Hmm…swipe. So, what's that?" she questions then, abruptly changing topics.

"What's what?"

"That? In your bag?"

"Ohhh… my AirBoard??"

As if being suddenly hit with a rancid smell, she cringes. "Your… Air-Board? I mean, you actually ride that thing – in reality?? But, but… why? That's really dangerous."

"Well – not really – maybe if you don't know what you're doing – it can be."

"But… I don't understand."

"Understand what?"

"Why would you even risk getting hurt? What about your SIV??"

"I'm not afraid of getting hurt."

"Uhhh… no offense, but you're extremely strange. If you just want an adventure, why don't you just create one in your World? Doesn't your assistant advise you against it??"

"Sure, he does…but I do it anyway."

"Your advisor tells you not to do it, and you just 'do it anyway'?? But – but I don't understand. That makes no sense."

"Well – I just like it."

Scratching the side of her head, Leema gazes blankly into Jolem's face. She's confused, but shortly her natural resistance against deep thought kicks in. "Hmm, okay … swipe," she replies with a shrug. Her demeanor shifts from concern to calm, as if the conversation was never had. It's an odd transition, but almost instantly, Leema's attention is pulled into her World, and she bursts into laughter.

"What's funny?" he asks.

"Oh – nothing. Not you. Something in my World. Hilarious."

This time, Jolem observes her with curiosity while she interacts with her World as if he's not even there. Gesticulating with her hand, she laughs melodramatically as if being filmed for a reality show. Ironically, her behavior is as bizarre to him as his is to her.

A few moments later, Leema's white compact Zumer pulls up in line in front of them, and she strides in its direction. "Oh, hey Jolem… this is me," she says, turning back towards him. As she approaches the Zumer door, it pulls out of the traffic line and then approaches. "You know I will collect that smile, right?" she asserts while slipping into her seat. She flicks a happy face emoji his way. "That's for free," she says, winking.

"Ah, okay. Thanks."

Her Zumer pulls off, and she flashes a huge smile. "It's a good life, Jolem!" she says as her darkly-tinted window slowly rises shut.

Jolem's feet seem cemented in the ground as he watches Leema's Zumer disappear out of sight. His thoughts once again drift, and he becomes almost oblivious to all the activity around him. For a long time, he's maintained a strong resentment towards high SIVs. He's felt they were mostly shallow, pretentious, and only concerned about their personal brands. They huddle among their peers, and with the exception of charity, he hasn't known them to socialize with lower SIVs. However, despite his disdain for members of this group, for some odd reason, Leema is intriguing.

A few more passengers slide into their Zumer and drive off, then Jolem's car is next in line. "Jolem, we're up," alerts Li'l J to his distracted companion.

"Huh?"

"Ride – your Zumer. It's here."

"Oh, my bad, Li'l J," Jolem replies, quickly moving toward the open car door. He plops onto the seat inside and nestles into its memory foam-like upholstery. "Okay... take us home," he sighs as his seat reclines. Without a word, his favorite tunes begin to play, and the vehicle's interior gels cool to his desired temperature. The symbiotic connection between his clothes' digital fibers and Zumer's integrated sensors work together to create his perfect environment. This seamless communication allows him to just sit back and receive personal treatment as if he were a celebrity.

His head leans against his window, and he begins to gaze at the cars zipping by. These sleek, white, mostly compact autos flow fast and efficiently through the interstates reaching speeds in excess of 100 miles per hour. Years ago, his short trip from New York City to suburban New Jersey would've taken him well over an hour on busy, congested roads and highways. Today's vehicle-to-vehicle communication technology makes gridlock a thing of the past.

Jolem's single passenger Zumer has one captain seat with a sloped dashboard console that swings around his side. With no steering wheel, the customizable console can transform to his right or left, depending on his preference. Many large family vehicles have interior seats in a U-shaped formation, curved around an open middle that allows passengers to interact face-to-face during their travels. Most engage in their Worlds during their trips, but Jolem just sits back and enjoys the soft vibration of the smooth motor-less ride.

While glancing at nearby cars, he flashes back to one of the many stories of his long-since-deceased grandfather. With a smirk, he recalls the chaotic descriptions of combative roadways with raging drivers, honking horns, and fender-benders. The wild scene fueled by negligence and misdirection is so far from the systematic roads he knows. He considers how challenging it would be to take control of his speeding Zumer and attempt to navigate through the sea of autos. The archaic idea seems so unimaginable that he snickers at the mere thought.

For the time being, he continues to live with his mom and sister, but within months, he'll be in his own place. It's an awkward transition for him, but the historically stressful move arrangements will all be made almost without his involvement. Besides virtual walk-through tours, everything is handled by Li'l J, who understands Jolem's likes, dislikes, budget, and other considerations. Locating the perfect home is elementary for his more than capable digital helper. When the time comes, Li'l J will purchase furniture, solicit movers, and set up home services.

As Jolem continues down the street, digital billboards and signs are vibrant. They beckon to him, displaying custom messages and independent pitches for products he'd like while using reviews from his World network of friends and family to aid. "Hmmm, that does look good," he comments softly to himself as he reaches up and pulls an item into his storeroom. He peeks to his left, and his attention is grabbed by an advertisement high up above. The augmented view of a giant, beautiful woman savoring a bite of one of his favorite veggie burgers is hard to overlook. Seductively, she swipes the sauce dripping off the sandwich's side and licks it with her finger. "You know you want it, Jolem," she suggests in a low, enchanting whisper as she points to a blinking "Open" door decal below.

Jolem grins, lays his head back, and rests his eyes as his therapeutic music hums. He passes on the meal and just relaxes. Moments later, his AllVu temple orbs vibrate, and he hears three familiar soft sounds. It's the routine ping of Rony's World tone that nudges his eyes back open. His seat twists slightly towards his right-side console, and then he calmly calls out, "Accept Rony." Instantly, Rony's LiveView emerges.

"What's new, Sola?" Jolem asks.

"What's not new?!" exclaims Rony. "Sola, The Path is GREAT!"

"You're funny, man," Jolem chuckles.

"C'mon – you don't agree???"

"It's going – alright, I guess."

"'Alright' my ass! This World evangelist Track is perfect for me. PERFECT! I was already sharing everything with my World, and now I get paid to help people with theirs. What more could I ask for??"

"Sounds like you."

"You damn right. I still can't believe you passed on simulations. Jo, wait 'til I show this spot I found...well Juko found it. It's STELLAR!"

"Okay, okay, man. You know you should've taken the Path 'cheerleader' Track," jokes Jolem. "Do I have to hear your Path praises every day?"

Rony grows quiet as his smile drops. With a stone expression, he remains still staring at Jolem during an awkwardly silent moment. "YOU DAMN RIGHT," he erupts and then bursts into laughter. "C'mon man, let me show you this place."

With a few words, Jolem follows Rony into his virtual World to tour the apartment. As if being in the actual building, he touches walls, fixtures, and other parts of the simulated structure.

"This is the color I'm going to paint," Rony comments as a light grey spreads over the bare white walls. "And here's this stellar bed I'm about to buy," he continues as the bed, and other furniture items begin to fill the empty rooms. "I have it ALLLL planned out!"

"NICE Sola," Jolem remarks, nodding approvingly.

"But wait…" interrupts Rony. "There's more." He backs out onto the terrace and swings open his arms. "Check out this view." Overlooking tall trees, they see the open green landscape of a small park. The scene is outstanding.

"This is the life. Soon as I pass the three-month Path probationary period, I'll be eligible to move in. As long as I get through without any deviations, I'm in there. How about you? What's up with the spot you were looking at the other day?"

"Uhhh – I'm not sure yet. We still have a couple months before the end of probation, so why rush it?"

"Okay – Mr. Indecisive. Just let Li'l J decide for you."

"Yeah…yeah."

"Okay, Sola, I'll catch you later. My dad keeps disguising himself and walking around my World," Rony chuckles. "No matter what mask he wears, I can spot him a mile away. I'm about to send him into a rabbit hole," he laughs.

"Alright, later man…"

Jolem's conscience returns to his ride, and before long, he pulls up to the curb in front of his house. "Enjoy the rest of your day Mr. McKay," pleasantly salutes the Zumer as he steps out onto the pavement. A flash of antiseptic UV light cleanses the car's interior, and then off it goes to pick up the next passenger.

Jolem stands on the sidewalk facing his home. There's a recognizable calmness to the neighborhood that's only interrupted by the Zumer's soft hum as it disappears in the distance. He looks searchingly down the tranquil street, and random thoughts about the conflict he witnessed between Mr. Perry and the Compliance Control Officers run through his mind. Curiously, there's been silence about the encounter, and he hasn't seen Mr. Perry since. "Hmmm," he murmurs to himself as he continues up the walkway.

"Hey, Li'l J, is my mom home?"

"Yes, she's in the kitchen."

"OK."

When Jolem blusters into the room, Kirame is gazing peacefully out of the glass wall that overlooks their backyard. As she slowly stirs honey into a cup of warm tea, her eyes follow the morphing clouds in the calm blue sky. Just recently, she left the World of her younger sister, who lives in upstate New York. Kirame is still giddy to have just witnessed her niece's first steps, even if the actual event occurred hours ago.

"Hey, mom!" Jolem calls out to her backside, but even his sudden entrance doesn't slow the robotic swirling of the spoon against the inner edges of her mug. Her eyes flutter shut, and her chin lifts high. She wants to hold on to the peaceful moment, but judging from her son's tone, she anticipates the calm will soon come to an end. After taking a small sip, she turns towards him, smiling tenderly. "Hey, Jolem... how was your day?" she inquires softly.

"It was actually pretty good. But – hey...have you heard anything about Mr. Perry?" he inquires. Sure enough, Kirame's state of bliss comes to an abrupt end as her mug slips from her loose grasp and cracks against the pearl floor. "Oh – uhhgh, look at this," she mutters. "Jolem – what are you talking about?"

"Well, Mr. Perry – the Compliance officers...what happened to him?" While gritting her teeth, Kirame rolls her eyes. "I don't know what you mean."

"C'mon, Mom – you know what I'm talking about."

Quickly their HumanAid drifts over and lifts the mug off the floor. A plate-sized orb spins slowly out of a low cabinet compartment and moves over the spill. Within seconds, the small puddle is cleaned and evaporated dry. Kirame lifts upright and places her hand on his waist while she surveys Jolem. "Mr. Perry's deviations got him into some trouble – period! What more is there to say??"

"Is it really that simple??" Jolem shoots back.

"Yes. It is THAT simple," Kirame lashes out. "Follow The Path, and you won't have any problems. It's as simple as that!"

Jolem and Kirame stare at each other silently in a brief showdown. Each is unable to truly empathize with the other's position. Kirame has always felt she wouldn't be able to contain the strong will and great desire for understanding Jolem inherited from his father. Jolem, who can see the fear and concern in his mother's eyes, knows her views will not budge. While they stand firmly at an impasse, neither utter a word. It's a foreboding sign of things to come.

The moments of silence creep by while Jolem and Kirame awkwardly try to escape the contentious conversation. However, they are in luck. When Liz suddenly bounces into the room, they receive the timely break they were both searching for. "Hey...uhhh...did I miss something," Liz asks hesitantly as she notices their stony expressions.

"Oh, hey squirt. What's goin on?" Jolem asks as the tension in the room deflates. Seeing his sister immediately changes his mood. He grabs her and throws her over his shoulder and then playfully swings her around as she cracks up. "Put me down!" she screams while kicking her feet. She loves horseplay with her big brother.

Kirame settles back into her seat, watching them interact. Almost instantly, her peace returns and the fight between her and Jolem becomes a memory. The evening continues without another coarse word spoken. Kirame wishes the felicity could remain always, but she cherishes the present. She's painfully aware, with Jolem, these moments don't last forever.

12

A couple of weeks have passed since Jolem's interesting run-in with Leema. As he idly chews a bite of his lunch, he ponders the missed opportunity to visit the Lunar Colony. Lost in his thoughts, he can see the slow movements of his co-workers' mouths, but he hears no words. After only a few months in The Path, the monotony of his daily routine has already settled in. He hasn't used Incubus since entering the Path, and as his boredom intensifies, he struggles against his cravings.

"Okay," he says, slapping his hands on the table. "I'll be right back." The beginnings of discomfort overcome him, and he thinks a cold splash of water to the face may help. He pops out of his seat, then makes his way toward the bathroom, focused singularly on its slowly approaching entrance. He feels a mounting tension in his temples as if his head is going to explode. However, while his destination is only a few feet away, he's stalled when he once again comes face-to-face with Leema.

"Jolem??" she says as they almost bump into each other.

"Oh – hey, Leema. My bad. I didn't see you."

"Is everything okay?? You look a little – weird."

"Oh yeah – I'm…fine," he says uneasily, straightening his posture. "Was just...on the way to the bathroom."

"Uhhh – okay."

"How are things going?" he asks.

Leema starts to reply, but before she can form a word, her assistant interrupts the incidental conversation. "Uhhh, excuse me, Leema — you should really be on your way," her assistant says. "We don't want to be late, do we?"

"Oh, Jolem, my assistant is right, I have a Lunch-And-Learn session I'm headed to. But it was interesting bumping into you again. Gotta run," she sings.

Leema starts off and then suddenly stops. "Wait, Jolem," she says, reaching out to him.

"Yeah??"

"I just had a thought. I have something I'd like to run past you. Can we meet up later?"

With his mouth open wide, Jolem stumbles to respond quickly. "Uhhh – ok," he finally mutters.

"Okay. Send me an invite to your World," she says.

"My personal World??"

"Yaaaa," she snickers.

"Well. Okay – I'll do that."

"Okay, talk to you later," she salutes and then continues her casual glide down the hall.

Jolem grumbles quietly, shaking his head. " 'My personal World??' Man, what an idiot." Something unexpected about their innocent and random encounters continues to engage the typically unimpressed young man. While standing in place, his meandering thoughts drift to a chat with his grandfather years ago in his adolescence.

"Papa, how did you and Mama Sara meet?" an inquisitive young Jolem asked as his feet dangled from his kitchen table chair. Even as a child, he noticed the ever-present glow in his grandfather's eyes with just a glimpse of his wife's presence. Papa grinned with whimsy while he rubbed the top of his forehead. "Jolem, my boy," he began, "Those days were very different before The Path. It was the late 1990s. I was working as a systems tech for a struggling internet startup. We were just a small group of people with the hope of changing the world, hmmm." Papa gazed toward the ceiling, rubbing his white goatee, and then began to chuckle. "Then, she walked in. She was the new account manager, and she was breathtaking. No one thought I had a shot."

For several minutes, he would tell the story of two people inexplicably bound by a connection that started with a simple "hello." She was five years his senior and, at the time, earning almost double his salary. Many thought it wasn't going to last, but over 50 years later, they still had the twinkle in their eyes and passion in their hearts lasting until the end.

"You okay, man?" asks a squirrel curiously looking up at Jolem from the floor. The little creature's question jolts Jolem out of his daydream. When he looks around, he's surrounded by his puzzled pod-mates watching him.

"Huh? Oh – yeah, I'm good," he says, curling his lips. "Just lost in thought for a min."

"Ahh, okay. Man, you weird us out sometimes. We're headed back up... you coming?"

"Nah, give me a sec. I'll see you guys up there."

"Okay, cool."

Once again alone, Jolem continues his silent contemplation. After his and Leema's brief encounter, his anxiety inexplicably disappeared. She has a unique calming effect on him, and he can't put his finger on why. He wonders what she wants to talk about. For moments, he remains stuck in place, absorbed in thought. Finally, he continues into the bathroom, and throughout the rest of the day distracted by his imagination.

That evening, while staring at the ceiling with his legs hanging loosely off the side of his bed, Jolem smiles to himself. To his surprise, for the first time in a long while, he is completely relaxed. With the exception of his earlier breakdown, the days and weeks since entering The Path have passed relatively smoothly...and as the most recent experience with Leema replays through his AllVu, he becomes enthralled by possibilities. "Play again," he says, then watches her lips as she giggles during their chat. "Send her an invite, huh? Hmmm...I should, right?" he comments rhetorically. He's been re-watching her parting words over and over for the past few minutes.

"Sooo Jolem, what are you waiting for?" asks Li'l J. "Should I send her an invite?"

The welcomed thought of a planned rendezvous is suddenly stunted. Jolem pops up and props himself on his forearms. "Wait," he cries hesitantly. "NO, not yet!"

"Okay, okay, but…" begins Li'l J until Jolem interrupts.

"Yeah, yeah, I know…but maybe it's not such a good idea," Jolem replies with a grimace. He looks out of his glass wall and then stalls. "I mean – what does she want?"

"Jolem, do you believe your interactions would be harmful?"

"Li'l J, as soon as she enters my World, she'll know everything about me. I know I can try to block experiences and design remote rooms to hide some of my past, but that's too time-consuming. If I let her in, I'm sure she won't like what she finds."

"Well, Jolem, there IS logic to what you are saying, but maybe you're getting ahead of yourself. She only said –"

Before Li'l J can finish, the pressures of Jolem's insecurities peak, and he finally gives in to his doubt. "Li'l J… No. Don't send her an invite," he relents and shuts down his World. "I can't stand those uppity high SIVs anyhow." With a little less than two months of The Path under his belt, its bounds have him tied into knots. "You know what Li'l J? I need to get out before my head explodes. What's going on tonight?"

"Well, Jolem, it's already almost 11. It's not wise to go out at this hour. You have to work in the morning."

"Yeah, I know. I won't stay out long, but I've been really good. I need some air."

"Okay then… but I recommend you use caution during your probationary period. You've been doing so well staying on Track."

"Li'l J – Okay, enough already. I'm going to Wyth."

"Wyth Island?? On off nights like this, many lower SIVs hang out there. How about –"

"Li'l J, let's go."

Jolem reaches under his bed and pulls out his AirBoard, lays it on his sheets, and drops down beside it. He knows his mom is sound asleep in her room, and when he leaves, the door activity will trigger an alert. In an attempt to avoid hearing her mouth, he pulls up the house's ecosystem operations. With his extended fingertips, he expands the illuminated 3-D blueprint in front of him. "I'm not a hacker, but I still have some old tricks up my sleeves," he chuckles as he taps away. Within moments, he's done. "There, that should do it. I just have to mask my movements, and she won't have a clue I'm gone. Okay, Li'l J, that's hit it!"

Using methods he learned as a teenage menace, he stages his environment so that it appears as if he's in for the night. Jolem grabs his board, slips it under his arm, and tiptoes over to his door. His monitor tells him his mother is asleep in her room. While he creeps through the house on noise-proof flooring, he doesn't make a sound. He has programmed the lights to not react to his presence, so they remain inactive as he passes. Even the door alert is silenced as he steps out into the dry evening.

Jolem is exhilarated as he flows freely through the mostly deserted streets. As the wind blows against his face and through his hair, his eyes glaze. His arms sway like a bird, and he beams. He had forgotten how much he enjoyed being out alone on his board. His eyes open to the bright half-moon marooned in the sky, and he howls like a wolf. "I'm still here, Big Eye!!" he yells as he clenches his fists toward the drones cruising above. He doesn't even attempt to hide his defiant rant.

"Jolem! What in the world are you doing? Are you okay??" cries Li'l J.

"I'm great, Li'l J! Haven't felt this good in a while!"

"Well – I..."

"I don't want to hear it; just play my tunes."

At Jolem's request, the pulsating bass of his favorite music begins to blare in his ears. While winding around corners, his improvised movements make the empty road his personal dance floor. The euphoria of the moment is like a jolt of adrenaline. "Rony's world!" he commands, and suddenly, as his board shifts to autopilot, the dark skies and gravel pavement beneath him transforms into the bright endless space of Rony's open and public World. The many flowing conversations and magical interactions make the scene appear like a summertime amusement park.

"Rony!" Jolem calls out, and Rony pops up in front of him.

"Jolem! What's up, Sola!??"

"Where's Teri?"

As soon as her name is mentioned, Lateria also appears next to Rony. "Jo, what's upppp??"

"I'm headed to Wyth," he says as they slap hands. "Meet me out there."

"Wyth!?? Tonight??" Lateria replies, recoiling.

"Are you sick?" asks Rony.

"C'mon'! I'm on my way," Jolem replies with a nudge. "Let's go."

Rony and Lateria look at each other, confused. "Joe – what's with you?? It's late. We're almost out of the probation period?? I'm not going to Wyth," Rony replies.

"Yeah, Jo. I'm sorry. I can meet you there through LiveView, but I'm in bed." Lateria echoes.

"Nah, forget it. I'll catch you later," Jolem comments, swiping his hand, and instantly Rony's World disappears.

Before long, Jolem glides up to the Wyth Island entrance. Outside, in the shadows of the structure, mood fabrics, and AllVu visors stand out. Worn by kids immersed in the sensory experiences of their own Worlds, they glow in the dark like raccoon eyes. This group of mostly low SIVs silently tests the boundaries of the Cyber Ethics Rules by ignoring virtual reality time limit restrictions and wearing prohibited virtual masks. Cyber Ethics Rules were established to protect from VR addiction, manipulation, and abuse by hackers, but these wayward adolescents feel they are just another method of government control.

Jolem enters the grungy building, filled with flashing lights, then weaves through the eccentric crowd. The youth lay back against walls or reclined in oddly-shaped seats and sectionals that line the open hall. Some reach out and react to invisible partners and structures only their eyes can see, while others dance to the live musical performers. It's an escape for those looking for some action in the mind-numbing realities of a machine-driven existence. For most of their days, many of their Worlds are on autopilot and almost completely navigated by their assistants. Others, despite the constant advice from assistants, go out of their way to do the opposite. VR is the only way they feel alive.

Jolem spies a long auburn chaise lounge and plops down into its conforming upholstery. As he leans his head against the seat-back, a panting young woman in an irradiating, lined bodysuit falls into him. Twisting and squirming, she erotically massages the air as if her boyfriend was secure in her arms. Her tongue extends, and her body contorts when she experiences the sensation of her partner's touch. The lovers share an intimate moment even though they're miles apart.

Edging to the side, Jolem moves out of her way. He cradles low on the sofa and slips his hand in and out of his pocket. Again, he pulls out his tiny container. He said he wouldn't use Incubus again, and this time Li'l J's pleas for resistance are even more impassioned. The evidence tells Li'l J Incubus has a hold on Jolem. However, this time, to Li'l J's relief, his protests work. Instead of swallowing the pill, Jolem hesitantly returns his receptacle to his pocket. He reclines into the soft memory cushion and instead replays his experiences with Leema.

About an hour later, sluggishly camped alone in a dark corner, Jolem slumps over in his seat. His erratic thoughts criss-cross through his mind like bumper cars at an amusement park. He's physically tired, and as time creeps past midnight, his eyelids grow increasingly heavy. Moment by moment, they begin to slide shut while slowly, his body tips forward. Suddenly, a quick jolt snaps him back awake. "Huh…?" he mumbles incoherently while his bloodshot eyes scan back and forth. "Li'l J??" Expecting to hear the voice of the companion, he pauses, but it's not Li'l J who is vying for his attention.

"Hi, Jolem; this is SEE with your first Path Advisory Alert. It's 20 minutes past midnight. It is wise to start heading home so that you may receive proper rest for tomorrow."

Jolem's eyes pop open, and his back stiffens straight after the unexpected suggestion. Looking around suspiciously, he's not sure if he's awake or asleep in bed. "Li'l J, what's going on??"

"Jolem, I told you this was a bad idea. Let's go home," says Li'l J.

"What!? I'm not doing anything wrong. To hell with that alert!"

"Jolem! Please – be quiet. The Path." A second later, Jolem's SIV ticks down a point.

"Jolem, look what you've done. It's time to go."

"Li'l J. I don't care. I'm not goin' to be quiet, and my life is not goin' to be controlled like I'm some bot. I go to work and do my job. I don't bother anybody. I can sit here as long as I want!"

"Okay, okay… we can stay a little while longer, but please lower your voice," begs Li'l J. Defiantly, Jolem falls back in his seat and doesn't move from the spot for nearly another hour until he finally makes his exit. When he returns to the house after 1 AM, his unsuspecting mother is none the wiser than when he had left.

13

"Good morning, Leema," salutes the sweet voice of her assistant Mariela as soft acoustics chime in the background. "It's 7:15 AM and a beautiful 68 degrees. I'm sure it's going to be another WONDERFUL day in The Path."

Leema's eyes pry open to the amazing view seen through the glass wall of her bedroom. The low-lying sun peaks above the horizon, painting a beautiful portrait of the new day. She stretches out her arms from under her silky mauve sheets, squirms like a baby, and then sucks in a deep gulp of air. The captured breath settles for a brief moment and then breezes out through her lips like a whistle. "Whooooooo. Good morning Mariela," she says girlishly, grinning as she props up on her elbows. "I agree – it's going to be another WONDERFUL day."

Leema flips off to the side of her bed, hops down onto the floor, and slips her toes into a pair of fluffy slippers. For Leema, it's the carefree beginning of a typical day in The Path. "So, what's going on in my World?" she says as she floats towards her connected bathroom. Her head gently bobs side-to-side while beginning to hum along to the automatic stream of her morning music. The tunes commence soft and low but intensify with the passing seconds.

"Well, Leema, we have a lively day full of meetings and activities," Mariela begins as the mirrored wall in front of Leema's sink becomes active like a television. Mariela speaks, and corresponding optics appears. "First – a friendly reminder; today is Solia's birthday, and this evening, you're all meeting at McCarles at 6:00 PM."

"Oh, I wouldn't forget that for the world. It's going to be sooo much fun," Leema replies as a recent experience of the two friends enjoying a latte on an outside café terrace overtakes the interactive mirror.

"Yes, it will. Her gift is ready to send to her World."

"LEEMA – can't wait to see you girl!" exclaims a message from her friend, who lifts open her palm and blows a 3-D smooch.

"Great!" cheers Leema.

"Okay – now on to work," continues Mariela. "At 9:15 AM, you have a peer review meeting; at 11:00 AM – you have your Atlanta presentation. During lunch, Jenaha is excited to share her California experience with you, and at 2:00 PM, there is a collaboration session with the team in Albany."

"Wow, we do have a busy day," Leema responds while the infrared sensors of her electric toothbrush oscillate strategically around her teeth. She postures in the mirror like in a photo shoot, tilts her head and flashes a huge smile to showcase her pearl-white teeth. "Perfect!" she sniggles.

"After you went to sleep, your World was pretty lively," continues Mariela. "The release of the long-anticipated leg-length boot you were waiting on generated much chatter. There were 260 mentions by your friends. I've added a pair to your storeroom to try on later."

Leema's face lights up as a model donning the shiny, chocolate leatherette boot steps forward and strikes a pose. "They are BEAUTIFUL," she proclaims.

"Shoe Talk Group had an interesting discussion over them that you might want to experience later," says Mariela. "Most rated them very highly for style and comfort. However, others believe they're a little overpriced. Overall, they're rating is at an 8.9 out of 10."

"Okay, thanks, Mariela; pause updates till I get out of the bath, please."

Leema moves into her shower's therapeutic chamber, and automatic drops from the ceiling begin to fall like rain.

"Sure, Leema, but one last notice, if you will. While you were resting, you received a very late-night World invitation from – Jolem McKay."

Leema curiously stalls before stepping completely in.

"Jolem? Late night? Hmm, that's – odd. Did he leave a message??"

"No. No voice or visual, just an invite."

"There's definitely something – unique about him. Okay, thanks! Accept it in a few hours."

"Are you sure? His SIV is only 5.2."

"Yes, yes, and I think he's just what I'm looking for," she sings as she steps under the heated stream of her personal spa.

"Okay, sure. And what is your desire this morning?"

"Hmmm, how about a…Brazilian rainforest."

Leema's eyes slip shut, and the walls of her shower chamber transform into an exotic paradise. "Mmmmm," she murmurs as the intrinsic fresh aroma of wild plants and flowers penetrates her nostrils. In the background, echoed lullabies of tropical songbirds, indigenous creatures, and a canvassing waterfall fill the room. The staged environment transports her far away to a foreign land.

Meanwhile, across town, Jolem straddles the edge of his bed, feeling a little sluggish after a long evening. "Li'l J…tell me it was a dream, and I didn't actually send Leema an invite last night," he says, scratching his head. He already knows the answer to his rhetorical request, but Li'l J's comments pinch all the same. "Sorry, Jolem. This time, Incubus had nothing to do with it, I'm afraid."

Jolem wallows in contemplation about his late-night bout of spontaneity. It was a gut instinct he had when he got home sleepy and irritated. He was tired of being told what to do, so he did exactly what he felt like doing. Now the ball is in Leema's court. "Okay, Li'l J – what's up in my World?" he mutters.

"Well, Jolem, I'm still waiting on your responses to the apartments I've selected for you. I think you'll love the locations. No rush, but when you're ready, I'm sure they'll be to your liking."

"Li'l J, I promise to check em' out later."

"Sure, Jolem. FYI we're running a bit behind today. We should probably pick up the pace a little."

As he climbs out of bed, he peeks at the illuminating time etched in the air. "I'm not worried about that Li'l J," he replies nonchalantly. "We'll be fine."

Li'l J begins to inform Jolem of his daily schedule and World events as Jolem slowly strides to the bathroom. It's a routine day with nothing new or particularly exciting on the agenda. Standing at the bathroom sink, he splashes water over his face. Like Leema, the edges of his mirror also pan experiences that span through his World. Most pass without any interest, but one, in particular, grabs his attention.

"Hi, Jolem, it's Mrs. Mable," whistles tenderly from the soft and fragile voice of an elderly woman. Her tiny, frail frame quivers while her rosy red lip-gloss puckers. She pauses for a brief moment, clears her throat with a few dry coughs, and then continues, "Ehh hmmm, Excuse me…I know I'm a little late, but I have a graduation surprise waiting for you. You're going to love it. Bye-bye."

Typical World communications linger until either deleted or moved by their owners, but at the conclusion of Mrs. Mable's thoughtful message, her's evaporated as if it was never there. To the casual observer, Mrs. Mable would appear to be a sweet family member or close associate, but in this fantastical digital playland, things aren't always what they seem.

"Hmmm, that was strange, Jolem. Mrs. Mable didn't register," remarks Li'l J.

"Ha, don't worry about it Li'l J. Another one of those…bugs."

"Ahhh, okay,"

Following Mrs. Mable's message, Jolem has a renewed pep in his step. He rushes through his morning prep and darts down the stairs. In his rush, he almost bumps into Kirame as she passes down the hall. "Ohh hey – sorry mom," he says, slipping to the side and planting a soft kiss on her cheek.

"Whooo, hey, Jolem. Someone's running late this morning."

"Yeah, yeah, no worries… my Zumer will be here in a sec."

Kirame crosses her arms and smirks as her eyes follow him. "Well, maybe next time you won't stay out all night," she calls out, which freezes his movements.

"Huh??" he grunts. Embarrassed, his eyelids slide shut, and his chin drops to his chest. "How'd you know?"

"Let's just say, I have my own Halcyon tricks."

"Mom, I just needed – needed to get out for a while…"

Kirame takes a few steps forward and then lays her hand on Jolem's shoulder. "Jolem, honey. I know you, and I don't always see eye-to-eye," she says as she begins to softly pat. "I won't pretend to understand why The Path bothers you so, but I can understand that it does. And as much as I want to protect you, I know it's your life, and I can't live it for you. The decisions you have to make are yours and yours alone."

Jolem is so ashamed he's unable to look his mother in the face; instead, he continues blindly staring at the ground. It breaks his heart to disappoint her. His mom tenderly slips her fingers under his chin and then turns his face toward her direction.

"Jolem. I know you'll do the right thing. I trust you," she comforts. "Everything is going to be fine."

With responding puppy dog eyes and a childish grin, he nods his head. "Thanks, mom," he softly replies. "I know it will be."

Kirame smiles, shuffles his hair, and then plants her hands on her waist. "Now, Jolem…your probation period is almost over," she says, squinting her right eye while lifting the other. "No more crazy stunts, please. Okay? Your SIV needs a cooperation boost, not a drop."

Jolem looks through the glass wall out into the sky and then back to his mom. He releases a deep depressing sigh, "Okay, mom. No more – for now," he says with a devilish wink. It's a heartfelt moment that is short-lived. Seconds later, Li'l J alerts Jolem that his Zumer has arrived. Jolem swings his bag over his shoulder. "Okay, mom, I'm out."

"Okay, Jolem," she replies and then extends her arms open for a hug. She closes her eyes and holds on to him like she doesn't want to let go. "Have a great day in The Path, sweetheart," she says, shuffling his hair. "It's a good life!"

Jolem zips to his two-seat passenger Zumer waiting at the end of his driveway. Soon as he slips into his seat, a slow technotronic stream of low rhythmic beats starts to flow. His head falls back, and a mumbled sigh spews out of his mouth like a motorboat. This is one morning he wishes he were still at home, wrapped in the comfort of his bed7/7========covers. It was an interesting evening at Wyth, but being accustomed to eight full hours of rest, he feels the effects of the long night.

Jolem rubs his dry, tired eyes and leans his head against the window. Most would take the trip opportunity to interact with their Worlds, but not him. He instead prefers to rest in thought as his sights follow the random movements of tree leaves and scattering creatures of nature. The ride begins just like any other day; however, after about ten minutes, curiosity sets in. He casually notices a difference in his usual route.

Detours are common during Zumer rides. When they recognize upcoming obstacles or roadway hazards, they efficiently redirect to alternate routes. Nevertheless, something about the auto's inexplicable turns and maneuvers doesn't feel quite right to him.

"Li'l J?? Where – where are we going??"

Jolem scans back and forth, taking note of foreign buildings and unfamiliar structures. He has no idea where he is. "Li'l J??" he repeats when the call to his digital sidekick goes unanswered. "What the hell is going on?" he murmurs. His AllVu is still activated, so he can still see the augmented, but he's unable to reach Li'l J or access his world. Abruptly, the soothing sounds of his music transform into fragmented samples of unique and distinct laughter. Jolem finally becomes aware of his predicament. Like his buddy Rony months ago, his World has been hacked and his ride is under a stranger's control.

Once again, Jolem cries out to Li'l J, but still no response. His mind begins to race, and his breaths grow heavy. He doesn't know what to do. Car takeovers are uncommon, but they do occur. Most are a small part of a larger scheme and seldom leave the hostage harmed. However, in rare cases, their hackers' motives are much more sinister. As Jolem sits on edge, he awaits his fate to be determined by some unknown hacker. He knows he's at their mercy.

The tense seconds pass like hours as the annoying cackling continues. Jolem grits his teeth and grips his forehead while attempting to remain calm. He's been riding for about fifteen minutes now, and as his anxiety builds, his foot taps relentlessly against the floor. Suddenly, the awful chuckling stops.

"He-hello??" he tepidly stutters. "Who is this??"

A few silent moments pass, and then, finally, the quiet is interrupted. "Jolem. Jolem McKay," a deep digitized voice begins.

"Yaa…yeah."

Out of nowhere, the elderly woman from earlier appears. Puckering her large red lips, she shoots his way. "HEY, YOU SEXY BOYYY! THIS IS MRS. MABLE. ARE YOU READY FOR A RIIIDDDDE??!"

Instinctively, his head propels backward, and his hands spring up to block his face from the spooky vision. "HIDE, ALLVU!" he yells, and instantly Mrs. Mable and her protruding lips disappear. Slumped back in his seat panting, he's comforted by the realization he was just the latest target of a not-so-funny joke.

"G you bastard!!" he snickers. Moments later, his dormant AllVu re-animates on its own. "What??"

When Jolem saw the message from Mrs. Mable earlier in the morning, he knew his friend Gank would catch him off-guard at some point, but he wasn't expecting the gag to come so soon. He recognized Mrs. Mable as one of the many masks his crafty pal uses to disguise himself as he navigates anonymously through The Path. Finally, Gank's digitally distorted voice cracks up. "You should've seen your face, Sola!! Imma play it back for you," he wails.

"G--- what the hell, man?? I had no idea what was goin' on," chuckles Jolem.

"That's the point, my man. That's the point."

"Sola, I've got to get to WORK. I'm ridiculously LATE! Where's Li'l J?"

"Work? What's that? Nah, I've got something special planned for today. Time to celebrate."

"And – how'd you reactivate my AllVu like that? I hid it."

"I got all kinds of tricks," Gank laughs. "Don't worry. Li'l J is just sleeping for now."

"Huh? What about work? The Path?"

"Bro, do you really have to ask? SEE is my bitch!" he cracks. "Don't worry about Big Eye! I've planted some false experiences in The Path to mask your movements, so ya boy got you covered. There are so many holes in the Halcyon OS you wouldn't believe."

Jolem nods in silent deliberation. He just told his mother he'd be on good behavior, and he wants to stick to his word. It's a challenging decision, but in the end…he can't resist. "Well, Sola, let's do it then!" he agrees.

"Sit back and relax and get ready for the ride of your life."

A short five minutes later, Jolem's Zumer slowly pulls around the corner and down the street of a quiet, unassuming residential neighborhood. Modern, dome-shaped single-family homes line the road. The light from the morning sun glistens against their wood-inspired sunroof panels. To the observer, it appears to be an average middle-class avenue in a typical suburb. Little do most know that in the basement of Hazel Street house number 24, a quiet operation is at work.

As the Zumer slows to a halt along the street in front of the house, its door slides up like normal but without the expected farewell. Jolem slips out onto the curb, and before his feet are even set, the Zumer door swings down and off it speeds.

"Damn, this is weird…Li'l J? Are you there??" Standing still, he momentarily awaits a response, but the elevated sounds of nature are all he hears. With a shrug, Jolem starts up the walkway towards the front door. His AllVu remains activated, but he still can't access anything in his World. This entire event has been one surprise after another, and he can only imagine what's to come.

"Gank you mother f…" he mumbles with a grin as he scratches the back of his head. Since they were children, Gank was always the head of mischief. During the period following his father's death, Jolem was reaching for answers he couldn't grasp. Gank and his juvenile cronies gave him something to latch on to. Their childish pranks were notorious in his community, and the group loved the notoriety. Deciding The Path wasn't the way for him; Gank left education to join the enticing ranks of the local black hacker group Divergent Society.

Jolem steps up to the door, and it slides open. "Welcome, Gim," greets a sultry baritone. "Please follow the illuminated path, which will escort you to your destination."

"Gim??" Jolem mumbles. He slips his hands into his pants pockets and continues down the hall, guided by amber halos above. They lead him to a door and then down a set of stairs. "Yo Gank! Where are you??" he shouts as he descends the dark and narrow stairway, but there's no answer. Jolem's foot falls onto the floor after the final step, and he stands mesmerized by the unexpected. The scene looks as if he has just stepped back outside. Off to the right, he views a suburban scene; to the left, a city block, but without end, they seem to converge in the center. His eyes drift up, down and around, and then he begins to wander.

"What is this?" he questions as his brow crinkles. Squinting, he notices an object in the distance drifting forward in his direction. As it approaches, he realizes it's a bird. Jolem instinctively lifts his left hand and then cautiously twists it open. The vibrant canary lands on the tip of his pointer finger and begins to tweet. Its head swings from side to side, looking Jolem in the eyes, while continuing its song.

"Uhh...are you talking to me??" Jolem whispers, staring into its dark glossy eyes. Suddenly, like a lost video signal, the feathered creature flashes in and out and then vanishes.

"Huhh??" Jolem grunts while gently rubbing together his fingers tips. The realism of the strange encounter is mind-blowing. He spies around and then calls out. "Gank? Where are you?!"

Following Jolem's cry, the virtual environment fades away and he's standing in an open basement family room.

"Jo! Welcome," greets him from the integrated surround sound. The echoed voice remains altered, but he can tell it belongs to Gank.

"Sola, where the hell am I? And who is Gim??"

"Relax. You're just in one of our safe houses."

"And you're sure I'm protected from The Path??"

"Jolem. Jolem. Jolem. All these questions. You always have so many of 'em. Try being in the moment. You're missing what's right in front of you."

Jolem's head swings around. "Man, you know there's so much that I don't understand. It drives me crazy. I just want to make some sense of it all."

"You 'want to make some sense of it all' huh? Jolem in The Path, nothing is what it seems. You create your reality."

"I don't get it. Help me understand."

"I'm sorry, bro. At some point, you'll be there. As for now, you're not ready."

"I AM ready."

"We've been friends for a long time. And although you don't see me, I'm always around. Trust me – you're not ready."

"So then…why'd you bring me here?"

"Like I said, bro. This is a celebration."

The basement darkens, and the subtle lights of a small side room illuminate. "Okay, my friend, this is just for you," Gank says.

Jolem moves closer and peeks inquisitively inside the room. It looks like an intimate outer space-inspired lounge with a solo red captain's recliner set in the middle. His head swings up to the ceiling. "What is this Sola?"

"More questions. Jo, now that you are officially a cog in the machine, I designed something special just-for-you; to send you out with a bang," he says with a sinister snicker. "You'll find everything you need inside."

Slow and hesitatingly, Jolem continues forward until he's standing at the room's entrance. Sitting next to the recliner is a clear cylinder side table with a tiny glass container centered on its top. Jolem slips into the room, extends his hand, and grips the box. When he sees what's inside, he cringes. "Incubus??" he squeals. "I don't know, man. I promised myself

I was done."

"Listen, Sola. I spent hours working on this beautiful program. It's flawless and completely harmless. It'll help you see things differently. Believe me – it's a trippy adventure," he affirms, laughing.

"Gank man – I …"

"Jo! Do this for ya, boy. Trust me. You'll thank me later. It'll give you a whole new perspective."

"What about Li'l J?"

"Anything relating to this morning will be disguised from Li'l J. When you get home, it'll be as if none of this ever happened."

"You can do that??"

"Jolem – you don't know the half."

Jolem eyes the clear pill again while struggling to resist its temptation. He clears his throat and takes a deep breath, hoping the stall will mimic calls of restraint from Li'l J. This time, however, he hears no pleas, and his resolve is too weak. While adjusting his slumped posture, he stands tall and reaches for it. "Seriously – this is the last time. I could use the thrill though," he proclaims.

"Whatever you say, Sola. Welcome to The Path."

Jolem slips down in the autonomously adjustable seat, and as it reclines almost horizontal, the already dim lights darken. Embedded in the ceiling above, tiny flashes blink like stars on a clear southern night. The glass case in his hand flips open, and he studies the clear pill, holding it aloft. He closes his eyes with resignation, tilts his head back, and promptly drops it into his mouth. The pill's gossamer structure melts like molten chocolate as it dissolves on his tongue. In a succession of quick twitches, Jolem's muscles relax, and he's gone into the cosmos.

14

"Hello, Jolem! How are you feeling?" asks Li'l J, moments after Jolem's eyelids slowly open. To his surprise, he's at home, stretched out on the sofa. Normally, he wrestles with confusion for the first few minutes following an Incubus experience, but this time is different. Almost instantly, he's fully aware. His eyes bulge, and he pops upright. "Huh?? What the? Li'l J?" he cries, looking around. He begins to tap his fingertips together in a unique pattern and questions if he's truly awake or still under Incubus's spell. "Is this real??"

"'Real'? Jolem...are you ok? Your vitals seem fine... but do you need medical attention?"

"No. No...I – I actually feel - STELLAR. But 1:35 PM? How'd I get home?"

"You don't remember? This is worrisome. Maybe I should do some tests."

"No – I'm fine. Li'l J, this has just been a very weird day. Summarize it for me."

"Well, okay. You left for work this morning around 9 AM. Instead of going to your work pod, you were summoned to a Living Learning session for a few hours. You then received an unexpected exception at work and left early. We arrived home about an hour ago."

"Hmmm...okay." Misled by Gank's false scenario, Li'l J has no record of the morning's true events.

Something about this latest Incubus experience was unique. The

THE PATH

mere thought of the strange encounter sends chills of pleasure down Jolem's spine. His arms stretch high in the air, and he nestles back into the sofa cushion. He's unusually relaxed as if all anxiety has been magically washed away. He wants to stand up, but dueling parts of him desire to remain still. His mind is enraptured, and his body feels stuck in place as if an invisible force is pushing against his momentum. He feels as heavy as a rock.

In slow, cinematic motion, the room begins to sway until he hears Li'l J's low, drawling voice. "Jolem? You're acting extremely weird."

Channeling his inner strength, he reaches for the sofa and battles against the strength of gravity. When he's finally upright, everything speeds up to normal. "What the hell??"

"Jolem??"

"I'm good – I'm good," he says, shaking off his sluggishness. He runs his fingers through his hair, and he releases a long exhale. "Whew! That was wild!" His arms flutter, then he stretches his neck from side to side. Okay, now what's goin' on in my World?"

"Hmmm…well, it looks like your World has been buzzing… and good news: Leema has accepted your invite!"-

"Hmm.. okay."

After a strange morning that he can hardly remember, Jolem is relieved to be back home, trading barbs with his constant companion. He leans against a wall and takes a brief moment to reflect. Just being able to interact with his World again is refreshing. His thoughts shift to Leema, and a large grin overtakes his face.

"Li'l J, I'm hungry. What've we got?"

"Well…there's a delivery landing in approximately 1 hour and 5 minutes. How about a fresh chicken Ready-Meal? It can be available in 3 minutes and 24 seconds. And, of course, lemon water. Would you like it prepared?"

"Surely do."

Jolem moves into the kitchen, scanning his running list of messages and experiences in his World. "Jolie, what's good?" asks Lateria in one of them. "I hope we're still on. Hit my World later!"

Jolem notices his prioritized "to-do" activities, and he sighs. "I've got a few things I need to knock out."

"Yes, you do. You have a full apartment's worth of furniture to review. You're going to love my choices. Aren't you even excited??"

"Hmmm...well, I guess. I'll take a look after I eat – promise!"

While Jolem's thoughts trek through his World, a message alert interrupts the activity, "Meal's ready!" When his conscience returns to reality, his family HumanAid is a step ahead of him. In sync with the silent timer of Jolem's meal, his aid shoots to the camouflaged wall cook unit, retrieves Jolem's meal, and lays it down in front of him. "Here you are, Jolem. Is there anything else I can get for you?"

"Ahh, noo. But I thought I changed my preferences so I could get my own food."

"Hmm...no. Please enjoy your meal," he says, tipping his head, and then leaves the room as swiftly as he entered.

"That's odd."

"Jolem, I actually reversed that decision," comments Li'l J. "You were having a difficult day, so I didn't want you to be bothered."

"Li'l J, please don't override my decisions. LiveView, Lateria," he instructs, with a mouth full of food. Within moments she appears.

"Jolem, baby! What's good?"

"Everything, and yep we're still on. Gotta kick that ass this time."

"Not even in your dreams! Ste – lla. Hit you later."

"Cool."

After gulping down his meal, he glances out his back-window wall, then suddenly, he slams his fists on the table. "Play music!" he shouts. He pushes back, then begins to idly tap on its surface while his head bobs to the rhythms of the internal beats. "Now switch it up!" From slow to fast, the heavy base-inspired sounds blare progressively. With spirited movements, his head swings up, down, and around. "YEAAHHHH!" he moans, in the groove. "I can't be held down, Li'l J! Not me!"

"Jolem?? Are you okay?"

THE PATH

"Hell yeah, I'm okay. I'm invincible! Play throughout the house!"

His enthusiastic command sends his private tunes from his ears out to the home's unified sound system. From room to room, the surround sounds boom like a live band. Gank's suggestion about him being in the moment sits in his mind. He's tired of conflict and just wants to be. His family is jubilant, and so are his friends. He considers perhaps there's a future happy place in The Path that he lacks the foresight to see.

While home alone, he moves throughout the house, taking note of all the modern conveniences he enjoys. He considers some of history's challenges. As he peeps at his HumanAid gathering laundry, he thinks back to tales from his grandfather. He recalls a description of first-generation HumanAids from decades ago. Their puppet-like characteristics and movements were far from what they are today. They required massive amounts of energy to operate and needed to be plugged into an overnight power source. His HumanAid's wireless charging station keeps it on the go non-stop. Like most technologies, HumanAids were initially considered luxuries. Today, it would be hard to find a household without at least one.

"You know what, Li'l J?" he calls out while scratching the back of his head.

"What's that, Jolem?"

"Set up the apartment on East Spring Avenue with the furniture in my storeroom. Maybe you're right - this room is a little small for me. Time to make some decisions."

"Great idea, Jolem! That's the spirit."

He sinks into his sofa, then prepares for his apartment tours as if settling into a movie's opening trailers. Within seconds, his potential new home begins to build around him. Soon, he's standing in the middle of the empty one-bedroom loft.

"Rony thinks his place is nice. Wait 'til he checks this out," he snickers.

Li'l J is intimately in tune with Jolem's likes and dislikes, however, some of the furniture design choices don't quite hit the mark. "Hmmm... trash that," Jolem remarks as he grabs a throw pillow and tosses it into his glowing virtual can. "Li'l J, what's up with those, dude??"

"Oh, Jolem, all you have to do is change the colors, and they'd work out great."

"I don't know – let me see that sofa in a dark grey," he instructs while pointing from location to location, "and find a long red lamp for that corner."

As he speaks, items matching his requests pop up in a scrolling list. "Not that one – that one – no, no no…" he utters. One by one, he swipes them out of sight until something grabs his satisfaction. "Stop! This one is it! Keep."

After gripping the selected pillow, he places it atop the sofa... "PERFECT."

"Well done. Jolem, you have great taste," comments Li'l J. "I'll describe some of the many wonderful amenities of this apartment."

Jolem begins to move through the loft, imagining a life, calling it his home. Many of the old challenges for young adults seeking their first place, such as budgeting, decisions of location, moving complications, etc., are no longer concerns. Smart systems prevent overspending by allowing people to take on only as much as they can afford. With Li'l J's helpful assistance, narrowing down the options is almost a perfect science.

Jolem spends the next hour quantum leaping through the short list of apartments Li'l J selected for him. With all of them being great options, he faces a difficult final choice. "Wow, Li'l J," he exclaims. "I can see myself in each one. No more hiding stuff and dodging my mom. I'll be able to do exactly what I want."

"That's the spirit, Jolem. The Path has made all this possible."

"Whooooow. Oh no, not you too! Kill that, Li'l J."

"What?? Jolem, I don't understand."

"J, I'm just tired of talking about The Path. I mean – enough already."

"Jolem. Please consider all you know. Our history, our present, and our future. The Path makes everything work together for the good of all. It's wise that you drop all the resistance and begin enjoying your new freedom of The Path. Your world can be everything you want it to be if you'll only allow yourself to relax and experience it."

"Li'l J…? You actually sound a little different. What gives?"

"Hmmm, really? Well, there was a small update to the Halcyon operating system this morning. Interesting."

"Interesting for sure. Anyway – I can't make up my mind. Take me back through East Spring and Alcorn. I need another look."

"Sure, Jolem. As you wish."

A couple of hours later, Jolem's mom and sister return home. Liz had been away at a Future Path Stars camp for days, so he heads downstairs to greet her. As he rounds the corner into the open living area, he sees Liz's backside standing next to his mom. But before he can say a word, he receives a LiveView message from her.

"Hey, Jolem - WYD??"

"Oh, hey squirt…you know I'm right behind you, right?"

"Yep."

"Liz – okay, this is crazy," he says, stepping closer. "I told you to stop talking to my World when we're right next to each other. Turn around."

Giggling, Liz spins. "Hey, Jolem," she says as they bump fists.

"Welcome home – I missed you."

"Jo, you're so silly," she laughs, "I just saw you yesterday."

"Yeah, yeah. Well – World experiences are no substitute for the real thing. So, you were into it, huh?"

"It was stellar! My simulation was waaaay cooler than anyone else's. I want THAT Track!"

"You can do anything you want, squirt. If you want to be a simulator, then that's what you'll be."

"I know, I know…"

Jolem's hand rests softly on her shoulder. "But don't rush it. Enjoy being young. The Path can wait," he says, then turns off to the side. "Hey, Ma."

Standing nearby, with arms crossed and a tender grin, Kirame watches the natural affinity between her children. She loves witnessing the close affection they share.

"Hey, Jolem. How was your day, honey?"

Jolem's drift to the ceiling. "Ya know...normal," he replies, scratching the back of his head.

"That's good."

"Yeah, and guess what? I'm close to choosing an apartment. Down to two."

"Wow, really?? I'm impressed," she says proudly, ruffling his hair. "See. All it takes is a change of attitude. I knew you'd come around."

"Okay, okay, Ma - let's not go overboard."

"No, seriously. I see a change in you. You don't seem as uptight today. Nothing special happened?"

"Oh – no," he remarks awkwardly, rocking back and forth on his heels. "Just a normal day."

His mom glances suspiciously without words. She doesn't buy his story but doesn't push him. "Well, this all makes me ecstatic," she says. "It's truly a good life."

AN UNLIKELY FRIENDSHIP

15

That evening, Jolem and Lateria squirm in their reclined gamers' lounges like a fish out of water. For the past two hours, the close friends have been at Lateria's house, tackling an onslaught of adversaries within the virtual gaming experience, "Travail." The popular activity is one of their favorite pastimes together, and they often spend hours locked in the dreary adventure.

Lateria's battle-weary SimMe peers out into the horizon. She can see a hint of the auburn sun and knows she's close to the power source. A soft dusty wind brushes against her cheek. She smirks, then her body slowly materializes from her decimated car-hiding place.

"Jolem! I see it – we're close!" she proudly proclaims. She releases a relieved breath and then reaches out to retrieve her fallen armory bag. Suddenly, the fine hairs on her back raise as the shrill chuckle of a familiar voice echoes right behind her. Timidly, she turns to confront her mysterious adversary, whose appearance is unique each time she sees him. Her previous attempts to permanently expel him from her World have apparently failed.

"What the – this mother------!" rages Lateria, before clenching her fist tight. Gritting her teeth, she opens her legs wide and propels her body forward. "Take this, scum!" she yells, releasing a force of energy that blasts him into a thousand pieces.

"PAUSE!" she shouts. Instantly, her frustrated command suspends the simulated encounter and transforms her back to her home. "HIDE

AllVu," she says and pops up.

"What's up, Teri??" questions Jolem as he also halts his play. He leaps to his feet to find out what has bothered her.

"Sola, it's that bastard!" barks Lateria. "He tried it again, even after I knocked him out the last time. He keeps touching my body. I played my VPower and blew his effin' head off."

"What an asshole."

"I just can't stand that shit. I know it's a game, but it feels REAL as hell."

Jolem steps slowly over to Lateria and gently slips his arm around her shoulder, but she pulls away. "I'm good," she says, tilting her head off. "It's just... I keep blocking him, but he just changes his identity and gets past my security. I don't know what to do. I should report his ass to Cyber Crimes."

"Well – the last thing you want is them patrolling your World."

"Yeah – whatever…"

The soured thoughts of the two friends quietly guide them into Lateria's kitchen. They stop next to the long, curved window wall that wraps around the back of the room, and she looks out into the sky. Her cyber stalker's harassment is still festering in Lateria's mind. She's never met him and considers what she might do if he were actually standing in front of her. Turning away, she attempts to mask her pain. She crosses her arms, then asks, "So Jo – how's The Path?"

Caught off guard by her sudden shift of topics, Jolem averts his eyes. "Oh – good," he awkwardly remarks.

"Huh? Jo, you okay??"

"Oh yeah – sure. Wait, hold on a sec," he says, holding out his hand. "Li'l J's telling me something…"

"Jolem, she's here!" exclaims Li'l J.

"Who's here??"

"LEEMA. She's in your World."

A quizzical grin grows on Jolem's face as he slips down into the nearest chair. "Really?? Show me," he says, leaning back.

"Will do."

Jolem's sights move throughout his World, then his brim crinkles. "Uhhh – I don't see her. Where??"

"Jolem, can't you tell?? She's right there with the bunny mask."

"Ha, J! You're right…"

The use of elaborate digital masks can be a very effective method of perusing Worlds undetected. However, in this case, Leema's basic pink nose and fuzzy ears are not so clever. Bewildered, she wanders the unique passages of Jolem's World, looking around like a spectator at a museum. His many intricate and obscure doorways, tunnels, and hidden rooms fill her with the astonishment of a child at an amusement park. He's not sure if her mask was designed to actually conceal her identity or is just a cute way of getting his attention, but it's not much of a disguise.

"Looks like she's made her way into my hidden corridor. I guess she's savvier than I thought," Jolem huffs. "Oh weeell…"

Engulfed in his World, Jolem almost forgets Lateria standing right next to him. "JO! What's going on??" she questions while giving him a solid tug. She's more than curious by his unusual excitement.

"Uhhh… nothing – nothing," he quickly replies after being snapped back to reality. Instinctively, he tries to reclaim his cool. Showing his soft and fuzzy side might earn him a good amount of playful ribbing from his tough friend. Lateria stands with arms akimbo and then suspiciously peers into his face. "'Uhh nothing' huh? Do you think I'm some idiot?" she snipes. "Okay, what the hell's up??"

"Okay, Okay," Jolem says, tightening his lips. "Well – it's nothing, really. But, but there's…there's this girl at my job…"

"A girrlll? Go, Jolem! Are you a match? Is she hot?? What's your probability?"

"C'mon, listen – seriously…"

"Okay, okay, I'm sorry. Tell me about this girrrl," she says, grinning.

"Nothing's to tell," he grumbles, turning away. "She's some dumb, high SIV doll. We're not a match at all."

"High SIV?? Seriously Jo? I mean really… keep that bitch outta ya

World."

"So, that's the thing. She's in my World right now."

The rings on the front of Lateria's shirt light up as her eyes grow wide. "REALLY?? Imma go there and check her out!" she shouts, and her AllVu reactivates.

"NOOO!" Jolem quickly reacts, holding her back. "I won't identify her right now. She's wearing a crazy mask anyhow."

"Jo, ya know, you're being a jerk. What gives man??"

"Nothing. I just don't want to make a big deal of it. I'm just gonna lead her into a rabbit hole."

"Do it then."

"Damn, get off my back."

"Wow, Jo! My bad…my bad. I forgot you were always this difficult. I don't get you, Sola; for real. This is a waste of your time, and you know it. Be logical. If you want to meet someone, just hit PerfectMatch."

"Yeah, yeah – whatever. Let's just get back to "Travail,"; ok?"

"Okay, cool then," she says, shrugging. "You're sure you don't want to go play kissy with your girlfriend??"

"Screw you, Teri. C'mon, let's go back so I can kick some mo' ass."

"That bastard better have gotten the message this time. I can't deal with him anymore. If I ever identify this fool in reality, he's goin to have a baaad day."

"I hear you."

Lateria punches Jolem in the arm and they slide back down onto their gamers' lounges. Within moments, they're back on the urban battlefield, fighting off monstrous foes. They put in a valiant effort, blasting and bombing their way through rough and dangerous terrains, but they never reach their goal. Unfortunately, after an extended period of fierce gameplay, they are both finally blown into pieces by their play-along rivals.

An hour or so later, on the north end of town, socialite Leema is stretched peacefully in her World chamber, welcoming her World's interactions. Her luxurious glass-domed encasement provides a cozy sanctuary and a physical block from outside interferences. As she nestles into its puffy, soft coral cushions, she laughs uncontrollably as a girlfriend describes an earlier experience. While the humorous footage plays, Leema squeals, "Girl, stop! Please!" to the reenactment of the embarrassing exchange. The entire virtual room of her World is rolling in tears.

"I almost ripped off my shirt so he couldn't see my blush – DAMN YOU MOOD COLORS!!" her friend yells, with her fists clenched high in the air.

"You are CHAOS," laughs one of the women.

Gushing and joking, the group of girlfriends share experiences, products, and services from their Worlds. It's an animated exchange as they attempt to outdo one another with comedy, bravado, and showmanship like a cast on a live morning talk show. Enthusiastically, they apply ratings to everything from co-workers to clothing and save items to their storerooms. It's a pretty typical, enjoyable evening in Leema's life of leisure. While chuckling, she notices an alert hovering. "A new friend has entered your World," it says.

"Exciting. Mariela, who's our guest?" Leema asks, taking a break from her room chat.

"It's Jolem McKay. He's walking down the halls just looking around."

"Hmm, Jolem? Is he wearing a mask or anything?"

"No mask. He's just casually browsing. Of course, due to his SIV, he has limited access."

"Ahhh, okay."

"Hmmm Leema – I sense a peculiar interest in this individual. From what I have evaluated from his background, you may want to keep your distance. Remember, his SIV is hovering around a 5, you know."

"Yes, yes, I know. Oh, Mariela, stop worrying. I don't have a 'peculiar interest'. I just find him 'curious,' that's all. Like a social experiment."

"Hmmm," hums Mariela before a short pause. "Have you ever heard the term 'curiosity killed the cat'?"

"No – what does that mean??"

With his hands stuffed in his slim pants pockets, Jolem slowly canvasses the colorful and vivacious atrium of Leema's World. Up and down, his sights extend to the towering walls and endless flows of activity throughout. The lively spectacle is like being in the middle of New York City's Times Square mid-day. With a simple thought, Leema appears right behind him.

"Boo! What are you doin' here?" a bubbly voice questions. Startled, Jolem pops up on his heels and then spins around. "Leema? Is that you??" he asks with the first glimpse of his friendly stranger's bunny nose and matching fuzzy ears.

"Of course, it is Gizmo," she giggles as her mask dissolves from in front of her face. "I bet you didn't even know I was in your World earlier."

"What?? Are you serious? You know those bunny masks don't fool anyone," he laughs. "My assistant found you the moment you entered."

"REALLY!?? Hmmm. I thought it was convincing!"

Peering at Leema, Jolem brandishes a coy smirk. "No," he remarks and starts laughing. "You're joking, right??"

"Well – I thought so. Hmmm," she says, pondering. "I guess not."

"But I must admit – this is some World," he comments as his eyes drift around. "Impressive."

"Yeah, it is, isn't it?? I worked very closely with my simulator," she comments proudly, tipping her head. "And what's up with yours?? So dark with all those hidden doorways. It's as if you don't want anyone there."

"Well – often – I really don't."

"Hmmm…that's weird. Everybody wants people in their World. The positive activity helps boost your SIV."

"Weird, huh…" he shrugs. "So, what's up with the bunnies?"

"What do you mean?"

"Well – you like the bunny masks."

"Hmm – I just like rabbits. Sometimes I work a gig at an animal shelter."

"Uhh, okay. Cool."

They walk, side by side, moving slowly down her white, open hall in casual conversation. Accustomed to the presence of like-company with similar manners and actions, Leema finds Jolem's quirky nature fascinating but also extremely bizarre. His unpredictability and creative thoughts challenge her in ways she's rarely experienced.

"Why do some people do all the right things and still have low SIVs?" he asks, then turns away. He's not expecting an articulate replay but wants her to think outside her box.

"Hmmm…" she murmurs in contemplation. "I would say low SIVs are low because they DON'T do the right things."

"Is that right?" he questions, lifting one eyebrow above the other.

"How did you get like this?" she asks. Jolem begins to respond, but before he can form his words, he suddenly freezes. Looking him in the eyes is an illustrious monument devoted to a currently popular and polarizing political figure. As he stands rubbing his chin with his right hand propped on his waist, he cringes. "Oh shit. I thought your name was familiar!"

"Ohhh. My father??"

"Your father is DIRECTOR DALIO? How didn't Li'l J detect this?"

"Well – Dad just thought it would be best if this was hidden information. You know, with all the protests from those maniacs calling him 'Director Diablo.'"

"I guess I can understand that. I mean – doesn't he basically run the FDEC??"

"No, he doesn't run the FDEC. He's Director of the North-Eastern Region."

"Yeah, that's his title, but from what I've heard – he is the man."

"Well, the early generation Path was very clunky. He helped streamline its logic. But now he just oversees some operations. Does this bother you?"

"Uhhh – it's just a little surprising, that's all. All the controversy."

"Well, I don't pay attention to any of that nonsense. My father's a genius and a great servant to this country. It's all just hype from those crazies. It's all fake. They're sick."

Turning away and looking upward to the ceiling, Jolem fights the desire to defend the group. He decides this debate is wise to save for another day. His sights return to Leema, and he begins to speak, but her relaxed demeanor abruptly morphs.

"Leema?? Is everything okay??"

"Well…hmm. I just received…a Path Alert," she replies, smirking.

"Really?? What did it say?"

"All it said was, 'Please exit your World, and you'll be informed when you can return.'"

"Ohh, I'm sure it's nothing," comments Jolem nonchalantly, waving it off. "There are always glitches with the Halcyon OS and SEE. Probably just need to reboot your World."

"I suppose so. Gotta say this is a first for me."

"You've never had to reboot your World before?"

"Well, yes – of course. I mean – this is my first Path Advisory Alert. I knew I'd receive one at some point, but – ahh nothing."

"Ahh, okay," Jolem mumbles quietly without offering anything further. He's already received a few.

In an abrupt transition, Leema reclaims her cheery disposition. "Well, okay Jolem… I guess I'm going to exit and wait for instructions," she says, smiling. "There is still the reason I wanted to talk to you in the first place. It'll have to wait till later."

"Umm…okay."

"Okay then. We'll talk soon. BYE."

With those parting words, Leema disappears. Jolem takes in an extended panoramic view of his energetic surroundings, then pauses. Interactive rooms filled with popular products, fun games, and celebrity personalities line the moving walls. Live discussions produce dynamic and fluctuating ratings. With a command, he also vanishes from her digital domain, and his thoughts return to the tranquility of his bedroom, where he's stretched on his sofa.

16

"Good morning, dear," says a gentle but rough male voice as Leema slides into her kitchen the next day. With a full head of curly, grey hair, a speckled beard, and a gracious smile, Leema's father, Director Fitz Dalio, peers into the clear sky. "It's another beautiful day in The Path, isn't it?"

Leema waltzes around the room and into the seat next to her father at the table. "Good morning, Daddy. It sure is. Isn't it?"

After snuggling back into his seat, he places his hands behind his head, turns to her, and grins. "Soooo... anything exciting going on in your World today?"

"Are you serious??"

"Yes, I am."

"Daddy! You know what today is," she pouts, but jokingly he continues with the ruse.

"Hmmm... I don't have the slightest idea what you're talking about," he chides, clearing his throat. "Aliza, is there anything special happening today?"

"Director, don't you think you've teased her enough?" scolds his assistant. "You know today is the final day of Leema's probationary period."

"You're right," he snickers. "I apologize. You know that I'm aware of EVERYTHING that happens around here. Well, at least Aliza is... ha ha. I don't see why high SIVs need probationary periods anyhow."

"Well, Dad. I'm sure if they offered no value, the policy would've been eliminated long ago."

"You're such an insightful young woman," he chuckles. "I'm very proud of you."

"Dad, you're not so bad either. I don't understand why some of these people say the things they say about you – The Path. It doesn't make any sense. Seriously, how can they not see how The Path has set us free and made life so rewarding?"

"Well, Sweetheart...your wit and good judgment are some of the reasons you have such a high SIV. The delusions these protesters and low SIVs hang on to are just that; fantasy. I'm glad you have the wisdom to see the truth. Without The Path, this country and the world would be in shambles."

Leema smiles at her father with the youthful charm of a five-year-old. "If you ask me, you're far from 'Diablo' or 'devil,'" she laughs. "You're a good man – a noble man. You are doing such a great service for this country."

"Thank you, Darling," he replies modestly, smirking. Director Dalio lifts his morning tea mug and softly blows over its rising steam as he begins to review a World message. It's a routine beginning to the day. However, after a short lull in the conversation, Leema breaks the silence. There's an unusual tinge of unease in her voice.

"Dad, let me ask you something."

"Yess…"

"Well, there's this co-worker. A rather unique individual. He said something to me yesterday that I couldn't get out of my head."

Following Leema's words of curiosity, the felicitous gleam of Director Diablo's expression disappears. As he sits up and twists in her direction, concern suddenly spreads across his face. "And what's that, sweetheart??" he inquires.

"Well – he suggested opportunity is not always equal in The Path. Of course, it was a ridiculous notion, but it still had me thinking. Do more of the lower SIVs feel this way?"

Director Dalio pulls himself up out of his seat and begins to pace in a small circle. "And who is – this co-worker?" he asks, rubbing his chin.

"Nobody, Dad. Just one of the AllVu systems technicians."

"A systems technician?? Why are you chatting with a system's tech?"

"Okay, Dad, I have my reasons. Never mind; forget it."

"Okay, okay…, Leema, listen," Dir. Dalio remarks before sucking in an audible gust of air that then seeps out of his nostrils. "These are the kinds of ideas from which your mother and I have always attempted to shield you. They are dangerous and, in weaker minds, can grow like weeds."

He takes a step forward toward the window wall, stops, grips the back of his neck, and looks reminiscently out into the clear morning sky. With a sullen tremble in his voice, he begins, "You know, it actually pains me – in my core, when I hear things like this. The protests, the deviants, the false information. This country has come such a long way."

As he takes another gruff breath, he pauses for reflection and then looks her way. "History has taught us many lessons," he continues. "And one very important lesson I want you to always remember is that there will always be those who fight against what's good for them. But do not be upset with them or their narrow-minded ideology; pity them. Their thoughts are selfish and shortsighted. They are mentally ill, and WE must help save them from this sickness."

Listening to his foreboding tale like a child at a night campfire, Leema grimaces with disgust and awe.

"Do you know, years ago, many people abused a product called cigarettes," he says, frowning and looking sullenly into her eyes. "Before we outlawed these death sticks, many inhaled poison directly into their mouths and through their helpless lungs, despite the grave warnings enshrined on the very packages from which they were drawn. Cancers corrupted and crippled their bodies. Countless people died."

After stalling during a few heavy breaths, he continues. "Until we implemented DTH taxes, millions would also consume foods they knew were full of sugar, salt and harmful chemicals, which lead to obesity, disease and death. This created havoc in our healthcare system. Now healthcare is focused on prevention and people are healthy. Pity them, my dear, and it will give you the courage and strength to make the decisions that can, at times, be difficult to make. We high SIVs have a responsibility to help those who are otherwise incapable of helping themselves. This is our burden."

Leema stands proudly, shaking her head after being energized by her father's motivated speech. "You're right, Dad. I will do my part," she declares.

Director Dalio walks up to Leema and grins tenderly. "You're all grown up, and I can no longer save you from the world. It is time YOU help save IT. And fortunately, there is a guide. In all of your ways, follow the infallible instruction of The Path, and it will direct you."

"Thank you, Dad. I will."

"I know you will...I know you will," he mutters as he hugs her tightly. "And I know it is a tad premature, but let me be the first to congratulate you, sweetheart. Tomorrow you will be a full-fledged Path Ambassador! I'm sure you will represent this great country with the honor and dignity The Path has afforded us."

"Yes, of course, I will," she proclaims proudly.

17

Later that afternoon, with his arms stretched over the back of an office park bench, Jolem watches people sail by. As they float back and forth, interacting with their assistants or Worlds, the scene resembles an antiquated roller-skating rink. He humors himself by augmenting fire breathing dragons and two-headed gargoyles menacing the crowd. He's trying to find anything to add a little excitement to an otherwise uneventful day. "Li'l J, go to my World," he says, and within moments, he'll get the jolt he's seeking.

As soon as he enters his World, he's hit with a barrage of impassioned reactions to the recent indictment of Mr. Perry for treason and espionage. He hadn't seen or heard a word of Mr. Perry since the dramatic run-in with the Compliance Control Officers months ago. Now, his besieged neighbor appears to be public enemy #1.

"Mr. Perry is scum and a traitor!" one person shouts.

"I always knew there was something off about him," comments another. "Always talking against The Path. He'll get what he deserves."

One-by-one, vicious attacks on Mr. Perry's character resonate throughout Jolem's World. Without evidence or even knowledge of his wrongdoing, he's become a social outcast. Jolem notices a discussion in Rony's World dedicated to the subject. "Rony's World," he calls out, and he's immediately transported into the open forum. The one-sided gathering of angry participants slanders Mr. Perry, his actions, and his beliefs. His merely being an open critic of The Path brings out their ire. As Jolem navigates the large group, he suppresses his urge to speak. He recalls Mr. Perry as a kind and decent man...someone who used to console him after his father died. It's disturbing to witness the vitriol from typically even-tempered people. Abruptly, Rony appears at his side. "Wowww, Sola--- this is way out, man! I told you!" he says. "Can you believe it??"

"Believe what? What happened to Mr. Perry or this angry mob??"

Rony's eyes widen in amazement, and he lunges toward Jolem. "Sola, what the EFF?? Don't say stuff like that. Are you crazy??" he whispers.

"But – what did he do??"

"I have no idea, but clearly, he was a deviant. I told you."

"Rony... I've got to go, man," Jolem sighs, shaking his head. He swipes his hand and disappears. Instantly, his thoughts return to his office park reality. However, after what he just experienced, he's uneasy again. As he surveys the area, observation drones and cameras, exposed and hidden, seem to be everywhere. The eerie feeling of The Path following his thoughts and movements grips him like a glove. He wants to move beyond this place of malcontent, but every time he finds a small place of comfort, he gets pulled back in.

"Put your smile back on, and let's go home," he mumbles to himself, attempting to block out the distraction. He begins to lift up off of his seat until he receives an unexpected communication.

"LiveView call from Leema," alerts Li'l J.

"Hmmmm," he moans. Feeling somewhat apprehensive about their differences, he's not sure if he should respond. However, again his curiosity gets the best of him. "Okay, accept." Instantly through her world cam, she's right in front of him.

"Hi, Jolem. How are you?"

"Hey, Leema. What's up?"

"Welll, that was an awkward end to our experience last night. I was thinking about something you said?"

"...and what's that??"

"Ahh – can you meet me in my World tonight – let's say 7 tonight?"

"Okay...sure."

"Great! See you in a bit. Bye."

"Bye…"

Leema disappears, leaving Jolem with mixed emotions. He's not sure if he should smile or frown. He can't deny that there's some inexplicable, kindred connection with her, but he can't avoid the clear contrasts in their thoughts and beliefs.

"I'll need to replay our experience from last night, because I have NO idea what she wants to talk about, J."

"Would you like me to evaluate the conversation and give you suggestions?"

"Uhh…nah, I'll do it myself."

"Well, your Zumer will be here in approximately one minute. You can view it on the way home. But Jolem…,"

"Yeah, Li'l J?"

"I have some advice. Leema is a high SIV and a legacy of Director Dalio. The two of you have virtually nothing in common. I sense interest of a personal nature; however, that might not be wise. Based on this and other factors, I recommend this relationship would be better kept professional."

"Well, I DON'T have an interest of a 'personal nature,' but thanks. She's the one who called me…remember?"

"Okay, Jolem."

Jolem continues through his afternoon, anticipating his upcoming experience with Leema. Although he examined their earlier discussion like a detective, when seven o'clock arrives, he's still unclear of her angle. Circulating his room, he carefully rehearses prepared lines hoping he can control their approaching conversation. He clears his throat and begins to call her World, but before he can, he receives an untimely Path alert.

"Hi Jolem, this is SEE with a Path advisory alert. We've detected unusual activity in your World. As a precaution, please remain out of your World until you receive further instructions."

"Hummm," he hums. "What the hell is that all about?"

For the next ten long minutes, he impatiently sits on his sofa, mind-navigating two mini drones throughout his room. They crisscross, bob, weave and spin in the air until he's tired of stalling. "Forget this!" he grunts. "Li'l J, Leema's World."

"WHATT?? Jolem?? SEE instructed you to wait – what are you doing??"

"Li'l J, I'm sure it's nothing. Just do it."

"Jolem, I HIGHLY recommend against this. Please reconsider."

"I've already made my decision...Leema's World."

"Okay,...as you wish."

Within moments of his ill-advised command, Jolem finds himself standing alone in the middle of an empty white space. No walls, no ceiling or floor, just empty white space. "What the," he mutters as he looks around. "Leema??"

"Hi, Jolem," she speaks softly from behind him, and then he spins around. About ten feet away and donning a shiny white bodysuit, Leema nestles at the end of a velvety white sofa. "Here, come have a seat," she says, patting the spot next to her.

Jolem's fingers slowly rake his cheeks as he laggards over. After all of his prep, he's suddenly lost his thoughts. "Leema? What's going on?"

"Just sit next to me, please," she says quietly. "I just want to talk to you."

As he creeps closely, Leema follows him, smiling patiently. "Relax, you don't have to be uptight. Please sit."

Following his uncomfortable but short walk, he finally reaches the sofa. He plants into the opposite corner across from her and then twists in her direction. "Leema, what's going on? This is all too strange."

For a few moments, she peers into his eyes without saying a word, continuing to grin. "Jolem," she begins before pausing again. "You said something to me the other day which concerned me. I just couldn't get it out of my mind."

"Really? What was that?"

Long silences space out her responses as her toy-like expression continues. "You said, 'opportunity is not equal in The Path.' That is a very profound statement, but you made the comment almost in passing. I sensed…unhappiness."

"Oh yeah – that."

"Well, I know we just met, and I don't know you very well, but there's something about you – I find very fascinating. I don't have many associates like you. Actually, I don't have any like you. I want to understand the root of these emotions. I feel a responsibility to help you stay on Track."

When she finishes her intro, Jolem is confounded. Staring at her like she's an alien, he's speechless.

"Did you hear me?" she asks.

"I'm sorry. Of course, I did. But – I don't understand. Is this some kind of intervention? Ya know, you really don't need to worry about me. I'm good."

"Jolem, I only want to help. Why are you so guarded? It's weird."

"Ya know; you call me weird a lot??" he says, wincing. "Well, compared to what is normal, I'd rather be weird."

"And that – that's what I wanted to talk to you about, Jolem. I believe you're a good person and don't want to see you get into trouble. Life in The Path is so AWESOME!" she says as her face lights up. "Why are you trying to find fault in it?"

"Leema – you just wouldn't understand."

"Well, help me understand. When I wake up in the morning, I just feel…I feel WONDERFUL! This life has so much to offer. Our worlds are just so full of joy and peace. The Path has made it possible to just be happy. Don't you want to be happy, Jolem? Don't you want to smile?"

"Of course, I do. But I guess I just don't see things like you do."

"But why Jolem?? Your World can be whatever you want it to be?"

As her thoughts slip into the cosmos, Leema's dreamy eyes drift up and her expression beams.

"Sometimes I'm a navigator of a huge aircraft that stretches into the clouds," she says as a modern aviator's uniform replaces her white bodysuit. "Or an action star with millions of adoring fans," she continues as the white space fills with endless aisles of clapping fanatics and gushing paparazzi. "You are the designer of your own reality, Jolem! You can be who or whatever you want to be!"

"But Leema – you're NOT an aviator nor an action star. It's NOT real."

She cuts her eyes to him, lowering. Her head and demeanor drop. "Wow, you don't have to be cruel."

"But – but I wasn't – I…"

"You know, you may choose to live in negativity and cynicism, but it's foolish!" she lashes back. "It's a good and beautiful life, Jolem! It's all how you see it. You ARE the designer of your own reality. If you'd only stop fighting and enjoy, you'd see a world where anything is possible. Why can't you see this??"

After her dramatic plea, Leema's eyes cut sharp enough to cut metal. Like auditioning for a soap opera, she spins her back to him and melodramatically drops her head. Watching her angry sulk, Jolem shakes his head again. His lips twist, and teeth grind as he struggles with a loss of productive words to offer. It feels like he's debating his mother all over again. Finally, he reaches out, gently grips her shoulder, and then draws her near. "Leema…I'm sorry," he says. "Maybe you're right. Sometimes while I'm in my own little funk, I – I get caught up in my head. I really didn't mean to offend."

Leema turns slowly and peers into his puppy-dog eyes. She can see sincerity. For better or for worse, Jolem wears his heart on his sleeves. The tight crinkles of Leema's forehead relax, and the rigid edges of her mouth bend upward as she wavers from her silent protest. "You know, Jolem. I apologize, too," she says. "I shouldn't have yelled at you and taken what you said so personally."

Jolem tilts his head and grins back. "I really got to you, didn't I?" he chuckles.

"Honestly, Jolem, you're like no one I've ever met before. You're just strange."

"Ha. Well, at least this time, you didn't call me 'weird.'"

"C'mon seriously, Jolem," she laughs, tapping his arm. "You know you're different."

"Well – I take that as a compliment. And I suppose I could lighten up a little."

The tender moment calms them both. Jolem's sights swing out into the beyond, around, and then down. While scratching the back of his neck, he glances back at Leema and then smirks. "You know – you're not too bad for a high SIV," he cracks.

With two fingers, she swipes back a strand of hair that had fallen into her face and then returns the joking sentiment. "You can be an asshole, but not bad for a," she begins and then teasingly winces, "ughh 'mid-SIV.'"

They snicker during the playful and flirtatious exchange. Suddenly, Leema grips his wrist. "Jolem – come with me," she says, tugging him forward. "I want to show you something."

"Huh?? Okay."

They lunge ahead, and Leema swings her arm in a wide circular motion as if painting on the air. "THIS is one of my most favorite places to go," she says, glowing with excitement. "Follow me."

Vivid colors grow around them, and their environment transforms into the swaying tall grass meadows of a wide-open Midwestern prairie. Jolem delights at the sight of endless plains and picturesque blue sky. Its naked peacefulness is a far contrast from the technical freeway of Leema's World. "So, you DO like to get away from the noise," he wisecracks.

Leema opens her arms and spins around like a ballerina as the slow wind brushes across her face. "Yessss, I doooo," she cheers. "I looovvvve being out here. I saw it in an old movie once and had this alternate designed juuuuust for me."

While she races out into the distance, Jolem calls out. "So, do you bring a lot of people here??"

She looks off into the vast sky, and her pace slows to a stop. "No. No, I don't," she says, moving back toward him. "You're actually – the first."

"The first?? Really? Why me?"

With her eyes closed and hair flowing softly, she inches closer until she's standing in front of him. "Honestly, Jolem – I'd be embarrassed to take anyone else here besides you."

"Embarrassed? Why?"

"Well…don't get me wrong; I absolutely adore my World," she remarks, biting her bottom lip. "But sometimes…sometimes I…I just enjoy the peace, the quiet. And something makes me feel you're the one person who knows exactly what I'm talking about."

For a tranquil moment, they catch each other's eyes, and then she spins off again. As she dances to cinematic background music, Jolem is completely at ease. Smiling, he watches her with his arms crossed. Unfortunately, the tender interaction is interrupted once again.

"Hello Leema, this is SEE with a Path Advisory Alert. Please terminate this alternate and exit your World for a mandatory security update."

"Oh wow," utters Leema. "That's a coincidence."

"What are you talking about??"

"Well – I just received another Path alert; a security update, and I need to exit my World."

"Really??" Scratching his head as Leema's simulation transforms into her World atrium, Jolem fights suspicious thoughts. "Do you really just have to go? Just like that?"

"Jolem," she says matter-of-factly. "Have you not listened to a word I said?? Trust the Path and follow its instruction. It will not let you down; I promise you. I have to go now. We'll talk later."

Reluctantly, Jolem gives in, and they're forced to exit her World. Now back in his room, he sits silently marooned on his sofa with his chin resting in his palms. Leema's impactful pitch replays in his mind and he continues to question the goals of his resistance to The Path. He doesn't want to end up like Mr. Perry, and he can't imagine joining the protest of the Freedom Fighters. His thoughts return to the evolving relationship with Leema and he envisions unlikely possibilities. Despite the fantasy, the idea feels good.

18

Two days have passed since Jolem's unexpected but interesting World experience with Leema and he's been on a roller coaster ride of emotions. As he wrestles with his feelings, one minute, he wants to block her from his World; the next, he wants to visit hers. This morning he awoke with unusual vigor. He hopped out of bed, ran through his World updates, and trotted downstairs. For the time being, his cynicism is put to rest.

With a huge grin, he swings around and plops in the seat next to Kirame at the table. He grabs an apple and flips it into the air. "Morning, Ma," he says, planting a soft kiss on her cheek as the airborne fruit falls back down into his hand.

"Jolem – what's gotten into you?" his mom asks, squinting suspiciously.

"What do you mean?"

"You know what she means," interrupts Liz. "You're acting super weird lately."

"Weird? What is it with this word with everybody??"

"Yes, 'weird,'" confirms Kirame. "But in a good way. You're floating on air, and your SIV has lifted. Maybe The Path isn't so bad, huh??"

Jolem turns off to the side and smirks devilishly. His expression mimics a house cat with a long yellow feather hanging out its mouth.

"It's a GIRL, isn't it?" calls out Kirame. "That's what it is."

"What? Jolem's in looooove?" pokes Liz.

Jolem cuts back at Liz and sneers. "C'mon, you guys, there's no 'girl.'

Seriously. We're co-workers; that's all."

"Yeah yeah, sure," laughs Liz while augmenting exploding hearts and kissy lips around his head. Tickled, she takes full advantage of the opportunity to rib her brother.

"What??" Jolem cracks, swiping at the floating love symbols that quickly dissolve at his swing. A frown grows, and he glares over at Liz. "Okay, you want to play, huh??" Suddenly her eyes pop open, and she leaps out of her seat. "Aaaaahhhh!!" she screams and then darts out of the room as if it were on fire.

"Jolem! What the…" cries his mom. "What did you do??"

"That's what she gets for being funny. She just met my mutant spider," he chuckles. The menacing four eyes of his own augmented insect sent Liz running.

"Jolemm!" scolds Kirame, shaking her head. "You might traumatize that poor girl. LIZ honey…"

"What? What??" he says, shrugging smugly. He knows he's gone overboard with his retaliatory use of AR. "Don't worry, mom, she's used to creatures," he laughs. "Okay, well, I'm gone." With movements propelled by an unusual glide to his stride, he slips out to his awaiting Zumer.

"Li'l J, how do we look on time?"

"Looking great. Should arrive approximately 10:06 am."

"Stellar. You know…take a detour. I want a chocolate pastry from La Dulce."

"Wow, you're in a festive mood this morning?? What's the occasion?"

"C'mon Li'l J. Every now and then, you just have to treat yourself. Plus, I was thinking about sharing one with a friend."

"Ahh, I see. Jolem, Jolem, Jolem," slowly chastises Li'l J. "I again reiterate it's not wise to go down this road with Ms. Dalio. Your probability is extremely low."

"Yeah, yeah, Li'l J. I know. Believe me; we're just 'friends. Nothing more."

"Okay then, as you say. However, you do realize that I know you as well as you know yourself; maybe even more."

"Whatever."

"Okay, well, I must remind you that the DTH tax on those pastries is very high."

"Of course. All good."

"As you wish."

Jolem's Zumer changes directions and sets for La Dulce bakery, which is about five blocks off-course. As he sits back in comfort, he peruses the bakery's virtual menu that launches in his face. Sweet delights dance in his mind while his morning music sings him a relaxed ballad. It's a perfect morning, and the thought of the delicious treat has him captivated.

They pull up to the modern, white brick building and his order is already packaged and waiting at the side door. "Buenos dias, Mr. McKay," greets the Spanish-accented friendly work bot. She grins and then extends her arms out toward him. A small red ribbon, wrapped box sits in the middle of her open flat palms. "Your chocolate pastry is hot and flaky, just the way you like it. I've even added a couple of those caramel-coated air balls that you've enjoyed, just to show how much we appreciate you."

Jolem lifts the box out of her hands and gently pulls it forward. "Mmm, this smells amazing," he moans. His head slips back, and his eyelids fold over. "Li'l J, I don't care what anyone says; nothin's like the real thing."

"Ha ha ha," cackles the overly amused work bot. "I hope you have an excellent day in The Path!" she salutes, waving as they drive off. Within minutes of their first arrival at La Dulce, they're back on their way to the office. Jolem peeks over his right shoulder out of the window. Suspended in air, hovering above the bakery is a flashing personal sign of gratitude. "Thanks, Jolem! You're the BEST!" it reads.

Laid back with his morning treat on his lap, Jolem is on cloud nine. The pastries' savory vapors spread throughout his compact space filling the air with sweet expectations. Sealed in a heat-protected preservation container, his toasty meal could remain freshly baked for hours.

"Well, Jolem, are you happy now?" asks Li'l J.

"More than happy, my friend. I'm STELLAR!" proclaims Jolem as he takes another enchanted whiff.

"Good. And your bonus was just enough to cover it. I hope Ms. Dalio appreciates the sentiment. Jolem – please be careful with this course of action. You know her father – the director, would never approve."

"Approve of what?? We're only friends."

"Okay, Jolem. Friends or not, she's a high SIV, and you are not. If you're interested in companionship, PerfectMatch will find you a compatible partner," Li'l J suggests, but Jolem just stares out the window. During the remainder of the ride, he doesn't speak another word.

About forty-five minutes later, in the Icon office building, Leema swipes casually at her digital dashboard. Catching her by surprise, a white cartoon rabbit peeks his head into the room. When she curiously glances over, the bunny quickly pulls back out of sight like a child playing peek-a-boo. "Hmmm," hums Leema. She leans forward to the edge of the seat and crosses her arms. "Hi, cute little fella. I wonder who you belong to."

Hesitantly, the little animated animal walks into the room with his hands remaining tucked behind his back. "Okay, I'm game. Are you hiding something?" Leema asks.

He hops in front of her and then pulls out a sign with his right hand. "I HAVE SOMETHING FOR YOU. MEET ME??" it reads.

Leema smirks, slowly reclines back into her seat, and then begins to tap against her desktop. "Meet whom?"

The little bunny tosses the sign in the air, and as it disintegrates, he pulls out another. "JOLEM"

"Jolem??" she sniggles. "Weeelll, I'm actually pretty busy right now. I should probably focus on my work."

The rabbit's nose twitches and lips twist as he ponders. A second later, he throws the note away and pulls out another. "PLLEEAZZ!!!"

"Okay, okay. Since you're practically begging, but only for a minute," she agrees while the rabbit leaps up and down with joy. "When and where?" she asks.

"9th FLOOR STATION 20, 5 MINS," inscribes the last sign and

Leema confirms with an amused head shake. The excited rabbit throws a thumbs up, then shuffles out of the room as colorful fireworks follow in his footsteps.

Throughout the floors of this tall, circular building flows a continuous pattern of glass-walled rooms, interrupted by open nooks called "floor stations," slightly offset from the halls. These dim, secluded areas contain cushy, squared seats, like solid beanbags, that provide perfect sanctuaries for small group conversations or independent thought retreats. When Leema turns into floor station 20, Jolem is comfortably stretched out in the corner with his leg propped up on the seat. When his eyes set on her, he can't contain his smile.

"Hey, Jolem. So, you used the cute bunny trick, huh? You know, using your World like that at work is a violation," she playfully scolds.

"C'mon, do you ever break the rules? Plus, I knew you couldn't resist haha. Here, have a seat," he says while swinging his leg to the ground to make room for her by his side.

"Well – no, I don't," she winks. "Okay, Jolem - but only for a sec, ok?"

"Okay, that's fine. I got something for you."

"Really??"

"Really, really."

Apprehensively, she slides down next to him, peering. When she's seated, he pulls the breakfast box from his side and places it on her lap. "It's nothing, really. I stopped for a treat this morn."

From the moment the sealed package lands in front of her, the instant enchanting smell of sweet chocolate rises up through her nostrils.

"Jolem! I can't accept this," she quickly replies, pushing it back. "I'm sure whatever is in this box was pretty expensive for you. You eat it!"

"C'mon Leema. It was nothing. There was a sale, so it's not a big deal. I got one for myself and thought you might enjoy one too. I wanted to apologize for the other day."

"Well…that was sweet…I guess. Thanks."

Jolem unlatches the encasement and the full magnificence of the pastries spreads through the space. "Jolem, you didn't have to do this –

but I'M GLAD YOU DID!" she laughs. Like being unable to contain themselves, both Leema and Jolem dig into the box and take captivating bites until there's nothing left but crumbs.

Leema giggles while dabbing her lips with a napkin and then glances over to Jolem. "Okay, Jolem, I must admit – that was great! How can I repay you?"

"Nahh, it was nothing. Really. Well...actually, you can do me a Li'l' favor."

"A favor? Like what?"

"Disable your AllVu."

"Huhh??"

"Disable your AllVu. Just for a second. I've never actually seen your real eyes."

"Well...okay...I guess. For a sec."

After a short pause, Leema's face drifts to the ground. "Hide AllVu," she softly utters and her digital visor evaporates. As she turns back to him, she gently swipes back the long strands of hair that again had fallen over her forehead. Her chin lifts and then her eyelids fold open like a flower pedal.

"Wooow," he whispers when he witnesses the rare beauty of her greenish-grey pupils.

"Jolem – please...that's not funny," she says, shuffling to restore her AllVu. "Sho..," she begins, but before she can complete her command, he blocks.

"No, I'm serious," he says, quickly reaching out to her. "Your eyes... they're beautiful."

Jolem and Leema remain motionless, glaring into each other's eyes as they share a celestial second. It's a charming Solace for Jolem, who has found a place of peace, a loving friendship, and a renewed sense of hope. In this seemingly endless instant, he is happy. But once again, the bliss doesn't last long.

"Hi Leema, this is SEE with a Path Advisory Alert," alarms her. "You have an important peer review session this morning. It's wise to return to your office and resume your preparation."

"Hmm, well, I have to go," she immediately says, putting a frigid stop to their lighthearted conversation.

"What the?? Again?? Do you really have to go – this second??"

Leema laughs as she stands up and reactivates her AllVu. She's confident he's joking. "Jolem, didn't we just have this conversation? I don't have a choice," she giggles. "SEE said I should go, so I'm off."

Jolem pops up and softly grips her wrist. "Leema – of course, you have a choice," he pleads. "We always have a choice."

Leema's lips curl into knots as she considers his comments like trying to solve a game show riddle. "You're not joking, are you? You're serious." The idea of not following The Path's council is unheard of.

"I mean really – what was the alert?" he asks.

"It said I should return to my office and get back to my report. My timeline suggested I was well prepared, but I guess I underestimated."

"So why not just trust your own instincts? A few more minutes won't hurt, right?"

As Leema slides back down into her seat, the bizarre idea takes her for a loop. "Well...I suppose...not. Buttt..." she rambles.

"But nothing. 5 more minutes. It's settled," exclaims Jolem as he moves back.

"Uhhh – okay."

"Leema, I recommend you follow SEE's instruction," comments her assistant Mariela.

"Uhggh – right now I'm completely confused, but I guess – a little bit longer won't make a difference, right?" she stutters.

"Once again, I recommend against this decision Leema," Mariela continues. "Please return to your office."

Leema turns hesitantly toward Jolem, puzzled. "I...I think I should go," she says.

Looking into her concerned eyes, Jolem questions if he should let her go or push for her to stay. His overwhelming desire for her companionship wins. While his fingers nervously fidget, his eyes insecurely spring around to avoid contact. "Leema, I'm not sure what's going on, but I...I really enjoy your company," he says softly. "Most of the time, I feel uncomfortable or out of place and I have no idea why it's different with you – but it is. I know this is a very unlikely friendship and we're from different worlds, but please – just a few more minutes."

Leema also feels an inexplicable affinity for him. For the first time in memory, she follows her emotions instead of her instruction. "Uhhhh... okay," she tepidly whispers.

Awkward moments of silence pass until Jolem breaks the ice with a timely but corny joke. She smirks and then softly giggles while he blows an upside-down bouncy smiley face her way. Her smile grows, she covers her eyes, and then she laughs some more. For the next several minutes, Jolem and Leema chitchat, continuing to play. It's an unlikely harmony, but the stark contrasts in their personalities and backgrounds are equally fascinating.

It's a refreshing exchange. However, Leema is stunted by a unique sensory zap. "Huh," she utters to the foreign sensation. "Hi Leema, this is SEE with an urgent message. Apparently, you have veered off-track therefore, you are required to contact the FDEC within 24 hours for a Track Realignment. Thank you."

Leema's eyes budge as if she has just seen a ghost, and then she pops up out of her seat.

"Leema?? Is everything okay??" Jolem quickly responds.

"Well...I don't know. I just...I just received a summons for a – Track Realignment."

"REALLY?? WHAT?? But - why??"

Terrified, Leema slowly gulps. "I – I don't know. I knew I should've gone," she whispers anxiously, peeking back and forth. With guilty thoughts running rampant in her head, the delusions of passers' judging eyes heckle her like she's the town outcast.

"Leema, it'll be okay – trust me," assuages Jolem. "It's probably noth –," but before he can finish his comment, he receives his own chilling sensory zap. "What tha'...??"

"Hi Jolem, this is SEE with an urgent message. Apparently, you have veered off-track therefore, you are required to contact the FDEC within 24 hours for a Track Realignment. Thank you."

Jolem stands momentarily paralyzed with a sudden realization. As he quietly contemplates, it's clear the dual alerts are no coincidence.

"Jolem?? What?" cries Leema as her head jerks in his direction. His distracted expression has her concerned.

"Oh – nothing. Nothing," he says, attempting to mask his anxiety. "Li'l J – just said something – that's all."

"Okay – uh well, I'm – going to run," she stutters. "I need to get back to work."

As Leema steps off, Jolem reaches out but says nothing. The confusion surrounding all the unexpected events has him out of sorts and his tongue tied like a pretzel. Now the questionable series of interrupted communications replay in his mind. And as those random pieces form together so seamlessly, he can't believe he missed their connections before.

DISAPPEARING

WONDERLAND

19

A little more than twenty-four hours have passed since Jolem received his Path Realignment summons. Nervously, he again sits in his local FDEC office waiting room. As his fingertips rapidly tap against his thigh, he's clueless as to what comes next. In fear of how Leema would respond, he kept his summons a secret but scheduled his Realignment at the same time as hers. She was already freaked out, so he didn't want to alarm her anymore. Realignments are typically rare, with mid to upper SIVs who usually stay in compliance. Most who have received them keep these taboo experiences locked away tight. His right knee shakes uncontrollably, and his imagination wanders.

"Good morning Mr. McKay," remarks Mrs. Bolder as she slides up to his side. They haven't spoken since his Path Advisement, but their earlier interaction was unforgettable for them both. "I can't say it is a surprise to see you again," she comments with a cracked, patronizing smirk. "Hopefully, this will be short, and we'll have you on your way in no time at all. Please follow me."

As before, Jolem glides behind Mrs. Bolder down the glowing halls en route to her office. The journey is very similar, only this time, the experience has a shrilling foreboding like the appearance of dark clouds before a tornado. Being reprimanded for unwise deeds is not new for him, but not being sure of his wrongdoings has him on edge. He's bewildered.

Soon, they are seated in Mrs. Bolder's office. There is an awkward silence as the tense moments pass. He's been waiting for minutes, and she has barely said a word. While engulfed in her digital dashboard, it's almost as if she doesn't notice him there at all. "Uhh, excuse me," he says after a short period of looking around. His feet continue to tap nervously. Mrs. Bolder turns her sights away from her display, tilts her head, and peers toward Jolem. "Yesss?"

"Well – I was just wondering when we'd get started."

With a whispered sigh, Mrs. Bolder looks him in the eyes "Hmmm," she slowly hums. "Don't worry, Mr. McKay…we will begin…shortly."

For an extended moment, she continues staring straight ahead as the connecting corners of her lips lift robotically into a photographic smile. "And for today's visit – we have company," she grins.

"Huh??"

The faint swoosh of the sliding door sounds like a canon and a dark silhouette, steps forward out of the bright light. As he encroaches, the click of his shoe heels pressing against the marbled floors echoes throughout the room. The light reflects off the folds of his shiny dark grey uniform as he moves. Jolem etches up to the edge of his seat and locks eyes with the approaching stranger. The fine hairs of his arms rise. At this surprising moment, he realizes he's in a much deeper mess than he had imagined.

"Hello, Mr. McKay," the man's croaked baritone begins. "My name is Director Dalio – is it okay if I call you Jolem?"

"Director Dalio??" Jolem questions softly before his jarred eyes shift to Mrs. Bolder and then back to Dir. Dalio. "Ahh – sssure..."

"Okay…Jolem," he continues and then nods to Mrs. Bolder. "Mrs. Bolder – good day," he politely remarks before refocusing his attention back to Jolem. His foreboding smirk and slow hissing breaths between words put Jolem on guard. For Jolem, the room seems to squeeze distressingly tight, as if it's compressing by the second.

"I do apologize for my unannounced visit today, but under the circumstances, I felt it appropriate we meet – in person."

"Okay."

While listening intently, Jolem sits upright in his seat, awaiting the director's next move. Anxiously, his fingers grip the edge of his seat.

"So where do we start?" the director rhetorically asks. His animated facial and hand gestures speak more volumes than his words. "Jolem, you have an interesting background, Son... and a potentially prosperous future. I understand you are progressing nicely in your first gig at GreenView Industries. Is this correct?"

"Yes."

"Good...good. A very fine company. I'm also aware there was some early hesitation towards The Path. Is this correct?"

"Well...yes."

"Hmmm..." deeply murmurs the director while he firmly rubs the fine prickles of his chin. He pauses to take a sputtered throat-clearing cough. "Now, I'll be honest. While the entire country revels in the prosperity The Path has created, there have always been those who have instinctively resisted this good fortune. Fortunately, over a short period of time, most of these people have overcome this inclination and have begun to enjoy life like the rest of us. But – there are few – and let me emphasize FEW, who never come around. They are the ones who struggle and FIGHT like a stubborn virus battling an antibiotic. These are the ones who find themselves in a world of trouble. I'm hoping you are a member of the first group and not of the latter."

Dir. Dalio slips his hands into his pockets and then rocks back on his heels. His head tilts towards the ceiling and his eyes slide shut. Slowly, he sucks in an extended breath and then leisurely blows it back into the air. "So, I ask you, why would I engage in a matter typically handled by one of our numerous, more than capable associates? Why would I personally get involved – in your case?"

Jolem puffs out his cheeks as he peaks around. "Uhhh...Leema?"

"EXACTLY!" Dir. Dalio dramatically replies, clamping his hands as if he'd just heard the winning word.

"But – I don't understand," says Jolem. "Leema and I barely know each other."

Stiffening his back, the director erects solid like an oak tree and takes a long pause before speaking. "Okay, Jolem, let me skip right to the chase. Your personal relationship with my daughter, however small it may be, has forced you off track with The Path. You've received several Advisory Alerts, but they've gone ignored; therefore, you have been summoned in order to receive a Track Realignment. My first question to you is; is your AllVu functioning properly?

"Well…yes."

"We thought so because you've been interacting with your World just fine. Our records indicate no problems at all with your communications and/or Advisory Alerts. So, the only conclusion we can deduce is that you are intentionally ignoring them. Which IS a problem."

Director Dalio inhales deeply and then exhales with a gruff hum. "Okay, so do you remember when you originally pledged allegiance to The Path during your Initial Decisions?'

"Yes."

"Good. Well, you agreed that 'I understand my total compliance with the rules of The Path is necessary in order to be successful.' Do you also recall that?"

"Yes, I do."

Dir. Dalio slips his hands back into his loose pant pockets and creeps towards Jolem. "Jolem, what I'm about to say to you is for your own good. The relationship between yourself and my daughter must end now. The Path apparently sees it as a potential problem."

"With all due respect Dir. Dalio, none of this makes any sense to me," snaps Jolem. "I don't understand what our little conversations have to do with The Path. We enjoy each other's company and that's it. How can that be so wrong?"

"Hmmm…" murmurs Dir. Dalio. He finds Jolem's resolve intriguing, while also threatening. "Jolem – son, I have nothing against you personally. You seem to be a fine young man. But as you know, The Path was designed to see what we cannot see and understand that which we could never understand. The Path's decisions are for the greater good of all. We are a connected chain of unity and prosperity. It is not our job to question

The Path's logic. It is only our responsibility to follow it."

After his words, the director moves confidently across the room as if he was a lawyer who had just delivered his final arguments. Typically, just a mere encounter such as this would've been enough to persuade compliance, but Jolem is not typical. He grits his teeth and spies Dir. Dalio. "Shouldn't we have something to say about this?" he unexpectedly challenges.

With his back towards Jolem, the director abruptly stops as a sudden fit of irritation cripples his movements. Accustomed to being in complete control, he sputters even to respond. As he breathes deeply, he stands still until he reclaims his composure and then turns around. Stepping slowly and steadily, he moves into the intimate space directly to Jolem's side and sits on the corner of the desk. "Jolem, let me put it to you this way," he begins as his head moves even closer, so close that Jolem's face recoils from the warmth of his breath. "You may be comfortable with stepping out of line and putting everything and everyone you know at risk, but Leema is not. Trust me; this is over."

With those ominous words, Director Dalio lifts up off the desk, straightens his jacket and moves towards the exit. Like when he entered, his rhythmic stomp echoes while he slowly steps across the quiet room. In passing, he takes one last glance at Jolem. "Let this be a warning to you," he offers sternly, piercing ahead. "You will be wise to follow your Track and not give us any more problems. Have a pleasant day, and long live The Path. It's a good life."

20

Jolem anxiously leaps out of the building into the early light of day, stops and then looks around. The charms of the beautiful world he had begun to see have suddenly disappeared. He had started to believe he could exist within the rules of the controlled wonderland, but after the contentious exchange, he awakened from his dream. It was a fantastic illusion full of hopes and opportunity that had now evaporated as his eyes once again opened to his subdued cynical reality. And as his broken heart begins to race, he fears Dir. Dalio's words are indeed true. Inside he knows that the budding relationship is finished, and the fond feelings he had developed are about to be chilled.

"Li'l J – call Leema," he hesitantly calls out, but her World is dark. As his head tilts up to the endless sky, he grips the back of his neck in disbelief. Her passionate words of optimism now have no meaning. What a difference a day makes.

Not too far away in an uptown Manhattan FDEC building, excruciating seconds tick by as Leema sits terrified, awaiting the first comments from her advisor Mrs. Carr. They've been seated for almost five minutes without more than a few words of salutation between them. Leema knows no one who has ever had a Track Realignment and her confusion is only rivaled by her fear. The entire bewildering experience is like a surreal nightmare. Her allegiance to The Path and the accepted way of order has been her guiding principle. Just a day ago, even being in this fateful position would've been unimaginable.

While leaning loosely over her digital dashboard, Mrs. Carr slowly rocks from side to side. Then after a few moments of dead silence, she slips her rolling chair tightly under her desk and lays her hands flat on its surface.

"Ms. Dalio, is everything ok?" she asks tenderly. "You seem very uneasy."

"Well – I just don't understand. Am I in trouble?"

Mrs. Carr reaches towards Leema's hand, which is resting on the edge of the desk. "Relax, sweetheart. All will be just fine, and you should be out of here in a few minutes," she comforts and then returns to review the dashboard.

Leema's thoughts are rampant as she nervously gnaws at her bottom lip. She's heard the horror stories of deviants' punishments and knows the social stigmas. Merely seen leaving the building could have lasting consequences for her World of family, friends, and acquaintances. The suspense of the moment has her flustered.

Without additional delay, Mrs. Carr again lays her palms on her desk and finally directs her attention completely to Leema. The eerie mechanical happiness in her smile mimics that of a child's doll propped up in a seat. As they look into each other's eyes, there's an odd silence, which causes Leema's arms to tremble. In the hollow room, she can hear the sound of her swallow as it wrenches down her dry throat.

"Sooo Ms. Dalio...shall we begin??" asks Mrs. Carr.

"Ye – yes..."

"This is sort of a unique situation, considering who you are and your legacy."

"Did I do something wrong??"

"Oh no, no, no. Please relax, my dear. Of course, you know you are – shall we say 'special' and due to this, the Path views you through a slightly different lens – for your protection, of course."

"I – I don't understand."

"Believe me; you don't need to worry at all. I'm going to give you some simple advice. Follow my instruction, and this will all go away as if it never happened."

"Well…okay."

With a sudden breath of relief, Leema's tense limbs loosen as she drops back in her seat. She's feeling about as unnerved as she's ever been in her life. Anything she can do to quickly bypass this dreadful experience is all she cares about. Now sparking a huge smile of anticipation, she pops up intently, awaiting direction. Mrs. Carr's hands move together and then slow to a stop as her head props atop her pointed fingers.

"Okay, Ms. Dalio I understand you have developed a friendly bond with a co-worker named Jolem McKay. Is this correct?"

"Jolem?? Well…yes."

"Okay, this relationship has triggered concerns in The Path and, unfortunately, must come to an immediate and complete end."

Jarred back, Leema's expression drops. "But…I don't understand."

"Ms. Dalio, I know this has come to you as a surprise. Sometimes The Path asks us to take directions that are counter to our instincts. During these times, we may be conflicted with the decisions we must make… and that is natural. We are merely human," she chortles. "However, we can't allow our emotions to take the place of our wisdom. The Path does not make mistakes, as you well know. So as difficult as it might be, we MUST follow its guidance precisely. It is not only the law, but it is our moral obligation. Now, do you understand the direction you have been given this morning?"

After a slow sigh, Leema affirms her posture. Her response is not only swift, but it's also without struggle. Looking straight ahead to Mrs. Carr, she promptly replies. "Yes, I understand."

"And will you have any problems with compliance?"

"No, I will not."

6 YEARS LATER

21

The soothing digital hum of Jolem's wake-up music begins and his faithful companion welcomes him to the new day. "Good morning Jolem," fondly greets the former Li'l J, now simply referred to as "J." Jolem's toned arms lift out of his silky silver sheets and stretch high into the air. "Uhh mornin' J," oozes out of his mouth as the corners of his lips slowly curve upward. "Today's the big day, huh?" he says, peering out of the glass wall of his 10th-floor NJ apartment. In the distance, the hazy New York City skyline resembles a large mural.

"Yes, it is. Today is Liz's graduation ceremony. How exciting!"

"Wow, class of 2063. Mine seems like it was eons ago. I can hardly remember those days. My baby sis is all grown up now."

"Well, you were a very different person back then, Jolem. I'm so proud of how far you've progressed."

Jolem's bed responsively props him up as he leans forward. He reminisced of a painful period years ago that felt like a dream. While tilting his head back, he runs his fingers through his short dark hair. His long curls are a memory like many of the immature and rebellious instincts of his youth. A vague image of Leema passes through his thoughts and then disappears. "Hmm…I wonder what ever happened with Leema," he says as his hand continues across his cleanly shaved face.

"Well, after her transfer to Atlanta a week following the incident, most of her Track has been blocked. You hid all of your experiences –,"

"I know, I know J, I really wasn't expecting an answer. No need to bring all that up again. Fast forward, please. Anyhow – what's going on today?"

"I'm sorry, Jolem. I understand completely. Well – it's another pretty light day at the office. Besides the team meeting, you can cruise through your workday. We are moving into the final month of your gig. Your next gig is awaiting your acceptance, but you must complete your AllVu training course to be eligible. It'll only take about an hour to download and learn the required skill. Liz's graduation ceremony begins at 6:30 pm and Pati is more than elated to accompany you at this exciting milestone."

Jolem twists off the side of his suspended platform bed and sighs. He's approaching the year mark in his relationship with his girlfriend Pati, and lately, she's been pushing to live together. They were paired through PerfectMatch's compatibility matrix, like most relationships. Their long-term connection probability scored extremely high. He's finally settled into a loving bond with a complimentary and like-minded soul. His mother and sister adore their relationship, but he's hesitant to move forward.

"Hmm…okay. Anything new in my World?"

"Well, Jolem. Of course, you know there continues to be great enthusiasm around the release of The Path Version 10. The buzz is all about the Director's upcoming announcement."

"Interesting," he utters dispassionately, twisting his lips.

"Hmm, Jolem – I sense there is more to your indifference. Are you still bothered by Dir. Dalio's rise to National Director of the FDEC?"

"J – I'm not 'bothered'…it's just; no matter how deep you hide experiences, some things you never truly forget."

"Well, Jolem – of course, I was asleep during your track realignment, so I'm not aware of the exchange between you and the director, but maybe someday you will finally see that he was only acting on behalf of the country and The Path. If you remove yourself and your feelings from the equation, you will realize his words and actions were for the good of all and not personal."

"Well…maybe."

"You can always replace the experience completely."

"J – ya' know how I feel about replacements. We learn from history. Replacing bad memories with good ones doesn't help."

"Yes, I am aware of your position. Just presenting options."

"Okay well Show AllVu."

Jolem hops out of his bed onto his warm cement floor and then extends down to touch his toes. His head and neck bend from side to side while his arm wraps around his back. Cued by his routine morning warm-ups, his bedroom reactively transforms into an energetic exercise facility. In an instant, dark concrete walls, flashing lights and thumping beats surround him.

"J Jessi O," he calls out, and a simulated version of the popular fitness trainer appears in front of him. With her muscular tattooed arms planted on her waist, she cracks her neck from side to side and then grunts. Jolem continues stretching, and other virtual exercisers appear around him. Grinning, he peeks over to his right at his cross-town rival and nods. The two competitors go at it almost every morning. The raspy-voiced instructor points into the small crowd. "Okay, softies, are we ready to go??" she yells. "Let's DO IT!"

In his vibrant alternate, Jolem's competitive workout begins. Back in the reality of his room, his HumanAid initiates her daily tasks. She arranges objects and furniture into proper position, tightly folds bedding into place and carefully lays out his work outfit. Within minutes, she's off to do other household chores. When Jolem later arrives at his kitchen table, his breakfast is arranged artfully on his plate. "Hmm, this looks and smells great," he declares with his utensils clinched upright in his fists.

"Jolem, you say that every day," his HumanAid quips. "And it's that time again," she sings.

"Oh, okay," he sighs. His eyes slide shut while his back stiffens straight.

"Now take a deep breath annnd…"

As his body relaxes, Jolem's HumanAid holds a clear cylinder contraption next to his AllVu temple orb and then a quick light flashes.

"Ahh okay. All done," she says with the sweetness of a pediatrician.

His twice-per-week government-prescribed sedative called Opeateazone is administered. For the past six years, it has helped subdue his impulses while he's become a settled member of society. During this period, he hasn't received any further deviations and his SIV has sharply risen to a high 6.

For a few moments, he stares straight ahead in a daze. His dark brown pupils dilate wide, turning black and then returning to normal. A second later, he's back to himself again. Nestled in his seat, he peers into the summer dawn sky out of his kitchen window wall. He takes a small bite, chews slowly and smirks. It's an enjoyable solitude enhanced by subtle jazzy sounds and echoed electric beats in the background. Just the start of another normal morning in The Path.

Within an hour, Jolem's flowing down the road on his way to the office. He's worked gigs throughout the city but prefers projects at GreenView over most. Settled snugly in his Zumer seat, he interacts with friendly experiences that scroll through his AllVu. He chuckles and swipes while occasionally sending cheers to those he likes. During Zumer rides in his youth, he'd get lost in the simple amusement of nature-watching. Nowadays, he spends his journeys immersed in the cocoon of his World. While narrowly focusing on his close digital community, he's become insulated and iSolated from the broader society.

"LiveView, call Pati," he instructs. Moments later, he's viewing his girlfriend head-on as she sits in front of her bathroom sink mirror. With her back perfectly erect, her make-up mask sprays a beautiful blend of colors and designs across the curves of her face.

"Good morning, Cielo. How are you?" she asks in a soothing monotone while staring straight ahead. Around her, a light lullaby of chimes sings a mystical song.

"Gooood morning. I see you haven't left for work yet."

"Nooo. Remember, my Expressions of Love campaign is ending in a couple of days. I have one session today and will join it remotely."

"Okay. When's your next gig start?"

"Welll – I don't have another lined up just yet, soooo I'll just sit in some education pods until the pool calls. Until then, there's always love to share."

"Okay."

"So, what's going on with your team today, Mr. Lead?"

"Really, not much. But, hey--- I received an unexpected gold star yesterday."

"Wow, look at you. Hmmm, maybe you can buy something special for someone special. Hint, hint," she jokes.

"Yeahhhh, right," he grins and then abruptly shifts back to the subject. "Seriously though, sometimes I think my 'TEAM' wouldn't notice if I just disappeared one day. I have no idea what I did to earn another reward. Honestly, sometimes everything seems too good to be true."

Pati smirks softly. "Well just enjoy the tranquility, sweetheart. There's always reason in The Path. You lead an effective team and that's all that matters. They are happy, right?

"Yeah."

"Management is happy, right?"

"Well, yes."

"Then you're doing a great job."

"I suppose."

"Gooood. Now has Liz's gift arrived?"

"Not yet. It will be delivered to my place in 2 hours and 13 minutes."

"Can I see it again?? Please?"

"Sure."

As Pati slips back, her make-up mask dissolves and her dark auburn hair flows to the side. A thin white, AllVu wristband encased in a clear, glowing bubble materializes in front of her. The popular silicone-like band glistens in the light as she moves it around softly with the edges of her finely manicured fingertips.

"It's gorgeous. Jolem. She's going to love it."

"Of course, she will. It was the number one item on her World wish list. Everyone rates them highly. It was a bit expensive, but she's excelled in her education and deserves the best."

"Jolem...,"

"Yeah?"

Pati calmly turns away from the gift until she's looking directly into his eyes. Her tight manikin-like caramel skin is embellished with fine dark eye lines and vibrant airbrush accents. "You're a great big brother and she loves you so much," she begins softly. "Tonight – it'll be okay if you show – some emotion."

"I don't understand. I always show emotion."

"Jolem, as long as I've known you, I've seen three expressions," she says and then starts to count leisurely with her fingers.

"1. It's a nice day.

2. It's a happy day.

3. It's a peaceful day.

Tonight, maybe you add one more...

4. It's a momentous day."

"Hmmm," he murmurs in thought. "Perhaps."

"Ahhh, your uniqueness is one of the qualities which draws us together," she pokes. "One day, I'll break through that wall. We ARE a beautiful pair, Jolie. All my friends rate our connection very highly. I cherish us."

"I do too," he says with a slightly forced smirk. "And I will let you continue to enjoy your morning."

"Okay, Jolem. Well, put a little more thought into what we discussed...sweetheart. It's a good life."

"I will. Yes, it is. Talk to you later."

"Okay love."

Pati's WorldView disappears and Jolem stares ahead with his hands resting on his thighs. For a period, he shows no reaction at all. A moment later, he's back in his World, swiping experiences, messages and personal advertisements. Although he attempts to ignore the hype, most excitement is surrounding the director's imminent announcement. Speculation about The Path's latest features and life accommodations has been the hottest topic for months. Everyone's talking about them. This has been the normal public frenzy preceding the previous nine major releases.

After the short trip enthralled in his World, Jolem arrives at GreenView Industries right on schedule. Like an assembly line, the Zumer door slides up, he slips out, it zips off, and the next car repeats the experience. Jolem smiles stiffly as he flows from the front of the building through the grand lobby. People robotically glide back and forth while visual salutations spring above their heads as they pass. Along with the others, he now willingly functions among the ranks of the GreenView "Happy Team."

When he enters his work pod, he stops and then looks around at his small team of young system technicians who are immersed in their Worlds. As they sit back in their recliners, they swipe at images only they can see until they're systematically alerted to his presence. "Good morning," he calls out. Like a synchronized dance routine, they look in his direction, smile, and wave. "Good morning Jolem," they echo and return to surfing their Worlds. Their movements are so mechanical that he sometimes feels he's surrounded by NonHumans.

"What's got everybody so wrapped up this morning?" he asks. They glare confusingly at each other; then, all turn to him. "The director's announcement," one says, and the other four nod in agreement. "There's new speculation."

Quietly, Jolem scratches his head as he watches their bewildered expressions. They're truly amazed he's not feeling the same enthusiasm.

"Well...long live The Path," he proclaims, to which they repeat and continue in their pursuit of information. It's a routine that will continue over the following days until the highly anticipated event arrives.

22

"Graduating class of 2063. I welcome you to a universe of opportunities. A vast and limitless ethos of personal exploration," shouts the spirited headmaster in front of a large virtual and in-person audience of graduates, cheering family and friends. On the high digital walls behind her, shining stars shoot from the floor to the ceiling like fireworks. "I'm sure this is a very exciting time as soon you'll all be selecting your Tracks in The Path. Adolescence is over and now you must rise up to assume your patriotic role as productive and responsible Path ambassadors. YOU are the present. YOU are the future. The baton of truth and happiness is being placed in your hands to run into tomorrow. And as you consider the directions you'll take, always remember…The Path is with you; The Path is for you; The Path IS YOU! LONG LIVE THE PATH!" she vigorously extols to a rousing ovation.

Looking down from the second level of the extravagant dome-shaped auditorium, Jolem graciously claps to the headmaster's dynamic oratory. Next to him, Pati and his mother's reactions are not so measured. As soon as the headmaster's final words are spoken, they and the rest of the audience leap to their feet in thunderous applause. Jolem peeps around; it seems he's the only one still seated. He pops up and energetically claps like everyone else. After years of adjusting to the ways of The Path, his natural instincts are still that of an outsider.

Throughout the hall, flutters of high ratings and excited emojis shoot in the air like confetti. "Whoo ooo yah," yells Pati, swinging her fist in the air. She glances over to Jolem, winks with a giant grin and then continues clapping. She's more than excited for Liz and to celebrate another graduating class into The Path. Recalling Pati's morning suggestion, Jolem attempts to match her enthusiasm. "Yeah!" he shouts, pumping his fist. "GO LIZ!" The Jubilant cheer goes on and on.

The crowd finally settles down and the ceremony moves forward. With her head held high, the headmaster looks out into the masses as she prepares to pay tribute to each graduate. She calls out the first name and the walls of the wide-open room display 3-D visuals of the student dramatically waving and blowing kisses appreciatively to the adoring audience. The spectacle is a testament to the times as each graduate is celebrated like a superstar.

When the festive event finally comes to an end, the jovial gathering of mid-SIV families and friends seems in no hurry to leave. Without a care, they rejoice with their neighbors. Parents no longer worry about upcoming life dilemmas for their teens approaching adulthood. Mothers and fathers trust their children in the welcoming arms of The Path as they would a sweet grandmother's. It's a safe and cozy bubble to exist, free of stress from watching their children's mistakes and growing pains.

While Jolem, Pati and his mom wait for Liz to arrive, they gush over precious AllVu experiences of her younger days. Kirame has to fight back the tears as she watches young Liz stagger up and down during her first little steps. In the midst of the celebration, the sight of an old friend approaching from the crowd brings joy to Jolem's face. "Rony, my man! Thanks for coming," he calls out to his buddy as they lock hands in a familiar embrace. Over the years, they've remained in communication through their Worlds, but it's been a long time since they've been in the same space.

Since entering The Path, Rony has developed a throng of devoted fans in his large whimsical World. They follow his every move like he's the star of a constantly running reality show. Flamboyant and cheerful, he doesn't opt for subtlety as his bright, colorful outfit and gender-ambiguous accessories are designed to attract. When amused followers within the hall recognize his live presence, they gawk and share his actions with their Worlds. He loves the attention and can't get enough of it. His popularity has elevated his SIV significantly and he's been showered with The Path's rewards.

"What? Are you kidding?" remarks Rony throwing his arms up wildly, "I wouldn't miss this for the universe. Ya' know Liz is like family, Bro, and I wanted to be here – live."

"Yeah, I know 'Mr. Ronitus,'" Jolem laughs. "That outfit is outrageous, Bro! Well, I'm glad to see you out of your World."

"Ya' know, I can't let my fans down. Forget all that, though. I might have 5 million followers, but I'm still just me 'Sola.'"

Blown back with nostalgia, Jolem cracks up. "Wowww 'Sola'! I haven't heard that in a long time. Takes me way back," he says, patting Rony on the shoulder.

"Yeah, man – those times seem like millennials ago! Sometimes I check out the old experiences and laugh my ass off. YOU were something."

"Yep yep. I just wish Teri was here," Jolem says, shaking his head somberly. "When's the last time you've heard from her?"

Rony's expression also drops. "Yeah, man. It's been a few years. After her SIV took that major hit and mine elevated, we drifted apart."

"Same here. I've tried several times, but her World is blocked off. I don't know, man."

Reminiscing like old men at a reunion, they share memories by throwing out recordings of scattered historical experiences from their Worlds. "Man, we had some fun back in the day, didn't we?" grins Jolem fondly, looking off into the air.

"Man, right??" Rony chuckles. "So – how excited are you?"

"About what??"

Rony's eyes jar open with amazement. "About what??! Jolem, the Director's Path announcement is just around the corner."

"Uh yeah. Haven't thought about it too much, actually."

Slapping his forehead condescendingly, Rony sighs. "Jolem, Jolem.

Some things change and some things stay the same," he cracks.

"I guess," shirks Jolem.

"Well, I'm STOKED. V 10, man! V 10!" cries Rony jerking Jolem by the arm. "I mean, it doesn't get bigger than this!"

The childhood friends are so absorbed in reminiscing they almost miss their approaching company.

"So, I finally meet the infamous 'Mr. Ronitus' in person," remarks Pati as she moves to Jolem's side and slides her arm around him. "I love your World. So entertaining and engaging," she says, beaming like a starstruck teen.

"Why thank you – Pati. Your SimMe does you NO justice," flirts Rony and then softly tips his head.

"Okay, okay, break up the love fest," comments Jolem. He extends his arms and playfully separates them. "Yes Pati, this is my ole friend 'Mr. Ronitus.'"

"Please Pati 'Ronitus' is just my fan name – Rony," he interrupts, moving close again.

"Well, were you two just talking about the announcement?" she asks.

"Yes, we were!" exclaims Rony. "I can hardly contain myself! I'm having a private announcement watch party at my place. Just a small group and ya know, THE REST OF MY WORLD! I know you'll be there, right??"

"Well…I don't –," begins Jolem, until Pati tugs his arm. "Of course! We'll be honored to be there, Rony," she confirms and then cuts her eyes at Jolem.

Rony sparks a smile that could light up a room. "Ya' know Pati – I think you two make an excellent couple."

"Don't we??" she enthuses. "Everyone thinks so. Our compatibility is at 89%. Isn't that amazing?"

"That's great. Finally, someone's able to tame the beast," Rony jokes. He slaps his hands together and rubs like a magician. When his palms open, a glistening "10" unfolds. "Here., I think your connection is excellent," he says and pushes it their way.

"Thank you, thank you," she snickers.

"Oh people, please…" breaks in Jolem, shaking his head.

Pati pulls him close and laughs. "Okay, okay," she says, plants a soft kiss on his cheek and turns back. "So Rony, when are you going to get matched up? Your World wants to know?"

"Me??" he questions and then stops to ponder. "Hmmm…I'm in love with my World! Hear that WORLD??" he yells to his remote audience.

As the chummy trio chat, Kirame squeezes into the conversation. With comedic timing, she adds a humorous tale from the boys' unruly past that has them all tickled. Her arms swing open, and she gives Rony a motherly embrace. Outside all the glitz, he's still the wise-cracking little boy who basically grew up in her kitchen.

Jolem glances off to the side and is suddenly overtaken with emotion. Out from the crowd, Liz emerges forward in a shining silver bodysuit and matching cap. In his eyes, she looks like an angel. Grinning proudly, he notices her tall, regal frame and recalls when she was just a scrawny kid. He's overjoyed by the mature young woman she's become.

"Congratulations squirt!" he says as he clasps her in his arms.

"Thanks, big bro!"

"Liz?? Is that you?" Rony questions, dramatically falling back as if having a heart attack. "Wow World. The brat has grown up!" he yells.

"Rony! You jerk," she sasses, swiping like she's trying to make him disappear. "Yes World," she laughs, sticking out her tongue, and then points to Rony. "Mr. Ronitus is a big jerk!"

The enjoyable reunion continues until the crowded hall thins. Finally prepared to move the celebration to another venue, Jolem turns to Rony. "So, you comin' out to dinner with us?" he asks. "Headin' over to a spot in the thrill district."

"I wish I could, man," sighs Rony.

"But I have a big forum tonight dedicated to V 10."

"What??" pouts Liz. "It's my graduation."

"Liz, you know I'd love to ride. I can't let my people down, ya know?"

Liz looks off to the side and once again motions him away. "I'm not even hearing it," she says, twisting her lips.

THE PATH

"Jo, you coming to my party, right?"

"For sure, man, we'll be there – live. I don't care how realistic alternates are; they're no substitute for the real thing."

"I hear you, bro," Rony says as they lock fists and repeat their choreographed grip.

"Pati, once again, it was a pleasure," Rony continues, offering heartfelt goodbyes.

"Liz, congrats again! And don't be mad. Go to your World. I sent some special rewards. You can use 'em for all sorts of things. You know I'm goin' to shout you out in the forum tonight, right? Mrs. Mac, great to see you again," he says, launching a huge pink heart her way.

Rony slides backward through the dissipating crowd and graciously tips his head to some adoring fans. On a whim, he swings his arms and spins around like a top catapulting finger-blown kisses into the air. It's an example of the outrageous antics they love him for. As he continues to entertain, they shower him with hearts and positive cheer.

The graduation ceremony is over and Jolem, Kirame, Pati, and Liz move across town to one of Liz's favorite fast-contemporary restaurants. The laid-back vibe is casual but chic, with slow hip-hop-inspired beats streaming behind the soft dining room chatter. Lying low in her curved cubby-like seat, Liz softly swipes at a virtual carousel of eye-popping appetizers. Individually crafted based on her personal tastes, each one looks just as attractive as the others. "Hmmm," she hums while reaching out to one of them. When she touches it, the savory sensation of its taste, warm, crispy crust, and aroma become real. "Mmmm, I definitely want these, Mom," she says, giddily like a child.

"Whatever you want, superstar. It's your day," happily remarks Kirame.

"Well, I want this, this, and these," she continues pulling them aside. "Okay, order."

"Great choices Liz," comments the restaurant's congenial holographic host. His voice rings only through the ears of those at the table. "For your main course, we've prepared some great options we know you'll love. All vegetarian, of course, and no onions."

"EXCITING!" cheers Liz.

"So, Liz, when is your Advisement," inquires Pati and Liz's face illuminates.

"My Path Advisement is Tuesday morning, Pati. I can't wait!" she says as shiny stars explode above her head. Liz, Kirame and Pati swoon with joy, but an unexpected chill suddenly shoots down Jolem's spine. "Whoooow," he utters as his muscles jerk. He's temporarily confused, and as he looks around, he can't recognize his surroundings. "What's goin' on?" he questions.

Concerned, Pati turns to Jolem and grips his wrist. "Huh, Jolem, you okay?"

"Yeah, yeah," he rapidly responds. His momentary fog has passed. "Uhh, what'd I just miss?"

"Well, weren't you listening? Liz's Advertisement is Tuesday!"

Jolem props his chin into his palm and leans back. "You just graduated. Aren't you moving kinda' fast?" he asks, leeringly. "You know you have three weeks after graduation."

"Yeah, but I can't wait to choose my Track and enter The Path. And I'll be in the first class in V 10. With the announcement coming soon, it's like everything is aligning PERFECTLY!"

After six years of unquestioned compliance, something about Liz's passion for The Path ignites dormant emotions in Jolem like a bear just awakening from winter hibernation.

"'Perfectly'?? Don't you think you're exaggerating things a little?" he asks sharply.

"Huh? Jolem, what are you talking about," Liz lashes out.

"I'm just saying maybe you shouldn't be in such a rush."

As a child, Liz was accustomed to Jolem's rants and odd aversion to The Path. She was the ears for which he'd share the inspiring stories passed down from their father. For the past six years, his old rebellious voice has been subdued. So, when it unexpectedly resurfaces, she's shocked and annoyed. Their eyes collide during a brief standoff, and it becomes clear she's no longer a child.

"Jolem please...what's gotten into you?" jabs their mom. "This is Liz's celebration. She's worked so hard for this and her path awaits."

"Okay, mom. Not another word from me," Jolem relents, throwing his hands in the air.

Pati flinches as she quietly observes the sibling spat. Although she's fully aware of Jolem's wayward past, she's never seen this side of him before. She slips her hand on his thigh and lightly squeezes. "So, Liz, what Track are you hoping for?" she asks, which prompts a complete change of reaction from Liz. As she jumps up to the edge of her seat, her expression pops. "I want to work for the FDEC!" she proudly proclaims. "Simulations, Advisement, Enforcement – it doesn't matter. I want to give back to The Path. It's done so much for us."

As Liz gushes over The Path, Jolem's teeth grit at her every word. The young admirer that used to look at him like he was a king now dismisses him like he's a jester. Jolem follows the slow-motioned excitement of her, Kirame, and Pati. His thoughts begin to drift. Starting to lose focus, his eyes move past them and then throughout the room. He takes note of the happiness of others, enjoying fine food and company. Their mechanical grins all strangely mimic each other. His sights continue to wander and then suddenly, something odd captures his attention. A small gathering at a distant table appears to be looking back at him. "Huh?" he grunts. Slowly and cautiously, he spies around the room. The curious stares from table after table begin to all turn in his direction. "Do you – want…something?" he cries out. They point at him and whisper to one another, but no one responds.

"What do you want??" he yells, pushing up from the table, but just then, he's startled.

"Jolem?? Are you okay," Pati says, leering.

Jolem peeks at his arm and notices she has a solid grip on his wrist. "Huh??"

"You were…in another place. Is everything okay?"

Snapping back to reality, he realizes he's still seated and was only captivated by his imagination. He glances at his mother and sister. They're both stunned. He had a habit of zoning out when he was younger, but it's been a long time since they've witnessed an episode like this. Smiling, he tries to downplay his strange behavior. "Oh yeah, yeah. I'm fine. I'm fine," he says, shaking his head, embarrassed. "I think I'm just a li'l' overwhelmed with emotion. Ya know? What were we talking about?" Fortunately for him, his attempt to change the topic is aided by the timely arrival of the table's appetizers.

"Okay, let's get this party started," cheers Jolem as the flattering NonHuman server sets the plates in front of them. "But wait for it…," he continues holding out his hands. With a blast, a mini hologram of Liz's favorite musical artist bursts out of the table center, performing her latest hit. The applauding family is thrilled. It's a delightful meal, however, behind Jolem's excited exterior, Liz's unwelcome words linger, and painful hidden feelings return.

23

It was an unusually full day, but the night had finally come to an end. With Jolem's earlier outburst a distant memory, he and Pati kick back on his sofa, enjoying the tranquility of soft mind-stimulating music. The effects of the pheromonic sounds mimic an alcohol high. Pati snuggles into his side and brushes her hand down his thigh. "Ummm, this was a great day, wasn't it?" she asks, leaning in close to plant a kiss on his neck. "I love your family, Jolie. We are such a great group. Don't you think?"

Jolem grins and lays his head back. He feels good. As his eyes slide shut, his HumanAid sets a tray of healthy drinks and snacks on the coffee table in front of them. She stands straight, cups her hands together, and grins. "Enjoy your experience," she whispers and walks off. It's the perfect conclusion to the evening.

Pati peers into Jolem's relaxed face, sighs contentedly and then pats his leg. "Okay, I need to pee," she sings and hops up. "I'll be right back."

As Jolem watches her shuffle away, he grips a few carrots and then tosses them into his mouth. Nestling back into the sofa, he begins to casually swipe through the flowing activity of his World. Random acts of kindness, personal advertisements, and messages of goodwill pass. Inexplicably, his curiosity shifts to an iSolated door he hadn't visited in years. The hidden alternate is a hotbed for conspiracy chatter, dark news and shock experiences. For unknown reasons, tonight, he's drawn to it.

"Jolem?? What are you doing?" asks J. "I highly recommend against this room. Here, why don't you check out Rony's V-10 forum?"

Jolem's breaths progressively grow heavy as he reconsiders entering Pandora's box of activity, but he can't resist. "Yeah J...I know," he calmly utters, dismissing J's counsel. With a gentle hand gesture, he continues into the gloomy gateway. As soon as he enters, his forehead bends into knots when he's aroused by an unusual spectacle. "Stop," he commands, shooting out his fingers and lifting up from his seat. "View."

The rest of his World drifts off into the background and a vivid presentation burst out of the empty space in front of him. Multiple angular views of a major traffic accident from the vantage of eyewitness' Worlds launch around the main display. A woman racing toward the scene like an on-site reporter details the destruction.

"An unbelievable event just occurred near our nation's capital. This is something we haven't seen in many years. There was a car accident with fatalities."

"A CAR ACCIDENT?? With 'FATALITIES'?? Wow!" cries Jolem.

"I've never seen anything like this before," another woman gasps. "One car suddenly shot into another's lane. The grey car swirled to avoid being hit and ran right into another, knocking it off the road. It tumbled over several times and slammed into the rail."

As the terrified witness describes the disaster, the sequence replays over and over. The event results in the death of a family of four. Jolem clicks on different Worlds to get alternate perspectives, and they're all similarly horrifying. The durable car material and standard safety interior typically provide a cocoon of security, but these features were not enough to protect the couple and their two small children inside. Flowing at velocities of over 100 mph, any fender bender can be extremely dangerous. Fortunately, the passenger of the swerving vehicle walks away without a scratch. Most are relieved by his twist of fate, but to some, strange facts spark concern.

"The first car didn't have to hit the other. It should've run itself off the road and spared that family. Why didn't the Laws of Autonomy prevent this!?" the woman frantically cries.

Amazed, Jolem sits at the edge of his seat, firmly gripping the sofa cushion. Her question strikes a nerve. "Wait – J, she's right," he comments.

"Right about what?"

"According to the Utilitarian Laws of Autonomy, The Path should have protected the lives of the family over the life of the one man. 'Sacrifice for the greater good, remember?? But – his car clearly acted in his best interest!"

"Jolem, you know the Utilitarian laws of Autonomy are infallible and equal for all. I assure you there is a logical explanation. Please relax. I told you this was a bad idea."

"Hmmmm…it just doesn't make sense."

Looking out into the ceiling, Jolem wonders. "When was the last time there was a fatal crash in the U.S?" he asks.

"The last fatality occurred almost ten years ago, not too far from this one, in a suburban Washington D.C. town named Lower Marlboro, Maryland. Junior Senator Waslo was killed in this incident. There were no other cars involved. It was deemed the result of a Zumer system malfunction of the Elon S5."

"Hmmm…"

"Jolem –," says J tepidly. "I'm beginning to sense some familiar and disturbing feelings from you. These past six years have been a delight in The Path. You've remained on your Track and have been rewarded greatly for it. Look around you. Life is good. Please, don't jeopardize this progress."

"I know, J. I know. Some things are just not sitting well with me today, and I don't know why."

"You're just a little irritable right now. Maybe you're just having a little reaction to Liz growing up. It's absolutely normal. I'm sure Pati can help cheer you up."

"I don't know," he sighs.

"Maybe we need to up your Opeateazone dosage?"

"No."

"Jolem, is something wrong with your Opeateazone?"

"No, but – no."

"Jolem, please. Stay focused on the positive. Life is good."

When Pati returns to the room, she's startled when she notices Jolem slumped over with his face stuffed in his palms. She quickly slides down next to him and swings her arm around his back. "Hey baby, is everything okay?"

After a deep sigh, Jolem turns slowly in her direction, pauses, and then shrugs. "I dunno," he says and then continues sulking.

"But I don't understand. You were so happy when I left; what happened??"

Jolem awkwardly grimaces while he struggles with his own thoughts. He wants to change the subject however, he's unable to keep it inside.

"So – there was a car accident," he stutters. "– and a family of four died."

Pati's eyes and mouth spring open. "Wha – what?? An actual car crash? Died? That's terrible!"

"Yeah."

"You know you have to shield yourself from news like this. It can bring anyone down."

"Yeah, I know. I know…but there's something else. Something that's got me bent out of shape."

"What's that??"

"Well – a passenger in one car survived and it seemed his car ran the other one off the road in order to protect him."

"'To protect him?' But Jolem, you know the Laws of Autonomy wouldn't have allowed that. Everyone is treated equally in The Path. That's simply not possible."

"And that's what's eating me. I know what I saw. You should see it yourself."

"Oh, no, no, no!" she shoots back, shaking her head and hands.

Pati tilts his face toward hers until he's looking into her eyes. "Jolem," she begins softly. "I am completely aware of your history. You've always had an inquisitive spirit. I find it fascinating. I know some things are changing in your life and there might be a tendency to fall back into some of your old ways. I just want you to remember what you have in front of you."

Jolem slowly nods in silent agreement.

"Focus on the many wonderful things around you and block out this other stuff. You have a loving family, great gigs, friends, your health, and ME. Life is good. What more could you ask for?"

"O – okay."

"Don't go back there, Jolem. We are perfect. Stay with me in this peace."

"You're right, Pati. Of course," he says as they move together to tenderly meet lips. The mystique of her calm alluring voice and sultry gaze sedates him.

"Do something for me," Pati says while straddling on top of him. She looks deep into his eyes.

"And what's that?"

"Just close your eyes…breathe and…relax. I want to share something with you," she whispers.

Jolem's eyelids slide shut, and his mind opens. He inhales and blows out. Suddenly, a drop of water falls to his forehead. "Huh??" he mutters, fluttering his eyes. He looks up above. The ceiling is gone and replaced by an overcast evening sky.

"Shhh. Just relax," Pati murmurs as she leans her body against his chest. Another drop drips, followed by another and then a few more. A crack of thunder and lightning blasts and then rain pours down on them. As the mood shifts, Jolem and Pati spend an evening of passion under the AllVu semblance of a torrential thunderstorm.

24

After an unusually eventful Friday, Saturday arrives in a lazy fashion. While most people are laid out at home immersed in their Worlds, household systems auto-initiate and run themselves. Throughout neighborhoods, regular weekend chores such as laundry, clean up, and yard work are effortless. Self-propelled mowers hum softly as they navigate yards while intelligent sprinklers deliver the perfect amount of water to stimulate their beautiful green grass. Even smart dog collars escort the family pet out into the yard to do his business and then back in when it's done. Thoughtless activity is the dish of the day.

An hour ago, Pati left Jolem's home with parting words of positivity and encouragement. After the loving night, she rested like a baby wrapped securely in his arms. She believed her distraction was enough to quell his festering anxiety. However, as she slept without a care in the world, he couldn't keep his eyes closed. Now, sitting on his sofa swiping vigorously like he's trying to clean the air, Jolem attempts to connect loose ends like a private investigator.

"J, show me the accident survivor," he says, and virtual windows of public information launch all around him. Individually, he moves one in front of the others, scans and pushes it aside. "Tell me a little about him."

"Well, he is a native New Yorker…Chief Executive for Vanguard Innovations…46…single…no children and 8.3 SIV."

"What about the family – the family killed in the accident?"

"The Woodlands lived in one of the South Paterson Recovery Zones.

The parents have SIVs in the low 3s; children, ages 7 and 5, have SIVs even lower."

"Hmmm. The recovery zones are full of low SIVs."

"Yes. Years ago, during displacement, these zones were riddled with violence, illegal drugs, and crime. Today, their streets are peaceful, and people live in harmony."

"What do most do for work in the zones?"

"Well, many low SIVs have fewer on-demand skills. Since the resource pool has a lower need for their services, most spend much of their time in education pods between gigs. If their SIVs are under 5, the government allows them additional time in alternates. They also receive greater compliance rewards."

"So that means they spend the vast majority of their days in VR and even get rewarded for it."

"That would be true."

Jolem stops and contemplates as all the disorderly pieces swirl in his mind. "Hmm…what is the average SIV in the recovery zones?" he asks.

"The average SIV is…3.2."

"What??" he says, wincing like he's smelled something rancid. "Hide AllVu."

Jolem leans back, rubbing the building tightness in his neck. The deep crinkles on his forehead look like they've been painted in place. All of a sudden, he feels The Path's sensory zap.

"Hi, Jolem. This is SEE with a Path Advisory Alert. The Path recognizes an unusual increase in your blood pressure and recommends measures to reduce any new stress. It's a great time to use a reward to treat yourself. Maybe a New Adventure? You've earned it. Your assistant will present you with exciting options to consider."

Jolem grips his mouth and pulls his cheeks like he's attempting to pry the skin from his face. "Ya know, J," he sighs while trying to hide his agitation. "Maybe I am overreacting a Li'l'. Is my mom home?"

"Acknowledgment is half the battle, Jolem. Yes, she is."

"Okay, Zumer."

A short ride later, Jolem arrives at his childhood home. When he enters, his mom is seated comfortably with her feet up, head back and mind in her World.

"Hey, mom," Jolem says, leaning down to kiss her on the cheek. "What's goin' on?"

For a brief moment, Kirame remains stiff, staring straight ahead like a toy. Suddenly her AllVu dissolves, her muscles loosen, and then she turns to him, grinning affectionately. "Hey sweetheart, live two days in a row, huh? I feel special," she kids. "I'm just visiting with your aunt. Your cousin is such a cute little joker."

"Ah, okay."

Kirame lifts up to the edge of her chair. "Hmm, Jolem, your SIV has ticked down a bit. Have you been feeling alright? Yesterday you were not yourself. Is everything okay with you and Pati? Your gig?"

"No, mommmm…everything's fine. But something I saw the last night did irk me a bit."

One of Kirame's eyebrows suspiciously rises above the other. "And what's that?" she asks.

"So, there was a pretty bad car crash."

"Hmmm, really…it's interesting you'd mention that?"

"Why??"

"Well, you know I like to keep out of the gossip chat, buuut just earlier today, a friend was ranting about some accident…freedom fighter blah blah blah."

"And??"

"Jolem, I honestly wasn't paying much attention. She's always sooo dramatic," Kirame says, cutting her eyes. "I don't know why I even entertain her."

"But mom…there WAS an accident. And some people DIED."

Kirame tilts her head and smirks. "Nooo, sweetheart," she snickers. "Don't get all bothered, Jolem. I'm sure you're mistaken. Car accidents don't happen anymore."

"But don't you want to see it for yourself?"

"I have ZERO desire to see some – whatever you think happened," she says, shaking her head. "I'd prefer to keep my sights on more positive things." Her smile grows bright as she looks straight ahead. "And so should you," she quips. "Show AllVu."

With a giant grin, Kirame carefreely reclines back into position and re-joins her World conversation with her sister. As she lays idly in her virtual experience, her relaxed muscles begin to spontaneously flinch and jerk. Annoyed, Jolem stands near, gripping his waist. His lips curl in agitation from his mother's quick dismissal of his concerns. It's been years since he's had this level of disagreement with his mom and her disinterest brings back memories.

Jolem starts to nervously pace in tight circles while rubbing his chin. The house is so quiet he can almost hear his rambling thoughts out loud. Then after a few minutes of silent frustration, he glances back at his mom, stops, and exhales. His eyes scan the room from one side to the other. Almost embarrassed, he quietly acknowledges the stark contrast between his peaceful surroundings and the renewed conflict in his head. He questions the worth of his struggles.

Jolem lethargically moves to a stretched lounge to his mom's side and drops down. "J – take me to Mount Everest," he mumbles. The mountainous alternate is one of his favorite places for relaxation. He lies back and closes his eyes. Moments later, when they open, he's alone among the clouds atop one of these great peaks. As he panoramically views the amazing scene, he inhales a deep gust of unadulterated air. The hiss of the strong breeze blowing against his ears replaces any sounds of home. Carefully, he pushes up off the moist rock and stands at the apex overlooking the world. The simulated experience is a sight to behold.

25

"WE WANT THE TRUTH! WE WANT THE TRUTH!" passionately chants a larger than usual gathering of Freedom Fighters at the front steps of the Washington DC, FDEC headquarters. Only days after the car accident, the little-known controversy has moved from the shrouds of conspiracy into the public. The Freedom Fighters, wearing their signature all-white outfits with a big black eye planted on their chests, are in a fervor over the unexplained results. Pushing and yelling, they demand to know how the Utilitarian Laws of Autonomy allowed a family of four to perish while a prominent business executive survived.

Typically, the general population pays Freedom Fighters little attention. Their rallies can be disruptive but rarely garner much notice. They're often dismissed as radical idealists, lunatics, or traitors of society. This time is different. With the director's announcement looming, a concern has slowly spread throughout The Path. A small segment of the population is beginning to question if there was somehow a failure with the Utilitarian Laws of Autonomy. This system was seemingly fair and infallible.

The incident has become a growing trend in conversation, and watchful authorities have noticed. While the protest continues outside the FDEC building, a group inside convenes to discuss the developing situation. Director Dalio sits back at the head of his oval conference room table, silently tapping his fingers against its glass top. With an aggravated, stone-cold expression, he glares at his FDEC executive board members. Without moving his head, his piercing eyes scan the room, pausing as he meets them individually. They've all been sitting on pins and needles, almost motionless, awaiting his first word for what seems like an eternity. He finally blows a deep exhale out of his flared nostrils, and they wait no longer.

"Good morning, everyone," he drawls. The deeply cracked murmur of his voice sounded as if he had just awakened.

"Good morning, Director!" the room of eight salutes.

"It is unfortunate; we must deal with an event such as this," continues the director. "With my announcement of V 10 in one week, we have to end this quickly! This is a celebratory time, and the public should be more confident of their safety now more than ever before. The timing could not have been more – inconvenient."

As he pauses once again, he looks around the room. Slow and methodically, he makes discerning eye contact with each one. "We cannot allow any more dissension during this time of triumph. These distractions will not stunt our momentum!" he shouts while pounding his fist against the table.

Turning sharply to his left, he pinpoints his chief strategist, Mallard. "We don't want to harm them and create a spectacle, but what can we do to silence these Freedom Fighters?"

"Well – Director," Mallard begins before clearing her throat. "As you know, they wear computer vision distortion masks to camouflage our facial recognition, clothes made out of natural material instead of digital fibers, and they also don't use AllVu. Since most live off the grid in Unicorns, it's difficult to determine who they are or where they come from – sir."

Director Dalio scans the room again. "Ideas people."

"I – I don't think we should overreact. The news is fresh. It will probably blow away in another day…" hesitantly begins a member, but mid-sentence, he's interrupted.

"We can – discredit the authenticity of the accident," another argues. "Plant the idea. It is more fake news."

"But – there were many witnesses and footage," counters another. "That can easily be debunked."

"Yes," interjects the director grinning mischievously. "Yesss." That's a great idea! We don't have the luxury of time. We need to react now. People only care for an explanation. It doesn't matter if it's true or not. As long as it's plausible, they will accept our version, no matter what the so-called "facts" say. They WANT something to believe in. And they believe in The Path."

"So, how should we handle this?" asks Mallard.

"Like we've done before. Create a few Fakes; simulated witnesses and experts who discount the validity of the accident. Let them say there was indeed a small incident, but no one was actually harmed and most of the experience was embellished. Release their accounts into popular Worlds. THESE WORLDS will change the narrative for us. Fake News. Let the public fight over it. The notion will grow like wildfire. In the meanwhile, we must focus on the V 10 and the merger."

"And the Freedom Fighters?"

Director Dalio closes his eyes and shakes his head dismissively. "Ignore them. They're merely gnats in the park."

As the heightened tension in the room drops, agreeable grins grow on their nodding heads.

"Remember," continues the director. "We must, by all means necessary, protect the sanctity of The Path. Confidence in its ways cannot be challenged. This is of top national security. Long live The Path."

In unison, they all echo his allegiance to The Path, and then their holographic representations disappear from the table. In actuality, they're physically scattered throughout the country. The director remains seated, staring straight ahead while slowly rubbing his fluffy white beard. "SEE…" he calls out.

"Yes, Director," replies his AI counterpart, whose voice emanates through the room's amplified sound system.

"Is there anything I should be aware of regarding the merger?"

"No, Director. Everything is moving according to plan."

"Excellent. With the merger, we'll have much more control over destructive information like this leaking into the public. It does nothing but cause alarm and confusion. We must protect them from themselves."

Miles away in his New York office pod, Jolem's chair leans back while a ballooning idea has him captive. Initially, Pati and his mom's persuasion was enough to keep his rambling thoughts at bay. However, as news of the car accident has spread, the incident has him gripped. For most of his life, he's felt like a weirdo with an overblown imagination, something that needed to be tamed. He had convinced himself that his theories of contrived schemes were all just in his mind or exaggerated fables passed down from his father. This time, his concerns have moved beyond the shadows and out into the mainstream.

Earlier in the morning when his HumanAid attempted to administer his Opeateazone, he reluctantly refused her. When J called for reconsideration, he rebuffed him. He's unsure what soured him on the sedative, but he doesn't want it anymore. Without it running through his system, he feels his thoughts are much clearer.

Jolem rocks from side to side twisting his cheeks like dough. He hasn't had a productive moment all morning. It's only fifteen minutes to 1 PM, but his inefficient day has reached its end. "Okay, guys, kicking out a bit early," he hastily remarks to his team as he grabs his bag off the floor. "I'll be virtual tomorrow."

Jolem jumps up and dashes out of the pod and down the hall. With guilty thoughts, he glides past fellow employees, self-consciously smiling as if he had just stolen something.

"Whooow – Jolem?? Is everything ok?" asks J.

"I just can't sit still. Need some air."

Jolem breaks out of the building into the open, convinced he'd see the public concern. But as he surveys the office park full of people sailing about – nothing. Everything is normal. No outrage, hysteria, just normal. Birds chirping, vendors selling, blissful passers-by; no one seems to care. He can't understand why the collective is not at arms over this clear breach of confidence. Their apathy is perplexing to him.

With his hands gripping his waist, he contemplates until his thoughts are interrupted by another sensory zap. "Huh?" he grunts at the familiar sensation.

"Hi, Jolem. This is SEE with a Path Advisory Alert. Have you forgotten something? The Path has detected you have not taken today's dosage of Opeateazone. Remember, it's important you maintain a proper health regimen and keep up-to-date with your medication. Please take your medication as soon as possible. I've set a reminder for 8:30 PM this evening."

Jolem frowns but again attempts to hide his irritation. He takes a couple of deep breaths to control his composure, straightens his back, and clears his throat.

"J – let's go home."

Jolem glides among the orderly rows of sleek autos moving throughout the city roads. Grand digital billboards and signs pay tribute to The Path and the upcoming announcement. Typically, his ride from work is filled with World interactions, but today he opts for a journey less virtual. Like when he was younger, he stares out of his window, immersed in thought. J takes this opportunity to share his observations. "Jolem, if I might say – you've experienced a range of emotions these last few days and I recognize some of your old patterns have returned. It's completely understandable with all the moving parts in your life, but I recommend now is the time to reset. Let's get you restarted with your Opeateazone, take a day of relaxation and continue the great progress of the past six years. Pati is an excellent partner for you, and she'll do whatever she can to help get you back on track. Remember, you are on target for a beautiful future of happiness and prosperity together. Would you like to review your future long-term prospectus?"

"No, J. Not now. I'm fine," he utters. However, he's confused now more than ever. As his head leans against the door window, his AllView orbs subtly vibrate. "Message from Pati," says J. It's as if she had heard her name.

"Play," he says, which ignites a huge heart in the air that explodes into tiny dissolving mini hearts. The eye-catching display is followed by a sweetly spoken video message. "Jolem, my dear, I'm so excited to spend this announcement with you. I adore us. See you tonight." As her vision withers away, she puckers, then blows a kiss. For a quick second, the realistic sensation of her lips presses against his. She's seemingly everything he's looking for in a partner. It's a mystery to him why he hesitates.

26

For most of the afternoon since leaving his office, Jolem has avoided his World. The activities of the past couple of days have him befuddled. Slumped over with his legs stretched across a kitchen nook, he looks out into the setting sky. In this tranquil moment witnessing the raw beauty of nature, he has no desire to see it through his AllVu. With all of his mental strength, he's trying to fight his will and follow the advice to submit to The Path.

"Jolem? Are you okay?" asks J. "You've been very quiet tonight."

"No – I'm good," he murmurs. "But, I was just wondering."

"What's that?"

"My life changed pretty remarkably after Leema."

"In what ways are you referring?"

"Well, my SIV rose, and I was quickly designated as a team lead. Why me? What did I do to earn The Path's extra consideration?"

"I suppose The Path sees something in you that you can't even see in yourself. You should be honored."

"I guess…"

He leans back against the wall as his eyes follow the shooting lights of distant drones. "Any new info on the car crash?"

"Actually, there has been new activity."

"Aaannnd?"

"Well, there is a growing suggestion that the accident was actually fake."

"Fake?? What??" he gasps, leaping to his feet.

"Completely staged. I told you there was a reasonable explanation."

"But J...that doesn't make sense. I saw it with my own eyes??"

"Well, your World is full of fantasy; why can't this also be fiction??"

"What about the official record?"

"The record states they are alive and well."

Jolem stretches his neck as he starts to pace in place. His thoughts are riddled. "But...but, that's not what it stated the other day, J!"

"Hmmm... are you sure?"

"I...I think so."

With a thought, Jolem quickly enters his World. He's amazed at how fast this new theory has developed. Even his buddy Rony is taking advantage of the hype.

"The crash: Real or Fake. You decide. Hosted by Mr. Ronitus. Join the convo!" blings loudly.

"What??" Jolem says confused, as he hides his AllVu. "J, I – I don't get it."

Questions bounce around in his head like balls in an old pinball machine and he again peers outside. The setting sun shines across his shirtless frame casting a shadow on Pati, who silently appears behind him. Leaning against the wall with her arms crossed, she curiously watches him.

"Oh Pati – I didn't know you were standing there?" he says, surprised by her sudden presence. His sights drift to the ground and then back out the window.

Pati slowly moves toward him. She slides down into the seat to his side and also glares out into the colorful sky. "Hi, Jolem," she says quietly. "What're you doing?"

"Just thinking."

"Hmmm... 'just thinking' huh? You've been doing a lot of that lately."

She drapes her arm against him and then melodramatically exhales like she's auditioning for a high school play.

"Huh? Pati...you okay??"

"Welllll now that you ask. There is something concerning me."

"Really? What's that?"

"Well Jolem," Pati starts while twisting her face to him. She looks into his eyes, wraps her fingers around his and pouts. "Our compatibility rating has dropped. By six points."

"Really?"

"Yes, really. Aren't you monitoring it?"

"No."

"Jolem, you've not been yourself lately, and it's beginning to affect our relationship."

"Oh – c'mon Pati. Seriously?" Jolem shoots back. "A few days ago, we were perfect and now the sky's falling??"

Within an instant, Pati's demeanor shifts from discontent to outright upset.

"Well, Jolem, I'm beginning to think you're returning to your old ways and deliberately attempting to sabotage this relationship," she charges.

Jolem glares at Pati in disbelief. "Please, you're overreacting."

"Ooh really? So, this is my fault now?"

"Listen, I just need a little space to sort some things out."

"Well – I will give you your SPACE if that is what you need. But I don't like this new course we are taking. I received an Advisory Alert today, which was also very concerning."

"An Advisory Alert? About what??"

"Don't worry about it. But YOU need to get your act together because I can't go down this road with you."

"Really? Just like that?"

Looking tenderly into his eyes, Pati suddenly becomes relaxed. She gently brushes the back of her hand across his cheek. "Jolie, you know I adore us," she begins calmly. "but you are pushing me into a corner, sweetheart. I'll do all I can to help, but you'll have to meet me halfway. You'll have to do your part."

Jolem leers into her soulful eyes and deflates. "I'll try. I am trying. But something seems – off."

"'Off' with what?"

THE PATH

Pausing, he gnaws his bottom lip. "The Path," he whispers hesitantly.

"The Path? Is that what this is all about??" she questions. "What are you talking about??"

"I don't know…I don't know, the car crash…"

"Jolem. The car crash?? Are you still on that? It was FAKE!"

"You don't know that."

"All I know is The Path has set us free."

"I know, but at what cost??" he shouts, throwing up his hands. "Something is just not right. I can feel it."

"Jolem, have you completely lost it?" she snaps. "The FDEC and The Path have saved this country from ruin. Life is wonderful and peaceful. We used to share this peace, but now – I'm getting really worried. For the first time in a long while, I'm sad."

"Pati, I don't want you to be sad," he says, dropping his head.

"Then please…drop this…drop this now."

As the warning words of his mother echo from Pati's mouth, Jolem turns away defiantly like when he was a child.

"Pati for you, I will try," he huffs, looking to the ground.

"That's all we need, Jolem. As long as you're willing to recommit yourself, this can all work. We can do this – together."

Jolem tugs his cheeks and releases a heavy grunt. "So, you'll be happy to know I'm thinking about A New Adventure."

Suddenly, her face lights up as she moves to his side. "I think that's an EXCELLENT idea. This is your first time, right? Do you know what you want to do?" she asks, lifting up on her toes.

"No, I'm not sure yet."

With a breath of relief, Pati caresses her fingers through his hair. "Jolie, we're still a great pair. Take your New Adventure. The experience will do wonders, and when your subconscious takes over, you never know where it'll take you. If I were you, I would wrap up all these car crash memories and lock them away in a room far, far away."

Pati kisses him gently on the lips, winks and then slips off. "Come to bed, sweetheart," she says, motioning forward.

"I'll be there in a min," he mumbles.

A lagging gust of air blows out of Jolem's mouth as he plops down into his seat. Just as the room becomes quiet, his thoughts are again interrupted. The corner of his mouth cracks upward when he sees the LiveView call from his most favorite person in the world; his sister. "Accept," he calls, and instantly he's viewing her hanging out in her room. "Hey, squirt."

"Ya think maybe it's time for a new nickname Jolem? You know I'm not a kid anymore."

"Yeah, yeah, yeah. We'll see. What's up??"

"Well, first – are you okay? You were really weird the other day."

"Yeah, I know. Hey, don't sweat it. I'm fine," he replies, bouncing back. "Now, what's up?"

"Ahh okay. Well, I got it!"

"Got what?"

"I had my Track Decision Ceremony tonight. I selected my Track."

Jolem pops up in his seat. His face glows with intrigue. "Already?? What'd you choose?"

"Well, I'm on track to become an FDEC Life Monitor!"

"Okay, uh wow. Congratulations," he says, disguising his contempt.

Liz starts to rave about her future growing more animated by the moment. She's overjoyed, but as she speaks, Jolem's ears slowly become mute to her words. In stark difference to his elevating concerns of The Path, she aligns with the system he questions. While she details her Track, his thoughts slip back to her early years when she idolized him as a child. Abruptly, he breaks in. "Liz – ya know I love you," he professes.

"Oh – of course, I do. Are you getting all mushy on me?"

"No, no. I just wanted to tell you; again. No matter whatever happens in this world, remember that."

"Well, thanks. I love you too bro! Soooo, I just wanted you to be the first to know. I'm designing an announcement in my World. I'll talk to you later – okay?"

"Sure, squirt. I'll catch up with you later."

When Liz's LiveView disappears, Jolem sits back in his seat as nostalgia takes him on a ride. He thinks of the happy little girl who used to follow him around and listen to his stories with wide-eyed astonishment. He could've told her the earth was flat and she would've believed it.

"J…" he says calmly. "Replay Liz's third birthday party, please."

Following his request, the memories of his childhood kitchen launch vividly through the vision of his young, innocent eyes. As he watches along, his father, Michale, performs like a magician in front of a small gathering of children, delighted family and close friends. With his fingers, Michale swirls colorful light shapes in the air that dissolve quickly as an astonished Liz attempts to pull them from the sky. Their father chuckles, scoops her up, dips low and spins her high like an airplane while his mom adoringly hovers near. It was a beautiful, enjoyable time, and maybe a simpler time. Months later, Michale would be gone.

The virtual experience ends, and his thoughts return to the present. The sun has receded and the moon is settling high in the clear abyss, but the night is still young.

"Hmmm, J – maybe you're right – A New Adventure might be just what I need to clear my head."

"Great idea Jolem. I'm sure this will help you get back to yourself. What would you like to do?"

"I don't know… surprise me."

"Wow. How exciting. With these fresh experiences, you'll feel like a new person. Get ready. When your subconscious takes off, it could be a wild ride. When should we get started?"

"I suppose you can begin whenever you're ready."

"Sure thing."

Jolem tilts his head toward the ceiling and begins to rub the back of his neck. As his eyes slide shut, he releases a loud distressed exhale, "Ahhhhhhhh." Suddenly, his body flinches when he feels a subtle shock in the side of his head. "Whoooh," he cries. "What the hell was that?"

"Jolem – are you okay?" asks J. "I felt the sensation but have no explanation for it."

Jolem leans over with his hands clamping his waist, attempting to shake off the unexplained pinch. "Yeah, yeah – I'm good. That was… different." All of a sudden, he's filled with renewed ambition. "Hmmm," he murmurs. "Actually J, postpone the New Adventure."

"Jolem. But?? What's the problem?"

"I don't know, J. There are some things I just need to resolve first."

In deep thought, he paces the room until his AllVu orbs vibrate. "Hi Jolem, this is SEE with your 8:30 PM Path Advisory Reminder to take today's missed dosage of Opeateazone. Remember, it's important you maintain a proper health regimen and keep up-to-date with your medication."

Lowering, Jolem slides into the chair and props up on his elbows on the table. As his chin rests on his thumbs, his HumanAid creeps forward with the Opeateazone dispenser in her open palm. "Hi, Jolem. Are you ready?" she asks, slowly advancing toward him.

He glares at her and swipes. "No," he snaps.

"But…"

"Jolem," calls J. "Please take the medicine. You heard SEE."

Jolem peers angrily at his HumanAid as she continues at his side, etching her hand to him. "Let me see it," he mumbles.

She extends her arm and he tentatively reaches for the contraption in her hand. With the tips of his two fingers, he carefully lifts it. "Ya know," he says, nodding. "I'm done with this." His wrist flings forward, and the Opeateazone cracks against the floor.

"JOLEM! NO!" cries J. "What're you doing??"

"I don't want to hear it, J. I don't need it."

"Jolem, you know The Path will not like this."

"I don't care. I'm done with it…for good."

27

A few days after the height of public intrigue surrounding the car crash, interest dissipated like smoke in the wind. The stories from the fakes created enough doubt to put most concerns to rest. The public's short and flighty attentions have moved on to the next hot topic. However, while many have accepted the new narrative, Jolem remains stubbornly unconvinced.

Around 2:00 PM in the FDEC headquarters, Director Dalio reclines at his desk, monitoring the progress of The Path V 10 upgrade. His team has been laser-focused for months. "So, how's it coming along," he asks his remote chief assistant Mollard.

"Everything is moving as planned, Director. Regression Testing is underway and -," she starts, but without warning, all Worlds across the country are caught off-guard by a startling disruption. As a loud and shrieking beat commences, the digitally distorted view of three individuals wearing all white and standing firm against a black backdrop progressively becomes clear. They look sternly ahead through dark thin frames covering the eyeholes of their facial distortion coverings. With the big eye logo on their chest, they remain motionless and at attention until the short musical intro ends. Their allegiance to the Freedom movement is clear, but their appearance is more militant than the usual protesters at Freedom Fighter rallies.

"This is a public service announcement from The Divide," begins a deep altered voice from the man in the middle aggressively pointing forward.

"Don't try to shut down or disrupt this communication because you can't. What we have to say needs to be heard. Since the beginning of The Path, a faction of the nation has protested the federal government's FDEC's gradual, steady attack on the public's freedoms."

Gripping the soft cushioned armrest of his seat, Director Dalio is stunned. He leaps up. "What is this??" he barks.

As the director watches in anger, the masked man continues. "We railed against the law requiring all people to enlist in The Path. We pushed for more transparency in SIV determinations. We fought against overbearing oversight and excessive Advisory Alerts for low SIVs. This latest attempt to misdirect the public has gone too far. The car crash makes it clear The Path works for the few instead of the many. This blatant abuse must be stopped!"

In a frenzy, the director slams his fist onto his desktop. "How the hell did they penetrate our security systems so deeply?? SEE?!!"

Seething, the director yells to his cyber security forces as the antagonists continue. Together, the masked men lift their fists into the air and then the center spokesman makes a proclamation. "Citizens, while you sleepwalk through your days, being told what to do and what not to do, we are trying to wake you up to the realities of this so-called 'good life.' You can keep your eyes shut, but soon you will see. Director Diablo and his minions have a reckoning coming!"

When his short speech tails off, the charged music re-enters, continuing to play until the transmission distorts and disappears.

"I'm attempting to locate the message's origin director," accounts SEE's mild reverberating voice. "but they've manipulated compromised Zombie Worlds to misdirect us. The owners of these Worlds are completely unaware they've been used."

"These damn hackers are getting too crafty with 'zombie' Worlds," grumbles Dir Dalio. "They continue to piggyback on them and navigate The Path like ghosts, leaving no evidence to track. We've got to put an end to this!"

"The transmission was traced to the World of an elderly man in Alexandria, Virginia," informs SEE. "When interrogated, he was completely unaware his World was being used and lie-detection determined he was telling the truth. I'll continue investigating to see if the perpetrators left any digital footprints, but I don't anticipate we will find any. Their methods are too advanced for Freedom Fighters."

Locking his hands behind his back, Dir. Dalio saunters over to the long window wall and looks down at the streets five stories below. The rapid but orderly movement of Zumers, drones and rolling IGliders is a personal testament to his and his department's accomplishments. His anger and frustration by this resistance are only surmounted by his pity. He has little faith the small band of rebels can significantly disrupt The Path; however, this major breach is very concerning.

"These ingrates have been the bane of my existence for decades," he says, breathing heavily. "I don't understand why they are not kissing my feet and worshiping the ground I walk on. There would be no country if not for The Path, and they'd all be pledging allegiance to China."

With his head back, he sucks in a deep inhale and then blows it out audibly. "Today, they reached too close and we have to put a swift end to this. I'm sure they used vulnerabilities within Halcyon to attack us, which has been our greatest weakness. With this merger, soon this back door into The Path will be blocked for good."

"Director – there is one more thing," comments SEE.

"There's more??"

"Yes. There is a remote possibility they may have accessed the – list."

"WHATT?? Explain."

"During my investigation into this incident, I discovered another breach. I am unable to determine if they were successful, but there was penetration into the system. However, even should they have managed to break through our protective shields, it is extremely unlikely they have the capabilities to unlock the highly encrypted and safeguarded list."

The director pauses while staring blindly out of the window. "Okay," he says calmly. "I know the list would be extraordinarily difficult to crack – but not impossible. Send out snoopers to investigate all deviants, pre-deviants, their families, and their associates. Monitor their Worlds and conversations. We need to restore order and find out who's behind this, using any methods necessary – immediately!"

With his hands still clenched behind his back, the director lumbers over to his desk. He plops down and then starts twiddling his thumbs.

"SEE…" he says sullenly.

"Yes, Director?"

"Analyze and provide insight."

After a quick second pause, SEE begins. "Director, although bothersome, the acts of this relatively small group have had very little impact on public sentiment towards The Path. I've evaluated the activity of millions of Worlds. The initial response to this latest strike has been overwhelmingly in our favor. The general population is more annoyed with the interruption of their Worlds than distressed by the actual message. Their overriding fear of the unknown is much greater than any concern with The Path. They trust it and live by it. Even if they were aware of the list or any other classified detail of The Path, there is great data to suggest most will not care."

"So, you are proposing we should just let it ride?"

"I am advising that you not overreact. Continue the security protocol, and do not allow personal feelings to hamper your judgment. You are an effective leader and have an extremely loyal following."

"An 'effective leader,' huh?" he mumbles while gazing menacingly ahead. With his left hand tugging his cheeks, he ponders. "I'm not an 'effective leader,'" he rebuffs. "I'm a god. Prepare to respond."

In Worlds, homes and other live venues around the country, the Divide's transmission is the new hot topic. Gathered at a coffee lounge, Liz and a few friends were cheering the recently released date of the director's announcement when they were interrupted by the dreary message. The shocking one-time event has them in arms. Along with the masses, the group remains solidly loyal to the FDEC and The Path.

"Who is the Divide and why don't they just leave us alone?" comments Liz, perplexed. "The Path is not the problem; they are."

"Liz, they are terrorists and want nothing more than to disrupt our happiness. Don't even let them get you down," comforts her friend.

Liz's red shirt slowly transitions back to pastel blue as her frown flips up to a smile. "Ya know. You're exactly right," she confirms gleefully. "I'm not going to let them get to me. Life is too good to be upset. No matter how wonderful things are, there will be those stuck in misery." She turns to her girlfriend and flings a ten rating to the comment. "I hear ya girl."

"Liz, you've just said a million words," affirms her friend. "Divide, go away," she says, swiping at the air. "We must help those who can't see the light. I hope the FDEC finds out who these people are soon. Maybe they, too, can be turned around."

"That's the spirit," Liz giggles. "Rain happiness on everyone," she comments, flicking digital cheer to her friends.

THE ANNOUNCEMENT

28

Following months of intense speculation, the night of the highly anticipated The Path Version 10 announcement has finally arrived. Within a few short hours, Director Dalio will be unveiling The Path's latest life enhancements and people are thrilled. Around the country, watch gatherings fill up like New Year's Eve countdown celebrations. The nation is filled with joy.

A week has passed since The Divide's breach and they've gone silent. There hasn't been a word nor sighting of the intimidating group. Jolem and Pati discussed the incident and she dismissed it as a stunt. Jolem, of course, was affected more profoundly. He hasn't been able to get it out of his mind. En route to Rony's announcement watch party, he peers blindly out of his Zumer window, consumed in contemplation. He thought he was doing a good job hiding his lingering anxiety from Pati, but it was written all over his face.

"Jolem – are you okay?" asks Pati. She's been evaluating him in silence for the past few minutes and is growing impatient with his peculiar behavior.

"Huh?? Oh – yeah, I'm fine. What?"

"I don't know what happened but…you've been like a different person since the graduation ceremony. And our compatibility rating continues to drop."

"Pati, really, I'm sorry," he says, reaching to grip her hand. "I honestly have been trying. I don't know what else to do."

Well, have you taken your New Adventure?"

"No – not yet."

"Hmmm." Pati glances strangely at him. His oddity is impossible for her to understand. "Well, baby, the announcement is almost here and you know – The Path may have all the answers you're looking for, right?"

When Jolem twists in her direction, he recognizes the same distress he saw on Liz's face many years ago. To keep her mind and heart at ease, he smiles back gently and says, "You're right," and then pats her on the thigh. This comforting gesture, although contrived, is enough to give her temporary peace. She snuggles into his body, grinning as if she's solved the riddle, but again his thoughts wander.

It's a contrasting commute from Jolem's suburban New Jersey environment to Rony's exotic and spirited Brooklyn neighborhood. As they flow down the urban city street, the towering midtown Manhattan buildings loom in the distance. In this community of funky shops, restaurants, and trendy cafes, the bustling sidewalks are packed with diverse individuals wearing flashing neon-colored tributes to The Path. They gleam and throw digital cheer to passing strangers like confetti. It's a joyous time full of enthusiasm and anticipation for the evening's main event.

Jolem and Pati arrive at the front of Rony's renovated warehouse apartment building and Pati is electrified. As she looks out the window beaming from ear to ear, she takes note of all the activity and unique characters lining the road. The atmosphere is like a carnival. "Hi there, pretty lady," chuckles a clown-like masked man as he swings past the car. He lifts his open hand to his mouth and blows a barrage of tiny hearts in Pati's direction. "HAAAAAA, IT'S A GOOD LIFE!" he shouts, waving his hands in the air as he continues down the road.

"Ohhh!" stutters Pati recoiling. "Did you see that??" she says, pointing.

"See what?"

"The guy's face. In the mask. His name...identifiers, were all distorted. I couldn't see anything about him."

"Hmmm. Nope, I didn't see it."

"Strange…," she utters, spying back as the man disappears into the animated crowd.

When they step out of their Zumer, Pati pulls Jolem's arm leading him up the slanted walkway to the building entrance. "Hey, we'll get there. Slow down," he gripes, but his words have no effect.

"Jolem, I can't see how you're so calm," she calls with the eagerness of a child during the holidays. "The Director's announcement is almost here."

When they approach the sliding door of Rony's apartment, they're greeted by his extra-friendly assistant. "Welcome, Jolem and Pati! Rony will be so happy you made it. Please come inside and make yourself at home as we celebrate The Path V-10."

Pati slips her arm around Jolem's as they move through the intimate setting. Gushing like a star-struck teenager, she's in awe of the small eclectic gathering of about thirty of Rony's friends and fellow World celebrities. Leaning close, she firmly squeezes Jolem's arm. "Do you know these people?" she whispers while attempting to hide her excitement. "Some of their Worlds are – like…'lunar'." Our SIVs are ticking up just by being here."

"Nah, don't know any of them," he says, unimpressed. "Where's Rony?"

Jolem lifts a recycled paper cup off a tray carried by one of Rony's HumanAids that are circulating the room. His head drops back, and he swallows the THC-infused fruity drink. "It's a little stuffy in here, don't you think," he comments, pulling at the neck of his buttoned-up, collarless shirt.

"Relax, Jolem. Try to enjoy yourself," Pati comforts, bumping his side.

Jolem peeks around, casually surveying the room and then grabs another drink. As he lifts the cup to his mouth, Rony's bedroom door swings open. Then with blaring lights at his back, Mr. Ronitus pops into the crowd in a loud, spectacular fashion.

"Hello, World! Mr. RONITUS is HERE!!" he howls and the applauding guests love it. Rony, or "Mr. Ronitus," has a flair for the bizarre.

To kick off the V-10 announcement, he's taken it to another level. With a white-colored face and vibrant highlights accentuating his eyes and mouth, he looks like an Asian geisha and Vegas circus performer rolled into one. Reflecting lights glisten from his long multi-colored pigtails protruding out of his tall black hat. With charming one-liner greetings and witty gags, he makes his rounds through the amused crowd.

"Rony man, you really outdid yourself this time," laughs Jolem as he bumps arms with his buddy. "Are you wearing a suit, or is your skin colored silver?"

"Jolem, my man, I'm glad you made it! Whatttt?? This is the rave. Spray it on liquid digital fabric. After tonight, everyone will be wearing it!"

"You won't catch me DEAD in that," Jolem cracks.

In Rony's apartment and other festive assemblies across the country, people wait in suspense as the moments tick toward the beginning of Director Dalio's public announcement. When the hour strikes 8:00 PM, the main event begins. As all Worlds simultaneously become silent, everyone prepares for the director's much-awaited words. The moment is so quiet; one could hear a pin drop.

"Good evening, I'm SEE with an important Path communication. Everyone, please pause what you are doing and pay close attention to this very special update from The FDEC's National Director, Arturo Dalio. All Worlds will shift to sleep mode during his announcement."

Like a night show host walking out from behind the stage, Director Dalio's hologram slowly steps forward from virtual nothingness. Wearing the FDEC's shiny, grey body suit and a charming smile, he stands tall with his hands crossed in front of him. Nodding, he looks around as if he is actually in each room of the millions of households viewing. To the adoring fans of The Path all over the country, he is a national icon.

"Good evening, fellow citizens of this great nation. Once again, I am honored to speak on behalf of the FDEC and The Path," he begins, and the virtual audience goes wild.

"Like never before, I am so excited to share the great updates The

Path has for you," he says, grinning. He clenches his fists tight and exclaims, "This is, by far, the greatest advancement we've made in life experiences!" and the cheers persist.

"This is for YOU, my friends," he proclaims with confidence while he throws his right hand into the air. "All for YOU!"

Taking a moment to acknowledge the applause, he graciously nods before continuing. Softly, he motions down to settle the noise until the claps are replaced with complete silence.

"Now, before I get started with tonight's announcements, there are a few words I'd like to say." His head lifts high as he sternly gazes out into the distance. "Many of you are too young to remember life before The Path and the multitude of challenges that besieged our great country, our people. Violence, crime, poverty, sickness, foreign aggression, and a decaying planet threatened our very existence. Fortunately, it is a new day and those challenges are LONG GONE. There are those of you who thank me for the utopia we now live in, but I don't deserve this credit. Give your thanks and continued allegiance to The Path!"

Jolem stands at Pati's back, anxiously tapping his fingers against his thigh. He examines the room full of giddy and enthralled faces. During the previous announcement four years ago, he sat alone at home watching the spectacle. He followed the director's updates without much interest. This time is different. Fully engaged, he hangs on to every word said and those unspoken.

"Be wary of the naysayers," continues the director. "Those sick groups and individuals who would like you to believe the euphoria you are experiencing is a dream, a fictitious reality. They push false propaganda and misrepresentations. My friends, I am here to reassure you, what you feel, smell, and see is REAL. Real as the beat of your heart in your chest or the warmth of your child as you hold her close. Do not listen to the toxic words of a very few. The Path has set us FREE!" he extols.

"Now, my friends, as we approach another milestone within The Path, I'm pleased to say this is only the beginning of what we can achieve together. Because of your compliance with The Path, SIVs and promotions have increased at a significant rate. Reward earnings are more bountiful. Alternate experiences are livelier, and their memories are more vivid. We are enjoying life more and more. This is all because of YOU, my friends! This is the promise of The Path," he lauds, and again, the crowd cheers.

Director Dalio begins to pace in a small circle with a humbly satisfied smirk. His tight and forward clap is presented to the audience as a salute to their support. Elated observers everywhere share their excitement with their in-person neighbors. Even strangers slap hands and embrace like old friends. When the director's steps slow to a halt, he clasps his hands and then looks proudly up into the air. He looks like he has a secret he's been dying to reveal.

"SO, shall we get started?!" he asks, and the population explodes again. It's the key phrase he uses to kick off his presentations.

"Okay, great. I PROMISE you, this is the best version of The Path ever released and your lives are going to be more enjoyable than you can even imagine. Okay – so, this very first announcement is long awaited. Aren't you getting tired of trying to find a comfortable location to relax and enjoy your World? Wouldn't it be nice to stretch out in a comfortable World Chamber? I bet you thought World Chambers were only for high SIVs, well, I have a treat for you."

He steps to the side and an image of a plexiglass, basic encasement appears. "My friends, feast your eyes on the all-new Arcadia World Chamber Light."

To accompany his first notice, a NonHuman spokesperson surfaces to give a short breakdown of the product. Like attendees at a car show, audiences gawk at the sleek, clear chamber. Individually, they move it around with their fingertips and personally examine its craftsmanship.

"You might be asking yourself how much they cost…hmmm," Dir. Dalio remarks as the spotlight returns to him. He pauses, leaving the audience in suspense. "Absolutely nothing!" he laughs. "All you have to do is reach four straight months of full compliance, and it is yours, courtesy of your United States government," he says, and the national audience explodes.

For the ensuing period of about 30 minutes, the director delves into more updates, with each more grandiose than the previous. He follows the pattern of presenting a feature and then falling back while a Non-Human spokesperson appears to provide context and significance. One-by-one, the displays dazzle the wide-eyed masses. When the presentation comes close to the end, everyone knows to expect one more update. Director Dalio crosses his arms and looks firmly ahead before speaking.

"And last, there is just one more thing," he says, smirking. Rony's house fills with cheers and high-fives. Although, instead of boasting a new feature, the director sighs as he looks soberly ahead and then begins softly. "As you know, the Halcyon operating system and The Path have worked in conjunction to provide you with the best life experience imaginable. Unfortunately, the behavior of some rogue actors continues to undermine all the progress we've made. The other day, we all experienced the interruption from the terrorist group calling themselves the Divide. Many of these criminals use Halcyon's OS as a gateway into The Path to cause mischief, placing YOU at SERIOUS risk. Believe me, my friends, this is a GRAVE threat to our happiness and continued prosperity," he offers, clenching his jaws tightly.

The director looks around, nodding gloomily. For long silent moments, people wait anxiously for comforting words. He takes a deep breath and then wields his fist in the air. "BUT please do not be alarmed, my friends," he raves. "Your FDEC has an answer to this maliciousness. Therefore, to provide you with additional security, we are in the process of a complete merger of the Halcyon life navigation operating system into The Path. This unification will give us the capacity to better monitor and block unwanted visitors and fakes from your Worlds! Attempted attacks, small and large, will be sniffed out and obliterated before they even get started!"

When the director began his breakdown of the threat, faces across the country grimaced with concern. The FDEC's solution is received with relief and celebration. He begins to pace with his arms clasped behind his back, slowly nods, clears his throat, and looks ahead. "You may ask; how will this affect your life and daily activities?" he peacefully remarks. "And the answer. Not at all. This integration will be seamless and it will most likely go – unnoticed. Just continue your days as usual and know that your FDEC is working behind the scenes on YOUR behalf."

With his hands crossed, he lifts his head high and smiles wide. Worlds erupt in a boisterous ovation.

"Remember this, my friends," he declares loudly above the applause. "Life has never been more rewarding than this very moment. Our people have never been happier. There is peace and security throughout our lands. Long live The Path. It is truly a good life!" he lauds, waving his hands.

After his parting words, the director takes a thankful bow, turns and then walks until he fades away. When Worlds automatically become active again, they immediately begin to socialize their reactions to the announcement. Some think the updates were mind-blowing, while others yearn for more. The collective audience is elated, but Jolem's stoic demeanor doesn't change.

"How about that!??" yells Rony to his live gathering and large virtual following. "Quick ratings, please!"

Rony is hopping up and down with excitement as he impatiently waits. In flashing lights, the score tallies next to him in the air and then stops.

"9.8!! Wow!! It's a hit! The Divide is goin' dowwwwnnnn!!!" he howls, pumping his arms. A giant puff of psychoactive vapors blows through the room, and Rony's apartment ignites. "PARTAAAYYYYY!!"

Leaning against the wall, Jolem is vexed by the abandoned restraint of the exuberant crowd. Swinging their heads to the flashing lights and energetic beats, they are wild and free. "Come'onnn, Jolem," calls Pati as she seductively lures him to dance. However, like a stout tree in the middle of a storm, his feet remain planted in place.

"Jolem? Is everything okay??" she asks, confused. "Come dance with me!"

"Pati – this isn't right. I…I need to go."

"Go?? But – why??"

"Can we just leave?" he says, heading for the front door.

Pati reaches for his arm but comes up empty. "Jolem, wait," she cries and then chases behind him. "What the hell, Jolem?! I don't understand."

Jolem swings to her, agitated and breathing heavily. "WHY CAN'T YOU ALL SEE??" he shouts in her face.

Even through the blustering music, his bark draws the attention of party goers. Their movements slow as they peek over. With disturbed glances, they capture the experience in their Worlds' recordings. Unflattering ratings start to fly his way.

"Jolem, are you crazy? Lower your voice!" implores Pati as she looks into the faces of all the uneasy stares. She grabs his arm and pulls him. "Okay, let's go," she says, leading him towards the door. "I don't know what's gotten into you."

Rony notices them leaving and launches behind them. "Hey JO, what's going on, man?? Where're you goin'??"

Jolem slowly twists and shrugs. "Sorry man, but you know me. Some things change, and I guess – some stay the same," he says disappointingly, shaking his head and then glides out.

29

"Wake up, Jolem."

"Huh?"

Jolem's heavy eyelids crawl open and then slide shut. He slips back off to sleep, but a moment later, the gentle whisper calls again. "Jolem."

He springs up on his hands, and his blinking eyes spy from one end of his room to the other. When he sees nothing, he questions if he's awake or stuck in a nightmare that just won't end. Suddenly, a message like an old 3:00 AM anxiety commercial softly beckons from the shadows. Calm winds and soothing sounds of the elements whistle in the background as a woman's soft voice speaks.

"Do you sometimes feel – out of place?

In situations when everyone seems to be completely content, do you often feel – uneasy?

When you're in a crowd of people, do you still feel – alone?

Well, Jolem – you're not."

The mystical experience withers away, and only the dark silhouettes of his bedroom furniture remain. While lifted on his elbows, he stares ahead in a bewildered daze. The words of the short puzzling infomercial struck a nerve. He's not sure of its source, but his instincts point to an old character from his past.

While sitting up, he peeks over to the empty space in his bed, often occupied by Pati and then shakes his head. The evening ended far from how he had envisioned it would. His eyes slightly shut, and the night's events replay in his mind. His live confrontation with Pati was witnessed like a TV drama, and the negative reaction was overwhelming. Aside from the free fall of his SIV, his inexplicable behavior pushed her to her limit. On the ride from the party, she'd had enough and confronted him. As if beginning to formally present in front of an office panel, she cleared her throat, locked her fingers, and looked straight ahead with the calmness of a therapist. "Jolem, this isn't working anymore," she said straightforwardly.

Jolem listened in silence while she launched a logical case for why they were no longer a "good match." She pointed to their rapidly declining compatibility rating and his unwillingness to change. He attempted to pay attention, but as her words continued, they began to run together and muffle until he heard nothing. Watching her mouth move without sound, he zoned off until she was on her way out of the car. He didn't even try to stop her.

For the rest of the evening following his strange midnight message, he lay in his quiet room staring blindly at the ceiling. He couldn't get another moment's rest. Hours later, when the soft sounds of his wake-up music begin to play, he's in the same spot with the same blank expression.

"Good morning Jolem," greets J. "Looks like another beautiful day in The Path."

"Mornin' J," Jolem mutters. Without activating his World, he sits up, rubbing the thickening prickles covering his face. He hasn't shaved in days.

"Jolem, how are you?" questions J. "Last night was pretty rough."

Jolem sucks in a large breath until his cheeks fill with air, drops his head back and then blows it out like a canon. "I don't know," he grumbles. "I just don't know what's goin on anymore."

"Jolem, I know it seems like some things are unraveling out of control, but all you have to do is recommit yourself to The Path, and everything can go back to the way it was. Even your relationship with Pati can be mended."

Before he can even respond to J's words, a new Path message takes

Jolem by surprise.

"Hi, Jolem. This is SEE with an Advisory Alert. You've been awarded an additional day off today. Your Assistant will present you with some great alternate options to take you away. It's all for you, so sit back and relax. The work can wait."

"'An additional day'?" Jolem says, shocked. "What did I do to receive 'an additional day'?" Scratching his chin, he sits off the edge of his bed, contemplating the offer.

"What do you say, Jolem? How would you like to spend your day off?" asks J, but however tempting, Jolem reluctantly declines.

"Ya know J – I think I'll take another day off – later in the week. There are some things I need to do today."

"I really wish you would reconsider Jolem. This past week has had many challenges and it's time to reset. The Path is trying to help you get back on Track, but you must do your part. Advisory Alerts are more than mere suggestions."

"I understand, but not today."

As he hops out of bed on his way to his bathroom, he receives another curiously timed communication. His steps slow to a halt and he scratches the back of his head. This time it's from Liz.

"Hmmm…Hey Liz. Is everything okay??"

"Hi, Jolem," Liz begins calmly. "How are you?"

"I'mmm okkkk," he says suspiciously. "Ahhh, I see. You saw me last night, huh?"

"Well, of course I did. Everyone did. Mom is really concerned about you – and so am I."

For the next few minutes, Liz challenges him about his recent antics. Her loving words express fear but also worry.

"Jolem, everything I've said is out of love. Please listen to me. Not just as your little sister, but also as a soon-to-be Path ambassador. I don't want to bring up the "D" word, but your potential deviation horrifies me. Whatever is bothering you, remove it from your life and pleaseee recommit to The Path."

Liz's words penetrate deeper than those of others. She argued so passionately that he agreed to make efforts toward reconciliation. Although, he knew it was a promise he couldn't guarantee to keep. When the call ended, Jolem stood in place looking at the ground.

"Hmmm, J – I don't know what to do."

"Well, you can start by listening to SEE and taking the day off."

"J, I promise. After work, I'll do whatever, but – I have a nagging feeling… I need to go to the office."

Jolem rejects Li'l J's advice and ignores SEE's direction. A couple of hours later, he finds himself spinning back and forth at his office workstation. Since the strange night he experienced, ominous thoughts have taunted him. On edge, he scratches his neck as his eyes wander around his pod. He surveys for the unusual, but the mundane everyday activities of his co-workers are all he sees. As he rubs his prickled face, he questions his state of mind.

His insecurities mount and Liz's pleas scream louder and louder in his head. Finally, his body drops forward and the wind releases from his lungs. He's done fighting and ready to succumb to The Path. His fingers slide back through his hair and then start to rub the building tension in his forehead. Suddenly, he hears a familiar faint whisper, "Jolem."

"Huh??" he grunts, startled. Looking around, he realizes he's the only one who heard the soft call.

"Follow the hound. Go NOW," the voice instructs.

"The hound? What?"

Jolem sights cautiously pin-ball the room. When his eyes reach the door, he catches the back end of a small white dog with a red tail wagging. His breaths grow heavy, and his heart starts to race. He wants to make chase but doesn't want to cause alarm. Lifting slowly, he sucks in a deep breath and quietly blows it out. However, he's stalled again.

"Hi, Systems Technician Team 5. This is SEE with an Advisory Alert," plays throughout the pod. "Please stand by while we conduct a brief security update. It's important that you all remain in your pod until the update is complete. You will be informed when it is done. It should only take a few minutes. Thank you." The curious timing of SEE's Alerts continues.

"Jolem?? Is everything okay?" questions his co-worker when she notices his disturbed expression.

"Yeah…I'm cool," he quickly calls out.

Jolem glances to the exit and notices the dog passing through the door. His mind tells him to comply with SEE's instruction, but his instincts say, "Go." His insides churn into knots, and he feels he's about to explode. "Be back in a min," he says, leaping up.

"But – but SEE instructed everyone to remain in the pod until completion," cries his co-worker as Jolem passes by.

"I'll be RIGHT back," he shouts.

Jolem follows his gut out of the room in pursuit of the white hound. "Hi, Jolem. This is SEE with an Advisory Alert. Please return to your pod. Immediately," blasts in his ears, yet he's undeterred. He's not sure where he's going or why, but he scurries down the hall following his canine leader. When he turns around a corner, his momentum is stunted, as if he is colliding head-on with a speeding truck. No doubt he's shocked when his eyes and mouth stretch wide open. Gliding straight towards him, leading a small entourage, is a mature, confident, and in-charge, Leema.

"Le-Leema??" he utters in disbelief, but to his surprise, she doesn't recognize him. She looked right through him like he was a stranger.

"Uhh – yes. Can I help you??" she replies, flinching backward.

Standing still with a confused stutter, Jolem is tongue-tied. It's been six years, but he believes she has to remember him. "Huhh?? Leema, it's me…Jolem??"

Leema squints at his floating identifiers and then back into his face. "I'm sorry – Jolem, but I don't believe we've ever met."

"But, you're Leema. I don't understand. We…"

"Yes, I'm Leema Dalio. Perhaps you have me confused. I'm GreenView's Southeastern Director. And youu areee…," she replies while continuing to read his identifiers. "Uhh Jolem…McKay. ST Team Lead 5.

You've performed many gigs for us over the years, I see."

"Ah, yes."

"Okay, Jolem, it's a pleasure to meet you. I take it GreenView has treated you well?"

"Yes…sure."

"Great. Have a wonderful day, Mr. McKay. It's a good life."

"Okay, thanks."

Leema smirks, turns and then she and the crew proceed down the hall. Questions plague Jolem's thoughts as she flows out of sight. By the look of her expressions, she genuinely has no recollection of him or the experiences they've shared. She could've hidden their experiences deeply, but surely seeing him would have triggered something. Those experiences have either been blocked or supplanted. He shutters to understand why The Path and or the director would go through measures so drastic to keep them apart.

Jolem slowly returns to his pod, massaging the back of his tense neck. He's perplexed, but before he can catch his bearings, the saga continues. After six years of compliance, a dreadfully familiar sensory zap causes the fine hairs on his arms to rise.

"Hi Jolem, this is SEE with an urgent message. Apparently, you have veered off-track; therefore, you are required to contact the FDEC within 24 hours for a Track Realignment. Thank you."

His eyes slam shut, and he releases an agonized grunt. Although he's challenged The Path over the past couple of weeks, the advisory alert still takes him by alarm. He began the day in search of the truth, but the growing questions far outweigh his answers. The world that he knows continues to collapse.

With his head hanging low, Jolem drifts inside his pod. He instantly recognizes the odd demeanor of his team members. Curiously, they look straight ahead and ignore his presence.

"Guys?? What's goin' on?" he asks, but no one responds. During an awkward few moments of silence, they just look at each other.

"Jolem, as soon as you left, an alarm shot off," one of them calls out.

"What?? Where?"

In unison, they point to an illuminating dashboard and Jolem grimaces. SEE had informed them not to leave during the security update, but he disregarded the instruction. With his fingers, he extends the digital structure in the air to begin his security protocol. "Okay," he sighs and then reclines in his seat. "I'm entering the environment." His head leans back and his SimMe is transported to the virtual security sector.

He expects to be alone when he arrives but finds himself in the middle of a five-person holographic panel. Without expression, they sit still at a curved table around him.

"Uhh, what is this?" he stutters.

"Mr. McKay, we are a unit of GreenView's Security Force," the center man directly in front of him replies emotionlessly. "Unfortunately, we have some – not so great news."

"Okkk, and what would that be?"

"Because of some recent ripples in The Path, we have decided to go in a different direction as it relates to you. Because of recent non-compliance, you have been demoted from team lead and will once again serve as a systems technician. Your security clearances as a lead have been revoked."

"What?? But I don't understand."

"Yes, we're sure this is not what you'd like to hear, but The Path has taken many things into consideration, and this was a direct order. We have no choice in this matter."

"I don't believe this," he mumbles.

"Your current gig is terminated, effective immediately. After a probationary period, you will be considered for future gigs with GreenView. In your pod, security is waiting to escort you out of the building. We thank you for your service."

When Jolem's consciousness returns to his pod, the awkward stares of his team members are locked in his direction. His sights swing to the door. Two brutish building security officers stand just outside the room with their arms hanging to their sides. Jolem's head falls, weighted down by the burdens of his actions. Nothing makes sense anymore. The more he attempts to gather all the scattering pieces, the further apart they go.

Like a prisoner, he moves behind the stilted officers. It's a humiliating short trip through the building. Within excruciatingly long minutes, he arrives at the monumental glass front entrance. His head lifts, and he panoramically scans the long, lively lobby. People are moving happily about without a care in the world. His face drops again as he edges to the door, and his mind rewinds his surreal encounter with Leema. The day's events are hard to believe.

His thoughts wander farther into his World. He told himself he'd never review old experiences of her again. However, step by tentative step, he slips deep into rooms locked away.

"Jolem, are you sure you want to do this?" asks a concerned J. "You hid these experiences for a reason."

"I know, J," he whispers. "I'm not sure about a lot right now, but I want to see that look again."

With his words, he quantum leaps back to the day he asked Leema to hide her AllVu as they sat together sharing pastries. In that moment years ago, their SIVs didn't matter. They were just two young people sharing a singular space in the vast universe. Standing in the middle of a world falling apart, he willingly exposes himself to the hidden pain. He feels he deserves the punishment.

30

Later that afternoon, Jolem fidgets on his sofa, watching the moments creep past 3:30 PM. With nineteen hours left to respond to his summons, he's wrestling with a big decision. He has no desire to enter an FDEC building or reunite with Mrs. Bolder. He has even less interest in facing Compliance Control at his front door, should he miss his deadline.

"Jolem, are you ready?" asks J. It would be wise to reply to your summons. You don't want to risk deviation."

"Not now, J."

"What are you waiting for, Jolem? There's nothing else to consider. Respond to your summons and recommit yourself. The Path can set you free. Things can go back to the way they were before. All you have to do is recommit."

Jolem covers his ears and slams his eyes closed. "J! Enough! he yells, gritting his teeth. "I need time to think. Call Rony."

Tense moments expire as Jolem nervously taps his fingers against his thigh, but Rony doesn't answer. Surprisingly, even access to Rony's public atrium is blocked.

"What?? J, what's going on?"

"Jolem, you didn't consider how your actions affected Rony. His SIV also dropped after the party because of your relationship. As a show of disapproval, he was forced to temporarily ban you from his World. He had no choice."

Jolem shakes his head in frustration. "What? For how long??"

"It's indefinite. You must request re-entry."

"Do what you have to. I've got to talk to him."

For the following long anxious hour, Jolem awaits Rony's reply. He lies on his bed juggling five mirror-like floating orbs, attempting to occupy his meandering thoughts. Out of the corner of his eye, he notices his HumanAid uncharacteristically pause at his door. She glances into the room and then quickly shuffles out of sight. "That was odd," he murmurs, snapping up.

With a flick of his fingers, Jolem's virtual balls all disappear. He swings off the side of the bed and then props up on his palms. His sights begin to bounce around the room as he grows suspicious of every corner, object, and fixture. They all seem to be watching him. Just then, his cautious scan is disrupted by a World ping from Rony.

"Jo, WTF??" pops in the air in bold letters and then dissolves. "You okay??" follows.

Relieved, Jolem leaps to his feet. "Rony! Man, I'm glad to hear from you. I need to meet up," he dictates, then swings his words back to Rony's World.

Moments later, Rony replies. "I'll create a private room," he offers, but Jolem shoots him down. "No. Live."

Without an immediate response, Jolem nervously bounces around his room. The dragging seconds pass like hours.

"Jo. I don't think so. You caused a shit storm the other night."

"Please, man. I need someone to talk to. Someone I can trust."

Again, Jolem waits. This time even longer.

"Meet me at Prospect Park at the Audubon entrance in an hour. But Jo. Be cool."

"Okay. See ya soon."

Nestled only a short distance outside of the bustling city, Brooklyn's Prospect Park urban Audubon seems like a thousand miles away. With gorgeous views, nature trails and diverse wildlife, it's a popular local getaway for families and nature enthusiasts. During the day, children frolic through its acres of picturesque green landscapes as the sounds of waterfowl and migrating songbirds fill the air like a musical.

About an hour has passed since Jolem and Rony communicated. Leaning over on an old wooden bench next to the park's historic boathouse, Jolem waits for his friend. As he impatiently rocks, he spies parkgoers casually sailing by, mostly engulfed in their Worlds. His suspicious eyes leap from person to person. He trusts no one.

A small chipmunk creeps across his path, stops, lifts on his hind legs, and then with his nose in the air, glances at Jolem. "What are you looking at?" Jolem mumbles. He augments an imaginary hawk that dives out of the sky to attack the helpless creature. In reality, the oblivious chipmunk sniffs around, slowly turns, and hops away.

To Jolem's relief, before long, he spots Rony rolling around the corner. Without his typical loud, attention-grabbing apparel, Rony glides inconspicuously down the cobbled walkway with his head down. This time, he wants to go unnoticed.

"Jolem. What's goin' on?" mutters Rony as they meet. With his hands in his pockets, he nods instead of reaching out for their usual embrace. "You okay? You don't look so good."

"Yeah, yeah, I'm okay. Here. Sit down," Jolem says, motioning to the bench. Suddenly he pops back up like his seat is on fire. "NO – no, no, let's walk. Come on," he says, tugging Rony's shirt.

"JO Jo, what's up??" snaps Rony repelled. "I mean, you're acting stranger than you used to when we were kids."

Jolem inhales, drops his head back and expels it out into the air. "Hear me out before you shut me down," he cries. "I need your help."

"Uhh ohh, I don't like where this is going. What??"

"I only ask you this because you have a voice – a following. People listen to you."

"Yeah, annnnd??"

Jolem takes another deep breath in preparation for Rony's backlash. While his heart pounds, he slowly exhales. He cautiously scans the surroundings, turns Rony's way and then whispers, "The Path, Rony – The Path. Something's not right."

Rony throws his hands wildly in the air. "Are you out of your fuckin' mind, man??" he shouts. "People were BRUTAL the other night. My SIV took a major hit just because you're my friend. I tried to defend you and got crushed. I shouldn't even be here right now!"

With his hands raised, Jolem lunges to silence Rony. "Shhh man – shhh. They can hear you," he mumbles.

"Jolem, get off me, man," Rony snarls, pushing away. "And just for the record – I think you need help. I love The Path." He starts to glide off, but Jolem chases behind him.

"Rony, please. Just hear me out," he pleads. "We are being monitored and controlled like…like…MACHINES. We go where we're told to go and do what we're told to do. I know things are peaceful, but – but is this living? And what about the low SIVs? They sit at home and barely leave their Worlds. It's like they don't exist. With this merger, the FDEC will have even more power."

Moving a step ahead, Rony seems to ignore everything Jolem says. He finally swings his head back in frustration and glares. "Jolem, please… you're really losing it, bro. It's a good life. You need help."

Jolem pants as if he's just run a marathon. With arguments growing more passionate, his words are rapid and erratic. "And…and back to the accident. A fake?? Open your eyes, man! Someone's trying to cover up the truth. Something's going on!"

"Jolem, I don't know, man – I just don't know. And so what? The accident was extremely unfortunate, but it was an accident, and everyone's okay. I don't have the answers, but I don't care. Jolem, listen to yourself. You had the world at your feet. Good job, family, and Pati. Now look at you. You're a mess."

When he hears Pati's name, Jolem's discourse changes, and he becomes quiet. Drifting between his high and low feelings for her, he doesn't immediately have a response. "Hmmm. Sometimes…it's weird, and maybe it was just me, but…but sometimes, I felt she didn't love me; she just loved us."

"Jo. That's lunacy. Do you hear yourself?"

Thinking about his and Pati's relationship takes Jolem on a brief emotional ride. Quickly, his attention shifts back to his mission. He straightens sternly like a basic training drill sergeant. "Listen, Rony. You have the platform to reach people," he asserts, pointing his finger into Rony's chest. "To open their eyes. You can do something to make a change. Guess who I bumped into – Leema!"

"Leema??"

"Yes – and she didn't recognize me."

With desperation in his eyes, Jolem wraps his case. He's hopeful after his passionate plea; he's enlisted an ally in his pursuit of justice. Rony sucks his teeth and drops his head. His long, mangled hair falls in front of his face. For a period, he doesn't say anything.

"Rony??"

Rony's head theatrically flips up and his hair swings back away from his face. "Jolem, I say this because I love you like a brother," he begins gently. "Stop. I can't listen anymore. Just stop. The other night we heard some of the greatest updates and most inspiring Path announcements in history. Maybe the Divide got you…I don't know. But, for your own good, you need to recommit yourself to your Opeateazone, cling to Pati's side and realize how good life truly is. It's not too late."

Rony's odd dramatic speech causes Jolem to flinch. "Huh?? Rony, how did you know about my Op…what's goin' on, man??" Abruptly, his body tenses and his eyes grow large like saucers. "What a min – Rony, are you live??"

"Jolem – I'm sorry, but I had to show my people where I stood. It's a good life. You've got to stop this bro."

"Shit, man. SHIT! The FDEC, The Path, they're listening!"

"What?? The Path is not vindictive, Jo. The FDEC only wants what's best – for everyone. Let them help you."

"RONY, WHAT DID YOU DO??"

Shaking his head pitifully, Rony reaches out to his besieged friend. "Jolem, I received an Advisory Alert to help you. All you have to do is recommit yourself. Your SIV will tick back up and The Path will set you free."

"Rony, I can't believe you did this!!" cries Jolem beginning to slide backward. His SIV rapidly declines at the same time as positive support causes Rony's SIV to rise. Jolem turns and frenzies out of sight. He can't believe he didn't make sure Rony's World was silenced during their discussion. He was unaware their entire exchange was being publicly broadcast like an after-school drama.

Jolem shoots through the park as fast as his IGliders will propel him. He makes his way into a secluded forest area out of range from others. There's no escape from The Path's sight, but the wooded location could give him a little cover from some drones and cameras. Scurrying down, he slides under the branches of a large elm and then falls back against its solid bark. His head lifts and his deflated body slides to the ground. "J – I don't know what to do."

As Jolem slumps over, his mind is in a tailspin. Everything once secure is now slipping through his grasp. His SIV has been steadily slipping, Pati left him, he's been demoted, and an FDEC summons waits for his response. Virtually overnight, his life has been flipped upside down.

"Go dark, J," Jolem instructs and then grips his scalp like he's trying to rip into his skull. Moments later, he's more than surprised when his dormant World reactivates. While familiar calm winds and soft tones of nature again whistle, the woman's gentle voice returns.

"Jolem, when you reunited with a ghost from your past, were you confused?

When you parted with your girlfriend, were you conflicted?

When thinking about your future, are you concerned?

Remember Jolem – you're not alone."

The intimate message ends almost as it did before, but this time, she leaves parting words.

"There's help; call the Red Zombie."

When Jolem's AllVu returns to dark, he stares ahead, shell-shocked. There is no longer any ambiguity. It's clear now that the person responsible for his run-in with Leema is the same person behind these coded communications. His old hacker friend Gank.

Six years have gone by since they've last spoken. It's puzzling why Gank has popped back into his life. His eyes shut and he releases a long-burdened sigh. He's quickly running out of time and options. Gank's offer of help may be his last hope. He awakens his AllVu and then sends a coded message to the zombie World of a woman named Ms. Red. To a select few, she's otherwise known as the "Red Zombie."

Resting under the grand elm tree, Jolem watches the descending sun paint the sky a tinted orange. His fingernails spontaneously dig into the dirt around the edges of the highly exposed tree roots. He has no idea how and when Gank will respond to his call, but he knows to expect the unexpected. With his message out in cyberspace, all he can do now is wait. He fights to keep his heavy eyelids open as his head leans back. Before long, the day will come to an end, but the night is just beginning.

THE RED ZOMBIE

31

"Jolem, wake up," whispers softly like the gust of a calm autumn breeze.

He jumps up and peeks around, but all he sees is endless white. "Huh??" he mumbles, battling confusion. "Am I dreaming?"

"No, you're not dreaming," an unfamiliar voice continues. "You're almost woke."

"Who? What??"

"It's me, the Red Zombie."

Jolem releases a long-relieved breath. "Man, you don't know how happy I am to hear those words."

"Jo, listen. This connection is secure, but only for a few minutes. I've taken this communication into a room deep into your World and distracted SEE. Soon it'll recognize an abnormality and try to break in. Your assistant is asleep."

"Just tell me what to do."

"I fell back years ago to let you do ya' thing. When I saw what happened at Rony's party, I knew you'd soon need a hand. Staying in compliance for people like you and me is next to impossible. Sorry to say, we knew this was goin' to happen."

"We??"

"Yeah, you know, Divergent State. We've been talking about you bro. I had to make a case to bring you in."

"But why is all this happening now? For six years, I've been – okay.

Why now?"

"Jo, we don't have much time…were you taking Opeateazone?"

"Yeah."

"Opeateazone helps the government keep pre-deviants in line. Stunts your ambitions and intensifies your need for connections."

"Uhh…could it have made me feel closer to Pati?"

"Of course. It's designed to strengthen those bonds. Love, work, family. Once you stop, it takes days, sometimes weeks, for it to completely get outta' ya system. It could leave unpredictable side effects like hallucinations and insomnia. Are you still taking it?"

"No. I stopped – over a week ago."

"Is that when you started to feel different?"

"Hmmm…no. It was before then. I can remember some odd shocks. Afterward, I just felt I needed to stop."

"Okay. Okay. Those were neuro shocks. Happens when somethin' traumatic triggers your mind to reject Opeateazone's stimulants. Anythin' unusual happen lately?"

"I don't – I can't remember."

"Jo, THINK!"

"Welll – it first happened after Liz's graduation. At dinner. I…I thought I was losing my mind."

"Jo, you're not crazy. There's heavy stuff happening behind the scenes. You have no idea."

While rubbing his face, Jolem releases a heavy grunt. "I need to know what's goin' on. My life is falling apart."

"Listen – I'm goin' to be honest with you. For some reason, you're REAL hot right."

"What?? Why?"

"I don't know, but soon, you'll have some very important decisions to make. I've got the go to bring you into the Lore. From there, I can give you the information you're looking for."

Jolem's head slowly nods. "Let's do it."

Suddenly, Gank's pitch distorts high and then sharply back to normal. "Okay, Jo. Sorry to say, but our time is just about up. I can feel SEE breaking in. Remember – you're on their radar and being monitored – closely, but if you keep your cool, you should be fine until your summons deadline. Make your way to Prospect Park subway station and hang tight. Like before, I'll send a ride to pick you up."

"Got it."

"Jo…"

"Yeah?"

"Stay calm and try not to draw any attention. I'll do what I can to try to distract SEE. Now you're woke."

Gank's altered voice withers away, and the white simulated scene slowly morphs back to the reality of Jolem's woodland surroundings. As real-world sensations return to him, he feels a numbness in his legs from hours of sitting on the rough tree bark. With a breath, he pushes himself up off the ground and then brushes away the collected dirt and other debris from his pants. His head tilts to the side, and he stretches out the stiffness of his aching neck. He glances at the running timer augmented in the air. With less than fourteen hours to go before his summons deadline, time is not on his side.

Jolem carefully emerges from his tree hideaway out into the open. The darkened sky is speckled with lights of stars, drones and Zumer aircrafts. The earlier family noise and park activity disappeared with the sunset. They're now replaced with the intermittent whispers and creaks of nature's invisible critters. Jolem's head drops, and his hands slip into his pockets as he begins to roll through the quiet green landscape. It's largely empty with the exception of the slow drifter casually passing by, consumed in their World. Without making any sudden movements, Jolem flows to the meeting point, which is only a couple blocks away.

"Jolem – where are we going?" questions J. After reanimating, his sidekick's data is off-track.

"J, sorry ole' buddy, but I think we're about to go on a bumpy ride."

"Jolem, I don't understand."

"Well, J…that makes two of us."

Jolem carefully slides down the graveled, windy path toward the exit. His heart is racing. The short journey through the serene natural park seems to stretch and he doesn't feel he's getting any closer. In the horizon, you can see streetlights and city building silhouettes, but they appear miles away.

"Jolem, where are we going? You should stop for a moment and take some deep breaths," J recommends.

"No, J. I need to keep moving."

Anxious minutes pass, and Jolem finally leaves the wooded area behind. He approaches the sidewalk edge of the cross street between the park and his landmark. With the transit station a stone's throw away, he stands motionless, nervously viewing the old structure. There's an eerie silence in the air that causes his limbs to spontaneously flinch. Out of his peripheral vision, he carefully peeks down the endless, dark, barren road. First, he spies to his left and then to his right. He's alone but knows The Path's invisible eyes are watching his every maneuver.

A long dry breath seeps out of his barely cracked, open mouth as he prepares to get moving. The road appears empty when he slips out into the street in the direction of the station. Suddenly, a set of headlights beam out of the darkness and then moves in his direction. Quickly, he recoils back onto the sidewalk just as a dark mini Zumer van comes to a screeching stop in front of him. Its side door swings up and a slumped hooded figure dressed in all black sitting back in the shadows, gestures inward. "Jolem – slow and easy, get in," a deep digitally distorted voice directs.

"Huh?" Jolem utters reluctantly. "Who are you?!"

"This isn't trivia, man," the stranger croaks. "You either get in, or you don't. I'm leaving in twenty seconds."

Jolem again peers down both directions of the empty street. He straightens his posture and clears his throat. Cautiously, he moves into the van and into the seat across from his mysterious company. The door slides down and then off they go. Fidgeting nervously, Jolem canvasses the van interior. Before he can react, his escort launches toward him.

"Waooow – what's goin' on?" cries Jolem, bracing. His companion's hood swings back and to Jolem's surprise, she's a woman.

"I need you to sit still; I have to do something," she instructs and then pulls out a tiny contraption similar to the Opeateazone dispenser.

"What – Opeateazone??"

"Nooooo, but this is for OUR protection. It will prevent your World from leaving a trail to the Lore. We've already remote-scrambled your AllVu signal. If you're coming, I've got to do it. Your choice."

"Uhhh…okay…go ahead," Jolem relents, dropping his hands. After a quick flash, a second later, it's done.

"Okay," she says, falling back while her deep digitized voice returns to its natural tone. "I'm Mighty Mite."

Jolem nods. "Good to meetchu."

Leering at Jolem, Mighty Mite twists her jet-black lips. "Jolem, you're about to get a crash course in The Path. The world you know is about to get rocked."

Jolem glances at a passing street sign and flinches. "Brownsville Recovery Zone?? Is that where we're goin?"

"That's right. Sit back and enjoy the ride."

Dipped low in his seat, Jolem glares out of the window as they inch through the sullen East Brooklyn neighborhood. Still untouched by the sweeping gentrification seen throughout much of the country, Brownsville is like a ghost town. Its tall dilapidated, red-brick, old public housing buildings and shuttered storefronts have been vacant for decades. Trash and abandoned, broken-down vehicles still linger along the crumbling roads and sidewalks. Etched on the walls, old street art paints a painful story of a civil war of people against a technology invasion.

"Looks real lovely, doesn't it?" cracks Mighty Mite while Jolem looks on, astonished.

"I thought…The FDEC…said these zones were redeveloped and people were happy, comfortable," questions Jolem.

"That's what they say, right? We wanted you to see it for yourself. Have you ever met anyone from a recovery zone?"

"No."

"Didn't think so."

"Where is everyone?"

"Be patient; you'll see."

Without much more conversation, they continue from block to block until they approach a street of boxed glass buildings. With amazement, Jolem looks at the dull exteriors of the endless rows of single-family homes. The structures don't require much energy and their occupants receive little attention. Most of the inhabitants come from legacies of poor and struggling families, but today they need for nothing.

"Ahh... here we are," comments Mighty Mite. "Box O' People. That's what we call 'em."

"This is where they live?"

"Yep. These buildings are filled with low SIVs. They spend the majority of their days locked away in their Worlds. If you saw one, I bet you couldn't tell em' apart from bots. The government keeps increasing their time limits in their Worlds and they basically live virtual lives. As long as they're absorbed in their fantasies, they don't complain. In cities all across the country, they're out of sight and out of mind."

As they creep down the road, Jolem's face is glued to the window. They turn the corner and slow at the street side in front of an abandoned old church. The entrance of the one-level white-brick building is littered with a decayed cross and other fallen artifacts from a mostly discarded religion.

"Okay honey, we're home," wisecracks Mighty Mite.

"Here? This is the Lore?"

"Jolem the Lore is not a place; it's a state of mind. It's the TRUTH. This is just where we meet."

"And... The Path won't see us??"

"We're constantly misdirecting SEE to mask our movements. Jamming drones and cameras, adding false scenarios in The Path. For short periods of time, we can do anything. The Path is a program, so glitches happen. We patch everything back together with artificial data, so The

Path just overlooks these abnormalities." Mighty Mite stops and glares at Jolem. "Anyone ever tell you, you ask lots of questions?" she asks.

"Well – yeah."

"Hmmm."

The van pulls to the side of the curb and its door swings open. Mighty Mite edges up in her seat and clinches her jaws. "Take a deep breath and on the count of 3, walk past the front door to the side entrance. Okay?"

"Okay"

"Ready? 1 – 2 – 3."

Jolem slips out and cautiously hops around to the side of the building with Mighty Mite following closely behind him. Within moments they're at the entrance. The door is an older design, and it doesn't automatically open when they approach it. Without slowing his stride, he runs right into it.

"Ohhoww," he yelps, grabbing his head. "It's broken." Panting, he looks it up and down. "What do we do now?"

Mighty Mite cuts her eyes to him and then lifts her hand to the door. In a flash, fluorescent lights circulate her fingertips and then it slides open. "Jolem – the questions, man."

"Sorry."

"Let's go."

She shakes her head and then briskly leads him through the dull corridor. In no time, they make it into the open congregation hall. Sucking in air, Jolem tries to catch his breath as he scans the large room for Gank. Towards the front pulpit, he spots the backs of a few hanging in an intense conversation. It's been years since Jolem's seen his friend, but without a doubt, he picks Gank's stout presence out of the group.

Jolem edges forward, and Gank leaps up. While rubbing his thick scruffy facial hair, Gank sparks an award receiver's smile. The fluorescent tattoos that wrap his arms shine like reflectors. "Jolem, my man," he welcomes with a deep cracked northern accent. His arm spreads open to showcase the room, "Welcome to the Lore!"

The reunited duo moves together and lock fists.

"This is crazy," Jolem says as his eyes circulate the room. The repurposed scene resembles an old colorful Silicon Valley tech space.

"This is where the magic happens, Jo," Gank says, bobbing his head proudly. He points to the eclectic group of four he was just engaged with. Collaborated in a tight circle, they form 3-D holographic objects with their hands that they then throw in the air to illustrate their points. These shapes hover, expand and morph on demand and then quickly dissolve after being swiped away. It's a dynamic flow of conversation.

"The guy talking is Mitnic…" Gank begins, but as Jolem starts forward to interrupt the brainstorming session, Gank quickly shuts him down. He shoots out his arm in front of Jolem, stunting his movements. "Nah, nah, man – don't stop the flow. Don't ever stop the flow," he scolds, holding him back. "Give em' a minute. When they're finished – I'll introduce you."

Gank shakes his head and peers chastising to Jolem before continuing. "Sooo like I was saying – that's Mitnic; he's insane with simulations and manipulating alternates. Over there, to his right, is AdrianLulz. This girl is the shit; BELIEVE IT. Takeovers are her thing." He peeks back at Jolem, "You can thank her for getting you here," he quips with a smirk and approving single head nod.

"Next, on the other side, we have Nut. Don't get in his way – SERIOUSLY," Gank warns sternly. "This guy can make you disappear like you never existed. And lastly, you already know Mighty Mite. She got her name from an ol' school cartoon. The stuff she comes up with is stratospheric!"

"Wow, is this everyone?"

Looking back, glancing condescendingly, Gank again contorts his lips. "Bro, are you serious?? Divergent is everywhere! This is just a satellite location. We're squatting in this spot for a while and then we're out. This is our local crew, but we've got connections all over the country, my man."

"Damn."

"WOKE!"

Jolem and Gank are only feet behind the deliberating group, but it's like they're invisible. They don't even look their way. Jolem grins silently in awe of the collective talent in front of him. After years dragging through the dulled days of The Path, being in the presence of passionate conversation and unique personalities has him feeling a natural high.

"They're serious," comments Jolem. He's never seen a deep exchange like this before. Gank peers to Jolem, "Like I said – don't stop the flow," he chastises and then moves Jolem through the vibrant floor. Like a hiring manager conducting an interview, Gank proudly points out artifacts and the benefits of association. It seems the more he speaks, the more enthusiastic he grows for their cause.

After a few more minutes, the gathering finally breaks. Gank twists his lips and pats Jolem on the chest. "Okay bro, you ready to meet the crew?"

"I'm ready."

Reaching his arm around Jolem's back, Gank grabs his shoulder and pulls him towards the group. "Everybody, this is my boy Jolem. He's a straight-up genius even if he doesn't know it."

Jolem humbly nods as, one by one, they walk over to pay their respects.

"Jolem, you need to get them strings out ya back," Mitnic comments snidely as they fist bump. Lifting his head, he slips back his dark hood. "You not tired of Big Eye yet??"

Without a word, Jolem grips his hand and nods in silent agreement.

"Did you enjoy your ride here?" sarcastically adds AdrianLulz as she swings back the long multi-color dreadlocks that run down the right side of her face. The entire left side of her head is shaved, almost bald. At Gank's request, she was responsible for Jolem's Zumer escort. As a take-over expert, she can affect traffic as she wishes, misdirecting and manipulating routes without at all altering The Path.

"That was you, huh?" Jolem asks.

"Yup," she gruffly confirms as she crosses the arms of her petite but intimidating exterior.

"Well, it was not bad at all," he plays along, nodding respectfully.

She rubs her hands together and then cups them tightly. "You gotta be crazy special to make it into the Lore," she says. When she releases her grip, she exposes a vivid, glittering butterfly. Jolem is captured by its luminance as it flutters out of AdrianLulz's palm. Then, like a miniature firework, it blasts into infinite chromatic pieces in the air. His eyes swing back to AdrianLulz and catches the extended middle finger on the backside of her t-shirt as she drifts away.

The tribal ribbing continues like a college frat initiation as Mighty Mite, and Nut each offer their own personalized salutations. Not many strangers have mingled among their ranks or even stepped foot in their secret locations. Discretion and anonymity have allowed them to flow in and out of the Path like thieves in the night. Cynically and critically, they've questioned Gank's judgment about bringing in an outsider. However, after years of dedication, he's earned their trust and the benefit of their doubts.

The eclectic group moves about, leaving Jolem standing alone next to Gank. "Okay Gank, lay it on me."

Gank stalls before speaking, takes an extended breath and then slams his hands together. His demeanor becomes serious. "Take a walk with me," he says, pulling Jolem farther away from the others. "Okay then. Stick with me because it's a lot," he begins. "You ready?"

"As ever."

"Okay. So, there are aspects of The Path few are aware of. The most important and unknown is the list."

"Huh? The list?"

"Yeah. Its actual name is the Sui Generis List and it is fundamental to the behaviors of The Path."

"The Sui Generis List?? What's that?"

"Okay, technically, the Sui Generis List provides legal protection for a unique group of individuals deemed essential to the continued prosperity of society. It was designed to preserve the "elite," the "crème de la crème" geniuses, and remarkable talents. Those with the highest SIVs. If someone is designated to the "list," The Path has a directive to protect their existence at all costs; even at the detriment of others."

"What??" gasps Jolem. The confirmation of his suspicions leaves him shocked.

"What happened in the car crash was a result of the list," continues Gank.

"So, it wasn't fake?"

"Woke. The Path was definitely acting to protect him. What happened with Leema years ago was a result of the list, and it's happening in incidents all across the country."

"So, The Path was protecting her – from me?"

"Woke. And she probably didn't even know."

"And yesterday – it was you who led me to her, but why?"

"I thought you should know – the truth."

Exhausted and relieved, Jolem's chin falls to his chest. The mounting weight from all his hysterics, for the moment, eases from his shoulders. "So now what?" he says, looking back over to Gank. "Something has to be done. The public needs to know."

For a moment, Gank scratches his head in thought. "Jo – most of the population has no clue and probably wouldn't even care. Many members of the list aren't aware they're on it or that it even exists."

"I don't understand. Doesn't this go against the binding Total Life Path's Laws of Conduct?"

"Yes and no. Let me back up a li'l' to try to explain," Gank says and pats Jolem on the chest." Stick with me. So, you know, The Path was originally designed as a strictly utilitarian system. Its doctrine was that an action is right if it promotes happiness and benefits the greater good of all. There was no bias. The Path was designed to treat every person equally. The list would contradict this.``

"RIGHT... and??"

Well, early architects of the system also knew this doctrine left room for future manipulation and corruption, so The Path was programmed to save its OWN existence as the exception. Survival of The Path was considered to be the greatest good of all."

"Yeah, the Total Life Path's Laws of Conduct exception."

"Well, Utilitarianism worked fine for a little while, but soon an internal debate began while designing The Path version 2 when many influential people proposed quality over quantity. They asked; why should individuals who contributed much to society receive the same consideration as those who added little. They argued that these high contributors were essential to the continued happiness and prosperity of society and the ultimate survival of The Path. Therefore, this new direction supported the exception. They won the debate and this was the birth of the first Sui Generis List. Leading this effort was…"

"Director Dalio."

"WOKE. At the time, he was a young Path Architect and came up with the original concept behind the Sui Generis List."

"Wow man; are you fuckin' kidding me right now?? How does someone get on this list?"

"Early versions of The Path were programmed to recognize "unique" individuals by a complex matrix which gave these people extremely high SIVs. If their SIVs met a certain threshold, they were deemed 'essential' and automatically added to the list. And if that was not bad enough, there's more. About twenty years ago, a back door was created so that the FDEC council could use its discretion to place individuals on the list regardless of SIV. Over the years, the list has ballooned to include business executives, prominent government officials, celebrities, and it goes on and on."

"And Congress is okay with this??"

"Jo – everyone in Congress and their immediate family members have lifetime appointments to the list. They're not going to do or say anything. People who know believe in all of this. It's their dogma."

Jolem stops to think and then winces. "How do you know all this??" he asks.

"A few years ago, we came across some information about a young politician who earlier initiated a report detailing his concerns. He saw rapidly increasing deviations while promotions were significantly decreasing. High SIVs were continuing to live richer, more fulfilling lives, while low SIVs were spending more time in their alternates being maintained like cattle in a herd. And last but certainly not least, the numerous suspicious deaths and disappearances of individuals in conflict with the FDEC. He called for an independent counsel to investigate corruption within the FDEC and manipulation of The Path. He wanted to challenge the merits of the list. The report directly implicated Dalio."

"And what happened with the report??"

"Nothing. One evening while riding home from his office, his Zumer malfunctioned, ran off the road, and he was killed. His name was Senator Waslo. The report disappeared."

"The Elon S5. So that's what happened."

"Woke."

"This is mind-boggling! Sooo – what can be done about all this?? We've got to tell people."

"Jolem, we're still trying to figure this all out. We're not Freedom Fighters; we're hackers. Here and there, we've been able to make an impact, obstructing The Path when we can, but…but – I don't know. People are happy. Everybody is in their own world, and nobody cares. How do you save people who don't want to be saved?"

"So that's it?? Are you connected with the Divide?"

Gank stops, grabs his jaw and emits a loud grunt. "Jo, that's a whole other story," he replies wearily, shaking his head. "No. We don't know much about them either. But their skills are top-notch, and they didn't go through all that trouble for nothing. We're combing the net for info and reaching out to our connects, but no one knows anything about 'em.' It's crazy."

"Wow."

"Woke. I told you there was a lot goin' on behind the scenes."

Gank pauses and pats Jolem on the chest. "Ya know it's time you made another decision," he says, peering sternly.

Jolem sways from side to side as his hands slip into his pockets. "Okay, what's on ya' mind?"

"You know Jo, unlike the brainless herd in The Path, you…me…" he pans the room with his open arm. "We…we're all different. We think – differently. You can feel it. You can see it. You knew something was not right, but you couldn't put your finger on it. Why don't you drop this charade and run with us?? We have a lot of work to do and could use your skills, man."

While releasing a slow gust of air through his lips, Jolem rocks back on his heels. As his sights circulate the inviting environment, the provocative idea of joining the group twists him in knots. He closes his eyes and his head drops lethargically forward.

"Gank, I don't know."

"You DON'T know what??"

"Man, I'm a wreck," he says, shaking his head. "Everything I do goes to shit. And…what about my mom…my sister? I can't put them at risk."

"Jo – do you really want to keep playing this game, bro? Look at yourself. They're already at risk. I'm going to drop something real heavy on you. During your realignment, you'll be forced to recommit yourself to The Path and take a high dosage of Opeateazone that will help you forget your anxieties. You'll be lulled back to how you were weeks ago. You won't have a choice. Is that what you want?"

"And if I refuse?"

"'If you refuse'??! Man, I don't know what's goin' to happen. But The Path does not have loose ends."

Gank glances over his shoulder to AdrianLulz, who's leaning against the wall. He shakes his head, and she nods in return. "Bro, you have one of two options," he continues. "Either you become one of The Path's puppets, or you become a deviant outcast. There's no in-between."

"I need some time to think."

Like a phantom, AdrianLulz slides next to Jolem and grabs his arm. Unlike Gank, she's a lot more direct. "Jolem, are you serious??" she gripes.

"AdrianLulz, you just don't understand."

"No, YOU don't understand," she lashes back. "I told GHotz bringing you here was a bad idea…"

THE PATH

Jolem shifts his body and looks up into the ceiling while Gank silently stands near. With his arms crossed and again scratching his beard, Gank monitors Jolem's reactions as AdrianLulz continues to tear into him. "Lulz!" Gank finally interrupts, "That's enough," he calmly says. "It's cool. You can't wake someone who doesn't want to be 'woke.' Get him a Zumer."

Blaring at Jolem, AdrianLulz shakes her head in dismay. The colorful rings of her mood necklace turn fire-red. She connects her fingertips and then extends them, pulling out a large holographic dashboard in the air. "Okay, Jolem, your ride will be here in 3 minutes," she says after a few swipes and plugs. "Just like before, we'll misdirect The Path. None of your communication or tracking mechanisms will be active. When you make it home, I'll mask you and jam near drone or video signals for about 5 minutes, giving you enough time to get in the house without being visually detected. Your World will re-activate at that point. We'll throw a few false experiences in your history so your assistant will have no record of anything out of the normal. You got it?"

"Yeah, I got it."

"Okay, Cool – Gank…"

"Jo," Gank utters before taking an extended pause. Rubbing his beard, he pats Jolem on the chest again. "Listen bro; there's one more thing."

Jolem's breaths become more rapid as he holds on to the edge of Gank's words. He doesn't have a good feeling about what's to come.

"Jo, by being here, you now have a lot of sensitive information stored in your brain. Intel that could be devastating to my organization if it were in the wrong hands."

"Gank – you know I wouldn't rat on you!"

"Yeah, I know, I know, but there's too much at stake here. We MUST be protected. I had to agree to certain conditions to bring you here."

"Conditions??"

"So, listen – have you ever heard of a blue bomb?"

"Uhh – no."

"Okay, well, decades ago, when we had physical banks and before our credit system, robbers would enter these buildings with guns blazin' and demand the workers fill up their bags with paper currency they called 'money'. So, it's a wild, crazy scene and everyone's spooked out. At some point, while these thieves are distracted, the worker dumps a little bomb in the bag."

"Okay…"

"Sooo these robbers are riding down the street giddy with all this money they just stole, but a few minutes later, the bomb explodes and there's this blue ink all over it. Now it's useless. They can't spend it, and all their effort went for nothin'. You get me??"

"Uhhh – Gank, what's this got to do with me??"

"Jo – that shock we gave you in the ride over… it was a blue bomb."

"WHAT??"

"Believe me – I hated to do it. Buuut, should you get compromised and someone attempts to extract today's experiences, it'll blow. All of our interactions will be completely replaced from your memory and leave no digital footprints. There will be no signs this ever happened, plus, it'll send a virus back to the extractor."

"Are you serious, Gank!?"

"Sorry, bro. This is the way it had to be."

Jolem seethes like a raging bull fuming with anger. He feels just as manipulated by Gank as he has been by The Path. "Gank, I gotta go, 'bro'. You know, I didn't ask for any of this."

As Gank steps backward, his tight squint remains locked with Jolem's eyes and then he coyly remarks, "Jo – you've been asking for all of it for a long time." He shrugs, turns and steps away. "I thought you were awake, my friend, but I was wrong. You're still sleepwalking. I guess after tomorrow's realignment, you won't remember any of this anyway. If you come to your senses before then, you know how to find me," he caustically swipes as a parting dig. "If not, it was good knowing you bro."

Without words to say, Jolem stands in silence with his jaw dropped. From his backside AdrianLulz grips his arm, nudging him backward.

"Your Zumer is waitin'," she growls. "C'mon, let's go."

During the gloomy trip out of the room and down the hall, there's no conversation between the two. AdrianLulz follows a step behind, escorting Jolem to the front door like a guard releasing a captive. Ironically, when he steps out into the still evening air, the outside feels more like the prison. He's uncomfortably stuck between two worlds which both welcome and reject him at the same time. As his Zumer sits at the end of the walkway waiting, Jolem looks out into the vast sky, confused more than ever.

31

The short quiet ride to Jolem's apartment was torturous for him. Gank's words pierced deep. Now at home, leaning over on his sofa, his head hangs low. Nervously, his finger taps against his knee as he considers his next move. While wrestling with this new-found knowledge of the Sui Generis List and confirmation of some of his greatest fears, he wonders how he could possibly shun his responsibility to help the resistance. His father's words of action echo loudly in his mind. Contemptuously, they taunt him like a bully, barking in his ears.

"Hi Jolem, this is SEE with a Path Advisory Alert," interrupts his deep contemplation. "It is now 10:30 PM, and you have only twelve hours remaining before your summons deadline. Please stop what you are doing and make this your top priority. Remember, if you do not reply by 10:30 AM tomorrow, you will be in Deviation."

He exhales, and then his hand moves from his hair down his face past his eyes, nose and over his lips.

"Jolem, are you feeling okay?" asks J.

"Hmmm J, honestly, I don't know. Tired and anxious, but I'm okay."

"You haven't slept well for days. Do you know sleep deprivation can lead to memory issues, lack of concentration, hallucinations and all sorts of other physical problems? You need your rest."

"I know J...I'll be okay."

"Well, one thing is not Okay. You have only twelve hours to respond to your summons. What are you waiting for??"

"I'm just trying to figure some things out."

"Jolem, we went through this hours ago. Let's respond to the summons and reclaim your happiness. The FDEC is waiting to help you."

Jolem doesn't say a word. Instead, he lifts up and flounders through his apartment and into his bathroom. Standing in front of his mirror, staring at his reflection, he thinks about his younger self. That impulsive soul wouldn't have been hard to convince to join Gank. However, today is different. He has so much to lose and not sure what he has to gain. Overwhelmed, his face drops into his palms, and his fingers run through his hair. He wishes he could just disappear.

Slumped against his sink counter, he's so tired he feels he's about to tip over. He's startled when his AllVu calls. It's Liz and he knows she's fully aware of his impending deviation. "Ahhh…accept," he reluctantly mumbles and then her LiveView appears.

"Hi, Jolem. How's it going, big bro?" she asks. She forces a smile, but he can tell it's a lie.

"I'm…ok. What's up? You sound – funny."

"Jolem. I could never get anything past you. I need you to do me a favor."

"Annnd, what's that?"

"Jolem, please contact the FDEC. For me. My SIV is ticking down. Mom's too. We're very concerned."

"Liz…" he begins, dropping his head, "you know I'd do anything for you."

"Then please contact the FDEC and recommit yourself. It's the only way to escape this hell you're in. You look awful and you need help. In The Path, there is so much peace and joy. Please recommit yourself. Trust me. It's best for everyone."

Liz disappears and he's left standing with a stranger staring back at him in the mirror. With bloodshot, swollen eyes, he looks drained and almost unrecognizable. It's as if he's aged years overnight. Like a zombie, he slides into his room and slips onto his bed. Just like Gank said, he has a choice to make. And regardless of what he decides, it'll be both right and wrong.

Following his intense Lore visit and Liz's call, Jolem had another sleepless night. As the dawning sun shines through his glass wall, he remains almost in the same position he's been since he slipped under the sheets. It's early morning and he has a little more than three hours to respond to his summons. This nightmare can end with a simple call to the FDEC, or he can test his fate with Divergent State. He's still not sure what he should or will do.

"Good morning Jolem. Looks like it's going to be another beautiful day in The Path. Are you ready to reply to your summons?"

Jolem slogs off the side of his bed and drags to his window wall. Rubbing his irritated eyes, he watches the rising sun peek over the New York City skyscrapers. He thinks about his mother and Liz.

"Hi Jolem; this is SEE with a Path Advisory Alert. It is now 7 AM and you have only three hours and thirty minutes remaining before your summons deadline. Please stop what you are doing and make this your top priority. Remember, if you do not reply by 10:30 AM, you will be in Deviation."

"J…" Jolem begins hesitantly and then pauses. He drops on the bed and his sight falls to the ground.

"Yes, Jolem?"

Painfully, words drudge out of his mouth. "Reply to…," he begins resigned to his fate, but before he can finish his sentence, his AllVu vibrates and a very unexpected call ices his movements.

"Call from – Leema Dalio," alerts J.

"What?? Leema?!" he questions as his lips curl. The connecting pieces of the complicated puzzle have once again just shuffled.

"Ahhh a – accept," he stutters.

Tense moments extend like rubber bands as he anxiously waits for her first words. Just the day before, she responded to his presence as a stranger and now she's contacting him first thing in the morning. He's curious, but also suspicious.

"Good morning, Mr. McKay," she whispers formally. "I apologize for the early call. Is it okay if I call you 'Jolem'?"

"Goo – ood morning. Lem – ah Ms. Dalio. Yeah, sure. Uh sorry, I sound a little confused, but your call is a real surprise."

"Leema, please," she insists rigidly. "I understand completely, but I was hoping you could assist me with something."

As his anticipation grows by the second, Jolem's brow knots and breaths speed up. "Sure. How can I help?"

"Well, yesterday was, let's say, 'interesting.' I must admit when we met…there was a strange familiarity to you."

"Really?"

"Yes. I was initially stunted due to the obvious. But I saw something in your expression. I could not recognize you; however, I felt we were already acquainted."

"Okay…"

She swallows before continuing because her following words are a challenge for her to even speak. Being a high SIV Regional Director, having unexplained kindred feelings for him is disorienting.

"I'm embarrassed to say, a couple of times throughout the day, I had strange memory flashes. They included you."

When she finishes, Jolem is tongue-tied. She waits for a reply, but he says nothing.

"Uhh Jolem. Does any of this make sense to you?" she asks.

Jolem clears his throat and then inhales slowly. "Leema," he begins while softly releasing the pinned-up air through his nostrils. "Yes – we do know each other."

Leema absorbs the hard-to-believe information during another long, uncomfortable pause. She's experiencing unique feelings somewhere between confusion and disappointment.

"I attempted to reach out to you yesterday," she quivers. Her voice is softer and unsure. "But each time, The Path redirected me. This morning it happened again. Against my assistant's advice, I contacted you. I don't know why, but I needed some answers."

The slow-moving conversation continues to lag with intermittent breaks and soundless delays. Jolem is cautious and distrusting as their past haunts him. Neither really knows what to say.

"I – I have more questions, but I'm being pulled away again," she continues.

"Leema ah I can help, but – but not in our Worlds. It has to be live and it must be this morning."

"Live?? Why live?"

"I – I can't explain."

"Jolem, I don't understand."

"Listen Leema, I can't say much. Not here. And I don't have much time. Can you meet me in an hour?"

"An hour? I don't know. What's going on?"

"All I can say is – I realize you don't think you know me well, but I can explain all this. If you really want the answers, you'll have to trust me."

"I," she begins, but inexplicably, the message is cut short.

"What the?? J – reconnect!"

"Sorry, Jolem. Her World is blocked."

Jolem leaps to his feet and begins to pace his room. A jolt of ambition runs through his body like ice in his veins. He can't give in to The Path. Not like this.

"Jolem, are you ready?" asks J.

"Huh?"

"Weren't you about to reply to your –"

"Not now, J."

"But??"

"NOT NOW!"

The clock is ticking, and precious moments continue to pass. The race is on. Using his thoughts, Jolem pieces together an encrypted World message and sends it to Ms. Red. He's made up his mind.

For almost another thirty excruciating minutes, Jolem nervously glides from room to room, waiting for Gank's reply. Based on the way they parted, he's not even sure his old friend will respond. His thoughts are wild and his fingers erratically tap on his thigh. When he moves out into the hall preoccupied with worry, he almost collides with his HumanAid standing outside his door. "Whooo!!" he shouts.

"Hi Jolem, your breakfast is ready," she says happily, lifting a tray of food to him. "I made your favorite."

"What? No, thanks. I'm not hungry," he says, attempting to move past her. "Jolem – please stop!" she demands and then her voice returns to its soft, cordial tone. She tilts her head and grins. "You must eat your breakfast."

Jolem curiously gazes at his HumanAid's still happy expression. Remaining solidly in his way, her presence blocks him from moving forward. "I said I'm not hungry," he shoots back. Even as he squeezes around her, she doesn't budge.

As he finally eases past her, he glances back. With the tray still raised, she creeps towards him determined. Suddenly, he begins to blink uncontrollably, and his body stiffens like a board. His eyelids slam shut and when they lift back open, his surroundings are again white. "Huh? Gank??" he calls out. This time he realizes he's again in a hidden room in his World.

"Took you long enough, Jo. Are you finally woke?"

"As I'll ever be."

"Ya know time is almost up, Jo. Soon, Compliance Control is goin' to be on your ass."

"I know. Bring me in, man. I'm ready!"

Jolem waits for instruction, but there's a quiet break in the conversation. "G – you there??"

"Man – things have gotten a little more complicated since we spoke. GHotz thinks you're too hot. He wants to cut ties."

"Huh... cut ties?? GHotz??"

"Yeah, you didn't meet him. GHotz's the REAL man around here. He actually recruited me to the crew."

"But why??"

"Jo, with this merger and the Divide – we're all scrambling. He thinks you might bring too much heat our way."

"But then I'm screwed – what can I do now? I'll be a sitting duck."

"I think I can work things out over here, but I need a li'l' more time.

I just need you to take cover for a while. Uhhh…what aboutttt…THE UNCON? The one you went to years ago??"

"Refugio??"

"Yeah, Refugio! Can you go there and hang low?"

"But – it's been so long. They might not even remember me. What about another safe house??"

"That's not wise. I can stick you in a safe house, but like I said, you're hot right now. I'm not sure how long I can keep you hidden from SEE. You'd need a sophisticated persona and I don't have the time to program it right now. We need you outta' The Path ASAP."

"Well, whatever we got to do…let's do it."

"Okay. I need to make some connections to get you out there. Sit tight."

"Gank, wait! There's something I have to do first."

"Jo, you don't have time!"

"I know, I know, but – I need to meet with – Leema."

"What? Leema Dalio? Are you outta ya damn mind, man!? That's LOCO!"

"I know, I know – it's risky, but I promised her. Can you help?"

"Jo man, 'risky'? You're flirting with disaster. A deviant with Diablo's daughter? Do you have any idea what he'll do to you??"

Jolem sucks in and then blows out a deep sigh. "I know. But – I'll be okay."

"Alright then…like I said, sit tight."

Within an instant, Jolem's consciousness returns to his home. "How about some warm tea," offers his HumanAid, propelling a mug his way. Her persistence is startling.

"Uhh…okay," he utters cautiously, lifting the drink from her hands. He slides into the kitchen and leans against the wall. As he carefully blows the steam over his hot drink, paranoia slowly settles in. His suspicious, canvassing eyes see spies in every cabinet and appliance. His HumanAid eerily watching him sends chills down his spine.

"J, I need to get outta here," he cries and drops his mug in the sink.

"Jolem? Where? What about your summons??" J cries, but Jolem ignores his call.

"Do you want a Zumer?"

"NO!" he yells, running to his room. Scurrying to the back of his closet, he reaches down and pulls out his old AirBoard.

"Jolem! What are you doing with that?? It's been years since you've ridden that dangerous contraption."

"J – please!"

Jolem blows past his HumanAid and rushes out of the front door. Without any direction, he leaps on his AirBoard and propels forward. In his mind, observation drones, small and large, seem to appear everywhere.

"J, they're out to get me!" he yells as he speeds off into the street. His thoughts are running ramped. He sees cameras in the trees, neighborhood yards and building signs. Everything and everyone is fixated on him.

"Jolem," shouts J. "Look out!" However, as Jolem maneuvers erratically, J's warning is too late. His head spins around to see the front of a Zumer staring him in the face. Although J is able to alert the Zumer, it can't react quickly enough. As the car screeches to a stop, Jolem runs right into its front side and then he flips over its hood. A stunned gathering, records the latest rare car incident as Jolem lies motionless on the asphalt.

"Jolem! Jolem! Wake-up."

Minutes later, Jolem sluggishly regains consciousness. His scattered thoughts shift uncontrollably, which makes reality hard to grasp. For a brief period, he has no idea where he is, how he got there, or if he's stuck in a dream. "Uhhghh, what happened?" he mumbles incoherently. The Earth is spinning.

"Jolem – please relax. Rescue is on the way," a piercing sound echoes in his head.

"J…I have to keep moving," he mumbles. He can hear the faint noise of rescue sirens racing his way.

Jolem plants his palms on the ground while people implore him to stay still. As he presses up onto his hands and knees, he grimaces with each movement. He's determined to leave the scene, so despite the pain, he continues his struggle. Rescuers are close, but before they arrive, a compact Zumer pushes its way through the throng of people and stops at his side.

"Jo – get in!" shrieks in his ears. "Hurry!"

With all his energy, Jolem wills his way onto his feet and falls into the open Zumer door. And as soon as he's in, it speeds off.

"What the hell, man?!? I told you to sit still and not draw attention," gripes Gank. "You're not making your case any easier."

"You know me man…"

"Listen, there's an old warehouse right on the edge of the Jersey Turnpike. It's a known dead zone for Path signals and observation drones only pass by every few hours. There's a supply shipment going west and you can hitch a ride. We'll try our best to keep SEE off your tracks, but it's becoming trickier. There's been some recent updates to The Path, which is causing us problems with takeovers. We can only interrupt signals for minutes at a time. Leema has a Zumer picking her up in a few minutes. We'll hijack her ride and bring her to you. You'll have a few minutes to talk and then we'll Zumer her out. I can't promise this'll all go down smoothly."

Still trying to catch his bearings, Jolem absorbs Gank's instruction. "Well…let's do it."

"Woke."

THE RACE IS ON

32

When Leema and Jolem's call inexplicably dropped earlier in the day, she immediately attempted to reconnect it. However, his World was blocked to her just as hers was to him. Moments following the interruption, she received an advisory alert. SEE recognized abnormal anxiety levels and recommended Leema take the day off for reflection and relaxation. To help reinforce the suggestion, her assistant reminded her of the beauty and prosperity of her life in The Path. Together, they convinced her to block out the recent events and return her focus to positivity.

It didn't take long for the allures of Leema's World to recapture her. While she sheltered in her world chamber, The Path stroked her subconscious. She's always had a soft spot for nature's furry creatures. Her World's frequent messages and convenient visuals of adorable animals persuaded her that timing was perfect for an animal shelter visit. The welcome idea distracted her thoughts away from Jolem and subdued her.

With her mind in her World, Leema flows down the city streets. Seductive lavender aroma and ambient lullabies fill the air. She's mesmerized by the sight of lovable pups and fluffy kittens frolicking through tall grass. She's suddenly startled when the show stops, and her music is replaced by a strange digitized voice.

"Hello, Leema."

"Huh?? Who's this?" she cries, springing up.

"Who I am is not important. No need for alarm; you won't be harmed."

"Who – who is this?? And what do you want?? Where's Maribelle??"

"I'm sorry, but we had to put your assistant to sleep for a while. Until this is done, you won't be able to communicate with your World."

"Turn me around now! Do you know who I am?!? My father will-"

"Relax. You and I have a mutual friend."

"A 'mutual friend'? Who??"

"Jolem."

"Jolem?? Jolem? Is he responsible for this?"

"We are taking you to him now. For our protection, we must mask your movements from The Path. Please sit back and try to relax. After your visit, you'll return to life as usual. We'll be there shortly."

"Where am I going? Hello…hello??" she continues calling out, but the remainder of her ride is ominously silent. The trip only lasts about ten minutes, but it's the longest she's ever gone without her assistant. Without the comfort of her companion's voice, she's terrified. She's never felt so powerless and alone.

Leema peeks through her window as her Zumer bumbles down the dilapidated graveled road leading to the abandoned warehouse. It curves the roundabout in front of the old building and then slows to a stop. "Hell – hellooo??" she calls, but hears nothing. She flinches when the door she's leaning on swings open to allow her out. She's not sure what to do but hesitantly steps out onto the crumbled ground. As soon as her feet are planted, the Zumer door swings back down and it slips off.

"Wait!" she says, reaching out to the vehicle, but it disappears, kicking up dust, and she's left all alone. ISolated in the still wind, her body trembles with insecurity. Questions swirl and she frantically glances around for Jolem. Without her AllVu, she's fearful he won't make it, and she'll be stranded in the middle of nowhere. "Jolem??"

"Leema! Leema!" softly calls from her rear. "Over here." When she swings around, she spots Jolem crouching and waving next to an old trash bin.

"Jolem!?" she cries, racing to him. "I'm soooo relieved. Wait!! What's going on?? And why is my AllVu deactivated? Jolem, do you know who

I am?? If you're planning –"

"Leema, please!" he shouts, interrupting her. "I'll explain everything. But this was the only way we could talk without being monitored."

"Monitored?? I don't understand. What are you talking about?!"

"Listen, what I'm goin' to tell you, will be hard to believe. But you'll have to trust me."

"Trust you?? You just abducted me. And you want me to trust you?"

"Look! You called ME this morning looking for answers and I promised I'd help," he shoots back. "I'm putting my ass on the line for you. I'll give you the info you want and then a Zumer will swoop you up and take you back to your good life. After that, you'll never have to see me again."

"Okay, I guess you're right, Jolem. I apologize. For some reason, our conversation this morning seems like ages ago. But you're right. I just need to know – who are you?!"

"Leema…" Jolem says as he grips his waist. He sucks in huge breaths of air and, with his head back, releases it like chimney smoke. He knows his coming ideas will not be received well. Slow and cautiously, he begins to detail their brief history together from the beginning. He shares some of the warm feelings he experienced six years ago and how devastated he was when she disappeared without a word. Silently, she listens with empathy and a painful ignorance of it all. She wishes she could feel guilt but has no recollection of any of it.

Fast forwarding to their reconnection a few days ago, he explains to her how shocked he was to see her and how confused he was when she didn't recognize him. He suggests the memory flashes she experienced are side effects of a memory replacement. He speculates seeing him again may have triggered the remaining fragments in her subconscious.

Hardly blinking, she absorbs his story like a sponge. His words are indeed challenging to believe.

"But Jolem…I don't understand. Replacement?? But my memory report doesn't show any replacement? That's impossible."

He takes a pause from his tale and looks up into the air while rubbing his scruffy face. He's also perplexed by unanswered questions. He turns back to her and momentarily gets lost in her familiar eyes. They are so wide they appear as if they're being propped open with stilts.

"Have you ever heard about the Sui Generis List?" he carefully asks.

After a few moments of silence, her blank look and empty response say it all.

"'The Sui Generis List??' What is that?" she inquires innocently, as a child.

He's aware that what he's about to say will be impulsively rejected like the ramblings of the often-scoffed Freedom Fighters. To claim bias in a national system that is supposed to be impartial will be a hard sell and difficult for her to accept. Also, by introducing her to the list, he's implicating her and her prominent father as two of its primary benefactors.

As she sits on the edge, waiting to pounce on the words before they leave his mouth, Leema is experiencing an emotional overload. So much of what she knew to be fact all her life has been challenged and she's conflicted. She's unaware she was in a similar position when they first met years ago.

"Yes – The Sui Generis List. Leema – you're going to need an open mind to receive what I'm about to say."

"Continue…please."

For the next few minutes, Jolem repeats the story Gank told him about the FDEC, The Path and the list. Again, she's a good listener and doesn't offer much except for a slow head nod. When he finishes his story, he sits back and waits on a response, but without words, she just stares confusingly.

"Jolem, this is all CRAZY," she instinctively snaps. "Are you trying to say my father had my memories replaced off the record? That's ridiculous. All this sounds like the fake propaganda of the Freedom Fighters. I can't believe I allowed you to talk me into this. YOU must be one of them."

"Okay, believe what you want," Jolem says, turning away. "This was a mistake. Now I've got to get going."

"Okay, okay wait, Jolem," Leema calls, reaching for his arm. "I'm sorry – just give me a sec…"

In a typical situation like this, her assistant would analyze and provide guidance. Without Maribelle, she's unclear on how to process the information and, ultimately, how to respond.

"You have what you asked for," Jolem shouts. "I don't have much time. Just wait here. As soon as I'm outta' sight, a Zumer will come to pick you up. When you get close to NYC, your World will reactivate. You can go back to your utopia."

"But – where are YOU going??"

"Don't worry about me. I need to disappear for a while till I figure some things out."

"Jolem…" she begins, but as her lips move, her words become muffled. She suddenly feels as if she's going to black out. Everything slowly goes dark, and she gets another memory flash that takes her back in time.

"Leema, I'm not sure what's going on, but I…I really enjoy your company," she recollects a young Jolem insecurely saying as he looked around to avoid her eye contact. "Most of the time, I feel uncomfortable or out of place, and I have no idea why it's different with you – but it is."

A moment later, her recall disappears. Now looking into the same concerned eyes of a more mature and scruffier Jolem, she knows there's some truth to what he's saying. "Jo – Jolem?"

"Leema? Are you okay?"

Without another word, she grabs his shirt, pulls him forward and holds him tight. "I remember…I remember."

Jolem's eyelids slip shut while she's pressed against him. He can feel the rapid beat of her heart up against his. He wants to stay locked in this tender moment, but when his 9:00 AM reminder rings, he pushes away.

"Jol – lem??"

"I'm sorry. I know this is all heavy, and I wish circumstances were different, but I don't have any more time. I really must go."

"Just – just wait a minute."

"Leema! Wait for what??"

"How can you tell me all this – and just – leave??"

"You asked for information, and now you have it."

"Just like that? Sooo – am I going to see you again?"

"I...probably not. I – "

"Please just hold a sec and let me think..."

"Leema..."

"Okay. I'm coming with you."

"Whattt?? Noooo – Leema, that's insane!"

"I'm not asking. My head is all screwed up right now. I'm coming with you. We can figure something out together."

"Leema, that's impossible! You don't even know where I'm going! BELIEVE ME; you need to get as far away from me as POSSIBLE!"

"It doesn't matter. And we're wasting time here debating it."

"What about Diablo – I mean your father??"

"I can handle him."

Jolem slowly shakes his head in disagreement. "Okay then," he sighs. "Let's go."

They brace for the unexpected as they rush to the meet-up spot which is at the building's south parking lot. Leema's never done anything remotely like this before and begins to question her spontaneous decision. Before she has much time to think, in the distance, they spot a vehicle coming their way. An old four-door pickup truck with two passengers in the front seats pulls up and stops about a few feet from them. "Are you my cargo?" stoically asks a man, titling his head out of the left-side window. His untamed beard is so thick they can hardly see his lips. Looking them up and down, he quickly examines them like an old CIA agent. With Jolem's tattered appearance and her fancy, stylish garb, they look like complete opposites.

"Yeah," replies Jolem.

"I was expecting only one."

"Don't worry, she's good. She's good."

The driver rubs his beard, turns to his passenger, and looks back at Jolem and Leema. "Hop in."

When the door slides shut, the driver turns back to his new passengers. "All in? We're out. Names Caster," he remarks and then tips his head to his passenger's seat. "And this is 'Bo.'"

Caster's early-generation robotic friend mechanically turns his head, smiles and welcomes the couple with an exaggerated old mob accent. "Good to meetcha'," he says and then twists back. His puppet-like synthetic features are far from the realism of modern HumanAids and other NonHumans.

Twisting uncomfortably in her worn-out seat, Leema canvasses the strange grimy interior. "What is all this metal stuff?" she asks, wincing in disgust.

"The entire truck is custom lined with a conductive material to help shield my cargo from The Path's signals," replies Castor tapping the roof. "She doesn't look like much, but we'll definitely fly under the radar. While your AllVu is deactivated, SEE won't recognize you aboard. Let's go; it's goin' to be a Li'l' ride. Play beats."

Castor's command launches a melody of deep electric sounds throughout the cabin. The heightening music creates separation between him, Bo and their back-seat passengers. Jolem and Lemma sit uneasily against their prospective doors. There's a huge empty barrier dividing them. Jolem's sights crawl in her direction while hers do the same to his. When their eyes lock, they awkwardly turn back towards their windows. They're in uncharted territory and clueless about what they've gotten themselves into.

The moment Leema's AllVu deactivated, Director Dalio was informed. Back in his Washington DC office, he gazes out his office window wall. Standing firm with his hands locked behind his back, he follows the activity below like watching ants in an ant farm. Impatiently, he waits for SEE's update as to Leema's whereabouts. "So, my daughter has simply disappeared?" he bristles.

"Yes, Director. She was on the way to Happy Animal Society when her signal was abruptly lost and she hasn't been visually detected since."

"Insight…"

"Leema's had recent interactions with the pre-deviant Jolem McKay."

"Hmmm. Jolem McKay. And where is he now?"

"His AllVu has also been deactivated, so his location is unknown. There is also no visual detection. This morning at 8:15 AM, he was involved in a Zumer collision after shortly leaving his home. Another Zumer picked him up, and then, minutes later, both his and the Zumer's signals were lost. Someone is intermittently jamming our camera feeds, and they are most likely using zombies. Their methods are sophisticated. It's highly probable he and Leema are together. However, we can't determine if she is with him willingly or as his captive."

While listening to SEE's words, Dalio seethes as he glares out into the horizon. He's so agitated; he needs a series of slow breaths just to calm down.

"Here is an interesting note," SEE continues. "In fifteen minutes, Mr. McKay will be in deviation. An officer will soon be dispatched to retrieve him."

"So Jolem has finally chosen his lane. How unfortunate – for him. He used to be an itch on my back; a mere annoyance," Dalio murmurs. "We need to send a stronger message; to him and to all who are helping him. Leema's been tagged, so we won't need AllVu to find her. She'll just take a little longer to track."

33

It's 10:29 AM and one minute before Jolem's summons deadline. In mere moments, he'll become an official Path Deviant. As he watches the seconds tick by, his teeth grit and fingers tap uncontrollably against his leg. He's unaware if Castor, Bo, or Leema, know of his situation and the danger he's put them in. As 10:30 AM arrives, he holds his breath and closes his eyes tightly. To his relief, the moment comes and goes without notice.

Jolem's eyes pry open and then the captured air blows out his barely open mouth. He scratches his head and peeks over at Leema. Oddly, she's twitching and churning against the car door like a drug addict suffering from withdrawal. "Are you okay?" he asks.

"Yeah, I'm – okay. But the silence is killing me. I mean – I need to know what's going on in my World. I've never been without Maribelle before. How are you so okay??"

"I don't know. I like being away from all the noise. It bothers me sometimes."

Staring at him, she twists her lips. "Hmmm, weird."

"That word again, huh?"

"What??"

"You used to always call me weird."

Leema uncomfortably smirks. "It's because you are," she jabs. "Jolem, although I can't remember my Track Realignment or what followed; hell, it's hard to believe I ever even had a Track Realignment, but…I'm sorry for causing you any pain. I share joy. I don't like to take it away."

Looking over to Leema, he cracks a smile out of the corner of his mouth. "Ya know. That feels good to hear. Thank you. For years, I had no idea what happened."

With time, the caravan moves away from the city towards the Midwestern countryside, and the backseat ride becomes less tense. It didn't take long for the comfort in Jolem and Leema's communication to return. Without AllVu, all they have are their recollected stories and imagination to pass the time. Despite the dire circumstances, they find a semblance of peace.

"It won't be long now," says Bo as they pass a "Welcome to Pennsylvania" sign. Leema glances around cautiously, like driving through a Safari. Surrounded by only trees and the occasional rest stop, the scene is a stark contrast between metropolitan New York and her home in Atlanta. To Leema, it feels like she's in another world.

"And you've been out here before?" she asks Jolem.

"Yep, three whole days, and I was just a kid."

"And you weren't scared?"

"Of course I was at first, but when I got there, I felt more at home than at my real home."

They veer from the main strip and then slip deeper into obscure territory. Before long, they reach the entrance of a loose gravel and dirt road leading into the woods. Castor twists to the back and tips his head. "We're close," he happily calls out as they turn onto the bumpy terrain. Secluded and shrouded by forest, the village is completely camouflaged to most. Leema grasps Jolem's hand firmly as she inches closer to his side. For her and Jolem, all sense of direction is lost.

As they bobble down the narrow passageway through walls of towering trees, Leema's eyes shift toward every outside distraction. She's terrified. Jolem however, responds much differently. His body drops back and he grins nostalgically. Warm thoughts from his time in the unicorn years ago, eases the tightness in his muscles. To his relief, The Path is finally left behind.

The truck finally exits the obscurity of the woods and emerges out into the vibrant heart of the hidden community. "Refugio del Mundo," affirms Castor, throwing a thumb's up. "We made it." As they creep down the road, playful children run next to their slow-moving vehicle. These excited young recluses don't receive many visitors in their remote zone. Leema is astonished. The rudimentary scene of people walking about in cotton rags, street-side barters and intimate face-to-face conversations, is like a blast from the past. It's a completely different world from the digital mixed reality she's used to.

"Castor, you son-of-a bitch! Give me some," a man gags as he pops up to the blindside of Castor's window.

Castor's head snaps back and the truck comes to a jerked stop. "My man! Que pasa, amigo??" Castor chuckles.

"We were expecting you hours ago."

"Well I had to make a pit stop. Got some extra weight with me."

His host's jovial demeanor quickly shifts to concern before shoving his head into the truck. He glares into the back seat. With half smiles, Jolem, Leema hesitantly lift their hand and wave.

"Castor – did you clear them??" he quickly snaps. Unexpected visitors are as welcome as The Path's monitoring eyes.

"Sorry, man didn't have time. Big eye was on em' and G vouched. The guy says he knows Jeremiah and Salam."

"Really?!"

The man sticks his head into Castor's window again. "You know Jeremiah…and Salam? What's your name, bro?"

"Jolem," he says and then leans forward " – tell em 'smart guy'."

"Okay, pull over there and I'll be right back," he instructs, wipes his hands on his ragged old cotton jeans then jots off.

Minutes pass as they sit on the side of the road waiting and Castor begins to hum. Growing steadily impatient, he pats to his rhythm on the top of the car dashboard. He leers uneasily to the back seats and grumbles, "Are you sure everything is okay?"

Jolem gulps, but masks his insecurity. "Yeah…yeah…they'll remember me. Sure," he says, but he only hopes he's right. It's been ten years since he's been here.

"Something's wrong," Castor complains glaring at Jolem through the rear-view mirror. "I owe Gank, but I've got a strange feelin' about you."

"Don't worry. It's all good. Trust me."

While the atmosphere is increasingly anxious inside the truck, finally they see the man returning accompanied by two others. From a far, Jolem can't recognize either of them. As his heart races and he nervously taps his knee, his eyes closely follow the trio moving toward their vehicle. Shrouded by the sun's rays and their dark visors, he can't make them out until they're only feet away. They still aren't familiar.

"Castor, you know the protocol about visitors," sternly scolds the first man to approach. His long, thick salt and peppered dreadlocks fall forward making the features of his face difficult to discern.

"Hey, I hear you man. Like I said. It was a last-minute thing," replies Castor shrugging.

The man steps to the back row of the truck and knocks on the tinted window with the backside of his wrinkled knuckles. "Let it down," he instructs.

Jolem's hand hesitantly motions downward, and his window gradually descends. He grits his teeth while the intimidating man's frame progressively becomes clear. With his hands on his waist, the man tilts his head and peeks inside. His glower starts at the far side as he locks eyes with Leema and then drags over to Jolem. Looking straight ahead, Jolem doesn't move a muscle. His ogling interrogator's head is only inches away from his. Slowly, the man slips off his dark sunglasses and squints.

"Smart guy?? Is that really you?" he asks in a high pitch.

Jolem's head jerks towards the window. "Salam?"

"Ain't this a bitch," Salam laughs, "Get out the car man!"

With a huge smile, Jolem motions the door open and the two men embrace like old friends.

"Man, I thought I'd never see you again," cackles Salam. "You're a grown man now," he says, looking him up and down. Salam's a lot shorter than Jolem remembers. Now an adult, Jolem's a couple inches taller than he.

"Yeah man and you're all grey."

"And who do you got with you?" asks Salam, peeking back into the truck.

Jolem leans to the side. "This is Leema. Leema, this is my friend Salam."

"Hop on out Leema," comments Salam gesturing forward. "I'm sure you guys are hungry."

Tentatively, Leema pulls herself out of the old clunky truck astonished as if walking on the moon. The scene is surreal, like something she's imagined or seen in a historic documentary. "It's – a pleasure to meet you," she remarks relieved, but still overwhelmed by the whole experience.

Salam introduces the third guy, who turns out to be a good-natured comedian and head of the local security force. Alarmed, Leema notices he's wearing a concealed firearm stuffed in the back of his pants. He assures her the location is peaceful, but they govern themselves and are prepared for conflict if it arrives.

"Castor – you know where to take the supplies," says Salam.

Castor leans his head out of the window. "Hey, Bo's energy is a Li'l' low. Gotta' workn' charging station?"

"Hmmm… take em' to the Solar port behind supply room 3. It's fully charged, I think."

"Cool."

While Castor and Bo pull off, Salam leads the others through the village of gawking locals. Many smile, some cordially nod, while others quietly jeer with frowns and insulting remarks. Not all are happy to see unknowns in their midst. They're content keeping distance from anyone associated with The Path.

Salam directs the group past the open district of peddlers, markets and then off the main road. As they stroll down a dirt pathway in-between a hill of trees and large rocks, they move into the living quarters at the rear of the complex. It's a peaceful collection of single-story finely crafted square buildings with sun-paneled roofs and in-home water recycling systems. All their waste is recycled one way or another.

They continue beyond the first few rows of houses to the very back. "These structures are new," he points out to Jolem. "They didn't exist when you were here." Finally, they reach the biggest house at the edge of the compound protected by a seated guard at the front. When the group approaches, the man lifts up, nods to Salam and ushers them in.

"Look what the cat drug in," yells Salam as he steps into village elder Jeremiah's study. Surrounded by antique books and other periodicals, Jeremiah sits at his desk with his eyes closed and head resting in his arched palms. He gingerly twists his feeble frame towards the door entryway. "SMART GUY," he etches out exuberantly. Just the energy necessary to cry out forces him into a deep hacking cough.

"Jeremiah – you okay??" Jolem asks leaping to his side.

"Yeah, yeah – I'm just fine – for an old man," he chuckles. "You can't spring a surprise on me like that, I might have a heart attack," he jokes before another series of croaking coughs. He grabs a folded rag from his side and wipes it across his mouth. "And who's this lovely lady with you?"

Jolem moves out of the way and reaches for Leema. "Jeremiah, this is Leema," he proudly introduces.

"Hi sir, it's a pleasure to meet you," she says politely while extending her hand.

Jeremiah mischievously grins at Jolem and then back over to Leema. "Put that hand down and come show me some love," he says. "And forget that sir stuff and call me Jeremiah."

She leans forward, turns her cheek and gives him a dignified hug.

"The prodigal son has returned," Jeremiah continues in a dry raspy whisper. "I think this calls for a celebration."

During the pleasant afternoon, they meet others in the community and join together for a nice meal in Jeremiah's private quarters. While enjoying local delicacies served like she's never experienced before, Leema listens to humorous tales of a young, rebellious and inquisitive Jolem who found his way to their combine. Accustomed to her many luxuries, such as HumanAids, self-operating appliances and a state-of-the-art home, the archaic robots, outdated machinery and meager accommodations tickle her. She delights in the simplicity of an old school world and, for the time being, pushes aside the one she left behind.

While the intimate group of eight partake in the revelry, Jeremiah quietly observes Jolem and Leema. Everyone in the community has a personal reason for being there, so not too many questions are asked when people stumble in. However, this time something is unique. Leema is very different from those who've passed through on their way to wherever and those who've stayed. Her regal appearance, mannerisms and speech stand out in the grimy village of vagabonds. Jeremiah grins politely, but underneath, a foreboding feeling rests in his mind.

34

The sun begins to set and there's a cool comfortable breeze blowing through the rural Pennsylvanian hillside. Taking a break from the festivities of the congenial villagers, Jolem and Leema take a walk out of the trees and find a nice space alone in the flowing grass. With her head resting sideways across Jolem's thighs, Leema stares into the darkening sky. Her eyelids fold gently down and she cracks a subtle smile. Unexpectedly for her, she's completely at ease in this foreign environment. There's a unique sound in the air that is odd but also very charming. The wind is singing a peaceful lullaby, and for the first time in Leema's life, her trusty sidekick's voice is silent.

When she first disconnected from her World earlier in the day, the idea of being without Maribelle was unimaginable. As long as she could remember, the helpful advice from her assistant and other support systems had been her guide. Even as a corporate leader, she's never had to truly make decisions entirely on her own. And without the devices that have effectively run her life, she's questioned her own judgment.

Leema turns her head toward Jolem with eyes wide and inquisitive. Propped up on his arms with his head tilted backwards, he seems as native as the dandelions moving fleeing in the wind. "Hmmm…," she hums. His comfort in this strange place is more than intriguing. Jolem's head falls down looking back at her.

"Hmmmm, what?" he playfully inquires.

"Hmmm – you, that's what."

"Okay and what does that mean?" he says as he twists into a position lying on his stomach besides her.

"You're just weird. But weird in a good way."

"I guess I need to start taking that word as a compliment then."

"It's just – I feel like I'm in outer space somewhere. It's – weird. But not you. You seem at home. I don't understand it."

Jolem lifts a dandelion and blows its soft white stems across her face. "This is 'outer space.' A world right around the corner, but yet so far. I love it."

He flips on his back and lies with his head propped on his folded arms with a transcending smile across his face. At this moment he truly feels free. Leema crawls on top of his chest, closes her eyes and plants a tender kiss on the side of his mouth. He can feel her heart beating rapidly.

"Woo – I wasn't expecting that," he says jerking backward.

"Well, I guess the unexpected is expected. I don't know what's getting into me."

"Are you okay?"

"I think – I'm just a li'l overtaken with all kinds of emotions. This is – amazing, but…but at the same time it's terrifying. I've never done anything remotely like this before… and now what??"

Jolem takes a deep breath as his thoughts drift. Throughout his life he's been prone to situations that have satisfied his own adventurous desires; often at the expense and risk of others. Now as he looks back at her, with the full burden of her fate on his shoulders, he finally feels its weight. The last thing he wanted to do was to put her in harm's way. But after realizing that's exactly what he has done, he's overcome with guilt.

"Ya know Leema, maybe this was a bad idea," he abruptly says. He pops up and takes a few fumbling steps towards the setting sun. Staring out to the horizon, he folds his arms and contemplates. He's so lost in his thoughts, he doesn't feel Leema's presence until she is standing at his side. She moves close and crouches her chin on his arm.

"Jolem. What's wrong? A minute ago, you were on top of the world."

Jolem sighs and shakes his head. He begins to speak, but closes his mouth and shakes his head again. His emotions are so confusing he doesn't have words to say.

"Jolem? Talk to me. Please."

As he looks out into the rolling hills, he slips his hands into his pockets and rocks back and forth on his heels. "This was selfish. I shouldn't have brought you out here," he says contemptuously, kicking a rock across the grass.

"Jolem I don't understand. I'm the one who reached out to you and demanded I come. Annd…" Also tongue-tied Leema stands shell shocked. "I…I need Maribelle. I don't know what is going on or what to do. Jolem, help me understand. Please!"

"Relax, relax – it's okay," he comforts. "I'm sorry. I shouldn't have lashed out like that." He wraps his arms tightly around her and pulls her head close to his chest. "It's just that – I…I don't know what's waiting when we go back," he says as his eyes drift off into the sky. "They've replaced your memories once before. They'll probably just do the same thing again – to both of us."

Leema reaches up to his chin and gently pulls his face toward hers. At this moment, she is more relaxed than he. "Jolem, you've opened my eyes to a world I would have never known. I'm eternally grateful to you for that."

Jolem leers into her eyes and feels a longing desire he's never felt before. He's flush with emotion. As he clears his throat, words feel like rocks. "You – you've always been very special to me and you always will be," he says and then their lips press softly together. While the subtle songs of nature whisper them a sweet serenade, the intensity of their passion grows.

DALIO STRIKES

35

The unicorn slowly quiets when the long emotional day comes to an end. While Leema rests on an adjustable cot in a guest room of Jeremiah's home, Jolem is out alone among the stars. Standing at the edge of the hilltop apex, he closes his eyes as the breeze sways gently against his face. For a brief period lying out with Leema in the grass, he was at peace. However, the reality of his current predicament has him twisted.

He's now a deviant fugitive of the state. The pain of potentially losing his family, friends, Leema, and even his memories is almost unbearable. His fists grip tightly as he fights back, building tears, while the vision of Liz torments him. He promised to always be there to protect her, but he doesn't know how he'll even protect himself. His head drops in sorrow. However, his tender moment of grief is short-lived.

Without warning, an explosion booms from the community, lighting up the pitch-black forest. Its mere force shakes Jolem's foundation, knocking him off his feet. A dark, smoldering cloud of smoke spreads high into the sky, engulfing the area. He can hardly see beyond its murky bounds. Confused and dazed, he shakes his head, trying to regain his balance, while his ears ring like a siren. He still lacks full coherence but snaps up off the ground and darts towards the camp.

As he bolts down the loopy terrain toward the smoke, his heart races quicker than his breaths. What lies just beyond the bend is impossible to foresee and even more challenging to imagine. He etches through trees and rocky ground, getting whipped by limbs and unseen obstacles. When he reaches the outer edge of the compound, his eyes and mouth pop open startled by the horrific scene. "Compliance Control?? Butt...how'd they find us??" he gasps. The community is under assault.

Jolem spies from afar in awe, witnessing a combat scene straight out of the pages of a forgotten history. Laser shots ring out and blood curdling screams follow, while locals scatter aimlessly before meeting their own demise. Jolem dips low, slips behind a large storage bin and then peaks out from behind. Downed bodies of men, women and children are everywhere. He wants to run to their aid, but against the arsenal he's powerless. "DAMN why did we come here?" he bemoans, gritting his teeth in frustration. He can hardly believe what he's seeing.

The struggle doesn't last long as the village resistance is no match for the fully equipped assailants. Some return fire and fight back but one-by-one they fall, until eventually none remain upright. Jolem continues to crouch out of sight without making a sound. Should they catch him, all the lives taken in his stead, would be lost in vain. Although shock and anger temporarily push aside the surmounting guilt, he knows the attack is all because of him. There's nothing he can do. Staying out of sight is his only play.

As suddenly as it started, the conflict came to a swift and bloody end. Carnage is everywhere and the community remains ablaze. Compliance officers drift in and out of buildings clearing the rooms.

"Has he been killed or apprehended?" a muffled voice asks.

"Negative. He has not been identified within the wreckage, but we will continue to search for a positive match," a semi-digitized voice responds.

"Okay, I want it to be affirmed. Continue."

Without their Path connected wireless technology, Compliance Control must rely on other methods in their pursuit. However, their heat-seeking, DNA and facial identity technologies are much less effective in the wilderness. Obstructed by the heavy population of wildlife, conductive metal and thermal heat blockers, Jolem is almost impossible to discover. If he stays out of sight, he'll be protected.

With no recourse, Jolem retreats deeper into the woods and takes cover. He has no idea of Leema's fate, but he doubts she's harmed. However, the condition of Jeremiah and the rest of the villagers is much more dubious. While sitting low behind a large birch tree, his face drops into his hands and shamed tears fall in their honor.

"How did they find us?" he mutters. It is a question that will torment him. He remembers Castor and Bo left the complex shortly after delivering the cargo and wonders if they could have alerted the FDEC. While he plays out multiple scenarios, the activity in the distance grows quiet until he hears almost nothing. It's a deafening silence and he finally yearns for J's companionship. He's completely alone, clueless and frightened in an environment as foreign as the outer rims of the galaxy.

Jolem peeks back to the sight, but in the pit of night, he can't see anything. Slowly, he lifts up and takes a few hesitant steps towards the wreckage. All he can hear are the subtle sounds of nature. He considers returning to check on survivors, but his movements become paralyzed with fear. Undoubtedly, the assailants have gone, but still the risks are too great. After looking blindly ahead, he slips down to the ground and props his back against a tree. His chin falls to his chest, and he remains in place for hours.

When the crack of dawn sheds a little light, Jolem's sights are wide awake. It was the longest and most challenging night of his life. Cradled in the fetal position against the tree, he scans his forest surroundings. As far as the eye can see is nothing but trees and tall brush. Although he feels he can finally return to the scene of the disaster, he dreads what awaits him there.

Jolem carefully lifts up from the ground and begins toward the wrecked remains of the village. The rubble of toppled objects and burnt bush is scattered everywhere. He edges closer and an indescribable aroma penetrates his nostrils that causes him to feel nauseated. It's an awful smell he's never experienced before, but a scent he'll never forget. He covers his nose, mouth and then precedes forward through the residue of the unicom. He's heartbroken.

As he creeps past the destruction of buildings and play lands, he recalls the friendly community full of life and energy. With a large stick, he hesitantly pushes through ruined materials laying in the dirt. Just the day before, some of them were prized possessions locked in the hands of playful, young children. He bends to the ground, brushes through light rubble and lifts up the ragged remnant of a little doll. The one remaining eye is dusty, busted and spattered with dry blood drops. His lips quiver as he fights back the moisture building in the wells of his eyelids. It's hard to keep his composure.

In an attempt to remove the stain of all he's seen, he starts rubbing his eyes furiously. His body feels almost frozen, but he knows he must press on. With his head back, he sucks in deep, blows out and then lifts from his crouched position. Tentatively, he continues, but he's yet to see signs of any of the villagers. Inside, he's holding on to the slim possibility there could be other survivors, but he fears the idea is fantasy. Each time he pokes his head through the threshold of an open crevice or doorway, he braces for what lies beyond. He knows at some point he'll approach one of the fallen. It's a sight he's never seen before. To his surprise, as he moves from home-to-home, he sees none. In the middle of all the disaster, the villagers have all just disappeared.

He treads carefully out of the woods and into the open grounds of the residential complex. Suddenly, like walking into a glass wall, he's knocked backwards. After all he's already witnessed, he thought he was prepared for the worst. However, the awful sight of a smoldering mound of rotting corpses keels him over in a fit of sickness. While on his hands and knees, he painfully scans up the hill of lifeless bodies. When his bloodshot eyes reach midway, they spring open. Tears trickle over his cheeks, down to his chin and then drip onto the ground. "I'm so sorry," Jolem wails as the upside-down soulless face of Jeremiah stares back at him.

Jolem's seen enough. Stumbling backwards and kicking up dirt, he desperately tries to lift off the ground. When upright, he turns and darts back through the whipping tree branches of the woods. As he races, he can hardly catch his breath. He's exhausted, but can't stop until he escapes the madness.

Jolem finally breaks free from the bushes with twig lashes across his face and arms. However, as his feet skid to a stop in the dirt he's stumped. He's unsure if his eyes are deceiving him or if he's really looking at Castor's truck. It's parked close to the same location it was the day before. Cautiously, he inches over to the empty vehicle. He slides over to the open front door window and leans inside. He peeks around, but suddenly his eyes flare open and his body stiffens. Pressed against the back of his head, he feels the sensation of cold glass-like plastic.

"What the FUCK did you do??" a voice snarls in his ear. It's Castor and without even seeing his face, Jolem can sense his rage. "I awt' to blow your fuckin' brains out," he growls.

Jolem swallows the tiny bit of moisture remaining in his dry throat. He's so parched, it feels like rocks passing through his tight neck.

"Cast..Castor…please. I didn't do it," Jolem pleads, but the laser gun's barrel pushes harder into his skin.

"I know YOU didn't do this, but there's no doubt, you're the reason this happened!"

Castor grips Jolem's shoulder, flips him around and stuffs the gun into the middle of his forehead. While Bo stands near firmly gripping his waists, Castor seethes with anger staring into Jolem's eyes.

"You know I could blow your head completely off your neck and not feel a thing," Castor says. "Why are you here and where's the ice princess??"

"Castor please…"

"You better start talking. NOW!"

"Okay, okay, please…just don't shoot. I was in deviation. I was just trying to escape."

"So why would they do this?!"

"Leema – Leema…she's Dalio's daughter."

Gritting his teeth, Castor scowls. "YOU BROUGHT DIABLO'S DAUGHTER HERE??" His hand catapults backwards and then launches into Jolem's face knocking him into the truck. "You son of a bitch!"

Castor grips a handful of Jolem's shirt and throws him to the ground. Jolem's physical strength is no match for Castor and unarmed, he's helpless to defend himself. He's a sitting duck propped up against the vehicle's side as Castor cocks back his fist. His arm swings, but before landing the punch, Bo leaps forward and grabs Castor's arm.

"Castor, he's had enough," he says, pushing him back. "Enough."

"Bo, get yo hands off me! I'm not finished," Castor snaps, still charging ahead, but Bo's android strength is more than sufficient to guard him off. In the struggle, Castor's weapon falls to the ground.

"Castor – ENOUGH," says Bo.

Panting heavy like a boxer, Castor tilts his head to the sky and lets out a fierce holler. He's been making runs to this community for years and many of those who perished were close personal friends. "Diablo has gone too far!!" he yells, gripping his fists. His head swings to Jolem and unexpectedly looks down the eye of his own firearm.

"Don't – come a step closer. I'm serious," Jolem warns, pointing the gun in his direction.

Castor casually peeps to Bo, back to Jolem and then releases a loud, dull breath. "You have no idea what you're even doing," he remarks, shaking his head contemptuously.

"What?? I'll use it if I have to."

Fearlessly, Castor continues to Jolem, snatches his firearm out of his hand and then shoves it into its holster. "Biometric locks have been mandatory for decades. It'll only operate in my hands, you idiot," he says as he steps off.

Bo moves over to Jolem, who's beaten and exhausted. He reaches down and pulls him up off the ground. "Are you okay?" he asks, helping to brush dirt off Jolem's clothes.

Jolem grimaces, rubbing the left side of his face. "Feels like he broke my jaw," he mumbles, "but I'll live." He then glances over to Castor and drops his head in shame. "I'm sorry man. This is the last thing I wanted to happen," he laments. "I had no other option."

Castor's nostrils flare and his cheeks fill like balloons. He blows out and then glares toward Jolem. "You have a debt to pay; ya know?"

Nodding slowly, Jolem sternly looks back and confirms. "I know."

"So, what in the world were you doing with the devil's daughter? Did you kidnap her?"

"No, no of course not. We were…friends."

Castor cynically smirks to Bo and then back to Jolem. "Friends huh? Hmm – now that's a laugh," he chuckles. "Some dusty deviant like you and this ice princess. That's highly unlikely."

"It may be hard to believe – but it's true."

Twisting his lips dismissively, Castor again looks to Bo and asks, "What are we goin' to do now??"

"Well…" Bo begins, but Jolem interrupts.

"Director Dalio has to go down for this," he grumbles passionately pumping his fists. "He has to be stopped. The public needs to know the FDEC's secrets!"

Castor turns his head and spits out like a bullet. "Do you really want to go up against Dalio? The Path? Look around!!" he yells, throwing his arms in the air. "That's suicide."

Jolem clenches the top of his head and grits his teeth. "I'm still trying to come to grips with what just happened yesterday," he says sullenly, shaking his head. "I don't know but – we've gotta' do something."

"We?!" Castor shouts. "Why shouldn't we toss you aside and just get the hell out of here?! If it weren't for you, none of this would've happened."

Jolem's eyes drift to the ground and he sniffles. He balls his fists and frowns angrily to Castor. His eyes are fire red. "When I was 10 my dad died. Deep inside, I've always felt The FDEC had something to do with it. Now, I'm convinced it did. Please help me get back in The Path. That's all I ask."

While slowly scratching the back of his head, Castor again peers to Bo and then back to Jolem. "Many of those people who died last night were very important to me," he replies somberly. "Of course, I want Diablo to pay."

"I know Divergent State is working on something. I need to get in touch with Gank," Jolem says.

"We can make that happen."

"How do you make it past The Path?"

"Bo. He has a proprietary operating system I wrote a long time ago. It's old, outdated code that has never been updated to Path standards. His communication program encrypts messages and The Path can't read them, but Gank can. We use a backdoor into Halcyon and zombies to make the connections. We won't be able to send the message until we enter The Path though."

"Okay – let's do it."

"Jolem. I'll help you get back in The Path, but that's all I can promise. Dalio is out for you. Even with Gank's help, you probably won't last long."

After shaking his head, Jolem stands high. "I can't think of myself right now. I've got a debt to pay; right?"

36

Back in Director Dalio's Washington DC home office, Leema slumps in the middle of a sofa with her head hanging to the floor. She was earlier delivered extremely shaken but unharmed. Casting a dark shadow over her, Dir. Dalio looms above with his hands locked behind his back. For the past hour, he's been interrogating her like a homicide detective.

The unbelievable events of the day before, antagonize her like a nightmare she can't wake up from. Now a day after the bizarre overnight trip, she's having difficulty separating fact from fiction. Fortunately for her, she was quickly whisked away and spared witnessing the devastation that followed her departure. She has no idea of what happened to Jolem and the community. Repeatedly, the director told her the unicom inhabitants were all untouched and Jolem was never discovered. He knows these statements aren't all true.

"Leema there really aren't words to describe how completely disappointed I am with your actions," he scolds. "What you did was inexcusable, dangerous, and profoundly irresponsible. I expected much better from you."

Without words of defense, Leema is speechless. Glowering, the director slowly moves next to her on the sofa and then leans in close.

"Are you deliberately trying to hurt me or The Path? Has your allegiance faded?" he asks, continuing to glare at her between questions. She instinctively flinches as his words snap close to her ears, but her eyes remain locked on the ground.

"Version 10 will launch in just two days," he proclaims. "The Divide, your 'kidnapping' by Jolem and his cronies. None of these distractions will slow down our progress. The liberty and prosperity of The Path will endure."

Leema finally lifts her head during a silent break from his reprimand and looks over to her father. Out of her large puffy eyes, tears drip down her face.

"I have a question for you," she says calmly.

"Yes?"

She swallows and clears her throat. "Is it true? Does the list exist… the Sui Generis list?"

Taken by surprise, the director grips his jaw and slowly nestles deep into the sofa, by her side. "Leema, I don't know what you're talking about. Where did you hear this?" he asks, but his uncomfortable demeanor is more honest than his words.

"Don't lie to me dad!" she lashes back. "Please! Tell me the truth!"

The director pushes himself upright, straightens his jacket and lifts out of his seat. "OK – you want to know the truth, do you?" In silent contemplation, he takes a few slow steps around the room. Suddenly, he peers at her. "Leema, Leema, Leema," he comments, shaking his head pitifully. He pauses, rubbing his face resigned to the reality of the awkward moment.

"My angel," he says tenderly. "Yes, yes it does. You are one individual of a select group with special considerations in The Path."

"So, all these years – it's all been a lie!" Leema snaps as she pops upright. Her sorrow morphs into anger. "That The Path is fair and impartial. You told me we are the result of our own decisions."

The director begins to pace slowly from one end of the room to the other while gathering his thoughts. He knew at some point he'd have this conversation, but today he's clumsily unprepared. After a few minutes of silent deliberation, he stops and turns to her.

"Listen my daughter," he begins softly. "Throughout the world and history, our humanity has always been based on a simple principle; survival of the fittest. Undoubtedly the strong have been predestined to thrive, while the weak have been their burden. We are a selected group of elite individuals designed to maintain order and stability. It is our RESPONSIBILITY to manage the care of those who are incapable of doing it for themselves."

"But dad – people make choices. They change and grow. No one's perfect, but some get better – don't they? History has seen people rise from their circumstances over and over again. Wouldn't The Path's assistance be enough to give them the helping hand they need?"

"Don't be naïve, angel. Yes, SIVs rise and fall, but for the very most part, where you begin is where you end. Mobility of classes is a fairy tale. It's an inspirational and hopeful story fed to the starving hearts of the hopeless. For without hope, they would've truly had nothing. Today, even our low SIVs are – happy and content."

Leema's eyes again slip to the ground. She was initially confused, but now weighted with these profound ideas, her thoughts are even more disheveled. Throughout her life, she's followed a simple system of beliefs that has been shattered.

"So, isn't this unfair?" she asks.

"Fair? Hmmm. Fair…," he considers as his eyes lift to the ceiling. For another few moments, he quietly rocks back and forth on his heels.

"It's easy for us all to have short and selective memories, angel. However, don't forget, not too long ago, there were thousands of homeless and hungry citizens lining our city walls and shelters. There were many without occupation or dreams. Some were even desperate enough to force their way into houses and buildings, snatching whatever their grimy hands could hold. The few have always been required to solve the problems of the majority. It is our natural responsibility. Today we now have the most effective mechanism to do this. The Path, far more so than any other program ever proposed or implemented in this world, has given us the ability to help those who otherwise couldn't help themselves. We give the weak more than hope; we give them the means of self-sufficiency.

We release them from the bounds of welfare and give them individual strength. We give them direction. Fair you ask? Is it fair that we must bear this responsibility? FAIR is a concept we don't have the luxury to consider."

With so many things running through her mind, Leema feels her head is about to explode. Suddenly her thoughts shift. "And what about Jolem?? He didn't kidnap me. I went with him! It was MY idea."

"Are you so sure? If he hadn't fed you his lies and anti-Path propaganda, would you have gone? He tricked you to deactivate your AllVu. You were manipulated, Angel – like a fool."

Leema scratches the side of her cheek as she attempts to remember the beginnings of her and Jolem's conversations. "That's not…not true," she whimpers. "He wouldn't do that."

"Leema, Jolem is a deviant. His father was a deviant – you think you know him, but you don't."

Leema moves back down onto the sofa while her thoughts taunt her. "What's going to happen to him?" she asks softly, sobbing.

Leaning back, Dir Dalio gruffly twists his lips. "That is no longer your concern, but he is a deviant and suspected traitor. We have reason to believe he's connected to the Divide. He might even be the masked terrorist from their broadcast. As soon as he's recovered, he will be dealt with."

"What?? This isn't true. That's impossible," she cries, again jumping out of her seat.

"Leema, it is indeed true, and you are to stay as far away from him as possible. This is an order."

"This is ridiculous."

In complete shock at her defiance, Director Dalio's eyes budge as if they're about to pop out of his head. Furiously, he slams his fist on his desk. "ENOUGH LEEMA! RECOMMIT to your responsibilities and drop this NOW!" he shouts. But she doesn't back down.

"That is NOT for you to decide, and you can't force me to do anything!" she yells back.

Glaring at Leema, the director's stare is almost fierce enough to burn through her skin. Her audacious suggestion of his limitations enrages him. While breathing like an agitated bull, he inches close and then stops as the tips of their shoes touch. "I can't force you?" he asks eerily.

The director sucks in an extended breath of air and allows it to seep out of his nose. "Do you really believe that?" he sneers.

A cold chill, ices her spine as goose bumps lift the fine hairs of her forearms. For the first time in her life, she fears her father.

"You listen, my sweet daughter, and listen well," he says while pinching her cheek tightly. "I can do ANYTHING and EVERYTHING I want. Don't you ever forget this."

Throughout the quieted room, his deep heavy breaths echo. He's convinced his words are etched in her mind, and her resistance has finally fallen. After shifting the front of his jacket back into place, he turns and then begins out of the room.

"And what about me??" Leema calls out, which abruptly stops his movements. "Are you just going to replace my memories again? Turn me into a bot??"

With his hands at his side and looking straight ahead, the director slowly does an about-face. Smirking coyly, he looks her in the eyes. "Angel – Am I?" he chuckles sarcastically. "Is that what you believe happened?" he continues laughing progressively louder. "Oh, you begged me to replace those memories, but I refused. I wanted that experience to remain with you so you would always remember the consequence of The Path. It was you who went around my back and had them replaced."

"What?"

"See for yourself. Go on – your AllView is reactivated. I want to share something with you."

Leema sits up with her back straight like a board and then cautiously re-ignites her dormant AllView. With a quick swipe in the air, Dir. Dalio sends an old experience to her World. While visuals of his memories display to her like home movies, he begins to speak.

"You were perplexed and hurt when you disconnected from Jolem, but you did what you knew to be right. You followed the infallible instruction of The Path without complaint. However, the feelings you developed were not so easy to ignore. You asked for a transfer to Atlanta, and I made it happen. But that wasn't enough for you, so you had this done – to yourself."

"No...can't be," she whispers while witnessing evidence of his words.

"Oh yes, it can. You thought you could hide it from me by getting it done on the black market. However, even though it didn't appear on your memory record, I knew everything."

Leema tries to reject his words but knows they're true. Befuddled, she slides deeper into the sofa, and her face falls into her palms. Shaking his head pitifully, the director is without the need to say another word. He slips his hands into his pockets and again turns away from her. As he continues out of the room, he leaves Leema alone to wallow in the agony of her predicament.

Miles away in Jersey City, New Jersey, Gank lobbies to Divergent State leadership. The covert group has converted an elderly couple's rarely-used house into their temporary headquarters. Since he was last among them, Jolem has quickly become one of the FDEC's most wanted, and a heated debate rages over his return. Most believe they should cut ties with him, but Gank passionately argues on his besieged friend's behalf.

"Jolem is not only my partner, but his situation represents the type of corruption by the FDEC we've been fighting against," Gank charges. "We've got to do something!"

Divergent senior member GHotz crosses his heavily tattooed arms and mechanically twists the thick, silver ring protruding out of his bottom lip. He's stood firm against intervention and bringing Jolem back to the Lore.

"Gank. Like I've said before, Jolem is too hot, and we don't need this type of attention. We move like thieves in the night. I think this would be a huge mistake."

"I agree with GHotz," echoes AdrianLulz leaning back in her seat. "We need to focus on stopping this merger. We only have one day, and right now, our plan is shaky – at best."

"I understand your concerns," comments Gank. "But listen – I think Jolem could be the key to all this. Diablo's personal disdain for him could be his downfall. Jolem is the only one who can get close to him."

"What do you mean?" asks GHotz.

"We can go phishing with Leema Dalio."

"I'm listening."

"If we can get Jolem close enough to her, his AllVu can make a digital copy of her pupils. That'll be all we need to break into her World. When we do that, we might be able to attach a worm virus that makes it into the director's. Then if it gets through his quarantine, it can navigate into the core of SEE. Once there, it can quickly sniff out the integration code and destroy it before SEE notices a thing."

"Hmm," hums GHotz in thought. "That's a long shot but…not a bad idea."

"I don't buy it," snaps MightyMite. "We'd be pretty much betting the whole farm on this guy and his – relationship. She might even be working with or for Dalio. It's much too risky."

"I agree," AdrianLulz says, shaking her head against the idea. "This plan is ridiculous. It could all be a trap. Let's just go through Halcyon again, like we always do."

"Halcyon won't cut it this time," cuts in Gank. "The recent updates are causing us all kinds of issues. We have an opportunity to actually get into The Path's core. We have to take this chance!"

GHotz contemplates as he drops to the back edge of a nearby sofa. "He's right. Under the circumstances, it's the best play we got. The merger is tomorrow, and we've got to try." He turns and looks at Gank. "And if he's caught?"

"Well, he already has the blue bomb implanted. I can remote program it to cover recent experiences too. If he's compromised, he knows the risks."

While he twists the metal ring lodged in his lip, GHotz peers over to AdrianLulz, Mitnic, Nut and then to MightyMite. They all nod with skeptical approval.

"Okay then," he says before a long contemplative pause. "Lulz, let's get him over here."

Meanwhile, Jolem, Castor, and Bo approach the Eastern Pennsylvania border without a word spoken between them since they began their journey. During the extremely tense ride, Jolem's head leans against the window staring out into the morphing clouds. Jeremiah's tortured image replays over and over in his thoughts. He closes his eyes and wishes he could escape this awful misadventure, but when he opens them, the tragedy remains.

"So, what's our next move?" Jolem asks.

"We'll enter The Path's border soon and when we enter, we'll send an encrypted message to Gank. We'll take you to a safe house in one of the Recovery Zones until we can sort this out."

They're only minutes from The Path's boundary and they're all on edge. As soon as they crossover, any abnormally could trigger an alert, and the game's over.

"Well, everybody, strap on your seat belts," Castor remarks while tugging his hat tighter onto his head. "This ride could get bumpy."

With a confused glance, Jolem leans up to the front seat. "Caster, what's a seatbelt?"

Castor's rocking music blares as they mentally prepare like players in the final moments before a championship. Jolem's eyes clamp as the subtle evidence of The Path's signals ignite reactions around them. He's never been so scared in his life. He peeks out of the window and his muscles spasm at the return of the flashing drone's lights hovering in the sky. He's so anxious, he can hardly sit still. "Okay, message sent to Gank," confirms Castor. "Here we go."

The journey back into The Path stretches from seconds to almost two hours. It's so nerve-wracking it feels as if they've been riding for days. Fortunately for them, they've managed to fly under the radar and have remained undetected. As they move through eastern New Jersey, edging closer to the New York border, Castor veers off the interstate. He glances back to Jolem. "We're almost there," he mutters.

Pretty soon, they're flowing through another deSolate recovery zone neighborhood. Like the first time Jolem visited one of these zones, he's taken by its dilapidated condition. They maneuver down a few blocks and then drift into the driveway and garage of a decayed, old house.

"This is it. Let's go."

Jolem begins out of the truck and then stops. His head swings towards Castor. "How does The Path not see us??" he questions.

"The Path does see us. But, it just sees an old couple visiting their property. Divergent's got it covered."

"Ah, okay."

When inside the unassuming small house, Castor is ready to get started. "So, Gank responded with specific instructions for you. We're going to set you up and then hit the road. Go ahead, reactivate your AllVu."

"Reactivate?? But –"

"Don't worry; Gank has it under control."

Hesitantly, Jolem's finger slides up to his AllVu orb. As soon as he touches it, his World ignites like a blinding light. Once again, he's instantly transported to an empty white room.

"Jo, you look like shit, bro, but glad you're still standing," comments Gank's voice.

"Man, last night was – indescribable. I never in a million years would've expected anything like that. I'm still blown away," Jolem croaks.

"Bo sent me some footage. I can't imagine what that must've been like."

A lump grows in Jolem's throat as he begins to recount the horror he witnessed. He can hardly believe the thoughts in his head and the words as they leave his mouth. He knew there would be consequences for pushing Director Dalio, but this was beyond his wildest dreams. The guilt is overbearing.

"I just don't understand how they found us," Jolem continues.

"Jo, man, you still don't get it. She was never supposed to go with you, bro."

"What do you mean?"

"I'm sure she was tagged."

"Tagged??"

"Yeah. A tracking chip implanted in her wrist. A lot of high SIVs do. We do what we can to jam tag transmissions, but obviously, they found her. The mission was doomed as soon as she got in with you."

"Butt?? Congress shot tags down years ago."

"Jo – none of that matters. Don't trust ANYTHING."

"So…it really was…my fault."

"Man – what's done is done. We've got to try to move on."

"Gank, you didn't see what I saw!"

"Listen, man. I hate to drop this on you right now; you have a BIG problem. Your face is all over The Path."

"What??"

"Watch this. A nationwide bulletin went out, and all Worlds were interrupted last night."

Jolem's face appears like a 3D mug shot and a chilling recording begins.

"This is the FDEC with a special announcement. There is a nationwide lookout for Jolem McKay in connection with the Divide and last week's security breach into The Path. If you have seen or know of this person's whereabouts, please contact the FDEC immediately."

Jolem grips his forehead and then his hand slides down his face until it's covering his nose and mouth. "WHAT!? That's ridiculous!" he screeches.

"I know, I know – but we may have a plan."

"Please give me some good news, pleasee."

"Well, the good news is, I've been given the go to bring you in again."

"That might've been the best news I've ever heard," he says, exhaling slowly.

"We're going to figure all this out, but first things first. Right now, your AllVu is only being masked while we misdirect The Path. We can't hold SEE back forever. We're goin' to have to reset your AllVu."

"But – won't that permanently delete all my World?"

"Technically, no. Your World and all your personal experiences will remain hidden in the cloud. For now, the only memories you'll have are the ones in your brain. When this is all over, we'll restore your AllVu and you'll get your old World back."

"Ahhh, okay."

"Next, we're goin' to activate a new AllVu persona. You'll have a whole new assistant and World with a full 25-year history attached. As far as your assistant is concerned, you've been together all your life. It'll try to be helpful, but since it'll be pulling from a lifetime of false data, it's advice might not be too helpful."

"Okay…"

"Now, when you get here, we'll install GhostFace into your AllVu's visor and reprogram your voice. GhostFace technology reflects light, infrared or natural, to add skin tone and distort your facial features. So, anyone looking at you through AllVu will see a camouflaged face and so will surveillance drones and cameras. This'll prevent you from being visually detected. However, be careful. If anyone hides or disables their AllVu, they'll see your real face."

"Uhh okay. Got it."

"Last, we're goin' to give you underbody wear weaved with DNA Spoofers that will throw off thermal imagers. Keep em' on at all times."

"So, unless I do something out of the ordinary, The Path won't pay attention to me?"

"Exactly. To The Path, you'll be upstanding citizen Joyn Michaels going about your day. This gives us a narrow window of opportunity. We've had false people, businesses, and communities sitting in The Path for months, even years, undetected. To The Path, they are as real as you and I. Just don't do anything stupid. Stay inside for now, and you should be safe until I send you a Zumer. Don't try to contact anyone."

"What about Liz? My mom? How do I check on them?"

"For now, you'll have to just wait. Trust me."

"And Leema…"

"Her World is still blocked, but we have intel she's with Dalio. Officially she's on vacation for the next two weeks, but that's all we've been able to find out right now."

"Bro," Jolem says before releasing a heavy relieved sigh. "I can't thank you enough...for all this."

"Don't thank me yet, Jo'...we're just getting started. Give me a min while we work out a few things. We'll have a ride shortly." And just like that, Gank's voice disappears.

Jolem hides his AllVu and his consciousness returns to the safe house. "So, you're about to head out, huh?" he asks, peering over at Castor and Bo.

Castor takes a few steps forward and reaches out his right hand. "Yeah, we're goin' to lay low for a while," he says. "There's food in the fridge. Clean ya self up and settle in. Sounds like you're goin' to need your energy."

Returning his own, Jolem grips Castor's hand firmly. "Thanks, man."

"Jolem, take care," waves Bo and then they're on their way. Jolem falls back against the wall and looks around the almost empty room. The silence and uncertainty are agonizing. He slides down until his rear bumps against the floor. Worn out, he can hardly keep his eyes open. Before long, he doses off into a deep sleep. It's a rest his mind and body desperately need, but before long, his saga continues.

"Jolem."

"Huh?"

"Wake up."

37

Back in the Jersey City Lore, every second that passes creates greater anxiety. Time is quickly becoming enemy number one. When Jolem finally arrives at the front door, it's almost 10 AM. Gank ushers him in and down the hall with words of advice on how to engage the skeptical team. The stakes are much higher than the last time he was in among them, and he won't encounter a welcoming committee. He's urged to tread lightly when dealing with the edgy group.

When they step into the room, a hint of a smile doesn't exist on the faces of the pack. Jolem's sights pop around the room at the intense stares of AndrianLulz, Gonzalez Gold, Mitnic, Nut and MightyMite. They all mean business. Looking ahead stoutly, GHotz sits in the middle, rocking from side to side.

"Hi – hi everybody," hesitantly begins Jolem and then Gank leaps in front. "Jolem, this is GHotz," he says. "GHotz knows more about The Path than anyone I know. He's saved my ass more times than I can count and opened my eyes so wide I can see through walls. He's awakened us all."

"GHotz, it's an honor. I don't know how to thank you…" Jolem graciously begins before being stunted again by GHotz's extended hand. "Ahhh stella man. But before we proceed, I need to drop some things on you."

"Okay, okay, sure, sure," Jolem replies, bobbing his head quickly.

For a moment, GHotz stares at Jolem dubiously, turns to Gank and then back to Jolem. The magnitude of the responsibility about to be handed to Jolem is extraordinary.

"I wish I could say this is all about you, but it's way beyond you or me. Honestly, I've struggled to even intervene in a system we've been able to use and manipulate for years, but we've approached an inflection point."

Rubbing his fingers together meticulously, GHotz's stern and crinkled expression doesn't change. With an astute understanding of The Path, he begins to break down its inner workings while Jolem absorbs his words.

"Since its inception, there have been 9 major versions of The Path and countless updates. And with each one, Dalio or one of his predecessors have stood in front of the public and fed them a bunch of lies," he begins somberly. "We're not innocent in all this either. For years, we've selfishly sat back and watched all this happen. We've been able to do what we needed to do. But V 10 is different. After this merger is complete, our back doors and loopholes into Halcyon will be closed. Infiltrating The Path will be a hundred times harder. They are attempting to gain full control over life experiences. With this merger or takeover, the FDEC will virtually have no checks and balances. One entity should not have this much power. What's happening to you and many others will only get worse. We've got to disrupt this merger."

GHotz pauses and exhales deeply. "Jolem man, I feel for what you've just been through and believe me, Dalio will get his, but right now, our mission is to stop this merger."

"Well… what can we do??"

"We've written a worm program we could use to delete the integration code. It's a sneaky and unnoticeable virus that can secretly attach itself to Dalio's World, make its way past his quarantine and into SEE. When in her core, it will find and destroy the code without leaving a trace. From there, it will self-detonate."

GHotz's constantly moving fingers abruptly stop as he takes a contemplative pause. His grim expression becomes even soberer as he gazes toward Jolem. "I hate to be so direct, but I need to know now if you're in or out."

Jolem slowly spans the room of hopeful and concerned faces. They desperately need him and he knows it. "I have a debt to pay," he murmurs, stiffening his posture. "Whatever I can do to help. I'm in."

"Stellaaa. Now, here's the plan. You know we have to get this worm into SEE, but we can't break through her firewall remotely; the security is too tight, so that's why we have to go through Diablo to access the network. If we corrupt the code, we think we can force SEE to abandon the merger. If we're lucky, we can also cause Dalio to make a costly mistake."

"How're we goin' to do that??"

"This is where you come in. Leema. We need you to meet her in person."

"Leema?? I haven't talked to her since Refugio and her World is blocked. I don't even… know what she thinks of me now."

"Yes, it's a risk, but if you get her to hide her AllVu for one second, we can make a copy of her pupils. This'll allow us to break into her World remotely and attach it. Through her, it can spread to Dalio's World. Then as soon as he accesses SEE, we're in."

"But – as soon as I step outside, I'll be exposed. And Leema will be covered with Compliance Control. How will I get past them?"

"The same way you got here. Your new persona should protect you as long as you keep your cool. Compliance Control and everyone else will see and hear Joyn Michaels."

Jolem grips and rubs his forehead. "OK," he sighs.

GHotz crosses his arms and tilts his head while looking at Jolem. "Man, I'm not gonna' lie; this won't be easy. We have eyes everywhere and we'll do what we can to keep them off your back – but if SEE suspects ANYTHING, especially a threat, it will react swiftly to correct it. You will be vulnerable while outside and you won't have much time. However, you're our best shot."

Listening to the magnitude of the task ahead, Jolem begins to pace in place as he massages the stiffness in the back of his neck. The feat seems impossible, and his slim feeling of hope begins to wane. "This is insane," he mumbles.

"You're right. It is," GHotz says, sitting back and waiting for Jolem to absorb it all.

Jolem deliberates quietly, shaking his head. The possible fate of their efforts rides on his shoulders. His head tilts back and then down. "So, when are we goin' to do this?" he asks.

"It has to be done today. The merger is tomorrow, so we must plant this worm ASAP."

GHotz takes a step back, and Gank moves toward his embattled friend. He pats him on the chest.

"Jolem – I have to drop one more thing on you. I hate to remind you of this, but if for some reason you fail, remember what'll happen. The blue bomb is still active. Should you become compromised, it will detonate and erase all experiences relating to us, the mission, the list, everything. You won't remember any of it, and you'll be on your own."

Jolem sucks in and blows out like a propeller. "Okay – let's do it."

"Alright then. Let's go phishing."

It's early afternoon, and hours have passed since Leema's confrontation with her father. Back in his Washington D.C. home, she moves about idly. Their verbal battle is still festering in her thoughts and she desperately wants to get out of the house. Just moments ago, she received an invitation to a late lunch from a good friend, but the director is adamantly against the idea.

"Until this merger is complete, we are under high alert and I'd like you to stay put," he firmly instructs virtually through her World. "I know your little boyfriend is back in The Path and being helped by his band of criminals. It is only a matter of time before they slip up and he'll be in our custody."

"Why are you so certain the masked man is him? What proof do you have?"

"I have all the proof I need. With 100% certainty, I know it was him, and he will pay severely. I just want you to remember how easy life was before reconnecting with this – deviant. The Path disconnected you two for a reason and now his return has infected you with his sickness. Can't you see? You can have that ease once again. You can have that peace. You're GreenView's Southeastern Director, remember? It's time for you to recommit yourself and move beyond this awful period."

Leema listens to his words with nostalgia for her prior carefree and happy life. She would love to have it back. However, conflicted between her heart and her mind, she can't forget the knowledge that now taunts her. She moves out of the room into the hall and sends a World message to her friend. "I'll be there," she says in defiance of her father's demand.

Smirking, Leema replies to her father, "Meeting a friend for lunch. Be back later," she says and he fumes. "LEEMA! I told you not to leave the house."

"Dad – I won't be gone long. And I'm sure your pets will be following me anyway."

"I want you to remember – I see everything."

Back in the Lore, Mitnic reclines low in his seat and then winks to the group. "Done. The simulation worked and she thinks she's meeting her friend. We're a go."

"Okay," grins GHotz. "Get Jolem set up and to DC."

THE MISSION

38

Following a strenuous ride, Jolem is only minutes from his Washington D.C. destination. The full weight of Divergent State's plan rests firmly on his shoulders and he's petrified. Any tiny mistake could draw SEEs attention, and then the mission and his freedom are both done. He has a simple goal. All he needs to do is persuade Leema to hide her AllVu and then look directly into her eyes. He's hopeful she'll welcome him with open arms, but in the back of his mind, he's fearful she'll reject him, and his cover will be blown.

With the subtle waves of the Potomac River to his side, Jolem drifts down the cobblestone roads of the historic Georgetown neighborhood in the nation's capital. The picturesque, upscale community is awash with high-end shops, independent boutiques, traditional taverns, college bars and cafes. As he takes note of locals and tourists moving carefreely through the vibrant sidewalks and intersections, his fingers tap uncontrollably on his thigh. He used to pity their blissful ignorance, but at this moment, he envies it.

Finally, Jolem's Zumer slides up to the curbside of the restaurant meetup location. It's a charming open-front contemporary-style building with a gorgeous panoramic view of the river. The location was chosen because of its unique themed dining experience. In individual rooms, small groups of friends and strangers participate in virtual games to solve puzzles while enjoying their meals. The layout presented a perfect opportunity to seclude Leema from Compliance Control. This will give

Divergent State a small window to distract SEE without arousing visual suspicion from others.

When his car slows to a stop, Jolem peeps around, scanning the waterfront activity. Children are splashing in a sprinkler-like water fountain, and lunch-goers lounge on patio seats while boats on the water ease by. He doesn't see Compliance Control but knows officers are not far off. He's insecurely reliant on the protection of his false persona and Gank's remote direction. The door swings open, and his fate is out of his hands.

"Have a great day, Mr. Michaels," salutes the Zumer as Jolem gingerly steps out. His heart is beating like a drum, so he takes a deep breath to calm down. He's so nervous he's afraid he'll give himself away. Exhaling slowly, he looks straight ahead at the entrance, only feet ahead. He begins forward, but the short walkway seems to stretch farther with each timid movement. His breaths are fast as his legs teeter. He feels like he's about to pass out. The door appears so far off, it seems he'll never make it. He's plagued with dubious thoughts, but before long, he arrives.

Jolem's jaws clench to hold his jovial expression intact as he moves carefully through the festive crowd. Back in the Lore, the crew is monitoring his every maneuver. They're aware Leema is already inside one of the interactive rooms nursing a drink as she waits for her company. She's still shaken from the previous day's chaos and had lobbied her friend to meet at an intimate table for two. However, her "friend" was able to convince her a fun distraction could be just what she needed to get back on track.

When Jolem enters the room, her head turns his way and she cracks a soft courteous grin, but her sullen expression barely changes. Disguised by his digitally distorted appearance and identifiers, she believes he's the first of her dining companions.

"Hello, this should be fun," he says as he slips down into the seat directly across from her. "This'll be something new for me."

"Yes, it's my first time too. Should be fun," she replies, coercing a smile and then glances back towards the door. She's completely deceived by his appearance.

"Is everything okay?" he questions. "You seem – bothered."

"Hmm…that was – random," she comments, flinching. "You just met me."

Leaning in close, Jolem startles her. "Leema please, please relax," he whispers in his natural tone. "I'm not Joyn Michaels. It's me – Jolem."

When she hears Jolem's undistorted voice out of the mouth of a stranger, Leema is stunned. "Jolem?? But…your face. How?"

"Leema, I only have a minute to talk. Hide your AllVu, and you'll see. But be very – normal."

With a thought, Leema hides her AllVu and is shocked when his long nose, freckles and other distinct facial features morph into Jolem's. Now unobstructed by her AllVu visors, Jolem looks into her eyes, and a copy of her pupils is made. Quickly, the first part of the mission is successful.

"JOLEM. It IS you – but how?" she asks, and he's comforted by her expression; she still seems to be on his side.

"Shhh – relax, relax. I don't have time to go into it now, but I had to see you."

"So, my friend who invited me? That was you??"

"It was. I hated tricking you, but it was the only way. I'm sorry."

"But… you shouldn't be here. My father. He says you're with the Divide."

"I know, I know. I just need you to know everything you've heard about me is a lie. I need you to believe me. It's all untrue."

"I knew it. I couldn't believe it. But you risked everything just to tell me this??"

"I needed you to know the truth."

Jolem exhales as he's momentarily lost in her large luminous eyes and soft smile. He'd love to preserve the tender moment, but once again, the pressure is on.

"Jolem, they're on to you!" yells Gank, and Jolem's face cringes. "Get outta there now! You've got less than two minutes."

"Okay, Leema, sorry I gotta' go," Jolem says discreetly, lifting up.

"But –"

"I'll try to contact you later. This experience has been masked from your assistant; just act normal. I was never here," he whispers and then strides out of the room. "G – where do I go?"

"Head to the back; next to the bathroom there's an exit. I'll kill the alarm and distract them. Hurry, the officers are moving in fast."

Jolem leaves the room and casually slides past the unwitting patrons on his way to the lounge's back exit. He approaches the door, but it remains sealed. "It's locked," he says, panicking.

"Hold a sec…now." Within a moment, it slides open.

Jolem peeks outside, panting like a track runner. The pound of his heart feels like it's about to burst through his chest.

"Go, man. GO!" shouts Gank.

As Jolem escapes out of the back, Compliance Control appears at the front. Moving in unison, the unarmed trio of shiny masked officers storms past the lobby of gawking guests and into Leema's room.

"Ms. Dalio, where is he?" robotically asks the lead while the others stand a step behind on each side.

Leema slowly drops her glass of water onto the table and twists her lips. "Who??"

"We know Jolem McKay was here. Where is the deviant?"

"Jolem?? I haven't seen Jolem since the unicom, and I hope I never see him again."

"Ms. Dalio, I detect deception."

The lead officer strides out the door, and then his sights circulate the room of stunned faces. His scan stops, and then, with two fingers, he signals to the back. "That way," he calmly instructs and the two other officers make chase.

With slow rhythmic steps, the lead moves back to Leema's side and then stiffens like a mannequin. "The director requests we escort you home," he says without almost moving a muscle. Moments later, as he stands firm next to her, two more officers appear at the room door. "Good day in The Path," the lead says, tipping his head and then follows the back-door pursuit.

Down the back alley, Jolem is on the run. He's worn out and being propelled by pure adrenaline. Above, he hears the low-flying buzz of unmanned FDEC hovercrafts. They have the vision of satellites to home in on the smallest target. Gank and crew do all they can to jam signals, but they can only provide Jolem intermittent retreats. The Path continues to pinpoint his location. Pretty soon, he'll be trapped.

"They're right on your tail, so go south to the end of the block. Six drones have locked on you, and I can only block their signals for minutes at a time. HURRY!"

Jolem races out into the busy waterfront sidewalk and tries to mix with others. From all angles, he can see officers converging, and he has nowhere to go. "Gank??!"

"Big Eye's locked in on your persona. They see you!"

"What do I do??!"

"Okay, okay I'm gonna' try somethin' we've been developing. It's untested, so I hope it works. Let's play a game of hide-and-seek."

"What's that??"

"When I initiate, your AllVu will randomly change to different personas. It'll confuse em'. Let's hope this works. 1…2…3…"

Suddenly, the officers stop in their tracks and begin to look around erratically. The swirling drones also seem to lose focus. Lucky for Jolem, Gank's trickery works to perfection. As Jolem's persona instantly changes from Joyn Michaels to someone else, the officers lose him in the crowd.

"Okay, move naturally into the coffee shop next to you and sit with your back to the entrance," instructs Gank.

"But?"

"Now."

Inconspicuously, Jolem slides out of the throng of people and into the unassuming café at his side. He drops his head and slips into the nearest bistro table away from the door. As he slumps in his seat, he can hear Compliance Control sirens rapidly approaching. Within mere moments, the loud activity sounds like it's just outside the building. Gank has gone silent and Jolem believes he's reached the end of his road. His eyes close and his chin falls to his chest as he resigns to the inevitable. But when the noise reaches its peak, surprisingly, officers don't burst into the coffee shop and apprehend him. Instead, the blare grows faint until it slowly disappears.

"Huh??" he grunts, lifting his head.

"Man! You owe me another one," laughs Gank. "Those idiots are chasing an empty Zumer. They think you're in the back seat," he hollers. "We have a Zumer craft on the river waiting for you. Good job, man. We're bringing you home."

39

Early the next morning, everyone in the Lore is on edge. There was little to no sleep the night before. With less than eight hours before the completion of the merger, Leema and the virus have yet to enter Director Dalio's World.

"What the hell, man?" questions AdrianLulz slamming her fist into a virtual punching bag. "She hasn't gone to his World yet? We need her to make that move."

"Relax, relax – she will soon," calmly comments GHotz as he watches the tracker. "Just relax."

Almost another hour passes and still no movement. At the mercy of fortune, not many words are spoken between them. All they can do is wait, and pessimism begins to slowly infect their thoughts. Tensions flare.

"I knew this wasn't gonna' work. Why'd we waste all our time with this joker??" AndrianLulz yells with her finger pointed to Jolem.

"You know, screw you, Lulz! I put my life on the line out there!" fires back Jolem.

The two continue shouting at one another until then it happens. "Hold a min," calls out Gonzalez Gold. "She just entered Dalio's World. The worm is on the move!"

"Yeah!" GHotz shouts, brandishing his fist, displaying an unusual level of emotion. "Now give it a sec to go through quarantine," he says, lifting his finger and the Lore becomes as silent as an old library. "It's in!"

After the intense waiting game, the second part of the mission is complete, and the group erupts into cheer. AdrianLulz and Jolem flash smiles of respect and, for the moment, put their personal differences aside. The feuding couple embrace and lock fists. However, as euphoria spreads throughout the room, GonzalezGold calls for quiet. "Hold up, hold up...I'm getting something strange. Wait...wait," he says, lifting his hands. "There's a message transmitting from the dark web. You all have got to hear this."

When he pulls the communication out into the air, attention focuses on the untimely return of the masked stranger from the Divide. This time standing alone, he addresses a different audience. His grim words are not for the general public but instead for his fellow hackers.

"To all my brothers and sisters in the struggle or those of you just stealing crumbs like rodents of the night, I have a message for you," he says sternly. "This country needs a revival, and the only way humanity can live again is for The Path to die. Things have gone too far to fix. It has to end."

While they look at each other with dismay, they attempt to locate the source. However, even with the collective skills in the Lore, they can't break through the treads of the clever transmission.

"We've already set in place a plan to take down The Path," the masked man continues. "As we speak, a virus is making its way through SEE, silently sabotaging Worlds. It's a very nimble virus. It hops around from World to World, duplicating. By the time SEE figures out the magnitude of what's going on, millions of Worlds will have been infected. Then when it's reached every World in this country; BOOM!"

As they listen to his gloomy announcement, the room is silent.

"We estimate it will take another six hours for it to replicate to all Worlds. The moment Version 10 is launched, Halcyon will crack, and The Path signal will simultaneously shut down. No more assistants. No more Worlds. No more Path. Confusion will follow, chaos, mass hysteria and ultimately, freedom. You will try, but there's nothing you can do to prevent this. Prepare yourselves."

The communication slowly fades into nothing, and the collective is stunned.

"They can't be serious!" cries Jolem. "This is insane!"

GHotz nestles into the back of his worn leather seat with his forehead resting on his fingertips. He releases a long breath that seems to take ten minutes to finish. "Wow, this just got really real," he says unemotionally. "This is even beyond the FDEC and the merger. If the Divide's virus is executed and The Path goes down, the collateral damage to society could be – catastrophic."

With ominous visions of doomsday swirling in Jolem's head, his thoughts immediately shift to Liz and his mom. Gank. I've got to check on my family. I need to know they're okay.``

"Jolem, are you crazy? We need all resources here right now. Millions of lives are at stake."

"I know, I know, but I'll just be in the way. I need to see my family. I won't be much help here."

Shaking his head, Gank sighs. "You know, when you step outside our firewall, you'll be vulnerable again. We need to focus on all this. We can't protect you."

"I'll risk it. Just get me to the house. I'll take it from there."

"Jo, Alright, man," he shrugs. "You know this is suicide."

"Gank," Jolem begins, then wearily shakes his head. "I've got nothing to lose."

Gank pats his exhausted friend on the chest and then reaches out his hand. "I hope I see you on the other side then bro."

Gank reluctantly reprogrammed Jolem's AllVu and sent him on his way. According to Liz's AllVu, she's in the house, but their mother is dark and can't be found. Jolem rides through the suburban streets on his way to his childhood home with the wind in his face. He was instructed to keep his windows closed to further shield him against facial detection, but he disregards the advice. He's exhausted from all the confining rules and strict guidelines he's had to follow. He just wants to be free.

As he rides, he takes note of the beautiful moment that's now being threatened by both The Path and the Divide. The clear blue sky doesn't have a cloud in sight. It's probably the most radiant blue he's ever seen. And the smell of the air as it blows gently against his face is alluring. It's a sweet fragrance like he's never smelled before. Today the simple pleasures of life have renewed appreciation.

When he turns the corner to his street, fond recollections of landmarks and events become vivid without the help of his AllVu. Even the large disagreements with his mom today seem petty and insignificant. He misses her and Liz profoundly. He's been without his World for days and hasn't been able to revisit any of his past experiences. They're stuck in the cloud, waiting for his true AllVu to be reactivated should he somehow make it through all this. All the madness of the last couple of weeks seems so surreal. He wishes he could go back in time and wash it all away.

When his Zumer stops in front of his childhood home, he's antsy to see his sister but also cautious. He thinks back to her advice from days ago that he didn't follow. His deviation has undoubtedly affected her, and his mother's lives. Like with Leema, he doesn't know how his surprise presence will be received. After his momentary pause, he advances to the door and his false persona is greeted by Liz's assistant.

"Hi, I'm here to see Liz," replies Jolem.

"Hmm, she's not expecting you. Is there anything I can help you with?"

"Well, actually, I really need to speak with her. It's concerning her brother."

"Okay. One moment please."

As he anxiously waits for his sister, Jolem must force his trembling fingers still. With all his power, he's attempting to remain calm. Thanks to Gank, local cameras and observation drones are temporarily muffled, but only for minutes. He needs to get out of sight. If she doesn't answer quickly and allow him in, he's sure to be noticed.

"Yes, can I help you?" Liz says, appearing on the door's video panel. Inside, he's bursting with excitement, but on the outside, he's collected.

"Hi, uh, I have a message fro – from Jolem."

"Jolem??"

"Ye – yeah. But...I need you to hide your AllVu first. Please trust me, Squirt."

When Liz hears her brother's commonly used nickname for her, her face lights up. "Hide AllVu!" she instructs. "Open door."

The door slides open, and as Jolem steps in, his true identity is exposed to her.

"Jolem!" Liz yells, launching towards him. Her head sinks into his chest, and tears of happiness trickle down her face. Jolem grips her tightly, his eyes close, and he lets out a labored breath of relief. The loving reception takes him back to when he arrived home from Refugio when he was thirteen.

"You look terrible, Jolem. What's happened to you??" she questions, pushing back. His deep sunken bloodshot eyes make him look like he's aged years in only weeks.

"Sooo much, I can't even begin," he croaks, dropping his heavy head. "I just needed to make sure you were alright. Where's mom?"

"Jolem – she's a wreck. She's dark and waaaay over her limit. Family...friends – they've turned their back on us. Everyone believes you are the masked man. Our SIVs have nosedived. No one likes us anymore."

Jolem grabs Liz and pulls her close. He stares into her eyes and pleas. "Liz, I'm sooo sorry for all this. But, please don't listen to anything you've heard about me – none of it's true. None of it! There's something big about to happen and...I don't know how this will turn out."

Liz gazes sympathetically at Jolem and smirks. "Jolem, you know when I was kid, I used to look up to you. I thought you had all the answers. You were my hero," she softly begins and then pauses. "But now...now, I just can't help feeling sorry for you. Life is sooo good and this sickness has you all confused. You need help. I'm trying not to believe the masked man was you, but...I don't know."

Jolem slowly steps backward, thrown by Liz's sudden demeanor change and unflattering comments. "Liz, these are all lies! Lies! Dalio is trying to set me up," he cries, but her pitiful stare continues. "Can't you see?? None of it is true. NONE OF IT!" he yells.

A small pool forms in the well of her eye, and slowly a single tear trickles down the curve of her cheek.

"Sorry, Jolem...but it's too late."

"Liz! What have you done?!" he utters, but her silence speaks volumes. As he gazes into her burdensome eyes, he knows he's been betrayed. His strongest strength has always been his most fragile weakness.

"Jolem – Compliance Control is on the way. It's time to stop running. You need help. I received an Advisory Alert warning me you would try something like this. The Path sees everything. Let the FDEC help you, Jolem. I'm sorry."

"Not you too, Liz. Not you!" he yells. He rushes to the kitchen window wall and presses against the glass. Down the street, a caravan of Compliance Control SUVs is racing his way. As he looks around feverishly, trying to find a way out, Liz reaches out to him. "Jolem, please stop running," she pleas. "Stay. Let The Path help you."

"I can't do that. And no matter what happens...I love you. Always."

With those parting words, Jolem jets for the back door, but it won't open. "Liz, release the door! Let me out!" he shouts, but she stands firm. "Sorry, Jolem. I have to save you from yourself," she says, extending her hand to him.

Jolem grabs the closet chair, swings it back and starts ramming it against the glass wall until it shatters. He tosses the chair aside, races outside and leaps off the second-floor balcony. After awkwardly landing on his shoulder, he grimaces in pain, but he can't stop. He leaps up and hobbles out into the street but comes to a chilling halt. Compliance Control is emerging from all angles. Twisting around frantically, he searches for an escape, but realizes he's cornered.

After evading Compliance Control for two days, Jolem is finally caught. Standing alone in the middle of a solid barrier of flashing lights from the street and in the air, he's out of options. Slowly, his hands lift in surrender while he turns his sights back to the balcony of his old home. Leaning against the rail, Liz looks down with tears dripping from her face. She truly believes the outcome will serve the greater good.

"Jolem McKay, you are surrounded, and there is no way out. Please do not resist," resounds from the perimeter of black-mated vehicles in front of him.

Jolem is heartbroken by the surprise double-cross of his beloved sister. With his hands high and away from his body, he releases a long-sorrowed exhale. Blinding lights shooting down from hovercrafts shine back and forth across his body. For long moments, the wall of Compliance Control officers stands firm, and it seems like an eternity before they even flinch. Then like a marching band, they synchronously begin toward him, and Jolem's head drops like an anchor.

Suddenly, an inexplicable loud screech from down the street draws all attention. Jolem's eyes swing open and the officer's movements are stunted in place. Maneuvering wild and fast, a large sixteen-wheeler truck heads straight toward them. Before they can hardly react, it barrels through their SUV barricade, sending the officers leaping for cover.

"Take that BITCHES!!!" howls AdrianLulz, remotely controlling the rig like a toy. At the same time, jammed signals send the circling hovercrafts into a tailspin. The welcome distraction provides Jolem with the opportunity he needs to slip away.

"Jolem, we can't leave you alone for a second, can we?" cracks Gank. "Tired of savin' your ass!"

"Can't thank you enough, bro! What do I do??"

"Third house on the right. Back door. It's open. Follow my direction, and we'll get you outta' this."

"OKAY! What's next?"

"Listen. We're goin' to get you to the Times Square V10 countdown celebration. You'll be among a million people who should give SEE fits trying to discover you in the crowd. Your randomly changing personas should hold. The bug is on the move, but we're still trying to figure out how to handle the Divide, so sit tight. One way or another, somethin' big pops off tonight."

"Got it."

"Jo – SIT TIGHT."

40

"The time has finally come, my friends. In a little more than an hour, Version 10 will be launched. Cheers to you all," Dalio congratulates as stimulating mists pass through the air. In tribute to the momentous event, an FDEC conference hall is filled with executives, spouses and esteemed guests. In a holiday-like atmosphere, the countdown has begun.

"As soon as V10 goes live, the fine people of this country will truly experience life enhanced like never before. This will be our greatest moment of triumph. Relish it."

With his head held high, the director proudly circles the room to vigorous applause. He brandishes his fists in the air. "And we are one step closer to crushing these hacking cockroaches like the pests they are!" he proclaims and the gathering hails. Nodding, he parades through the clapping crowd and their flattering emojis, accepting their praise with contrived humility. However, only moments later, his premature gloating comes to an unexpected halt.

"Director. We have a problem," warns SEE.

"Huh? What kind of problem??" he whispers. Behind his smile, his teeth grits.

"For an unknown reason, the integration code is – being deleted."

The director lifts his hand and chuckles. "Please will you all excuse me for a moment. Duty calls," he says chuckling factiously, as he moves out of the room into the hall. "What?? How?"

"I haven't yet determined, but 20% has been removed."

"Stop it! Stop it!"

"I'm unable to locate the source. 40% has been removed."

"NO!"

"60%..."

"What about our backups?"

"I've attempted to roll back or replicate, but the backup sources have also been compromised. It's a virus. 80%..."

"All this work, ruined," fumes the director.

"Director…100% of the merger code has been erased."

"No! What happened!?" he barks.

"It appears a worm program has somehow entered my system. Its purpose was to stop the merger. Its location has yet to be determined."

"Find that worm and dissect it! We need to know who's responsible for this and make them pay!" Instead of returning to the festivities, he storms down the hall to his office.

As Dalio's mood deflates, the Lore ignites. To their relief, the plan worked flawlessly and their improbable mission is a success. Spirits are high in their basement hide-away, however there's little time for back slapping. Stopping the merger will mean nothing if the Divide successfully launches its virus and shuts down The Path. The resulting breakdown in society could be disastrous. The Lore's ambitions completely shift to preventing this nightmare scenario from unfolding.

GonzalezGold swings open his hands and a digital algorithm appears in the air. "Wait, we already have the worm burrowing in SEE," he blurts out. "Can't we remote attach an antivirus program to go after Divide's virus? It can sniff it out and kill it before it can execute."

GHotz pushes out his lip and pulls at its protruding ring. "The idea is intriguing, but we don't have enough time," he sighs. "Their virus has been replicating through The Path for days. It would be impossible to reprogram our worm with an antivirus program intelligent enough to locate it. We also have no idea how much time it'll take SEE to find our worm; could be minutes or even seconds. It can't hide forever. We need it to detonate so that it's not caught."

"WAIT. Maybe we don't need it to," comments AdrianLulz leaping to her feet.

"What??"

"Hide."

"Lulz. What are you talkin' about?"

"Our worm's damage is contained to the integration code. Besides the Halcyon merger, nothing else was affected, so The Path continues as normal. But what if we unleash it out into the rest of SEE? The Path will be automatically forced into Safe Mode to protect itself."

"And in Safe Mode, The Path will immediately lock down and quarantine all Worlds," continues GHotz. "Their virus will be exposed and mitigated. Lulz you're a genius!"

"That I am, but we'll save the ass kissing for later," she says winking. "If the Divide realizes what we're doing, they'll most likely detonate their virus. We've got to be discreet and we don't have much time to set this worm free. Gonzalez, I need you!"

The team in the Lore quickly sets in motion action to obstruct the Divide's attack. They have less than an hour. While they reprogram the worm's directives, in New York City Jolem mentally prepares for the worst. With his new persona intact, he blends in among the massive Times Square crowd as they anticipate the launch of V10. The huge, mesmerized gathering, delights at an augmented light celebration in the sky. As colossal cartoon characters and vivid star-spangled images dance above the tall skyscrapers, Jolem moves slowly through the pack. He follows their enchanted expressions and feels sorry for them all. They have no clue of the potential disaster just around the bend.

Jolem's AllVu vibrates and then an anonymous message pops up in front of him. "We have a plan. Moment of truth soon." It's a short and hopeful note from Gank that will be overlooked by The Path.

There hasn't been a public word from the Divide since their ominous World interruption over a week ago. To most, their direful proclamation has been long since forgotten or just disregarded as hacker folly. Twenty-seven minutes from the scheduled 8PM release of V10, the country is in a happy frenzy. In-person gatherings are filled and grand virtual celebrations continue. Without warning, the booming anthem and slow digital entrance of the three masked men once again take over the nation's Worlds. Their images overtake the sky celebration and all other broadcasts. Like the first time, the two men on the side stand silently with their arms crossed while the middleman addresses the shocked national audience.

"My fellow Americans, this is my final address to you. The time grows near. Some of you will feel the following actions will be cruel, even inhumane, but believe me, what we do is for the good of humanity. The reckoning is here. Keep those you love near because you will not be able to depend on The Path. We, the people, are neither data nor bots. We have brains, compassion, and all capable of greatness. I can't say this will come without pain. Unfortunately, there will be a lot of it. But we are strong and resilient. We will endure. We will emerge out of this like a phoenix rising from the flames."

As the nation watches, millions become crippled with fear and confusion from the gloomy speech. The mystery man glances to his companion on his right, to his left, and then stares straight ahead again. While all eyes are glued on him, his digital mask dissolves exposing his identity to the world.

"I cannot allow history to be written by propaganda or lies," he begins. "I am NOT Jolem McKay and he has no connection to my movement. Although we wear the Freedom Fighter symbol, we have no affiliation. I've been liberated from my identifiers, so simply remember me as X. The release of The Path Version 10 will be YOUR liberation."

Jolem is stunned and as he scans the bewildered crowd, he doesn't know how to react. Dueling parts of him want to laugh and yell at the same time. The imminent threat from the Divide is gravely serious. However, no matter whatever comes next, he's assured Liz, his mom, and Leema are aware he was telling the truth. His vindication is unmeasurable.

As suddenly as they appeared, the fearsome trio flash out of sight leaving the Times Square masses perplexed. People look to their neighbors with clueless expressions while animated thought bubbles spring above their heads. They're disturbed, but some begin to question the reality of what they've just seen. Curiously, the celebration gradually returns to normal and the Divide's grim words are again pushed aside. Jolem is blown away by their apathy. It's as if they all had just watched a commercial or movie trailer.

Jolem wants to be alone and far from everyone when the moment comes. He recognizes the time quickly elapsing and pushes his way through the packed crowd. With only fifteen minutes before eight o'clock, he has to hurry to find sanctuary. When he finally pries into the open, he spots an empty waiting Zumercraft shuttle preparing for takeoff. He dashes for it and hops through the closing door, despite not even knowing where it's going. "Welcome Mr. Ryte, I don't see you on the party's list. You're not authorized," comments the Zumer.

"Must be an error. I'll correct it at the door," Jolem replies. "Override."

"Sure Mr. Ryte. Enjoy your ride."

The Zumercraft lifts up and floats away. Jolem peeks down out of the window as his ride quickly moves in the distance of the massive colorful gathering. With only minutes to spare, the Zumercraft lands on a tenth-floor landing pad of a high rise, blocks off from Times Square. "Right in time for the celebration, Mr. Ryte," remarks the Zumer as the door slides open. "Please hurry to assume your viewing position for Director Dalio's announcement."

"I will. Thanks!"

The Zumercraft pulls off the launchpad and Jolem heads into the building toward the private party hall. The Divide's attack is set to coincide with the V10 launch and only seconds remain before the ceremony commencement. The moments pass in slow motion as five o'clock approaches and Jolem diverts into an open office. He slides back against the wall and cradles his legs. Solemnly, his eyelids slide shut. When his AllVu orbs vibrate, his jaws clench, and his muscles tense. He knows the time has arrived.

All Worlds are simultaneously interrupted just as they were during Dalio's V10 Announcement. "Good evening, I'm SEE with an important Path communication. Everyone, please pause what you are doing and pay close attention to this very special update from The FDEC's National Director Arturo Dalio. All Worlds will shift to sleep mode during his announcement."

Director Dalio's hologram moves forward out of virtual nothingness. Wearing the FDEC's shiny, grey body-suit, he smiles and waves to the adoring national audience.

"Good evening fellow citizens of this great nation. Once again, I am honored to speak on behalf of the FDEC and The Path," he begins and the virtual audience goes wild. "The wait is finally over," he lauds. "In mere moments we're going to launch V10 and your lives will never be the same again. Remember this is your FDEC going to work for you. We'll never stop pushing to make your life happier, more fulfilling and protected. You've undoubtedly watched the Divide's mutinous threats. Let me assure you these terrorists are just within our grasp!" he charges, clenching his fists and gritting his teeth. "We will not be persuaded by fear or intimidation. The Path has set us free. It is here now and FOREVER MORE!" he proclaims.

During a long vigorous applause, Director Dalio stands firm pumping his fists in the air. He moves from side-to-side punching like a prize-fighter and the crowd's adulation continues. The nation is wrapped in his charms. When the loud praise diminishes, he settles with his arms to his side. A large throbbing green button with the word "LAUNCH" inscribed in its middle, appears next to him. He displays his pointer finger to the audience. "Are we ready??" he yells and they cheer him on.

Back in the Lore, tensions are high. GonzalezGold wipes away the dripping sweat from his forehead as he moves interlocking holographic images into place. He grips the final piece and then slips it into the fitting space in his puzzle. "Ahh…OKAY!" he stutters stepping back. "That shooould do it."

At the same time, the director's hand slowly moves in front of the button. As the anticipation reaches its peak, he pauses teasingly. "LAUNCH! LAUNCH! LAUNCH!" they chant. He flashes a great big grin to the public, turns back to the button and then – presses it. Rejoice erupts as vivid light displays shoot in the air like fireworks. Then abruptly, everything stops.

To the amazement of all, in households across the country an eerie silence replaces the activity of The Path. People look around speechless into the undigitized faces of friends, family and neighbors as all mixed reality disappears. No more Worlds, assistants or connected technology. HumanAids and other NonHumans fall idle. In the twenty-eight-year history of The Path, a stoppage has never occurred. It's a moment of despair and panic that's shared by everyone, no matter the SIV.

Long seconds stretch into minutes and panic spreads like wild-fire. Like the end of days, horrified individuals suddenly find religion and pray to the skies above. Some begin to weep, while delirium corrupts the fragile minds of others. The Divide's doomsday scenario is realized.

The Lore is dead silent. As they mire in disappointment, their puzzled and defeated expressions fill the room. Apparently their strategy to stop the virus was not good enough. They've failed and without any answers, even the fortitude of these hardcore personalities, breakdown. They know it's only a matter of time before society begins to fall apart and pandemonium erupts.

Jolem remains squatted on the floor with his head sunk into his folded arms. He's paralyzed with despair. He doesn't hear a sound and the quiet is deafening. Without AllVu, he has no idea where he is or what to do next. Like being stranded on a desolate island, he's hopeless and alone.

Suddenly, like the power returning after a thunderstorm, the lifelessness of The Path inexplicably re-activates. The lights and electricity resurrect, his World re-ignites, and augmented images and sounds are renewed. Within the Lore, eyes and mouths spring open and the collective explode into a volcano of tears and cheers. Although late, it appears SEE has discovered and stunted the Divide's attack. GHotz, Gank, and the crew embrace like never before. A small band of hackers and a deviant, ironically worked together to save the system they've been fighting against.

Jolem rattles his clenched fists in triumph. After the longest days of his life, he can finally breathe a little easier. He's unsure what tomorrow holds, but in this monumental moment, he's more hopeful than ever before. All seems possible. He stretches his aching neck from side-to-side. He's emotionally overwhelmed and can't believe it's finally all over. Liz and his mom appear in his thoughts, followed by Leema. He titters at the vision of her smile and large brown eyes. As he shakes his head in disbelief, his light laugh progressively grows into a crack-up. With his scarred and swollen hands, he presses up off the floor until he's upright. All of a sudden, his body trembles when he hears an unwelcome voice.

"Hello, Jolem," speaks, as coarse as sandpaper."

"Dir – director Dalio??"

"You seem surprised to hear from me."

"But how?" Jolem whispers.

"It took us a little while, but we were able to isolate similar abnormalities in your changing personas. This little AllVu trick won't work anymore. Believe me, there's nowhere to run. It's time to give yourself up."

"Give myself up? But it's over. The Divide failed."

"Jolem please," the director condescends. "It's far from over. There is a matter of the destruction of the merger code. The non-release of Version 10 is a huge disappointment and a major setback for the nation. You should be proud. You and your cronies were successful, where so many others have failed. But now, someone has to be held accountable."

"But...but we helped you. Without us, there would be disaster!"

"Jolem don't be so naïve," the director snickers. "Did you actually think you and your friends were responsible for the return of The Path? We've known about the Divide's so-called plan for some time."

"What?? That was you? You were behind the Divide??"

"Oh no. The Divide's threat was real and could have caused enormous damage. But we discovered and shut it down days ago. Then they became our patsy. They played the roles of the perfect boogeymen. It was actually SEEs idea; brilliant. We have such a wonderful Human-Non-Human partnership."

"Huh??"

"WE stopped The Path, or shall I say, suspended its non-essential functions. We just needed to show the public a glimpse of a world without The Path. You know, just to scare them a little. Like it or not, our lives are much too dependent on it now. It's a fusion of existence that is here to stay. However, the integration with Halcyon was essential to the Version 10 upgrade. When the code was deleted, we were forced to terminate or postpone the release. I could have you locked up for life for this act of treason."

"This – this can't all be true."

"Now, we will release a statement to the public claiming to have foiled the assailants' plot, restored The Path and captured those responsible. They will be disappointed V10 will be postponed, but they'll love us for saving the day. Their faith in us will be unwavering. We could've admitted failure, but wouldn't you say this was a much better outcome? Everything you've done, I'm afraid to say, was for nothing."

"OKAY, then, you've won! So, what do you want with me? Why can't you leave me alone?!" Jolem yells.

"Jolem, we've actually been monitoring you for some time now. As a matter of fact, ever since you developed a bond with my daughter, we've made sure you were close. You are different. The Path doesn't have room for different. We thought your promotion would keep you quiet. We've tried awards and exceptions, but still no. It's amazing to me the resolve of unique minds such as yours. Life could be so easy if you'd just enjoy it like most, but something drives you to want more. To challenge authority. It's in your blood. Jolem – come in and end this peacefully. I promise you a fair deal."

"Me a fair deal?? You killed all those people in Refugio!"

"Jolem, I have no idea what you're talking about. Are you referring to all those Path-hating Unicom scum? I don't know if I despise them or the Freedom Fighters more. However, I did nothing to them."

"You're a liar and a monster!"

"A monster, you say??" Director Dalio chuckles menacingly. "That's funny. You think I'm a monster, and your friends, your family…they believe I'm a GOD."

"No. You won't get away with this! And I won't turn myself in. If you want me, you'll have to come get me."

"Have it your way. Just take a look outside."

Jolem lumbers over to the window wall and hesitantly peeks out. On the ground, there's a black sea of flashing lights. In the air, Compliance Control aircrafts circle the building. His head drops like it's too heavy to hold upright. There was peace for a few minutes after the return of The Path. That brief period of tranquility seems like a distant memory. His head slowly lifts, and his eyes pry open. "Okay. Come and get me," he murmurs.

"Very disappointing. I offered you a fair deal, but you refused it. You should hope I'm in such a generous mood when you're in my custody."

When Dalio's transmission breaks, Jolem knows he doesn't have much time before officers storm the building. Now that his false persona has been detected, he's aware there's nowhere to hide, but he won't give up. Soon, they'll arrive to arrest him, and he doesn't want to be a sitting duck. He doesn't know what he'll do next, but he won't be taken without a fight.

Jolem drags out of the room, down the hall, and into the stairwell. Painstakingly, he pulls himself up stair-to-stair and floor-to-floor. Every inch of his body aches, and it seems his arduous climb will never end. Finally, he turns the corner, and the moon's shine alerts him that he's reached the top level of the tall building. He pauses to take a long-relieved breath and then braces for outside.

A mild early evening breeze meets Jolem as he presses out onto the rooftop. He's so tired that he's barely able to remain upright. As he attempts to catch his breath, he closes his eyes and leans back against the wall. The structure is the only thing keeping him from falling over.

Precious moments pass as he rests with the wind softly blowing against his face. Needing to kick back into gear, he forces his heavy eyelids apart. From his right over to his left, he spies the full landscape of the flat rooftop. In the clear blue sky, the flashing dual-color lights of FDEC's aircrafts hover near the corners of the building. They have him pinned.

Jolem swipes away the beads of sweat cascading down his face and fills his lungs with a deep inhale. His frame drops, and the captured air audibly expels out of his hoarse throat. Looking straight, he can see the building's edge about fifty feet ahead at the end of a paved walkway. He pushes off the wall and twists the kinks out of his sore arms and shoulders. Staggering, he starts forward through a path of large illuminating Solar panels to his right and huge industrial exhaustion fans to his left. When he reaches the ledge, he carefully leans over the short glass rail and looks down to the ground. It is an amazing spectacle all devoted to him.

For minutes, Jolem surveys all the activity in the sky and below. Dejected, he considers leaping over the railing and ending this nightmare on his own terms. Suddenly, the rooftop door slides open and his head jerks in its direction. Three Compliance Control officers step outside and form a line next to each other. The trio pull out their hand-held stun guns and slowly begin forward. "Jolem McKay, please do not resist," calls the middle officer. "You are under arrest for Non-Compliance Code 56.23. Place your hands in the air."

As the officers inch closer, Jolem etches down the ledge. His sights swing up, down and around, but there is nowhere to go. Little by little, he moves toward the corner of the rooftop with his arms straddled on top of the railing. The wind from the propellers of a near black metallic hovercraft, knocks Jolem slightly off balance. Its so close he can almost touch it. "Resistance is futile," the middle officer cries as he and his crew continue forward. "Stop, or we will be forced to disable you!"

With only an arm's length separating the officers and Jolem, the lead reaches out to him. "Jolem McKay, resistance is futile. Step down from the ledge. You are under arrest."

Jolem's eyes shift back and forth between the craft and the officers that are advancing to his side. With no other options, he spontaneously dashes for the hovercraft and leaps toward it. "STOP!" commands the officer as he extends his weapon and quickly sends a flash across to Jolem. With two hands, Jolem grabs the craft's wing and is almost able to evade the officer's zap. Still, it grazes his side. "Uhh," he glowers.

As Jolem hangs onto the sleek hovercraft, his weight and momentum send it sailing out of control. Quickly, it propels away from the building and wobbles through the open air. With all his remaining energy, Jolem desperately holds on for life as he suspends twenty stories above the ground. The unmanned vessel dramatically spins off and then shatters through the window side of a neighboring office building. Like a bowling ball toppling pins, Jolem tumbles through the floor of office furniture until he slams against the wall.

The wrecked office looks like the aftermath of a bomb site. Across the open floor, the warped siren of the damaged hovercraft sputters and then dies. Lodged under fallen debris, Jolem remains motionless. He's lucky to be alive. Disoriented and wincing in pain, it's a chore to even open his eyes. His worn clothes are shredded and drenched with blood. They are so damaged; the recuperative mechanisms of the digital fibers are feckless. He attempts to move his arm, but it doesn't respond. He thinks it's broken. As he tries to will himself onto his feet, he shrieks in agony. When he peeks at his leg, he sees a long shard of glass protruding out of his thigh. The pain is intense.

Jolem closes his eyes and reluctantly prepares to dislodge the sharp fragment from his leg. His jaws clench so tight he can hear his teeth grind together. His hand is shaking uncontrollably as it moves down his side and slips his fingers around the glass. On the internal count of three, he snatches it out and wails before tossing it aside. Blood gushes down his thigh, and the suffering is even worse.

The room is in a daze, and Jolem's not sure if the blood loss or the gun's stun is causing him confusion. He rips off the remnants of his shirt and ties it around his leg to stop the bleeding. With one arm, he agonizingly drags himself across the floor, almost blacking out along the way. After the painful pull, he makes it into an executive office and hides in a closet. With desperation, he holds on to the idea that the mangled electrical structures might cause some interference with The Path's signals.

While sitting in silence, the rapid beat of his heart pounds as if it's about to burst through the wall of his chest. He softly wipes the beads of sweat racing down the contours of his trembling face. With the back of his head against the wall, he has to battle his eyes from closing. The sedative shock from the rooftop is challenging his fortitude. He doesn't think he can fight much longer. With each passing second, his slim hope of escape gets dimmer.

As Jolem begins to move in and out of coherence, he recalls the events that led him to this fateful position. He grips his brow in discontent, wondering if he achieved anything. Should he have fallen in line and played by the rules? Should he have heeded the repeated warnings? Should he have just walked away? As his breaths intensify, a tear forms and slowly drips down his cheek. The room goes dark, and his thoughts become disheveled. Suddenly, he can't even remember how he ended up in the closet. Like a distorted radio transmission, he hears a faint but familiar voice.

"Jolem! Finally found you."

"Gank, is that you?? They've got me. There's no way out."

"Jolem, you're confused. Wake up!"

"I guess I won't remember any of this tomorrow, huh? Either they'll erase me, or the blue bomb will."

"Listen, something went wrong. Wake up!"

"No, I can't. Can't keep my eyes open," he mumbles. "I'm done. Well... thank you – for everything."

Just as his friend's voice withers away, ominous footsteps enter and circulate the room. They come to the door of Jolem's office and abruptly stop. "Jolem McKay, you are surrounded, and there is no way out. Please do not resist."

After being on the run for so long, he's finally out of space. There's nowhere to jump, no secret hideaways, no last-minute persona changes. The door slides open, and a blinding light shines on his face.

"You are being apprehended for Non-Compliance Code 56.23. Please do not resist."

Jolem's cramped hiding place starts to spin, and then his surroundings blur. His trembling hand lifts, and he follows the slow movements of his fingers. Finally, his arm drops, and he blacks out.

43

Jolem's heavy eyelids dredge open and the endless room is a hazy nothingness. "Huh??" he utters as he attempts to regain his cognition. He feels as if he's lying on a cloud. "Where – where am I??" he says, looking around. He rubs his fingers gently across his skin, searching for the unique patterns of his palms. All of a sudden, his muscles tense when Dalio's coarse voice sends chills through his spine.

"Hello, Jolem…"

While his head drifts hesitantly to his right, the blurry silhouette of Director Dalio flutters near. The faint whitewash of his presence appears in and out like a mirage.

"Director Da…lio?" he asks.

"Why so surprised? You knew we'd meet again."

Jolem's eyes close and he inhales deeply. Within a second, a lifetime passes through his thoughts. Channeling all of his strength to face whatever lies ahead, he releases the captured air out through his flared nostrils. He makes peace with his fate and then his head lifts up proudly. All the events of the last few weeks have culminated in this very moment.

"Yes. I knew this time would come," he says.

The director's right hand slips out of his dark pants pocket and swings open. "Here – you'd probably be more comfortable sitting down." Off to his side, it seems a chair appears out of nowhere.

Blinking his eyes in confusion, Jolem looks at the chair. "I don't understand," he says, rubbing his head. "Is this real??"

"Jolem...Jolem...Jolem. Your questions about reality, dreams, and altered perceptions have plagued your life. In many ways, it has placed you in this precarious position. What is real?? The events of history have been perceived as fact or fiction largely by our individual thoughts and beliefs about them. We ALL determine what is 'REAL' in our lives. If you feel it is 'real,' then it is. Do you believe this is real?"

Jolem slowly lifts up off the texture-less ground and pulls onto the dark seat. As he spies his adversary, Director Dalio's shadowed frame remains unclear. Jolem continues rubbing and blinking his eyes. Whatever has affected him, has him loopy.

"Jolem, you look at yourself and think somehow your existence has some grand meaning, that one day, purpose and reason will become clear. You think what you now know validates all the turmoil you've struggled with all these years. Now, you see yourself as a martyr for some greater cause. You think the world is just, and there's retribution for all. You expect the bad will see their day in court, and the good will be vindicated with reward. You think you are right, and I am wrong. Jolem, the fantasy is not The Path. The delirium is all in your head."

While Jolem doesn't say a word, the director paces in tight circles in front of him. Dalio's movements stop, and then, as he glares into Jolem's face, he continues proposing suggestions that send Jolem's mind in loops.

"And what about now? Do you think this is real, or are you at home asleep in your bed? What is real, Jolem? Do you believe your 'relationship' with Leema was real, or maybe it was a trap I used to get you here? What do you believe to be real? Didn't you request A New Adventure a few weeks ago? How do you know this is not all part of your dramatic journey? Isn't this what you asked for? Didn't you want some EXCITEMENT in your life??"

"But...no...I...told J no."

"Did you?"

"Uhhh..."

"You know – I never knew your father, but I knew of him."

"My father??"

"He was also someone who had a hard time functioning within the dynamic nature of The Path. He was consumed with an idea. The same idea that plagues you."

"What did you do to him?"

"You see, when your father was young, about your age, he had a thought. At the time, The Path was still in its infancy, but it had already transformed America. Most of the country was thrilled by what we were able to accomplish; the peace and happiness we created. We lifted the country from ashes like a Phoenix, but still, there were those who just couldn't be satisfied. A few disgruntled and sick individuals started the Freedom Fighter movement. But it was insignificant. Their relatively small protests were mostly invisible. That was until your father came along. For years he and Mr. Perry…"

"Mr. Perry??"

"Yes – Mr. Perry, your neighbor. They operated under our radar, advancing anti-Path sentiment. Soon, we noticed the rallies were getting slightly larger and more organized, but we still discarded them. Before long, their numbers grew too big to ignore. His voice had to be silenced."

"What??"

"Yesss. Your father sat in a room very similar to the one you're in right now and was also presented with an offer. He had a choice to make, just as you do."

Not able to keep his thoughts straight, Jolem continues to blink, but still, the director is a blur. Quiet moments pass, and his fuzzy form stands almost motionless.

"At this point, you've seen into a window that was never meant for your eyes. The burden of this new-found knowledge is much too heavy, and for that, I pity you. I pity your plight, your wasted efforts, and the position you're now in. Therefore, I'm going to do you a favor."

"A Favor?"

"Yes, a favor. I told you I would offer you a fair deal."

Dalio walks near, stands right in front of Jolem and looks down on him. "Like your hacker friends, we have capabilities that are still a bit controversial. First, we're going to extract from you whatever we can to help hunt down your associates. However, this will be of no consequence to you. As far as you're concerned, all of this will go away as if it had never happened. For you, we will change this nightmare into a dream. Your old memories will be replaced with a whole new life experience. Severed relationships will be repaired. In this new reality, you will see the world differently; more beautifully. You will feel nothing, and there will be no side effects. Your mind will be trained to love The Path. Your adventure will finally come to an end."

"I don't want your offer…"

"I'm sorry – did you *really* believe you had a choice?"

44

Silence. That's all Jolem hears. Finally, free from a mountain of complications, peace overtakes his mind and body. Like being cradled by the heavens, the serene emptiness holds him. He doesn't know where he is or how he got here, and he doesn't care. He's in Solace, far from his world of chaos.

His eyes slide shut, and a euphoric smile drapes his face. He's at ease in this charming solitude, without a worry of time or space. However, this is not nirvana. With a blink, he quantum leaps back into the world which he was disconnected from.

"Ahhhh," he yells as his eyes pop open like saucers. "What? I??"

"Jolem?? You're awake!"

"Li'l J?"

"You've been in and out for a long time. I've been trying to wake you. How do you feel?"

He begins to tap his fingertips together in a unique pattern and then looks around, scratching his head. "Is this real??"

"Jolem? Are you okay?"

"Mmmm, I think so. I'm a little confused. What the hell just happened?"

"That was a wild experience you had. Glad to have you back."

"I don't understand," he says, battling disorientation. "What happened with Leema?"

"Leema? Leema Dalio?"

"Of course. Is she okay?"

"Jolem, what are you talking about?"

"Huuumm – actually, I really don't know. She just flashed in my mind."

"Jolem, your vitals are fine, but maybe you need further evaluation."

"NO – NO! I really feel great."

"Okay. If you say so. But please contact Liz, she's concerned about you. Your mom too."

"I willll."

"And Lateria. Please contact her also; she's sent you three messages."

"Teri?" he asks, rubbing his face. "Seems like I haven't spoken to her in forever."

Jolem curiously scans his bedroom and takes note of all his familiar things. For some odd reason, they seem new. He glances out the window wall and sighs.

"Okay. Sooo…what's new in my World?"

CPSIA information can be obtained
at www.ICGtesting.com
Printed in the USA
JSHW022036250723
45290JS00001B/85